ANNIE SEATON lives near the beach on the mid-north coast of New South Wales. Her career and studies have spanned the education sector for most of her working life, including completing a Masters Degree in Education, and working as an academic research librarian, a high school principal and a university tutor until she took early retirement and fulfilled a lifelong dream of a full time writing career. From 2014 to 2017 Annie has been voted Author of the Year (2014 and 2017) and Best Established Author (2015) in the AusRom Today.com Readers Choice Awards. Each winter, Annie and her husband leave the beach to roam the remote areas of Australia for story ideas and research. One of her favourite destinations is the Whitsunday region where emerald green islands sparkle in a sapphire ocean. Secluded beaches, coral reefs and towering hoop pines are all part of the Great Barrier Reef World Heritage Area. It is a stunning and pristine landscape threatened by human activity.

Readers can contact Annie through her website annieseaton.net or find her on Facebook and Twitter.

Also by Annie Seaton

Undara

Annie Seaton

Whitsunday Dawn

mira

First Published 2018
Second Australian Paperback Edition 2019
ISBN 9781489284136

Whitsunday Dawn
© 2018 by Annie Seaton
Australian Copyright 2018
New Zealand Copyright 2018

Published by
Mira
An imprint of Harlequin Enterprises (Australia) Pty Ltd.
Level 13, 201 Elizabeth St
SYDNEY NSW 2000
AUSTRALIA

® and TM (apart from those relating to FSC®) are trademarks of Harlequin Enterprises Limited or its corporate affiliates. Trademarks indicated with ® are registered in Australia, New Zealand and in other countries.

A catalogue record for this book is available from the National Library of Australia
www.librariesaustralia.nla.gov.au

Printed and bound in Australia by McPherson's Printing Group

As always to Ian, the love of my life.
You are always there for me.

CHAPTER
1

April 27, 2018

The Front Street shopping precinct adjacent to the marina was abuzz with activity and noise. Electric-powered buggies whizzed along the wide street as tourists jostled past Liv Sheridan. She stepped to the side to let a group of young men in brightly coloured board shorts and T-shirts pass as they headed towards the bar.

'Livi!'

The shrill cry drifted across the street, rising above the noise of the crowd and the squawking birds. Liv glanced over her shoulder with a frown but couldn't see anyone trying to catch her attention. The busy thoroughfare was crowded with tourists and they all seemed intent on their own pursuits. She looked across at the people sitting outside the coffee shop on the corner, but they too were engrossed in their own conversations. She shrugged; she must have misheard.

The sun appeared briefly through the scurrying clouds, reflecting off the windows of the big inter-island ferry moving slowly across the channel. Liv lifted her free hand and pulled her Gucci sunglasses down from the top of her head. She knew no one here, and she'd told no one from Sheridan Corp that she was spending the weekend at Hamilton Island before catching the ferry across to Airlie Beach on Monday. And anyway, the only people who used the diminutive of her name were her family, and they were thousands of kilometres away.

She hitched the strap of her blue Boss briefcase over her shoulder and continued along the footpath that fronted the busy coffee shop, a couple of high end boutiques, and a bar already overflowing with noisy patrons, despite the early hour. A couple of groups of young guys she recognised from her flight were already swilling schooners of beer; it hadn't taken them long to get into holiday mode.

If only I could too. Be in holiday mode, relaxing and enjoying myself.

Liv's suitcase had been one of the last to be offloaded from the Virgin flight and by the time she'd found a trolley and walked out of the terminal, all the electric buggies that transported the new arrivals and their luggage to the hotels had left. After waiting for a minute, she'd gone back inside and organised for her bag to be delivered to the Reef Resort Hotel.

'Are you sure you want to walk, Ms Sheridan?' The young woman glanced down at Liv's Christian Louboutin shoes as she tagged her suitcase. 'The buggies will be back shortly.'

Liv nodded, smiling as she picked up a map of the island from the counter. 'I'm more than happy to get some exercise. And I'm looking forward to seeing the island. I've already spent most of my day sitting in a taxi and a plane.'

'It's a fair way across to the hotel, it's on the other side of the island.'

'A kilometre at most? I'll enjoy the walk.'

The young woman pointed to the street at the end of the terminal parking bay. 'Go along there and when you get to Mango Tree Corner, turn right and that'll take you over to Catseye Beach to your hotel. You can't miss it.'

'Thank you.' With another smile, Liv had picked up her handbag and briefcase—that wasn't leaving her sight—and headed out of the terminal.

Now, as she walked, she surveyed the crowded street that ran along the marina. Hamilton Island was nothing like she'd imagined from the promises of the glossy tourist brochures. The only blue Whitsundays water she'd seen so far was a brief glimpse from the plane window. The jet had broken through the heavy cloud as it approached the landing strip. The airport terminal could have been anywhere in the world, teeming with people and noisy with constant announcements over the speakers, with most of the tourists dressed more casually than she was. Liv looked down at her navy-blue pencil skirt and jacket with the discreet red Sheridan Corp logo pin on the breast pocket. She'd spent the morning at the office in Sydney, meeting with her father and then, on his instruction, updating the presentation for Monday's meeting, so there'd been no time to change before she left for the airport. Her swimmers and sarong were packed, and she was looking forward to an afternoon around the pool, although she would probably have to take her laptop and go over the presentation at least one more time.

'There's a lot riding on this community meeting, Olivia. Don't stuff it up.' Her father's words had stayed with her the whole flight. A niggle of worry lodged in Liv's throat and she pushed the nerves away. She would not let Dad—or the company—down.

As Liv walked past Mango Tree Corner, the clouds cleared and the sun came out. It would have been nice to have time to sit out here and watch the crowds go by for a while. As soon as she got this damn presentation out of the way, she would be able to relax. Maybe it *was* time to think about taking a holiday. The walk was slow and it took longer to negotiate the crowded street than Liv had anticipated. She was already regretting not waiting for the buggy to return. Time was short, and she wanted to make the most of it before she stood in front of a hostile community to convince them of the benefits of the Sheridan Corp development. She shook her head and dug deep for confidence; she'd done this so many times before. There was no need to be nervous.

Beneath her braid, perspiration trickled down her neck. Despite being late autumn, it was still hot and humid up here in the trop- ics. She stepped to the side of the street and put her briefcase down before shrugging out of her jacket, folding it neatly over her arm.

'Liv!'

Again. Someone *was* calling her name.

This time she turned around, taking more time to peruse the crowd. Her eyes settled on a plump elderly woman with perfectly styled silver hair hurrying towards her from the outdoor garden of the coffee shop. She almost ran along the footpath, heading to Liv, both hands outstretched.

'Oh my goodness,' the woman said, her voice quavering. Her face was wreathed in a huge smile as gnarled old fingers, loaded with diamond rings, took Liv's free hand, holding her fingers in a crushing grip. 'Oh my darling.'

Liv looked down as her jacket slipped from her arm to the gut- ter, the cuff of one sleeve settling in the only puddle in sight. The woman's hand was shaking and her smile disappeared as she tried to speak but her words caught on a sob. Liv's throat closed in sympathy as the woman held her gaze with sad, faded blue eyes. Tears welled and rolled slowly down the wrinkled cheeks as she shook her head from side to side. Even though she didn't have a clue who she was, Liv felt sorry for the woman.

'Oh, Liliana,' the woman said, her voice unsteady. 'You came back. It's been such a long, long time. Where did you go? Why didn't you come home?'

'I'm sorry. You must have me confused with someone else,' Liv said gently as she tried to remove her hand, but the elderly woman held on tightly. Her long, manicured fingernails pressed into the skin of Liv's palm. 'I'm Olivia Sheridan, not Liliana. My family calls me "Liv". That's why I stopped. I thought you were calling out to *me*.' She tried to ease her hand out but the woman's grip was surprisingly strong.

The woman shook her head and her voice rose, her mouth set in a petulant pout. She let go with one hand and touched Liv's braid. 'Look at you! You didn't even get your hair cut off, Lil! And you don't look old like me.'

Liv frowned, unsure of how to deal with the situation but a deep voice came from behind her. 'Come on, Aunty Tat.'

Liv looked away from the sad eyes and determined lips. Two men had caught up to them, and the man closest to the woman reached down and gently unfurled the tight fingers wrapped around Liv's hand. His voice was soft, yet firm as he placed his arm around the elderly woman's shoulders. His lips curved into a tender smile.

'Come and have your tea, Aunty. It's getting cold. And you know how much you hate your tea cold. I've ordered your scones too.'

Liv rubbed her hand against her hip to ease the stinging. The woman nodded and smiled, seeming to forget that Liv was there as soon as she looked away from her.

'Yes, I'm thirsty. I hope you ordered Earl Grey, and I want strawberry jam today.'

'I'm so sorry.' The man holding the woman shot Liv an apologetic smile and lowered his voice. 'She's not having a good day.' With a nod to the man beside him, he pointed in the other direction with his free hand.

Before Liv could move, her elbow was being held as she was steered away from the coffee shop. 'Wait. What are you doing?'

'Come on,' the man holding her arm said. 'I have to get you out of her sight.'

Liv wrinkled her nose as an awful smell surrounded her. 'Wait! My jacket's still in the gutter back there.'

'Okay. But keep your back to her while I get it. Aunty Tat will go happily with Byron, but if she sees you, she'll take off again.' He let go of her arm and walked back the few steps to retrieve Liv's jacket from the gutter. Before she could take it from him, he took her arm again in an attempt to steer her further away from the coffee shop. Liv felt uncomfortable with this stranger holding her arm, and her temper was building. 'Excuse me. Do you mind?'

'Come on, then.' He let go of her arm but stayed close to her. 'Where are you staying? Knowing Byron, he'll want to apologise to you later. Poor Aunty Tat's not been good lately, but this is the first time she's actually grabbed someone.'

'There's no need for anyone to apologise. I'm fine. My jacket, please.' Liv valued her personal space and this stranger was invading it. 'You don't need to lead me anywhere. Just give me my jacket and I'll be on my way.'

'I'm sure Byron will want to get it dry cleaned for you. It's wet.'

Liv shook her head. 'No, don't worry about it. I'll sort it at my hotel.' She held her hand out.

As the man held the jacket out, he looked down at the company pin on the pocket. His eyes widened for an instant, but the fleeting look of surprise was quickly replaced by a sardonic grin. He folded the jacket carefully over one arm, and even though his touch was now light, he took her elbow again.

'I'll take you there and I'll arrange for dry cleaning.'

God, he's so persistent.

'There is absolutely no need. I'll walk around the corner so I'm out of her sight.' Her patience was wearing thinner, and the closer he stood to her, the stronger the unpleasant smell became. 'I *can* walk unaided.'

'Perhaps not in those shoes.'

Liv raised an eyebrow as her temper finally fired. This situation was becoming ridiculous. It was as though this guy was going out of his way to annoy her, and his rudeness pushed her into a curt response that was totally out of character for her. 'My shoes are none of your business. Nor is my jacket.' Her voice was as glacial as the look she threw at him. She wrinkled her nose with distaste as the stench continued to pervade the air around them. His singlet T-shirt was stained—the red marks looked like blood—and his ragged-edged denim shorts had splotches of something solid— possibly fish— stuck to them. Beneath his shorts, his legs were muscular and tanned, and his feet bare. If he held onto her jacket much longer, it would absorb that awful smell.

If it hasn't already.

'Fish! Dead fish! And fish blood! Ugh. That's what I can smell.' She held her breath and lifted her chin as he finally passed her jacket over.

'Not *dead* fish. Fresh fish. *Poisson frais.*' His French accent was appalling and she frowned.

'Nothing beats it, darlin',' he said with a wide grin. The chiselled jaw and a nose that had obviously been broken at some time were surrounded by unkempt, long, blond curls. His eyes were full of mirth as she stared at him.

'Well, fresh or dead, whatever it is, it smells terrible.' She clutched her jacket to her chest and heat rushed to her cheeks as his gaze lingered below her neck.

'So how about a drink later tonight? An apology for Aunty Tat grabbing you.'

Liv couldn't believe his words or his audacity when he winked at her.

Is he for real?

'No, that's totally unnecessary. And please tell—Byron—there is no need at all to apologise. I'm sorry for the lady's distress but no harm has been done.'

Apart from a damp jacket, and a guy who was making her feel more uncomfortable by the minute.

'Whatever you say, darlin'.' With a casual flick of his hand and a waft of more fishy smells, he turned away. Liv stared after him as he sauntered back to the coffee shop.

As she watched, the woman appeared at the door, Byron close behind her.

'Lil, I'll come and see you later! I'll tell Mama and Daddy you've come home.' A gleeful smile crossed her face as she looked up at the tall man. 'See, I told you, Billy. I always knew Liliana would come home. I just knew it!'

Liv turned the corner and headed out of sight as she'd promised, but the woman's voice followed her.

'Billy, hurry up and take me home so I can tell them.'

Billy? Byron? What a strange start to her visit.

As she crested the small rise and entered an avenue of lush tropical trees, Liv felt unsettled and just a little bit sad.

CHAPTER
2

The Reef Resort Hotel was stunning. The reception foyer floor was laid with cream marble, the air was perfumed by tropical white lilies in tall vases. To the right was the entry to the dining room, and to the left, a sunken area opened out to an expanse of lush green grass with a hint of blue in the distance. Casual cane chairs and hammocks beckoned invitingly in the now sunny afternoon.

After checking in at reception, Liv entered her room, threw the security card on the marble table by the door, and carefully put her briefcase on a chair. She crossed the large living area, heels clicking on the shiny white tiles, and looked into the bedroom; her suitcase was already on the luggage rack opposite the bed.

Her eyes widened as an incredible view opened up in front of her. The whole northern wall of the bedroom was glass. Stepping across the room, Liv kicked off her shoes, slid open the door set in the glass panel, and stepped out onto the balcony. A sun lounge and a small table with two white chairs covered with brightly coloured cushions sat on either side of the door. A small hammock of cream macramé hung from the ceiling at the other end of the balcony, tucked out of the wind. Sapphire-blue water glinted as the sunshine played on the small waves whipped up by the wind. Pure white sand edged the water below, and palm trees swayed in the brisk breeze. The grey clouds had cleared, and the brilliant blue sky was rimmed by towering white clouds hanging over the small islands dotting the horizon. Liv drew in a deep breath of salty, fresh air and the tension that had filled her since this morning's meeting with her father began to ease.

Specks of white dotted the blue water as sailing boats made their way slowly up the channel between Hamilton Island and an island to the north. Hidden bays broke the shoreline of an island across the water, and a ragged volcanic peak a few kilometres to the north, rose from the centre of the island. As she stared at the beautiful blues and greens, an unfamiliar serenity filled Liv, chasing away the last tendrils of tension and the sadness that had tugged at her since she had encountered the elderly woman.

Happy cries drifted up to her seventh-floor balcony. Children splashed in a netted enclosure in the water on the narrow strip of beach below as parents supervised from a row of sun lounges set along the sand. More hammocks swung from the trees and as she watched, a waiter with a tray in hand made his way from the resort down to the beach. A flock of rainbow lorikeets swooped low as they flew past her balcony and she smiled. This was one of the most beautiful places she had ever seen. Not the hotel and the facilities, although that made for a welcoming environment, but the colour of the water and the sky and the lush verdant green of the islands in front of her were sheer perfection.

A tropical paradise, she thought. If only she could forget about the work she was here to do, pull on her bikini and sarong, order a cocktail and forget the real world for a while. She stared out over the water, mesmerised by the brilliant colours. She'd had no idea that it was so blue, always assuming the tourist brochures had been touched up to entice prospective visitors. She'd never tire of looking at a view like that; it was breathtaking. As soon as this Zenith project was signed off, she'd definitely make the effort to come back here for a holiday before she moved on to the next project.

A tap at the door caught her attention, and Liv opened it to a young girl in the hotel uniform, a tray in hand.

'Welcome to our Reef Resort, Ms Sheridan. A jug of freshly made lemonade for you. Would you like me to put it on the balcony?'

'Why not?' Liv smiled as she stepped back to let the girl enter the room; she could get used to this life very quickly. The girl placed the tray with a glass, and a jug of ice on the table outside. She held up a small plastic implement and pointed to the glass. 'Just use this to squeeze the lemon onto the ice and then tip the syrup over it too.'

'Thank you.'

'Is there anything else I can get for you?'

'No, everything is wonderful.' Liv pointed to the island across the channel. 'One question for you, though. What's the name of that big island?'

'That's Whitsunday Island, and that's where you'll find our famous Whitehaven Beach.' The girl smiled and accepted the tip that Liv held out to her. 'Thank you. Make sure you do take a tour there. It's listed as one of the ten most beautiful beaches in the world. We offer a day trip from the resort. You won't believe the colours of the water, turquoise, blue and green swirling over white sand.'

Liv shook her head regretfully and glanced at the girl's badge. 'Unfortunately, Sara, I'm here to work, as much as I'd love to take a tour.'

'You could always work at night.' Sara's voice was persuasive. 'There's so much to see out here in the islands. How long are you staying?'

'Only for the weekend. I have to be over on the mainland on Monday morning.'

'Don't miss the opportunity. The forecast has promised a brilliant day for tomorrow. It would be a shame to spend it in a hotel room.'

Liv laughed. 'You make a good argument.'

Sara crossed to the door. 'Well, think about it. It's as simple as selecting your tour and calling reception. You can't visit the islands and stay in a hotel room working all day.'

After taking a quick shower and pulling on a pair of long, loose pants and a T-shirt, Liv reluctantly opened her briefcase and placed the files beside her Mac Air on the inside dining table. If she stayed out on that balcony, she'd never get any work done. The light faded into a tropical dusk, the chatter of the birds filling the air as they swooped on the blossoms looking for food. Liv switched the computer on and logged on to the resort's network to check her email. Before she could open the messages, her mobile rang.

'Olivia!'

Her buoyant mood disappeared instantly at the brusque tone. 'Hello, Dad.' She sat on the bed and leaned her head back against the soft rattan bedhead.

'You haven't replied to my email. What are you doing?'

'I've been on a plane. I've just downloaded my email now. Give me ten minutes and I'll look at—'

Her father interrupted her. 'Don't worry about it. Your presentation has been amended.'

Liv fought the urge to grit her teeth and kept her tone even. 'Again?' God, she'd almost memorised the whole bloody thing and had a response prepared for any questions that the community could throw at her on Monday. Any changes would mean more work, and time was running out. 'I thought we went through the *final* PowerPoint this morning?'

'I've had a videoconference this afternoon, and we've moved forward a long way.' The short huff from the other end of the call relayed his usual impatience. 'Things change quickly in the corporate world. You should know that by now. Have I made a mistake trusting you with this project, Olivia?'

'No, Dad, of course not. You know you can trust me,' she said quietly. 'I know this data inside out. So, what's changed in the presentation now?' A glimmer of disquiet tugged at her, bringing back the tension she'd carried all the way from Sydney. If it was a major change, she would be working all weekend.

'Don't worry. It's all been updated for you. All you have to do is look pretty and change the slides.'

Liv closed her eyes and took a deep breath before she replied. 'I'll ignore that sexist remark. Now, tell me what's changed, so I can be prepared for any questions.'

'We've moved further forward with the local council for the new site approval—'

'New site?' Liv interrupted.

'I told you that this morning. Earnaldo Bay has been selected.' His tone was impatient. 'And, more importantly, the rail line has been approved.'

'That's good to hear.' Liv stood and crossed back to her computer. She was sure it was the first mention she'd heard of Earnaldo Bay. 'So, you've emailed the updated file to me?'

'No. The bloody thing's too big. You'll have to log on and download it. Rod's emailed you the file path.'

'Okay. I'll check now.'

'Make sure you do it properly. Now we've got the regional council on side, we're almost there. The state government's very close to signing off on the project. We are at an extremely sensitive stage of the negotiations.'

'So this community meeting is the last chance for any more local objections to be raised?' She clicked on the email icon.

'Yes. Now that we have the council in our pocket—'

'I won't be using an expression like that,' she interrupted.

'Don't be smart, Olivia. You know what I mean. I want the process to be seen as open and transparent, so the local community needs to feel well-informed.' His chuckle was out of character. 'They need to think they have a say.'

Liv frowned as she looked at the new messages. 'Yes, the email's here. I'll get straight onto it.'

'All you have to do is follow the link and copy the new Power-Point to your computer. Can you do that?'

Liv gritted her teeth.

'Make sure you use that one and not the one we looked at this morning. And don't make any other changes.' His tone no longer held amusement for what he considered Liv's unnecessary detail to her presentations. They'd had words about that on several occasions. 'I know how you like to "pretty up" your presentations. You're there to placate any objections.'

'Trust me.'

'I hope I can. I don't want this stuffed up, and I don't want any rabid greenies hijacking the meeting.' Her father's voice rose. 'I expect you to be on the ball with this, Olivia. One hundred percent. Replace the file and then don't touch it. Is that clear?'

'Quite clear.' She kept her voice patient, though her frustration threatened to spill out. Sometimes she wondered why it was so important to her that she please her father.

Not that I ever seem to. Liv scrolled through her emails as she listened to more instructions. She'd heard them all before, and it was simply a reiteration of what her father had gone through as she'd stood in his office overlooking Circular Quay before leaving for the airport only six hours before.

There was no doubt about it; Dad was a ruthless businessman, and anyone who didn't measure up would soon be cut loose—daughter or not. Liv swallowed down the lump that stuck in her throat. She knew that better than most; she'd been working to gain his respect—forget about fatherly love—for most of her thirty years, much to her mother's dismay. Liv had been an unexpected addition to her parents' marriage when they were in their forties, and it hadn't been easy having a father who'd never shown any interest in his only child. Liv had been trying to compensate for not being a son since the day she was born.

'Livi, it's not worth it. You have to realise that your father is a hard man. You won't ever succeed in pleasing him.'

How many times had she heard that from her mother? Life had been easier for Mum after she and Dad had divorced the year Liv had started high school. Years of trying to hold the marriage together, even after a succession of his extra-marital affairs, had made Mum stronger. She had found herself a new career and had run her own successful florist business until she'd retired a couple of years ago. While Mum had revolutionised her life, Dad had moved on to a later-model wife, but that marriage had only lasted eighteen months.

Strength was a trait of the women in their family, and Liv was thankful she'd inherited the gene from Gran and Mum. But despite her inner strength, trying so hard to please her father frequently had them butting heads. Sometimes Liv wondered if it was worth it. Maybe she should have stayed with Gran and Mum on the land.

When Dad had agreed—albeit reluctantly—to her joining his company when she'd finished university, Liv had foolishly assumed their relationship would improve. Mum had tried to persuade her not to accept the position, but Liv had seen it as the perfect opportunity to finally prove herself; to make amends for not being a son, and to show him she could achieve whatever he wanted her to. If anything, Dad's attitude had become more distant in the eight years she'd worked at Sheridan Corp.

She dragged her thoughts back to the present as his voice rose.

'I'm sending Phil and Rod to join you on Monday. They'll fly in Sunday night, and meet you at the conference centre on Monday morning.'

Liv stood straight and kept her voice level to hide the disappointment.

Nothing ever changed.

'Phil?' She knew Rod well and liked him; he was the first of Dad's PR people to treat her with respect.

'Phillip Garvan is the media liaison rep from Zenith. They'll keep the company line. Let Phillip answer any curly questions. You stick to the facts and figures.'

I'm obviously not capable. 'Gee, thanks,' she muttered under her breath.

'I'll email you his contact details now.'

This time it was bitterness that rose in her throat, but she stayed professional. 'Great. I'll wait for it.' She stared at the screen as the email dinged its arrival. 'And Dad. Trust me. I won't let you down.'

'Make sure you don't.'

The call disconnected from his end. Liv carefully placed her phone onto the table beside her computer as she came to a decision.

Sending two staff to the meeting to answer the community questions was further proof that her father had no faith in her ability.

She could spend all night going over the wretched presentation, and it would make little or no difference. She could bring in a multimillion dollar contract singlehandedly, and there would still be someone in the company who had done it better, or faster, or made more money for Sheridan Corp. Whatever she did wouldn't be good enough. The problem was, this deal was huge. It was in the national papers frequently, and the controversy of the Chinese company, Zenith, backing the Sheridan Corp deal was gaining more attention every day. But it looked like it was going to be another major success for Sheridan Corp—or more to the point, Andrew Sheridan.

I'm over it.

Padding across the cool tiles to the coffee table, Liv sat on the sofa. She picked up the hotel compendium and flicked through the brochures before picking up the phone and dialling reception.

'Hello, this is Olivia Sheridan in Room 726. I'd like to book a tour to Whitehaven Beach tomorrow.' After her reservation was confirmed, she opened the fridge and pulled out a small bottle of wine. As she was about to take her first sip, her phone buzzed again and she rolled her eyes. She hit the answer button and lifted the phone to her ear. 'Yes, Dad, I'm downloading it now.'

The lighthearted laugh that came through the phone brought a smile to her face.

'Don't tell me your father's still making you work up there in the tropics?' her mother asked.

'Hi, Mum. And you should know better than to ask. Of course he is.' With the phone to her ear, Liv crossed to her computer, opened the email and clicked on the link. The company network logon came up on the screen. 'Give me a second. I just have to download a file and then I can talk.'

'Okay. I'll go and pour a wine. I've got time for a good natter tonight.'

'I've just poured one.' Liv put her phone down and entered her company username and password. She frowned as the screen opened to an unfamiliar part of the network. Instead of taking her to the revised PowerPoint, a series of folders filled the screen. She glanced over them and nodded when she saw the one labelled Community Meeting. Clicking on the folder she looked for the revised PowerPoint but there were three rows of files in the folder. She flicked quickly through the names, unsure which file was the correct one to download.

God forbid she downloaded the wrong PowerPoint. She wouldn't have to worry about work; she'd be out of a job. Conscious of her mother waiting, Liv closed the Community Meeting folder and then clicked to download the folder it was sitting in. She'd sort out which was the revised presentation later.

CHAPTER
3

April 28, 2018

Fynn James stood on the deck of *Footprint* and looked out over the Hamilton Island marina. The gentle wind lifted the curls from the back of his neck and he took a deep breath of the clean, pure air. The sky was cloudless and the breeze was perfect for sailing, promising a good day around the islands. This would be the last charter he'd be taking out for a week or so; he needed to work through the last files that Greg had emailed last night. The sooner he could sail *Footprint* out to one of the bays and moor in isolation, and peace and quiet, for a few days, the happier he'd be. He had a lot of work to get through if they were to be successful in stopping Zenith.

'And bloody Sheridan Corp,' he muttered, thinking about the woman they'd met yesterday. Looked like Andrew Sheridan had sent his daughter in to do his dirty work again. Greg had predicted she'd be the one fronting the community meeting, and if there was anything worth knowing about Sheridan Corp, his journalist friend knew it.

Fynn unchained his bicycle and lifted it from his yacht onto the finger wharf. He'd spent too much time going over Greg's files last night, and slept through the alarm. He glanced at his watch as he pedalled towards the wharf at the other end of the marina. He was going to make it in time for departure, just.

Between the fishing charters, the sailing trips and the restaurant, he'd been needed on the island early each morning for the past couple of weeks, so *Footprint* had been berthed in the marina, side-by-side with other yachts. Byron had been trying to talk him into living in one of the apartments on Hamo, knowing how Fynn hated being jammed into the marina, but he preferred to stay on his boat. He'd spent his life living on boats, and the thought of being confined within four walls stifled him.

'I won't be available from Monday for a few days,' he'd told Byron when they'd walked Aunty Tat through the marina yesterday afternoon. 'Can you get Adam to fill in for me?'

'Yeah, he's back from his break today. I'll call him as soon as I get Aunty Tat settled at home. What's happening?'

'Greg's sent up a lot of useful data, and after the community meeting on Monday, I'm sure we'll have more questions. I'm going to sail out and go over what I have. Greg will come up in a week or so to plan our next move.'

Byron had looked at him as he and Aunty Tat had walked to the ferry wharf. 'It's going to be interesting, that's for sure.'

'Are you attending the meeting in an official capacity?'

'No, John is the council rep on this project, but I'll do my best to be there, don't you worry about that.'

'It is a worry. No matter whatever we raise or what hits the papers, Sheridan always comes back with a response. How the hell he's convinced so many people that this is beneficial for the region has me stumped.' Fynn ran his fingers through his hair and grimaced when the fishy smell filled the air.

'There's nothing to worry about. There's no way it will go ahead. The traditional owners won't approve the rail line across the land from the mine, and building a coal loader so close to a tourist town is ludicrous. The council will never approve the site, no matter how many times Sheridan gets the land usage rezoned.' Byron's voice was empathic but it didn't reassure Fynn.

'I don't trust them. Greg has uncovered some pretty murky things in their past projects, and they've managed to get them approved despite the environmental concerns.' Fynn leaned over and kissed Aunty Tat's cheek. 'You look after yourself, darlin'. It was lovely to see you again today.'

'Are you coming over to see me on Sunday?' Aunty Tat's smile was bright, and she'd forgotten all about the woman she'd accosted earlier.

'Of course I am. You know I wouldn't miss a Sunday at Poinciana House.' Fynn held her elbow as they stepped up towards the ramp onto the ferry. 'And my favourite lady.'

'You didn't come after the cyclone last year.' Her voice held censure.

Byron shook his head and caught Fynn's eyes. 'Her memory's there for recent events,' he said quietly.

'But she's already forgotten about that woman.' Fynn narrowed his eyes. 'Did you happen to notice the pin on her jacket?'

'No.' Byron held onto Aunty Tat's hand and paused before he stepped onto the ramp beside her. 'What was it?'

'Sheridan Corp. I'm assuming it was Olivia Sheridan.'

Byron had given a low whistle. 'Interesting. Here already for the meeting on Monday?'

Fynn nodded. 'I'd say so.'

Byron looked thoughtful as he led Aunty Tat towards the enclosed cabin on the lower deck. 'I'll see you at home on Sunday,' he called. 'We'll talk some more before the meeting. You can fill me in on what Greg's got to say.'

Now, Fynn was thoughtful as he turned his bicycle onto the last finger wharf at the south end of the marina.

Olivia Sheridan. The woman they'd encountered yesterday had been different to what he'd expected. Ms Sheridan certainly had the corporate look, but she'd been very kind to Aunty Tat, before she'd turned on him. With her tall, slim build, fine features and pretty coloured hair, she was certainly a stunning woman, even with the snarky attitude, but Fynn would bet anything on her knowing how to play the game. She'd switched from warm to ice cold in seconds.

Forewarned is forearmed.

Fynn was determined to fight dirty if he had to. There was no way that this proposed development would get approved. It would take more than a beautiful woman with a nice figure to get approval for a project that was so damaging to the environment.

He had the academic knowledge and contacts, and Greg had the inside on the company activities and the media contacts, as well as an ear to the mood of the state government. From what Greg had said, the corruption that abounded in both the corporate and government worlds was unbelievable.

Fynn allowed himself a smile as he jumped off the bicycle. Olivia Sheridan would need more than good looks and a snarky attitude to overcome community opposition to the Chinese-funded coal loader.

★   ★   ★

Liv had set the alarm to go off early, so she had time to look for the right file before she went down to the restaurant. If she didn't have the file ready to work on for when she got back this afternoon, she'd worry about it all day instead of enjoying the tour to the islands. She found the updated file and put it in her working folder. A quick flick through had confirmed that it was almost the same as the previous file her father had taken her through yesterday morning, and she noted the updated slides towards the end. She'd focus on them tonight.

She was being picked up at the hotel to be taken to the marina to board the *Lady May*, the yacht she was joining. Liv took the *Lady May* brochure to breakfast, and read it as she waited for the waiter to bring her coffee. Excitement curled in her stomach as the day ahead beckoned.

The choice of boats available and the level of sophistication had been wide ranging—from small, private mono-hulled yachts to large motor cruisers that took a couple of hundred passengers. She'd taken the advice of the receptionist and chosen a tour on a smaller sailing boat that took only twenty passengers. It was more expensive, but the privacy had appealed.

Dozens of options, from snorkelling trips to Blue Pearl Bay on Hayman Island, to underwater observatories and to the pontoon out on Hardy Reef, were available; the brochures outlined tours that catered for all needs and budgets.

A day on board Lady May *will fulfil your dreams of luxury. It is like no other sailing trip in the Whitsundays. A high-class service,* Lady May *promises luxury and comfort, with a highly attentive level of service. A gourmet lunch is included, along with champagne or beer served with antipasto through the afternoon until we return at sunset. Our attention to detail to make your day perfect is our highest priority and we aim to leave you with a joyously memorable experience of our beautiful Whitsunday Islands.*

It was certainly a more enticing option than staying in her room and reading over that blasted presentation.

Liv hadn't taken a holiday in the eight years she had worked for Sheridan Corp. When she'd talked about going overseas for a couple of weeks at the end of her first year, her father's disapproval had quickly put paid to the idea.

'You want to be a successful businesswoman?' He'd almost sneered as she'd broached the subject the week before Christmas. 'I suppose you intend to go swanning overseas with your mother. Do that and I'll know you're not serious about a career with Sheridan Corp. Your choice.'

So Liv had made her choice. The idea of a holiday had been put on the backburner, and there it had stayed for way too long. Despite working longer hours than most of the other staff and completing her MBA part-time, Liv burned with frustration that newer employees were promoted over her, time and time again.

Patience and one hugely successful project.

That's all it was going to take. She wanted this to be the one. Dad would recognise the quality of her work—not to mention her loyalty to the company—and this deal was her opportunity to prove she was highly capable. If she could do it before absolute exhaustion burned her out. She was beginning to realise that her working pace was unsustainable, although Gran's comment about 'having to slow down now that she'd turned thirty' had made her laugh. Gran was about to have her ninety-third birthday and she still managed to work around the farm as though she was fifty years younger.

The waiter placed a cup of coffee in front of her and Liv smiled her thanks as she turned back to the glossy brochure. She turned it over and looked at the back page. It was a map that she was very familiar with; one that she had stared at on her screen as she'd read the proposal for the new mine one hundred kilometres inland,

and the associated coal loader north of Airlie Beach. She looked at the names of the bays, all too familiar. It was different seeing them on a tourist brochure rather than on an environmental impact study. The rail route, now apparently approved, would wind its way east from the mine north-west of Proserpine to the coal loader. It wouldn't be far north of the town where she would be speaking on Monday. Liv frowned as she stared at the map.

Instead of chatting to Mum last night, she should have opened the revised file and had a close look at it. A niggle of doubt tugged at her; reading the names of the bays and the islands on a map was very different to standing on her balcony and looking out over the sapphire-blue sea. She traced her finger over the coastline to the north on the tourist map on the table, recalling the name of the bay where the coal loader had been originally proposed.

Liv put the brochure aside, wondering how far north it had been moved. Guilt flooded through her; she shouldn't have taken today off. She'd look at the presentation as soon as she was back this afternoon, and work into the night. But then she remembered her mother's words last night.

Don't let him suck you in, Livi. He's a master at that. Be warned.

No. Today was hers, a day to recharge her batteries, and she planned to enjoy every minute of it.

She pushed her chair back and walked over to the buffet, collecting a newspaper on the way. A colourful array of tropical fruits filled the first table—mango slices fanned into the shape of a huge flower, pineapples hollowed out and filled with yoghurt, the slices of pineapple interspersed with different types of melon and strawberries on another tray. She loaded her plate with a variety of fruit and went back to the table. When she was almost done, she glanced at her watch and opened the newspaper. There was still half an hour before she would be picked up for the tour. Flicking through the newspaper, Liv narrowed her eyes and put the spoon back on her plate as the headline on page four caught her attention: *Zenith Enterprises slammed by the Queensland Institute*.

Her appetite and complacency disappeared as she quickly read through the article.

'In its latest statement on the Chinese-funded project, the Queensland Institute asks why up to half a billion in loan funding should be provided by the state government for a rail link to the proposed coal loader on the Whitsunday coast. A financial modelling undertaken by the institute's economists concludes that government funding of the Zenith Enterprise rail line would have a negative impact on the coal industry state wide.'

Liv skimmed through the rest of the article, where there was a discussion of the potential multi-use of the rail line, although the economic reporter's tongue-in-cheek conclusion was that, as there were few tourists living near the proposed coal mine who would need transport to the coast, the multi-use justification could not really be considered seriously. It was already outdated information because the new rail line route hadn't been made public yet. Articles like this had appeared in the newspapers since the project had first been proposed. A tagline at the bottom of the article directed readers to the editorial comment on page two.

'*Bloodsucking journalists out to make a name for themselves.*' Her father's words had been heard many times at meetings over the past few months. He had no respect for the media, and somehow usually managed to keep some of the more damning reports out of the national papers. She'd often wondered about the honesty of his connections, but the one time she'd questioned him, disgust had curled his lip. 'And you really think you can make it in the corporate world, Olivia?'

Liv reached for her coffee, needing a caffeine hit before she read any more of the damaging conclusions. She flicked back a page and read the editorial.

Greg Coutts. She'd heard of him before. He was a tenacious reporter and had recently exposed an illegal plan to put a coal seam gas waste dump in a small national park in the central west of Queensland. After the report, the overseas company had quickly pulled out.

Green groups are not alone in their fear that our reef will suffer further.

Liv scanned through the editorial. The main focus was the damage to the reef and, secondary to that, the certain damage the coal loader would cause to the tourist industry in the Whitsunday region, not only in the islands but along the Queensland coast from Townsville to Mackay. Professor Ted Darnell at James Cook University, who also represented scientists at the World Conservation Congress, had been asked to comment and was vitriolic in his opposition to both the mine and the coal loader.

'It defies reason.' Coutts quoted Professor Darnell throughout his article. 'There is no single action that could be as harmful to the Great Barrier Reef as the Zenith proposal. Roughly a third of marine species have parts of their life cycle in coral reefs. So if you take out coral reefs, you have an ecological collapse of the oceans. It's happened before, mass extinctions through ocean acidification. The consideration of this proposal coincides with our increased concern over threats to the reef from land-based pollution, including sediments, nutrients and pesticides.'

Liv put the paper aside with a groan. Coutts had his eye on Zenith, which was a worry. Should she call Dad?

No. His minions would have read the report by now and alerted him to it.

Why this weekend? Why did the media have to get hold of all of these reports two days before she was presenting to the local Whitsunday community on the economic benefits to the local region when—if—the mine and the coal loader were approved? The current focus on tourism and the potential for damage to the reef, and the tourism industry, was going to make her presentation very difficult, and she suspected there would be strong opposition at the meeting. For the first time, she was pleased that her father was sending the other guys up from the company, and then she bit her lip.

Maybe Dad had been right all along, and she wasn't tough enough for the corporate world. Or maybe she'd been kidding herself that she wanted to be.

If only he would let her get involved in economic analysis and projection; that's where her strength lay. Instead, she got sent out as the public relations person with the figures and projections of other analysts in his company and the parent company. She would never forget a comment she'd overheard at the coffee machine in the office one night. 'Sherro's daughter's got the looks. Why else would he send her out there to do his dirty work?' She hadn't recognised the voice, but the laughing response had come from Dad's last PA. 'Whatever works, and a bit of eye candy never goes astray when you're trying to convince an audience.'

The comment had rankled, and she hadn't been able to let it go, then or now it seemed. Liv swallowed, focusing on the article in front of her. If it was accurate and supported by credible people, where the hell was her father getting his advice from? It was almost as though he thought the company was untouchable and could go ahead without any justification, apart from making millions of dollars. In one way, Liv was pleased she was up here in the islands. It certainly wouldn't be pleasant in the office at Sheridan Corp today. And it didn't matter that it was the weekend. Most of the Sheridan Corp employees worked seven days a week.

She bit her lip as her stomach churned. The more she saw of the islands, the less convinced she was about the very proposal she was up here to endorse. Pushing her coffee away, she picked up her napkin and dabbed her lips. Her appetite had gone.

She walked up to her room, quickly changed into her swimmers and slipped a white linen dress over them before packing her tote bag with sun cream, a sarong and her camera. She glanced across at her computer, and then her iPhone, tempted to log on and look at the new file. With renewed determination, she picked them both up, opened the safe next to the bed and slipped them inside, and reset the code to her date of birth. She had no doubt that her father would contact her again today, but she was taking the day off; she'd listen to anything he had to say tonight. There was sure to be a dozen or more emails from him, and she wasn't going to let anything spoil her day.

Today is mine.

As she crossed the large marbled floor of the foyer to wait for the buggy, the day receptionist came from behind the desk and handed her a message slip.

'There was a call for you, Ms Sheridan, while you were at breakfast.'

Liv's buoyant mood deflated quickly.

Oh God, already? The day of relaxation ahead had been a dream. She unfolded the message and read it as the receptionist waited.

Please call Byron Ellis. The name was followed by a mobile number. Relief surged through her.

Not Dad. Not yet.

'Would you please call Mr Ellis and let him know I'll return his call tonight?' She recognised the name, Byron, as that of the man who had been with the elderly woman yesterday afternoon. It would be rude to ignore his message; he'd been polite and considerate. It was the smelly fisherman with him who had been a total jerk and riled her temper. The guy who had tried to push her along the street, and held onto her jacket, had annoyed her at the time but Dad's call had pushed the incident from her mind.

'Certainly, Ms Sheridan. I'll pop a copy of the message on the desk in your room for you.' The girl in the brightly patterned tropical shirt smiled at her and pointed to the door. 'There's your buggy now. Have a great day.'

CHAPTER
4

The *Lady May* rocked silently on the glassy water. It was still early and there were few people around apart from crew pushing loaded trolleys towards the charter boats. Liv glanced around at the small group of people waiting to board the classic timber yacht. As they stood on the narrow concrete wharf, a few hesitant smiles were exchanged, the sort that strangers welcome each other with when they know, by the end of the day after their shared adventure, they will be exchanging emails and photographs.

Maybe not, Liv thought. Most of this small group was made up of young couples and she guessed some were probably on their honeymoons. There appeared to be only one other passenger taking the cruise alone and, as Liv glanced over, the girl caught her eye and wandered over to where Liv was standing at the edge of the wharf.

'Hello, I'm Inga.' Her voice was deep and her accent had a Scandinavian lilt. 'I am very excited to be travelling today on this beautiful boat.' She looked around curiously. 'Are you travelling alone also?'

Liv smiled and held out her hand. 'Hi, I'm Liv. And yes, I am by myself. And I'm also looking forward to the day. It's going to be a perfect day for sailing.' She gestured to the brilliant blue sky where fragments of wispy clouds were being pushed along by a strong wind up high.

'As long as it is not too rough. I do not wish to be … how do you say it? Ocean sick?' Inga frowned.

'Seasick,' Liv replied. 'I'm sure it'll be fine. The best part of the charter is there won't be smelly fumes from the motor, just smooth sailing. Hopefully, anyway, if there's enough wind.'

A young woman in a bright blue cotton shirt and white shorts stepped off the boat onto the wharf with a clipboard in hand. 'Hi, everyone, please gather around. My name is Sonia. Welcome to your day on our beautiful *Lady May*. Today we're going to indulge you with luxury and elegance on a journey back to a past age of classic yachting.' She moved through the group, and ticked off the passengers on the list, finishing with Liv and Inga. 'Ms Sheridan? And Ms Nordstrom? Fabulous, we're all here. Thank you, every-one, for being so punctual. We've got a great day ahead, and the wind is forecast to increase and promise a wonderful day of sailing.'

Sonia turned and nodded to the deckhand who waited at the side of the boat. He slid a wooden walkway from the deck to the wharf.

'Please take your shoes off. We'll stow them below deck when you are on board,' she said. 'You'll see *Lady May* has beautiful tim-ber floors, so it's barefoot for all of us until we go for our walk at Hill Inlet. Please take anything from your bags that you'll need on deck before we stow them below for you too.' She kept walking as she checked off guests, and continued speaking as the first of the group followed her up the walkway. 'Actually, there's really nothing you'll need. We've got plenty of sun cream and water on deck, so maybe just a hat. Don't worry about your mobile phone unless you want to use it as a camera because once we get out through the Solway Passage, there's no service.' She quickly ran through the safety procedures, the facilities below, pointed out the life raft and the water station, and told them to be careful on the steps if they went below deck to the restrooms.

Liv removed her sandals, slipping them into her small back pack, before taking out her camera and slinging the strap around her neck. Small waves were beginning to ruffle the calm of the marina as the breeze picked up, and sunlight sparkled on the blue water. She held her straw hat by her side so it wouldn't blow away.

Liv and Inga were last to board. They passed their bags to the deckhand as they stepped off the walkway and made their way to the raised section that ran down the centre of the deck. Large burgundy cushions lined the seats on the top of the cabin, and they found themselves a position up front, close to the bow.

A tall man stood at the large steering wheel on the left-hand side of the boat towards the back. Portside, Liv corrected herself. And stern.

One summer when she'd been in her teens, Mum had insisted on sailing lessons on Windermere Dam near Mudgee, not far from Gran's farm. Liv smiled; Mum had tried so hard to get her interested in a hobby. Sailing, horse riding lessons, gymnastics, the suggestions had been endless, but Liv had preferred to spend her time out on the farm with Gran, or doing her school work.

'Leave the girl alone, Rhoda. Let her enjoy her time out here with me.' Gran had always stood up for Liv. Since she'd been working in Sydney, visits to Gran's farm had been rare. A rushed weekend here and there had been all she'd managed to fit in over the past couple of years. Her grandmother's hatred of her ex-son-in-law didn't help and after a while, it became easier to stay in touch with Gran by phone rather than visiting. She promised herself to make time to go to the farm after this project was finalised.

She turned her attention to her surroundings. There was no point dwelling on personal issues while she was out here on this beautiful old sailing boat. In front of the steering wheel was an undercover sunken lounge area, and three of the older couples had settled themselves there out of the sun. Another young woman in the blue shirt embroidered with *Lady May* came up from below and made her way to the front of the boat. As the motor started, she, Sonia and the deckhand leaned over and lifted the fenders protecting the side of the yacht from the concrete wharf. As the boat backed out from the wharf, Liv tilted her head back, leaned against the bolster behind them and closed her eyes. The autumn sunshine was warm on her face and the serenity was relaxing her limbs already.

'Very nice,' Inga murmured quietly beside her.

Liv opened her eyes and sat up. 'What's nice?' she asked.

There was a clunk and the motor idled quietly as the boat stopped moving away from the wharf. A man in a blue shirt wheeled around the corner on a bicycle. Longish curls obscured his face as he jumped off and quickly chained the handlebars to a post on the wharf.

Oh, no, surely not?

'Now *that* is going to make our day even better,' Inga said. 'What do you think?'

Liv narrowed her eyes and leaned forward but the man disappeared below the front of the hull. It couldn't be. Of all the boats she had to choose from, her luck wouldn't be that bad?

A moment later, a couple of ropes were thrown over the side and the deckhand at the front of the boat secured them to a bollard.

'Sorry, guys. James had to go on the other charter, so I'm filling in for him,' the latecomer called to the crew. He ran past the bow

to the end of the wharf. The yacht was almost touching the concrete floating wharf. As soon as the voice reached her, Liv stifled a
groan.

It *was* him. Mr Smelly Fisherman from yesterday jumped from
the wharf and grabbed one of the ropes hanging over the side of
the bow. He hauled himself over the front of the boat in one lithe
movement.

Of course he did. From what Liv had seen so far, he was a show
pony, full of confidence. But there weren't any fish stains on his
shirt today—the same blue shirt the rest of the crew were wearing. With a wide smile, he made his way past the passengers to the
back of the boat and took the microphone from a holder next to the
wheel. Liv pulled the front of her hat down and looked the other
way as his smooth, deep voice filled the air.

'Hi, folks, sorry I held you up. I'm sure our gorgeous Sonia
here'—sexist too, Liv thought—'has told you all the safety stuff,
now it's my turn to tell you all about the *Lady May* and what the
plan is for our day ahead. I'm Captain Jay—and one of your deck-
hands today—and I'm looking forward to meeting you all after we
get underway.'

How many brochures had she looked at? How many charters
were there to pick from? Of course she'd picked the one this jerk
was on. She'd assumed he was a fisherman, but he obviously worked
a few different jobs.

Liv couldn't believe her bad luck; a whole day confined on a
boat in his company. Suddenly, the seventy-foot yacht seemed a lot
smaller. There was no way she'd be able to avoid him. She bit her
lip as the yacht motored out into the passage between Hamilton
Island and another small island in the middle of the channel.

'Now, Rick here is going to face us into the wind, and Chris
and I are going to hoist the mainsail. Your day is about to begin. As

soon as we are underway, Sonia and Liz will come around and take your coffee orders.'

Loves the sound of his own voice too.

For a moment, Liv considered getting off the charter, and then realised it was too late—unless she wanted to dive overboard and swim in. A glimmer of a smile tilted her lips; she was being oversensitive. It had been a quick—if strange—encounter and he probably wouldn't even recognise her. Even if he did, he was at work, and there would be an expectation of appropriate behaviour. She leaned back and forced herself to relax as the two men began to put the mainsail up. The huge white sail snapped in the brisk wind, the motors cut and there was silence. The yacht cut smoothly through the waves, and Liv turned to stare over the water as they made their way east.

Inga leaned over and nudged her. 'Does he remind you of someone?'

'Who?'

'The dreamboat, Captain Jay.' Inga put her hand on her heart and pretended to flutter her eyelids.

'No, I don't think so.' Liv forced herself to face the stern and watch him—Captain Jay—as he walked back and picked up the microphone.

'We're underway, so sit back and enjoy the sail. That's Fitzalan Island on our portside, and the big island behind that is Whitsunday Island. We'll head along here until we round the southern end of the island through Solway Passage. Keep your eyes out, folks, there's all manner of wonderful marine life to be seen if you watch carefully. Loggerhead turtles, dolphins, and maybe a whale or two. Our Whitsunday area is known as a whale watching hot spot. Between now and August, whales choose the calm, warm waters around here to give birth to their young each year. If we're very lucky today, you might even see a brand-new whale calf taking its first breaths and being taught how to swim by mum.'

He had a voice that was easy to listen to, and he certainly had a handle on the tourist patter.

Inga leaned forward. 'He looks like that cute American guy who was in the movie about the dog.'

'The dog?' Liv frowned. 'I don't think I know it.'

'I can't remember the title or the actor, but he really, really looks like him.' Inga pulled her phone from her pocket and smiled. 'Good. Still some service.' Her thumbs flew over the tiny screen and she nodded.

'That's him! *Red Dog*. I saw it on the bus when I caught the coach up from Sydney my first week in Australia. If I didn't know better, I'd say it was the same guy.' Her smile got wider. 'But I suppose it can't be. He has no American accent, but he really looks like that actor.'

'I haven't seen the movie.' Liv looked down at her hands clenched on her lap and willed herself to relax. She'd worked so hard at uni and then since she'd joined the company there was little time for even visits to the cinema. 'I must look out for it.'

'It is wonderful.' Inga put her phone back in her pocket. 'I cried every time I saw a dog from the bus window for days.'

Liv paid closer attention as Captain Jay outlined the plan for the day. She wasn't going to let him bother her, even if he did have movie-star looks. Now that he was dressed in clean clothes and his hair was a bit tidier, he looked more presentable than yesterday. With a shrug, she turned away; she was going to make the best of the day. It was an opportunity to see the Whitsunday Islands for herself—not on maps, videos or photographs in an environmental impact statement.

After the newspaper reports she'd read at breakfast, she was determined to improve her own knowledge of the area. She would take in her surroundings and be more familiar with the region before Monday. She needed credibility, a personal touch to convince the community of the benefits of this proposal.

The small niggle of worry was growing as Liv looked out at the pristine waters around them, but she refused to let it sink her buoyant mood. She turned her attention back to the man on the microphone and tried not to scowl. The smile hadn't left *his* face since he'd pulled himself up over the front of the boat.

'When we leave the Solway Passage, we're gonna sail past the beautiful Whitehaven Beach. You'll see how crowded it is there, but we have a special treat for you. We'll take you around Tongue Point and moor around the corner in the bay. After a quick trip to the shore in the tender, we'll walk up to the lookout overlooking Hill Inlet, and then have a swim at our own private beach. While you're on shore at Betty's Beach, the gals will prepare you a wonderful feast on board.'

Liv switched off again as some of the passengers began to ask questions; she couldn't hear what they were asking. Inga was speaking to the Danish couple on the other side of them. Bracing her hand on the cabin top against the rising swell, she stood and crossed the narrow deck, the timber smooth and cool beneath her bare feet. The wind was stronger, and the mainsail was billowing as the wind pushed the boat along. On either side of the Passage was an island, and ahead was a silver expanse of sea all the way to the horizon.

'As we turn away from the wind, you'll get your first glimpse of the white sands of Whitehaven Beach on the portside.'

Olivia started; she hadn't noticed Sonia come up to her. 'Once Captain Jay gets on the microphone, there's no stopping him.' The young woman smiled.

'He seems to know the boat well. Does he work on it often?' Liv attempted to satisfy her curiosity without being too obvious. 'I actually ran into him yesterday and he'd been on a fishing charter.'

'Captain Jay is a jack of all trades,' Sonia said slowly. 'He's a bit of an icon on the island. If you stay long, you'll see him everywhere.'

'I'm only here for a few days.' Liv pointed to the beach that was appearing across to the north. 'Wow, is that Whitehaven Beach?'

'Yes, it sure is. That first view of the white sand is always special, no matter how many times you see it. I'll leave you to listen to Captain Jay now. He does know the history of the place. Would you like tea or coffee?'

'Coffee, please.' Liv crossed back to the seat on the cabin top and listened as he described the cyclone that had decimated the Whitsunday region a year ago.

'Cyclone Debbie was a bitch, but we've all bounced back. The vegetation has regenerated and the reef is repairing itself. Nature can repair her own, but we're all worried up here about the proposed coal loader that's threatening the area. That would be the end of the reef if it got built, but there's no fear of that happening. We'll do whatever it takes to stop it.'

Liv's head flew up and a strange feeling ran through her. Captain Jay was staring directly at her. The perpetual smile had left his mouth and his expression was set.

Well, well. So *that* was his problem. No wonder he'd reacted to the Sheridan Corp pin on her jacket yesterday. If he was involved with the group opposing the project, he was sure to know Sheridan Corp was involved. That's why he'd been such a smartarse. Liv lifted her chin slightly and stared back, her eyes cool.

'Yes, we'll all make sure of that,' he repeated. 'Enjoy your coffee and scones. I'll come around and have a chat with each of you as we make our way down to Hill Inlet. So get those questions ready.'

Liv took the coffee that Sonia was holding out to her, but shook her head as Liz came along with a tray of muffins, and scones piled with jam and cream. Her appetite had disappeared. 'No, thank you. I had a huge breakfast.'

Liv sipped at her coffee and watched as a seaplane came in low in front of the yacht. It skimmed above the water for a hundred metres before landing with a huge splash.

As she watched it taxi across to the white sand and disgorge its passengers, a shadow fell across her.

CHAPTER
5

'Ms Sheridan.' The warmth and friendliness that had been in Captain Jay's voice as he'd talked on the microphone was gone. 'We meet again.'

'We do.' There was no point denying their encounter yesterday, no matter how much she would prefer to forget him. Liv was aware of Inga sitting beside her and listening with interest.

'Hello. I am Inga. It is nice to meet you, Captain. I have enjoyed your commentary.'

'Thank you.' His smile was dazzling, and Liv looked away.

When Dad had mentioned the issues with those opposing the project, he had dismissed them as coming from a small group of rabid greenies. She turned and watched Captain Jay, trying to align him with her father's unflattering description. So far, all she had seen from him was knowledge—and if she was honest, a love—of the local area.

She pulled her thoughts back and wondered why he was bringing out the worst in her. He had barely spoken to her today and she was feeling unsettled. It had to be the stress of this blasted presentation; she was attributing motives to him that he probably hadn't even considered.

'You already know each other?' Inga frowned, and Liv felt obliged to defend herself. 'Oh no, not really. Captain Jay was kind enough to pick up my jacket when I dropped it yesterday.'

'I hope you've managed to get it dry cleaned ready for your meeting?' Despite his tone, she received the same wide smile that he had bestowed on Inga. The guy really did have movie-star looks.

She forced a friendly smile to her face as she decided to give him a chance. 'It wasn't necessary. A bit of a sponge and it's as good as new.'

'I'm pleased to hear that. I didn't get a chance to apologise to you yesterday,' he said, his blue-eyed gaze holding hers, the smile staying as he looked at her.

'Apologise? There was no need. I felt sorry for her.'

'No, not Aunty Tat. For the state of my dress. And the smell of freshly caught fish.' His eyes were dancing now. 'I was half expecting you to sniff your jacket as you hurried away from me.' He turned to Inga. 'When I ran into Ms Sheridan yesterday—'

'Liv, please.' The formality made her feel awkward, and seemed to set her apart from the rest of the passengers.

'When I ran into Liv yesterday, I'd just come off a fishing charter. We'd bled the mackerel, and unfortunately, I was covered in fish guts and blood.'

'Bled the mackerel?' Inga's mouth opened and Liv was sure her expression was the same.

White, even teeth flashed, contrasting with Captain Jay's tanned face. Liv moved away slightly as he stepped up onto the cabin top and sat on the cushion closest to her. The man had no concept of personal space. She moved away a fraction more.

'What I meant was, we had a very good catch. I'd cleaned the fish and I'd delivered them to the restaurant, and I wasn't really in any fit condition to be talking to a woman as lovely as … Liv here. But we did have a situation.'

Inga smiled and then turned to speak to Sonia, who was collecting the empty coffee cups.

Unwelcome warmth ran through Liv as he held her gaze. He quirked one eyebrow, and she forced herself to smile back. 'We did, but it wasn't a problem at all. I was merely a little disconcerted by the encounter with the poor lady. Tell me, was she okay after I went around the corner?'

'She was. Poor Aunty Tat has dementia. By the time I got to the table, she'd forgotten all about you.'

'That's very sad for you and your aunt,' Liv said.

'Tat's not my real aunt. Aunty is just a term of endearment, but she is related to Byron. We work together sometimes.'

'So, he's on the boats too?'

'No. But I'm sure with your work, you'll see him again. Byron is on the regional council.'

'My work?'

'Sheridan Corp.' He held her gaze. She held his eyes steadily as she picked up on his subtext.

'Oh? And what about you? Will our paths cross in "my work"?'

'Me?' The white teeth flashed again as that perpetual smile dimpled his cheeks, and his reply was enigmatic. 'Who knows? I'm just a simple yachtie. But a man has to feed himself, you know.'

'Sounds like an interesting life. A simple yachtie and a jack of all trades. Island life must be good.'

'It is.' He stood and nodded to her. 'It's been nice getting to know you, but I'd better share myself around all of the passengers.' He began to walk away but paused and turned back to her. 'We're going on a different route home. Once we snorkel at Blue Pearl Bay, we'll head north. I'll point out Double Bay to you. You may be interested.'

She looked up at him. 'Double Bay?'

'The bay where your development is *proposed*.'

Liv shook her head as she watched him walk to the front of the bow. *What a jerk.*

The arrogance of the man! At least there'd be no more of the 'have a drink with me'.

The crew pulled in the sails as they passed Hill Inlet, and Captain Jay disappeared below decks. Liv was cross with herself for even noticing.

Nick steered the boat and took over the microphone. Inga came up to the bow and sat beside her as the boat cruised past the private Betty's Beach where they were going to swim before lunch.

'Don't forget, folks, stinger suits are a must if you intend going in the water,' Nick announced, and Sonia pointed to a large bag on the sunken area. 'If you're going to swim, please come over and get fitted before we take you to shore.'

'Have you been up to the islands before, Liv?' Inga asked after they had picked up their stinger suits and moved closer to the bow. The direction of the swell had changed when the *Lady May* turned into the bay and every time she dipped the bow cut through the water, sending a small spray of water over the young couple beside them.

'I hate to admit it, but no, it's my first visit. Can you believe it? I'm an Aussie and this is my first time up here. I've actually never been north of Brisbane before.'

Inga looked at her with her eyes wide and she waved her arm. 'Really? All of this beauty and so many Australians do not leave their cities. I do not understand them.'

'I guess it's because we all get caught up in our careers and our lives. What about you, Inga? Is this your first trip here?'

'I've been working over at Airlie Beach for six months, in a coffee shop. I've fallen in love with the place—the people, the atmosphere, but more than anything, the beauty of these islands. When I save enough each week, I take a day cruise out to the islands on my day off. I've travelled a lot of the world, but I have never seen anything as beautiful as here. It is a place I would like to live. If I won the lottery, I would live on a boat like this.'

Liv smiled and looked around as the yacht motored into the bay. On one side was a small beach dotted with large rocks, and along the inner circle of the bay were mangroves. On the northern side, a high volcanic peak shaded the bush. The morning sun was still low in the sky; the trip around from Hamilton Island had made good time, with the strong wind in the sails. The verdant green of the bush contrasted with the white sands and the light-coloured rocks on the ocean side of the ominous peak. In some places, the forest of trees went right to the edge of the deep azure-blue water.

'It's breathtaking.' Liv couldn't take her eyes off the island. There were no buildings in sight and it appeared to be uninhabited.

'Wait till we get to the lookout and you see the view from there,' Sonia said as she walked past. 'As soon as we pick up the mooring, please make your way to the back of the boat. Captain Jay will bring the tender in as soon as we're secure and we'll take you in to the beach.'

The passengers near the bow moved back as Sonia and the deckhand leaned over with a large boat hook and picked up the mooring.

'We're secure, captain,' Sonia called. Captain Jay turned around and gave her the thumbs up, his smile wide. Liv looked away as he vaulted over the back of the boat into the tender.

The passengers were divided into three groups to take the short trip to the beach in the inflatable tender. 'We'll be walking to the lookout, so make sure you have your cameras with you.'

Liv wasn't used to having such a lazy day. As she waited, her fingers went automatically to her pocket, feeling for her phone to do her hourly email check, before she remembered she'd locked it in the safe in the hotel room. A day without technology at her fingertips was rare; she smiled as she leaned back, relaxed.

As she looked out over the water, she wondered again why this area had been chosen as the site for a coal loader. The proposal outlined the advantages of the deep-water bay, where ships could come in beside the coal loader, and extolled the advantages of the proximity to the proposed coal mine. Surely, though, there were other suitable locations, further from the islands? She hoped the revised location and the revised rail route were as a result of those factors being considered.

But on the other hand, enhanced employment for the local area was one of the key features of her presentation on Monday. The more she saw of the islands and the Whitsunday Passage, the more her stomach churned with uncertainty. Surely the impact on tourism would take away any other economic benefit provided by enhanced employment? Liv chewed on her lip. She would revisit that part of her talk tonight. Her gut feeling was that her presentation—the presentation and the figures she had been given—wasn't going to go down well at the community meeting.

Monday loomed ahead like a black shadow, and Liv couldn't wait for it to be over. Since she'd arrived in the islands, this whole project was making her ill at ease.

She jumped as the motor revved and the inflatable tender turned in a wide arc, coming in close to the back of the yacht.

'Last group, come on over,' Captain Jay called. He held out his hand to each passenger as they stepped from the back of the yacht into the small boat that was bobbing about on the waves. 'We only take eight at most.' He looked up and caught Liv's eye and gave her a broad smile. 'The fewer passengers in the tender, the higher we are in the water, and the more chance of everyone staying dry.'

She shook herself mentally as she waited her turn to step down into the small boat. His hand was warm and his grip strong as he helped her into the boat, and the little shiver that went down her back annoyed her.

The front of the tender rose and fell in the small waves, and the passengers stayed dry as they crossed from the yacht to the shore. All went well until the boat stopped in the shallow water near the rocky beach. Captain Jay held it steady as the passengers swung their legs over the side and waded the short distance in to the beach.

'No!' The cry was full of fear. A young Japanese woman refused to step into the water. Her husband was out of the tender and stood in the water, waiting for her to climb out. He held out his hand but she didn't move. She sat with her arms folded and shook her head. 'Irukandji.'

Captain Jay stood in the back of the boat and let the motor idle, but the boat was being pushed closer to the rocks with each wave that pushed in.

'It's safe to walk that short distance. No jellyfish will get you, you'll only be in the water for a few seconds.' Liv sensed a note of impatience in his voice, but his smile held sympathy.

The woman's eyes were wide with fear and she shook her head again. 'No. Crocodiles too.'

Her husband raised his hands in frustration. A short conversation ensued, and Liv caught Captain Jay's eye as the woman sat back with her arms folded.

No amount of persuading from her husband or Captain Jay would entice her to get out of the boat, and the woman was blocking the way out for Inga and Liv.

'I don't suppose either of you can drive a boat?' Captain Jay turned to them, his voice low.

'Actually, I can.' Liv held back a laugh when he raised his eyebrows. 'I've done a lot of boating on Sydney Harbour.'

Another point to me, captain.

'Great.' He pointed to the throttle arm of the motor and gestured for Liv to take his seat. 'Just keep it idling. If the waves push it too close to the rocks, do you know how to put it into reverse?'

She nodded and took the throttle from him. Before she could speak, Captain Jay jumped over the side, and walked around to the back of the boat. He held his arms up like a cradle, and then gestured to the shore.

The woman nodded. He leaned over, scooped his arms beneath her legs and back before carrying her to the shingly sand, and putting her down beside her husband.

'I wonder if I pretend to be scared too, will the beautiful captain carry me,' Inga said with a smile before she climbed over the side. By the time she was at the beach, Captain Jay had jumped back into the tender and taken the throttle from Liv.

'Thank you. A WHS nightmare, but I appreciate that you helped out.' For the first time, his voice seemed sincere. 'You jump out now and I'll drag the boat up.'

'She's right, you know.' Liv looked over into the clear, shallow water. 'I recall reading a newspaper article quite recently, where somebody was standing in ankle-deep water, and bent down to wash the sand off their face, got stung and ended up in Mackay hospital for a week.'

His voice was laconic. 'You'd have to be pretty unlucky.'

'But it could happen,' Liv persisted.

'It could.' As she stood to get out of the tender, his gaze caught hers. 'I guess there's a serpent in every paradise, Ms Sheridan.'

★   ★   ★

The rest of the day on the *Lady May* was relaxed, and Liv managed to forget her concerns and enjoy herself as they snorkelled and explored the island. Captain Jay left Liv alone after his 'serpent in paradise' comment. In fact, he'd let the rest of the crew look after the passengers and steered the old sailing boat around the north side of Whitsunday Island with no time on the microphone. A couple of times, Liv caught him watching her. She'd looked away. After they'd snorkelled at Blue Pearl Bay, Sonia told them the history of the islands as the sails filled with wind and they almost flew over the water.

It was exhilarating. Liv tipped her head back, enjoying the wind rushing past her face. The variety of the sea life and coral had amazed her. When she had hefted herself over the tender and handed the flotation noodle to Nick after snorkelling in the bay, she'd raved about the colours she'd seen. Inga smiled at Liv as they dried their hair back on the boat.

'I cannot believe you have not been snorkelling before!'

'That was incredible.' Liv couldn't keep the smile from her face.

'Will you come again?' Inga asked.

'I will. As soon as I can take a holiday,' she replied as she tied her sarong over her wet swimming costume.

'We must exchange phone numbers. I could show you around the town if you come back here,' Inga said shyly.

'I'd like that.' Liv crossed to the side of the boat and listened to the commentary coming over the speakers as they travelled back to Hamilton Island.

The wind was brisk and the return trip was a fast sail, but Liv didn't mind. As they rounded Langford Island and headed out into the Passage, they turned south. The yacht rolled in the swell as waves rose up in the open water. Liv jumped as a firm hand gripped her elbow and she turned around. Captain Jay was standing very close to her.

'Take care there, Liv. We're about to turn into the wind. I'd hate to see you go overboard.' As he spoke, the boat slewed to the side and Liv stumbled. She gripped the rail firmly with both hands.

'I'm fine, thank you. I have my sea legs now.'

He let go of her arm. A slow glance dropped down to the bare legs beneath her short sarong and she lifted her chin. It must have sounded as though she was trying to get him to look at her legs. She bit back a smile as he nodded.

'And very nice sea legs, I must say.'

He's certainly a player.

Liv had always been impatient with the whole male–female flirting thing. She'd been working too hard to have time for any of that since she'd left university. She stared towards the mainland and ignored him. He moved close again and lifted his arm to her shoulder and she waited, but he extended his hand and pointed without touching her.

'See the second hill north of the township?'

Liv followed the direction he was pointing in and nodded. 'Yes.'

The sun was low in the sky and a small island appeared to hover over the horizon, burnished in a golden bronze. Several inlets cut narrow bays into the far hills that seemed to drop all of the way to the edge of the water.

'Follow that around and then cross to the next fold in the hills. See the hill with the small clearing at the top?'

She nodded again.

'That's the head of Double Bay.'

Liv nodded. 'Is it?'

'Oh, it is, darlin'. Double Bay East and Double Bay West.'

She looked back at the township and then to the inlet that he had pointed out. Double Bay had been the original proposed site for the development and she couldn't believe it was so close to the town, not to mention the islands.

'And your point is?' She stared at him but there was no friendly smile on his face now.

'I just wondered if you are aware of how close Double Bay is to Airlie Beach.'

'I guess I am now, seeing you've so kindly pointed it out to me, but—'

'But?' His gaze was intense and Liv noticed the unusual colour of his eyes; deep green flecked with gold.

'But I'm on a day off. I'm here to enjoy a day on the water. If you want answers, and reassurance about the project, I suggest you come along to the community meeting on Monday. That's a more appropriate place to have your questions answered.'

'Oh, I wouldn't miss it for the world, sweetheart.'

Suddenly, all of the pleasure from Liv's day was gone. A cloud crossed the sun, and the bright blue water looked dark and murky. When she got back, she was going to call her father. She wasn't just going to be the pretty face. If he wanted her to be able to persuade the community that this was of such benefit to them, she needed to present more information about the site relocation. He wanted the process to be seen as open and transparent so the community could feel well-informed, he'd said.

Why was Earlando Bay a more acceptable location?

CHAPTER

6

Liv threw her phone down onto the table in disgust. Her father was always available, all hours of the day and night—his PA had joked once that he'd still be answering his phone at his own funeral. He was overheard and dismissed—and she couldn't understand why he wasn't picking up his phone tonight.

As soon as she got back to the hotel room, Liv opened the file she'd downloaded before she brought up Google Maps on her Mac Air. The names of the bays were familiar now and she could picture many of them now after being out there today. The new location for the coal loader was only one bay north from Double Bay. She shook her head; it was still very close to the tourist town and the charter routes that she'd seen so many yachts and powerboats on today.

The new location was in a small mangrove-edged bay called Earlando Bay. Liv chewed her lip as she traced her finger over the map. There was a small island, Grassy Island, at the front of the bay, and even she could see that the coal ships would have to come in south of the island to access the coal loader. It was way too close to the main islands, and as she looked more closely at the map, she noticed there was another resort area not far to the north at Cape Gloucester.

How the hell were they going to persuade the community that a coal loader would go smack-bang in the middle of a busy tourist destination? And supposedly have no impact on tourism or the environment. She chewed on her lip as her eyes scanned the bays again.

Liv picked up her phone and hit redial. It went straight to her father's voicemail again. As she put the phone down, she sighed and flicked her braid over her shoulder. Her hair was stiff from swimming in the salt water, and in need of a shampoo and a good dollop of conditioner. She'd been tempted many times to have her waist-length hair cut short but had managed to resist so far. Confining it to a braid most of the time made it easy to look after.

Heading to the luxurious marble bathroom, she set the bath taps to run and perused the shelves recessed into the wall, choosing the orange blossom fragrance bath oil.

Liv glanced at the table beside the door. There were two messages propped up on a small wooden stand. She picked up the first note and unfolded it.

Tried to ring you, darling. Hope the island is beautiful. Have a great time, and don't let your father bully you. Love Mum.

She smiled. Mum had told her last night that she worked too hard.

And she was right. Lately, her job satisfaction at Sheridan Corp had been nonexistent. If she was honest, it had never been satisfying and she was beginning to accept that working hard to please her father and to get some recognition from him was a waste of time. Here she was: thirty years old, working long hours with no time for holidays to enjoy places like this and not even moving up any higher in the company.

Why do I do it? Is it really worth it? She'd never listened when Mum or Gran had tried to tell her. Mum's words were a little bit more restrained, but Gran's opinion of Andrew Sheridan was as low as it could go. Ever since Gran and Pa's farm had been resumed by a coal-mining company and they'd lost the farm that had been in the family for generations, Gran's words about her former son-in-law had been vitriolic.

'I hate that you work with him, Livi. He is a low-life, conniving bastard and I told your mother that before she married him. But like her, you won't listen.'

'Gran, don't worry. I'm good at my job and I know what he's like.'

'You might think you do, but trust me, sweetheart. I hope you will never know personally what he is capable of. He is a very dangerous man.' Her grandmother had snorted with disgust. 'With your education, you could get a much better job. And not with a company that's destroying the environment with every new project they take on.' Poor Gran had never got over having to move off her family's farm to make way for an open-cut coal mine. The story went that she'd chained herself to a bulldozer and wouldn't budge, but Liv wasn't sure if it had really happened. Gran was not one to talk about the past.

Maybe it was time to think about a move. Seeing the beauty of these islands had been a huge wake-up call. Thinking about them being compromised made Liv realise that she didn't want to be involved with the sort of developments that Sheridan Corp contracted. She sighed as she reached for the other message.

Please call Byron Ellis. As soon as you can. Many thanks.

This was his second message. She hadn't had a chance to call him back yet. There was a mobile number on the message slip.

Liv glanced at the time as she picked up her phone, but the call answered immediately.

'Byron Ellis speaking.'

'Oh hello, Byron. This is Liv Sheridan. We met briefly yesterday at the marina with your aunt.'

'Hi, Liv. Thanks for returning my call. I hear you went on a charter today?'

The front desk must have passed on her message to him. 'Yes, on the *Lady May*. It was most enjoyable.'

'I'm pleased to hear that. We like to see the visitors to our islands enjoying themselves.'

'Yes, I did. You asked me to call?'

Byron's voice was concerned. 'Yes. I actually have quite a favour to ask you.'

'Yes?' she said slowly.

'Just hear me out first and see what you think. Aunty Tat has been distraught since she saw you yesterday. We can't get her to settle and she didn't sleep at all last night. She usually lives alone but we've had to stay over. My wife was up with her most of the night, and then I took over so she could get some sleep. Sorry, you don't need all the details, but she's really upset.'

Liv stood and walked into the bathroom, flicking the taps off as she listened.

'So, I was wondering if you were planning on visiting the mainland at all,' he said. 'I … we were hoping you might come and visit her.'

'Do you think that's necessary?' Liv frowned. 'Would it really make a difference?' She looked down at the bubbles that were almost to the top of the bath tub. 'I'm coming over on Monday and I'm not staying after that, so I really won't have any spare time before I fly out.' She cleared her throat. 'Look, I really am sorry. If I could help—'

There was silence at the other end for a moment. 'I'm sorry, that was a selfish way to frame my request. Let me rephrase that,' Byron said. 'We're having a barbeque tomorrow, and it would be lovely if you would join us. If you could talk to Aunty Tat too, that would be a bonus. Do you have any plans yet?'

'No. But—' Liv bit her lip. 'I really do have a lot of work to prepare before Monday. I'm up here for work, not pleasure.' As soon as the words left her mouth, she felt like a fraud. He knew she'd been out on a tour today.

'How about I organise for you to be picked up, come over here for an early lunch, and then we'll have you back over there in plenty of time to work in the afternoon. Her dementia has been worse these past few days and we're trying to avoid having to medicate her again. A conversation might convince her that you're not her sister.'

'She's been really upset since she spoke to me?'

'Yes, very.' His voice was almost pleading. 'Sunday lunch is an event at Aunty Tat's. It's always busy. I can promise you a lovely meal in a beautiful old house and a fast trip across the Passage. And you'll be helping our family out.'

'Why not?' Liv tried to make amends for her comment about work. 'I'm only here for a few days, and it *will* give me a chance to see a bit more of the area.'

'Thank you so much. I'll organise for you to be picked up from the foyer at ten-thirty and be taken to the boat. I'll look forward to it, Liv.'

'Me too.'

'Have you chosen anywhere to have dinner tonight on Hamo?' he asked.

'I was just going to get room service while I waited for a call.'

'No way! You can't do that when you're visiting the island.' He quickly gave her directions to a restaurant and she smiled when she heard the name. 'I'm a part-owner of Fruits de Mer,' he said. 'I'll let them know you're coming. Enjoy your meal. It's on the house as a thank you for helping us out.'

'There's really no need—'

Before Liv could protest, Byron cut her off. 'I'll see you tomorrow.'

It looked like she was going out for a seafood dinner.

Liv shook her head with a smile. Grabbing a glass and a small bottle of wine from the mini bar fridge, she poured the sparkling liquid and set it carefully on the edge of the bath. Flicking the sound system to low, she picked a random mix of music to relax to.

After a long soak and a luxurious shampoo, she blow-dried her hair and left it loose over her shoulders. She pulled out a brightly printed jersey dress patterned with tropical flowers and slipped on a pair of blue sandals. A dab of perfume to her wrists and a final look at her phone for a message—there wasn't one—and Liv closed the door behind her.

The Fruits de Mer restaurant was on the lower ground floor of the hotel, behind reception. As she crossed to the entry to the restaurant, she glanced over at the tiki torches flickering on the sand. The soft light played on the fine bubbles of foam edging the sand, where tiny waves crept up the sloping beach as the tide came in. She waited in the doorway; there didn't seem to be any waitstaff free at the moment. The restaurant had an Italian feel, with red-checked tablecloths covering the tables, candles burning in the centre of each one. The music was soft and the low buzz of conversation created a welcoming ambience. Liv took a deep breath, enjoying the unfamiliar relaxed looseness of her muscles. If this is what one day in the islands did for your wellbeing, she vowed to come for a longer holiday as soon as she could.

And it would probably be sooner than later, the way things had gone today.

The door from the kitchen opened and she turned with a smile, expecting to be shown to her table. But her smile froze on her lips as the man crossed the room towards her, flicking a white napkin over his arm.

Captain Jay stood in front of her and his smile was cheeky. 'Ms Sheridan, welcome to Fruits de Mer.' This time his accent was perfect as he rolled his tongue around the French name. 'I noticed you had a booking.'

'So this is another one of your interests? Or were you just delivering the fish?' Sarcasm dripped from her words.

'Just helpin' out, Liv. A friend owns the place.'

'Yes, I know. I was talking to Byron earlier.' Liv frowned and stared at him. 'If I didn't know better, I'd suspect you were following me.'

'Now why would you ever think that? Besides, I was here first.' His eyes were full of laughter and Liv softened a little bit.

'I've been on the island for just over twenty-four hours and wherever I go, there you are.'

'Turning up like a bad smell. Go on, say it, that's what you were thinking, wasn't it?'

'Well, maybe the first time I saw you.' Liv was surprised by the chuckle that bubbled up from her chest; that glass of wine must have mellowed her. 'I heard you were a jack of all trades. Just how many jobs do you have on this island?'

'You'll have to hang around for a while longer if you want to find that out.' He led her over to a table by the window, overlooking the lawn and the beach, pulled out her chair and waited for her to take a seat before he picked up the napkin and spread it on her lap. He handed her the menu and the wine list.

'I'll leave you to decide. And'—another grin—'you've probably had enough of my company today.'

Liv looked down at the menu and didn't disagree.

As she ordered and ate her solitary meal, the restaurant filled up. The whole island seemed to be quite a romantic destination; like on the *Lady May* today, all of the diners were couples. For the first time since she'd left university, loneliness tugged at her. How nice it would be to be spending the evening with someone who cared about her. A beautiful meal, a bottle of wine shared in the company of someone who was interested in her, not just how much money she could make for a company.

The enjoyment of the day left her as the spectre of Monday's meeting loomed again. She pushed her plate away, stood and walked across to the counter. As the cashier looked for her bill, Jay emerged from the kitchen.

'I've got this, Kate.' His smile was wide as Liv held out her visa card. His sour mood on the boat seemed to have completely disappeared.

'No need. It's all taken care of. Byron said you're his guest.'

'Thank you.' Liv nodded and headed for the door without looking back. If he thought she was rude, she didn't care. She could feel his eyes on her as she walked across the restaurant, and a strange shimmy of warmth ran down her back.

As soon as she reached her room, she checked her calls and email, but there was nothing from her father. She tried again but the call went straight to voicemail. Frustration filled her, and she opened her email program and pulled up the details of the two others he'd said were flying up for the community meeting. Maybe one of them could give her a bit more information on the changes. When both of those numbers also went straight to voicemail, Liv hurled the phone onto the bed.

Liv set the alarm early to give herself plenty of time to call her father before she was picked up for the trip to the mainland, but the next morning, the call went to voicemail again. A niggle of worry tugged at her; her father was always available. She opened her laptop and checked her email but nothing had come in overnight.

Her mood was unsettled further by the prospect of the day ahead. A chance five-minute meeting with a stranger surely wouldn't have caused so many problems for the elderly Aunty Tat and there was really nothing she could do to help.

But she'd promised to help out. Once she'd logged off, Liv dressed casually in a pair of white capri pants, a loose midnight-blue sleeveless silk shirt and flat shoes. After she'd secured her Mac in the safe, she put her phone and purse into a small bag and slung it over her shoulder.

The bright sunlight shone through the glass doors fronting the water in the reception foyer. It was another cloudless warm day, and there were already quite a few boats in the bay. The water in the middle of the channel parted in a spray of white foam and she stopped, curious to see what had caused it. Liv's mouth dropped open as the silver surface of a huge whale breached the water and hung in the air for a moment before coming down with a huge splash. Another one rolled on the surface beside it, slapping a fin.

'Oh, how beautiful.' Liv couldn't help smiling as she walked outside to join the crowd gathered on the lawn. For a few minutes, she watched the whales playing, before heading out to the circular drive. This place was magical. It was going to be hard to fly back to the reality of a cold, wet and windy Sydney.

One of the island buggies was parked in the waiting bay and the driver beckoned her over. 'Ms Sheridan?' he asked.

'Yes, that's me.'

'Jump in, and I'll take you across to the marina.'

Liv slipped into the small buggy with a smile. 'Thank you.'

The trip down the hill and through the small shopping precinct and restaurant area only took a couple of minutes. She pulled out her purse to pay for the ride as he stopped at the building at the front of the marina, but the driver shook his head.

'All sorted. Fynn took care of it.'

'Oh, thank you.' *Fynn?* She wondered who Fynn was.

'*Serendipity* in'—he looked at the clipboard on the seat between them—'F seventeen. You go down past this main building, stay to the left of the fuel jetty, go almost to the end of the finger wharf and you'll see number seventeen on your right. *Serendipity* is a beauty.'

'Thank you. How long does it take to get over to the mainland?' Liv was bemused. She had no idea what the beauty was, but she assumed it was going to be some sort of boat.

'In her? No more than half an hour.'

She climbed out of the buggy and, a few minutes later, was thankful for the flat canvas shoes she'd worn as she traversed her way down a steep ramp to the wharf she'd been directed to. She counted her way along the berths before she realised they were numbered on a small post as well. The luxury cruisers she passed had to be worth mega dollars. It certainly was the playground of the rich.

Coming to number seventeen, she stopped. A sleek white motor cruiser with a fly bridge filled the berth. *Serendipity, Airlie Beach* was written in elegant letters along the back. She stood on her toes and peered over into the boat. The double glass doors were open but there was no sign of anyone on board. Making sure her bag was firmly over her shoulder, she stepped from the wharf onto the highly polished timber deck at the back of the boat.

'Hello?' she called. 'Is anyone here?'

There was a sound from above and Liv waited as footsteps tapped down the stairway leading from the fly bridge to the saloon.

'Oh, for God's sake! You must be joking. You again?' She rolled her eyes and folded her arms across her chest as she stared at Jay. 'Really? Yet another job?'

'Morning, Liv.' His smile was wide. 'No. This is a favour. Sunday is my day off. Byron asked me to take you over to the mainland.'

'And this is the best you could do?' She kept her face straight.

His brow lowered in a frown. 'The best I could do what?'

'A what? Sixty-foot luxury cruiser?' She gestured to the boat. 'Um, I was joking. Isn't this a bit of overkill? A boat this size just to take me across to Airlie Beach?'

'Well, Byron said you didn't have a lot of time. He did suggest his helicopter, but it was already booked for a joy flight when I asked at the office.'

This time his expression was serious and it was Liv's turn to widen her eyes. 'His helicopter? And *you* were going to fly it?'

He nodded. 'What's wrong with that? We'd have been over there in no time.'

Liv shook her head and muttered under her breath, '*Why me?*'

'Sorry, I didn't catch that,' he said.

'Don't worry.' Being rude was not something she usually did but this guy … she looked up and narrowed her eyes.

'Wait a minute,' she said. 'Who's Fynn?'

'Fynn? That would be me.'

Did the man never stop smiling?

'I thought your name was Jay?'

He put his hand on his waist and inclined his head. 'Fynn James at your service, Ms Sheridan. Captain J? Short for Captain James.'

'Oh. My mistake then.' Like she was thinking a moment ago, Fynn or Captain Jay or whatever, really made her uncomfortable. For a fleeting moment, she thought about saying she'd changed her mind about going across to the mainland, but he turned to go inside before she could speak.

'Come on in and drop your bag here. But before you do anything, would you mind taking your shoes off please. Boat rules.'

Liv obliged and followed him in, placing her bag on the coffee table beside a white leather sofa, and her shoes on the timbered floor in the saloon.

'I'll get you to give me a hand.' Fynn gestured for her to follow him back out to the deck and pointed to two white ropes holding the boat to the wharf. 'Once I start the engine, I'll call down to you. If you can stand on the wharf and just slip them off the bollards, and throw them to the back deck, and then jump aboard, that would be a great help. Can you do that?'

'Sounds easy enough,' Liv said with a nod and went back out to the deck while he ran lightly up to the fly bridge. Moments later, the engines fired quietly and he called down, 'Rightio, now.'

She jumped across onto the wharf and slipped the ropes off the bollards and threw the ropes onto the boat. She stepped back on board, rolled them up and stowed them in a side compartment before walking up the wooden stairway to the fly bridge.

'Thanks. Take a seat.' He glanced at her briefly as he manoeuvred the boat out of the pen and turned left into the main channel adjacent to the marina.

Liv took a seat at the table at the back of the fly bridge and leaned against the cushioned leather seat as they moved smoothly through the wide channel. Fynn's attention—it was hard to get used to thinking of him as anything apart from Captain Jay—was focused on the water traffic going in and out. It was a busy Sunday morning and the weather was glorious. Liv tipped her head back and let the warm winter sun play on her face. The air was clear, and the water in the Passage sparkled as the light wind whipped it into small waves. Once they were clear, Fynn turned around and called out to Liv. 'Come and sit up here. I can't talk to you all the way back there.'

Liv moved slowly—and a bit reluctantly—to the U-shaped seating opposite the seat where he sat perched high in front of the controls. She'd been enjoying her solitude and would have preferred to stay there by herself and not have to make conversation. It was the first time she'd been aware of a man in a long time, and if she wasn't mistaken, the interest was reciprocated.

He'd exchanged banter with her in the restaurant last night and already this morning, and he'd held her eyes for longer than necessary on the boat yesterday.

Whatever it was, she wasn't going to do anything about it. Half an hour across to the mainland—no, it would be an hour in his company, because he'd have to bring her back too. Surely it wouldn't be too hard to make small talk.

'Lovely day,' she said, and groaned inwardly.

Great conversation opener, Liv.

'It is. It'd be a great day for a sail. I hate these things.' He gestured around, and Liv followed the direction of his hand.

'What things?' she asked, frowning.

'Byron's playthings. Motor cruisers and their diesel fumes. Give me a sailing boat over a Cummins engine any day.'

'Oh.' *Great conversationalist, I am.* Liv racked her brains for a response but Fynn turned to her and his expression was closed.

'Tell me about what you do at Sheridan Corp.'

Liv thought carefully before she responded. 'I'm a project manager.'

'And what are you going to manage? Up here, I mean?' He stared straight ahead as they sped towards the coast.

'Public relations.'

'Ah, I see.' He was quiet for a while. His comment yesterday had firmly placed him in the opposing camp, but now that she'd seen the beauty of the place, Liv knew it would be difficult to convince her about a coal loader in the vicinity if this was her home too. Dad had said that the community meeting was to assure the community that they were well-informed, but she knew that even though he said it was close, the project still hadn't been signed off. She'd blithely accepted his words but now that she was up here and had seen the location for herself, she was beginning to wonder whether his certainty that he could get the project through was misplaced. As far as she knew, he hadn't been up here either. Visiting the location was very different to looking at maps, facts and figures.

'That's the *Derwent Hunter*.' Liv jumped as Fynn's voice pulled her from her thoughts. 'An old tall ship. If you have time, it's a great day out.'

'I won't have time,' she said quietly, and he turned his attention back to the boat.

The conversation from that point on was only to do with the docking of the boat, and the walk up to Abell Point Marina. Liv looked with interest at the conference centre in the marina complex. Lure was the venue for Monday's community meeting. She was pleased to see it was quite a small centre, so hopefully the crowd wouldn't be large.

Hopefully, it hadn't been publicised much and no one would turn up. But she knew that was a vain hope and an inappropriate wish from a public relations project manager.

Fynn called a taxi and walked her over to the pickup bay at the top of the wharves. 'I'll call Byron and tell him to call me when you're ready to go back,' he said as he went to close the door of the taxi as she slid into the back seat.

'You're not coming?'

'No, I've got some things to do in town.'

On a Sunday? Liv pushed away the disappointment that had settled when she'd realised he wasn't getting into the taxi with her. Why on earth should that bother her?

Fynn leaned into the front of the taxi. 'Poinciana House please, mate.' He passed over a twenty-dollar note and Liv protested. 'Really, there's no need.'

A flash of white teeth in a tanned face, a flick of a hand and Fynn loped away back to the marina. Liv watched until he disappeared behind the main building. She'd insist on reimbursing him when he took her back this afternoon. A person only worked so many different jobs if they needed the money. The taxi pulled away from the kerb and turned onto a main road, going past a small shopping centre before turning back towards the water.

With any luck, this wouldn't take too long, and she could get back to her computer. The taxi turned onto a quiet road that ran the length of a beach, and at each end of the bay was a small headland. Yachts floated lazily on the calm water just a stone's throw from the beach. At the western end, where the road came to a dead end at the bottom of a small hill, a lush green lawn ran to the edge of the sand. On the beach side of the street a wide-fronted low Queenslander house fronted the lawn, surrounded on each side by two huge spreading Poinciana trees. The soft cream colour of the graceful house contrasted with the greenery surrounding it. Cornices of dark green wrought iron lace filled the corners of an open verandah, where baskets of brightly coloured flowers hung in the sunshine. The verandah surrounded the house on three sides, and the lawn at the back of the house was separated from the sand by a low fence with a wooden gate.

The taxi pulled to a stop at the edge of the footpath. Liv climbed out slowly and looked at the cars parked on the grass verge. Laughter and happy voices directed her attention to a group of people on the lawn. A game of cricket was in progress on the beach at the back of the house, and a couple of small children were riding an old-fashioned three-wheeler bike up and down the path that led to the front of the house.

'Lily!' Heads turned at the high-pitched squeal.

'Here we go again,' Liv sighed, wondering why she had agreed to come.

Aunty Tat hurried down the path towards her, nimbly sidestepping the children and bike on her way. Liv held out her hand and took Aunt Tat's arm before the elderly woman could grab her again. Her skin was still healing where the manicured nails had dug into her palm on Friday.

'Lily! You came! Byron said you would. I've been waiting for *ages*.' Her voice was childlike, and Liv couldn't help but smile.

'I did come. You live in a very lovely place.' She looked around as Byron and a woman walked towards them from the group across the lawn.

'Hello, Ms Sheridan. Thanks so much for coming over. We really appreciate it.' He nodded to the woman beside him. 'This is my wife, Louise.'

Liv smiled at the woman who held her hand out.

'Lovely to meet you, Ms Sheridan,' Louise said. 'And yes, thank you so much for coming. We've had a couple of long nights here,' she added quietly. 'But when By said you would come over to visit today, Aunty Tat was much happier and she settled. We know it's only a short-term solution but it's very hard to see her so distressed.'

'Call me Liv, please.' Liv smiled down at Aunty Tat, who had looped her arm through hers and seemed quite happy to stand there listening to their conversation.

Byron took Liv's free arm. 'Come and sit down on the lawn chairs beneath the tree. It'll be cooler out of the sun for you, Aunty Tat.' He lowered his voice. 'And it will give you some space, otherwise she'll hang onto you all day.'

Louise was friendly as they walked together. 'This is all family. We'll do the introductions before lunch.' She waved an arm towards the group chatting on the lawn. 'Aunty Tat has six children. Most of them and their children, and grandchildren, and three great-grandchildren still live locally. Sunday afternoons are a bit of an institution here when the weather cools down. The barbeque will be fired up soon, and family will come and go all afternoon.'

Liv sat in a cane lounge chair facing the water and Aunty Tat took the one closest to her. She turned to face Aunty Tat. 'So, tell me, are you Byron's aunty or great aunty?'

Byron laughed. 'Now this is where it gets confusing. Everyone calls you Aunty Tat, don't they, sweetheart?'

Aunty Tat smiled. 'They do.' She leaned over to Liv and patted her hand. 'But, of course you don't, Lily, do you?'

'What would you like me to call you?'

'You call me Tat, don't you remember? And when you're cross with me, you call me Tatiana.' A wide smile lit up the old woman's face.

'Well then,' Liv said. 'I'll call you Tat!'

Byron mouthed a thank-you to her.

'Aunty Tat is actually my grandmother,' he said with a smile. 'My father is her youngest son, he'll be here later. But like I said, Aunty Tat is the name that she's known by to everyone. After her children grew up and left home, she took a number of foster children into her home, and the name Aunty Tat stuck. Our extended family, foster kids and all, comprises about half the town's population.'

Louise smiled at him. 'You exaggerate, darling. Maybe it did once but the population has grown a bit in the past few years.'

'It has.' Byron leaned closer to his wife. 'Lou, maybe you could take Aunty Tat inside and help her make Liv a cup of tea.'

'We'll make *Lily* a cup of tea, Byron.' Aunty Tat's voice was prim.

'Of course. Lily.' Byron helped his grandmother to her feet and she looked at Liv uncertainly.

'Promise you won't leave while I'm inside.' Aunty Tat held out a hand to Liv, and she took it and squeezed it gently.

'I promise. I'll sit here and wait for you.'

Once they were out of earshot, Byron leaned forward in his chair. 'Thanks so much for coming over. Like I said on the phone, she's been really upset since she saw you the other day. Tell me, Liv, do you have any family connection to the Whitsundays?'

'No, none at all. This is the first time I've been up here.'

'What about the rest of your family?' Byron asked.

'No, we're New South Wales stock. Why do you ask?'

'There's a photo I want to show you. The one that Aunty Tat thinks is you.'

'And her sister has passed away?'

'No. That is, I don't know.' Byron ran his hand over his short hair. 'It's a bit of a family mystery. No one knows what happened to her. Apparently, Liliana disappeared in the middle of World War Two. Some say she was taken by the Japanese—'

'Was she in the army?' Liv asked curiously when he paused.

'Sorry. Let me explain from the beginning. The family lived out on Whitsunday Island, their father—my great-grandfather—was a fisherman and timber-getter. He was a beaut old bloke. I can remember him sitting here on a Sunday afternoon, whittling away at a piece of timber when I was a child. He used to come over across the Passage in his old diesel launch, even when he was in his eighties.' Byron leaned back in his chair. 'Anyway, apparently some Japanese soldiers had been spotted on the island about the time Liliana disappeared, and that was one of the explanations put forward at the time. Aunty Tat has often talked about her sister, but she's never been upset like she has been this past couple of days.' He gestured at Liv's braid. 'When you see the photo, you'll see she had the same sort of hairstyle, and Aunty Tat says that it was the same red-gold colour that yours is.' He shrugged. 'Apart from that, there's really no likeness, but she's spoken of nothing else since she saw you. She's been talking nonstop about when her sister disappeared and how they looked for her. She's gone into great detail, things the family has never heard before.'

'That's so sad,' Liv murmured.

'It is. Most of it seems to be from her imagination. One day, she told Lou that the Japanese soldiers helped her brothers with their homework. Other things she's recalled could be true or part of the dementia'—he shrugged—'who knows. She had a mild stroke a few months ago and was diagnosed with vascular dementia. The doctor said that often seems to bring the past back as though it's the present. She's recovered well physically, and although she's occasionally called out to other women, she's never obsessed like this before. I think you'll understand why when you see Liliana's hair style. Ever since Aunty Tat's stroke, she's been talking about her sister coming home. And then you came along and with the same hairstyle and colour, it's all she can focus on.'

'Poor thing.' Liv shook her head. 'I'd love to see the photo, but honestly, there's no link at all to up here. My mother is an only child and my grandparents were original settlers out in central western New South Wales. My father's family are from Europe.'

She looked up as the two women stepped down from the verandah. Louise was carrying a tray and Aunty Tat was walking behind her, holding a small pottery jug of milk. Byron stood and pulled over a small table, and Louise carefully laid the tray onto the table.

After the tea was poured, Aunty Tat again took her chair closest to Liv's and sat quietly, a contented smile on her face.

'I wonder where Fynn's got to.' Byron glanced at his watch as Liv put his tea cup back on the table.

'Ah, he said you should call him when it's time for me to go back,' Liv said. 'He said he had some things to do.'

Byron raised his eyebrows. 'That's unusual. He usually spends his Sundays here.'

A glimmer of guilt ran through Liv. 'I think … I hope it's not my fault. I think he might have been giving me a bit of space. I … er … commented how he seemed to be following me around.'

'Don't worry about that. If he said he had something to do—'

'Fynn likes pretty girls, doesn't he?' Aunty Tat's innocent voice piped up and heat stole into Liv's cheeks. 'I was pretty when I was young, wasn't I, Lil?'

'He does like pretty girls, Aunty.' Byron drew Aunty Tat's attention away from Liv and looked at his wife. 'Did you get that photo, love?'

Louise nodded and reached into her pocket. She pulled out a small zip lock bag, opening it carefully, and Aunty Tat leaned forward and looked at the photograph through the plastic cover.

'Oh, Lil, remember that day? It was taken at the Boxing Day picnic in 1941. Jack took it so Daddy could be in the photo for a change. We were all over there.' She pointed to the headland at the eastern end of the beach. 'The very last one with our footprints before you left.' Her eyes clouded, and her voice rose, laced with a tinge of hysteria. '*Why* did you leave, Lily? Where did you go? Billy kept looking in his cave. We thought you were hiding from us but every time we looked you weren't there. Poor Mama. She cried like we'd never heard her cry before.'

Liv's eyes misted as the elderly woman's distress escalated. She reached over and took her hand, and the words seemed to come to her without thinking. 'It's all right now, Tat. I'm back here with you now.' Liv smoothed her fingers over the back of Aunty Tat's wrinkled hand. 'Don't cry. It's going to be all right.'

'You won't leave me again, Lil?' Aunty Tat's voice wobbled.

Liv looked to Byron for some backup. 'I think maybe she'll come and visit you again soon,' he said.

Liv nodded but she couldn't bring herself to put the promise into words. This was a problem that the family was going to have to sort out. It was sad, and she knew it was going to be difficult for them when she left, but it wasn't her problem to solve. It was too hard to make promises she couldn't keep. She leaned across and held her hand out. 'May I see the photo?'

Louise passed it over and Liv slipped it out of the plastic covering. It was an old photograph in faded sepia tones. One corner was slightly torn but it was easy to see the group of people in the middle of the photograph. It was a family standing on a beach.

'That's my great-grandfather, Boyd Ellis,' Byron said.

'And that's me, beside you, Lily.'

Liv stared at the photo, conscious of everyone watching her. It was faded and cracked, as though it had been held many times. The young girl standing at the right of the group had a long fair braid like Liv's, but other than that, there was little resemblance.

Sympathy flooded through her. How sad that the young girl had disappeared. It seemed so much more real, looking at a photo rather than just hearing the story.

Aunty Tat beamed at her. 'That was the day we met all the boys. Remember?'

CHAPTER

7

December 10, 1941

Don't they know there's a war on?

'This is so ridiculous,' Liliana Anastasia Ellis muttered under her breath as she walked slowly along Brisbane's Queen Street behind her partners-in-crime. Her cross mood was at odds with the happy, noisy Saturday night crowds surging around them. Soldiers in uniform and women in brightly coloured dresses, their belts cinched in so tight, Liliana wondered how they could possibly breathe, spilled from the hotels and clubs. Their laughter was loud and raucous, and the atmosphere was party-like. Most of the men were drinking beer from bottles, and several had a woman on each arm.

Disgust curled in Liliana's stomach. Ever since she'd stopped at the newsstand on the corner of Queen and Wharf Street and read the front page of today's *Courier Mail*, her worry about sneaking out of the boarding school dormitory had paled into insignificance.

Two days ago, Mother Vincent Reilly, the principal of All Hallows'
Convent, had called a special assembly. The hall had been quiet as
she'd told the students about the attack on Pearl Harbor and the
entry of the United States into the war. There had been quiet jubi-
lation in her voice as she told the girls the war would end quickly
now. Liliana knew the war news was filtered by the school to protect the girls. Now, the front page of the *Courier Mail* confirmed
her worst fears.

'The decision to call up an additional big quota of men for home
defence is believed to provide the best possible safeguard against an
invasion attempt.'

Invasion? Prime Minister Curtin seemed to be concerned, so
what was wrong with these people? Why was there such a celebra-
tory atmosphere in the city tonight?

The late news item on the top left of the front page had increased
her agitation. The bold heading announced: *US given warning of
attack*, and reported that a map recently discovered in purloined
Japanese naval documents had correctly foretold last week's attack
on Pearl Harbor. Liliana's blood ran cold as she read the rest of the
paragraph. Attacks spreading in a wide arc to the east coast of Australia were planned. Her home, her parents and her siblings were in
the north, so close to the action in the Pacific Ocean.

'Come on, Lil. Stop dragging your feet,' Peggy Armitage
called back to her as she forged ahead through the crowd. 'We're
almost there.'

Peggy and the other three girls from All Hallows' Convent
stopped outside a large, brightly lit café as Liliana caught up to them.
It was the first time she'd truanted from the boarding school in Ann
Street, not far from the hubbub of the city. The girls' excursions after
lights out had become more frequent as the soldiers came to town,

but Liliana preferred to stay in, not because she was nervous about being caught by the nuns, but she preferred to study and prepare for her final examinations. The glamorous enticement of soldiers in uniform held no appeal for her. Now that the exams were over, and the girls were counting down the days until the end of term and they could escape the eagle eyes of the nuns forever, Liliana had agreed to come out with them, anxious to find a newspaper.

She looked up at the sign over the door of the building. The large red block letters of the Red Cross Café were outlined in white. In the corner of the window was a small sign stating, 'volunteers always wanted'.

'Do you all want to come in with me, or do you want to wait outside?' Peggy smoothed down the plain navy-blue skirt and adjusted her white blouse.

'What for?' Amelia, usually as outgoing as Peggy, had been quiet tonight.

'I'm volunteering,' Peggy said.

'But you can't. You're going home at the end of the week,' Amelia said with a frown. 'We're booked on the Western Mail to Charleville on Friday morning.'

'I'm not going. I'm staying in Brisbane.' Peggy folded her arms. 'I'm going to cash in my train ticket.'

'Oh my gosh, and your parents agreed to this?' Amelia's eyes were wide.

'I haven't told them yet.' Peggy's smile held a slyness that Liliana had often noticed over the past four years.

Peggy pushed the door open and went inside. Liliana walked to the low brick wall at the side of the café and sat down to wait. A dark laneway led down to the river and muted voices reached them, interspersed with the occasional giggle.

'We're going across to the hotel. You two coming?' Anne and Claudia stood at the edge of the street waiting for a break in the traffic.

'No, I'll wait here for Peggy.' Liliana had her newspaper and she was ready to go back to the convent. Her mood was bleak, and there were another six days and nights to endure before she left for home.

'I'll wait with Lily,' Amelia said.

They sat there quietly, Liliana lost in her thoughts about the possibility of invasion in the north, Amelia unusually quiet beside her.

'Like to keep a couple of lonely soldiers company, ladies?' The slurred voice was accompanied by beery breath and Liliana leaned back away from the man whose face was too close to hers. 'Nice walk down the lane here.'

'No! Sod off!'

Amelia's fierce words were out before Liliana could come up with a suitably scathing reply. She lifted her chin and stared them down, her voice cold and haughty. 'My friend put it quite succinctly.'

'Oh, la de da. We've got a posh pair here.' A horn blared as the two men lurched away into the Queen Street traffic. 'Your loss, sweethearts.' It wasn't long before they found a couple of women on the other side of the street who were willing to talk to them.

Liliana turned away and closed her eyes as the earthy odour of the river wafted up the laneway. No matter how much she pretended, the smell of the water was nothing like home. Interspersed with the stale fumes of the traffic that wound its way along the muddy Brisbane River, the damp smell pervaded the whole school in the humid summer months. Her craving for the smell of salt air and the sound of the wind gently rustling through the hoop pines of home was as physical to Liliana as hunger.

'Lily?' Amelia's shaking voice interrupted her daydreaming.

'What's wrong?' Liliana looked at her with a frown. 'Are you okay?'

Amelia's face was pinched and white. Her eyes welled with tears as she shook her head. 'No.'

'Don't let those blokes upset you. They're gone now.' Amelia shook her head again. 'Or are you worried about the war? It should be okay where you are in the out—'

'Shut up, Lil. And stop being so bloody smart. I get so sick of listening to you prattle on sometimes.'

The comment was meant to hurt but Liliana shrugged it off. She was well used to what her fellow students thought of her, and it didn't bother her.

'I've missed my monthlies,' Amelia said quietly.

'What?' Liliana's eyes widened, and she drew in a sharp breath.

'I'm scared I'm having a baby.'

'How?'

'How do you reckon?'

'But you haven't—'

'I did.' Amelia's voice was glum. 'Twice. It certainly wasn't immaculate conception, although I've been thinking I could try that on Mum and Dad. They're going to kill me.'

'Oh no. Surely not.'

'Kill me? They will.'

'No, not that. I mean surely you can't be pregnant. You're only sixteen.'

'Don't be silly, Lil. For such a smart person, you can be really naïve sometimes.'

Before Liliana could think about the implications of Amelia being pregnant, Peggy came out of the café, her lips tilted in a huge smile.

Amelia leaned close and whispered, 'Don't say anything.'

'I got a job. Start next week and the lady in charge is finding me somewhere to board.' Peggy stood in front of them, smirking as she pulled her gloves off.

'Are you sure that's what you really want, Peg?' Liliana was still trying to deal with the shock of Amelia's news.

'You bet. They're looking for more girls too, if either of you want to stay in the city. She said there are thousands of American soldiers coming soon, and they're all going to be in Brisbane.' Peggy sat down on the wall beside them. 'I'm going to find myself a rich husband and go and live in New York. No way am I going back to the red dust of Charleville. No siree! Not for me!'

'Wait here for me.' Amelia jumped up and crossed to the door of the café, determination in her step. '*I'm* going to stay in Brisbane too.'

'What about you, Lil?' Peggy opened her small purse and pulled out a cigarette and a box of matches. 'Do you want to stay in the city too? Contribute to the war effort?' Her cat-like eyes narrowed as she lit the cigarette and inhaled deeply. 'Oh, silly me. I forgot you live in paradise.'

God, Peggy was a bitch. Six more days, Liliana thought again. Peggy had hated her from the first day they had met in the dormitory on the first floor of the old convent building. The girls had all shared where their families lived and when Liliana told them about growing up on Whitsunday Island, they had been envious.

'Oh, you are so lucky. Beats our dry and boring outback hands down,' Amelia said.

'It's very isolated and lonely,' Liliana argued. 'We get the newspapers days late. They're dropped off at Proserpine from the mail train, and then someone has to take them to Cannon Valley by dirt road, and then if we're lucky, the tourist launch will pick them up and drop them to us. It could be ten days before we get the news.'

'Oh, you poor baby. Late newspapers, hey?' Peggy's words had dripped with sarcasm. 'And tell us, what do you see from your windows, island girl? Dry red dust and huge emaciated beasts fighting over the scarce water that we might manage to pump if we're lucky? Black sticky flies that get into your nose and mouth and ears as soon as you go outside?'

'We have flies too.' Back then, Liliana had cared what the other girls thought of her. 'And sandflies. And dangerous creatures … like … like sharks, and jellyfish … and devil fish and moray eels.' Her protests were ignored.

'And you get tourists too! I would give *anything* to live in a place like that.' Peggy had kept her distance for a few weeks after that conversation, but always took the opportunity to have a dig whenever she could. Liliana soon learned to shrug it off and not let it bother her, but she was looking forward to going home and never coming back to school.

The longer she was at boarding school, the more she realised she was different to the other girls, and it didn't bother her one iota. This year in English her class had studied R.M. Ballantyne's *The Coral Island*, and the teasing had raised its ugly head again.

'That's where Liliana comes from,' Peggy had said to Sister Mary Catherine, throwing an innocent smile her way. 'Paradise, just like Ralph, Jack and Peterkin.'

Liliana had smothered a grin. Peggy's superficial acceptance of the story about an idyllic paradise was typical. She of all people should have picked up the theme of hierarchy and leadership.

The four years at the Catholic girls' school had been difficult, but if there was one lesson she had learned, it was resilience. Those four years had strengthened her character. When the war was over, Liliana was going to get a cadetship on a newspaper, and then she would travel the world. Her life would be exciting; talking to intelligent people, perhaps working as a foreign correspondent, interviewing spies and diplomats, maybe travelling to North Africa to interview a soldier from the French Foreign legion, and hopefully being published in the *Times*. Dreaming about her future was one way to push aside her constant worry about the war.

Their final days at All Hallows' flew by, and on the following Friday morning, the girls stood on the platform at Roma Street station. The Christmas crowds milled around them and it was hard to hear each other over the frequent announcements and the hiss of the steam engines. Peggy and Amelia had come to see them off. That morning, they'd both moved into a shared room in a boarding house at West End.

'Platform five, Northern Mail, ten minutes till departure. Passengers, please board.'

Liliana put her hands to her ears as the shrill whistle sounded over the loudspeaker.

Peggy raised her hand in a careless wave. 'Bye, island girl. I won't have anyone to keep me on the straight and narrow anymore.'

'Bye, Peg. Hope it all works out for you.'

'Yep, it will. I'm still waiting to hear back from Mum and Dad.'

Amelia was quiet and pale. Liliana hugged her and whispered quietly so the others wouldn't hear. 'Got them yet?'

'No. Not yet.'

'Make sure you write to me. If things get really bad, maybe you can come and stay with us on the island.' Liliana crossed her fingers behind her back; Mama would never agree to that.

'I will.' Amelia clung to her. 'I'll miss you, Lil.'

Liliana kissed Amelia's cheek and hugged her back. 'Take care, Amelia.'

She followed the other girls to platform five. Claudia and Anne were on the mail train north to Townsville with her. Liliana would be first off at Mackay, then change to the motor rail that went through Proserpine on the way to Bowen. Dad should be at Proserpine dropping off the fish catch to go south to Brisbane on the next train. If he was, she wouldn't have to spend a couple of days waiting for him at Aunt Beatrice's boarding house in Prossie. But Dad knew she wanted to be on the island for Christmas and he wouldn't let her down. He'd promised and her father was a man of his word. It was going to be wonderful to go home to stay. To be there with her family, no matter what happened in this blasted war.

'Which carriage are you in, Lil?'

'Second class sleeper.' She patted the calico bag hanging from her shoulder. 'I bought books for everyone at McWhirters for Christmas last Saturday morning, and I'm going to read them all before I wrap them up.'

Books were a precious commodity on Whitsunday Island. She'd also bought the early edition of the *Courier Mail* from the paper boy at the entrance to the station. The headline about a Japanese retreat had jumped out at her but she'd shoved it in her bag to read on the train.

'We'll say goodbye at Mackay then.'

Liliana hitched the bag higher on to her shoulder and headed for her carriage.

She was going home.

CHAPTER

8

December 26, 1941

'This is as far as I go.' The farmer had driven Jack Rickard and two of the ground crew he'd hooked up with on base down the bumpy, dusty road from Proserpine—or Prossie, as the old fellow had called it. He called to them from the cab of the old Dodge as the truck came to a stop and they jumped down from the back and pulled their kit bags from the tray. Jack came around and held out a ten-shilling note to the man but he waved it away, his leathery face wrinkled in a grin.

'Nah, lad, no charge. You boys are fighting for the country. Least I can do.' He jerked a thumb towards the mangroves on the south side of the beach and winked. 'If you want to freshen up for the ladies, there's a freshwater spring over there between the beach and the jetty.'

Jack followed the direction of the old fellow's thumb. A wooden launch puffing black smoke was pulling in at the end of the long stone pier on the eastern side of the bay.

'That's where you'll catch the launch to go to the islands tonight,' the farmer added. 'Gotta go. That old tub is taking my tomatoes. Bit like carrying coals to Newcastle, taking tomatoes to Bowen, ain't it?' His nicotine-stained teeth appeared as he laughed at his own joke. 'Enjoy your break, boys.'

With a loud crunch, the truck engaged into gear and lurched forward. It kicked up a cloud of dust that replaced the pungent aroma of tomatoes that had surrounded the three men for the past two hours as they'd leaned against the backboard of the truck. All the way from Proserpine to Cannon Valley, sugar cane and pineapple plantations, divided by seemingly never-ending rows of mango trees, filled the flat land beneath the Conway Range. As the truck had approached Cannon Valley Beach, a glimpse of sapphire water had beckoned. Riding on the back of that old truck had been uncomfortable. Jack had already decided they'd find a different way back to the base if they could.

'Reckon I could live down here after the war,' Roger Brooks said as he reached into his shirt pocket for a cigarette. 'What do you say, boys? Bit better than Bowen, hey?'

'Yeah. Don't mind it at all.' Jack cupped his hand as Roger held the match up to his cigarette. 'I'm with you, Rog. I mightn't even go home once this war is done.' He kept the bitterness from his voice. There was no point going back to the Hunter Valley. If he could convince Dad to lend him some money, he might think about starting a farm of his own up here. The old bastard probably would pay to keep him away from the vineyard—the bitterness pushed in again as Jack remembered their last argument.

'If you stopped sprouting your high-falutin' ideas and did a bit of real work to help your brother, maybe we wouldn't be losing money hand over fist.' His father's voice had been ice cold.

Jack's stomach had churned with anger and he'd held himself so rigid, the muscles in his shoulders quivered. The three years he'd spent at university studying engineering had opened up so many possibilities for the way they could improve harvesting and production at the vineyard with the implementation of modern technology, but trying to talk to his father was like talking to a brick wall. Heck, it wasn't even anything new that needed doing. It would simply mean bringing their production processes into the 1940s. Some of the methods his father used were the same as those his own father had used at the turn of the century.

Bloody pull my weight, he thought. *I know more about the grapes and the soil than my plod-headed brother ever will.* But he didn't say what he was thinking.

Maybe the truth hurt. Dad had to wake up eventually. Jack wasn't prepared to take the blame for the decline in the business. His father's thinking was so bloody narrow. Jack's great-grandfather had been one of the pioneer winemakers in the Hunter Valley, but their father was training Richard, his older brother, to take over the business, just because he'd had the luck to be the one born first. It wasn't bloody fair.

Second son, be damned.

Jack knew he had as much right to the vineyard as Richard. His older brother had always been the golden-haired boy, literally and in their father's eyes. Jack knew he was entitled to more than a secondary role but their father would have none of it. Since their great-grandfather had bought the land in the 1870s, the eldest son had always taken over the vineyard and their bloody father intended doing the same. It was the way things happened.

You'd think we were still in the bloody nineteenth century.

Why his father had ever sent him off to university, Jack had never been able to fathom because Dad wouldn't listen to any suggestions that Jack made.

'There's no need to make change for change's sake. There's nothing wrong with the way we've always done things. You need to pull your weight and things will improve if we work together,' was his father's constant catch-cry.

Who could blame a man if he went off to town sometimes when his father demanded his presence for the physical work? What was the point in making an effort when he could be at the horse races or in the cool of the pub? Richard would reap the benefits. Jack was bloody cheap labour, that's all they wanted him there for.

But the vineyard was Jack's life; he'd been out in the vines since the day he could walk. He loved the whole process, watching the grapes ripen on the vine and knowing exactly when to harvest; picking up the fine red volcanic soil and letting it filter through his fingers. He had a feel for the land that his father—and his brother—didn't have or understand. Even before his teenage years, he'd gone out to check the grapes as soon as he came home from school each afternoon.

'Have you ever considered the fact that our sales are down because of the blasted depression and the war?' Jack managed to keep his voice calm but the expletive had slipped out before he could stop it.

'Don't show disrespect in my house, boy.' Finally, his father's voice rose and satisfaction curled in Jack's chest. As his father had stared him down and Richard smirked, Jack gave in to the red hot anger that was simmering in his chest.

'It's bloody feudal, that's what it is.' He'd ducked when his father had raised his hand before launching into the familiar lecture on the rule of primogeniture.

Bloody primogeniture. Dad was an arse and Richard wasn't much better. It wasn't fair that Richard would get the farm. On that cold night, his father had yelled long and loud, and Mum had scurried off to the kitchen. Jack knew his mother was sympathetic to the way he felt, but she did whatever the old man said; there was no support coming from that quarter. That was the way it was, and the way it would always be.

'There will be no more discussion. My word is final.' Dad stood beside the dining room table, shaking the newspaper that he'd been reading before the argument had started.

'Well, Dad, you know what? I've had it up to here.' Jack sliced his hand in a chopping motion to his neck. 'You can stuff your grapevines where the sun don't shine. Fuck you and fuck Richard. I'm out of here. For good.'

Richard's mouth had been set in a firm line, but Jack knew he hadn't imagined the glint of satisfaction in his brother's eyes when he'd shoved past him into the kitchen and grabbed the keys to Dad's truck from the hook near the back door. Mum's eyes had widened; she knew him so well. One hand went to her bosom and she held the other out to him.

'Jack, don't be silly. Please.' Her voice tore at him, but he kept going. 'I'm sure you and Dad can work something out.'

'Where do you think you're going in my truck?' Dad had bellowed behind him. The door slammed with a satisfying crash and Jack took off for the pub in Cessnock, rage pushing his foot hard on the accelerator. The back tyres of the truck slewed around in the loose dirt at the end of the driveway and the truck rammed sideways into the gate post. Not only did it push the post sideways, the loud scrape as he drove forward indicated that Dad's pride and joy would need some panel-beating. Jack hit the brake and shoved the gear stick into reverse before deliberately backing into the fence post near the mailbox. Mum's white rose bushes in the small garden were collateral damage but he was too angry to care.

By the time he'd driven the fifteen miles to town, his breath was coming in short and choppy pants. Anger sat in his chest like a hard stone. The first thing he saw in town was the poster on the community board outside the post office.

Join the RAAF. It's a man's job.

He'd been thinking about enlisting since he'd left university last December. His final exam marks had been top class—not that Dad had ever asked—and Jack had toyed with the idea of joining up. A few of his mates from Sydney Uni had applied for officer entry but Jack had been itching to get back to the vineyard.

His wallet and his bank book were in his back pocket. Jack parked the truck in the middle of the main street, left the keys in the ignition and walked to the railway station.

Two weeks later, he arrived in Melbourne at the No 1 RAAF recruiting centre, took the Oath, and was enlisted and sent to Ascot Vale School of Engineering for three months before being sent to the Air Observers School in Cootamundra.

And only seven months later, here he was in the RAAF. When Japan had entered the war the same week he'd been posted to the Catalina squadrons at Rathmines, and then up to the base at Port Moresby, Jack knew he'd made the right decision. The men he worked with already treated him with more respect than his father ever had. He was a man here, not a second son.

It was just a bloody shame he'd left home the way he had.

Enough.

Roger put a hand on Jack's shoulder. 'Come on, boys. Let's go find this spring. We're not going to impress the local ladies covered in dust. And the odd bit of cow shit.' He brushed at his shirt. 'I was leaning against a bag of it.' He turned to the third man who'd got off the truck. 'You're as quiet as Jack here.'

'Checking out the talent,' Charlie said. 'But you know what? I think we've wasted the trip. We've come a long way for nothing.'

'Nothing? Look at that beaut view,' Jack said. 'Beats looking at the dry and dusty airfield.' He'd been sent down from Port Moresby to assist with the development of the Flying Boat Maintenance Unit. The base at Moresby was becoming untenable and the plan was to relocate the maintenance unit to Bowen, out of range of the Japanese bombers. Jack had jumped at the chance to come down to Cannon Valley for a break before he went back to Port Moresby. Roger and Charlie had invited him to spend his leave with them on the promise of a trip out to the Whitsunday Islands.

'The talk on the unit is that a squadron might be based here eventually. Word is that you're getting a lot of attention from the Japs up there now.'

'Yeah. We lost a Catalina a couple of weeks ago. We've had to leave the barracks a couple of times to avoid the air raids. I'd be happy to come back to the mainland.' Jack nodded and stared out over the water. It was a relief to be away from the constant tension of Port Moresby.

'I noticed some bullet holes in your Cat,' Roger commented.

'Yeah, they didn't tell us we'd be plugging bullet holes on the way back home when they trained us at Rathmines.' Jack's laugh held no mirth. He stepped away from them and perused the crowd as the park filled up. 'We'll have to find out if we can get a boat across to one of the islands this afternoon.' An assortment of trucks and cars were lined up at the edge of the grass, and there seemed to be more children spilling out of them than adults.

His eyes lingered as he spotted a tall girl walking towards the rocks with a couple of small boys, and another girl tagging behind them. She was slim and her shoulders were held straight. Long, lithe tanned legs were exposed by her thigh-length shorts and the sun glinted off her reddish-gold hair.

'Come on, let's find this spring and get cleaned up.' He grabbed his bag and hitched it to his shoulder.

The spring was at the end of the first bank of mangroves and, to their surprise, it had been piped to a tap. They waited as a couple of men in front of them filled kerosene tins before carting them along the beach to where the picnic was being set up. Jack cupped his hand beneath the cold crystal-clear water and drank before ducking his head beneath the tap. He ran his hands through his hair and pulled a small comb from his back pocket and flicked his hair back. As he waited for the other two to clean up, he stood and looked out at the water. It was so blue and bright, it almost hurt his eyes. In the distance, islands dotted the horizon. As he looked out at the view, he smiled. The tall girl with the children walked around the shore, peering into the rock pools. And she was as pretty as he'd hoped.

CHAPTER
9

December 26, 1941
Cannon Valley Beach

As the tide ebbed and the afternoon faded away, coral fangs of reef appeared. At Cannon Valley Beach, great masses of oysters clung to the salt-streaked rocks exposed by the low tide. Several men stood in a circle around the small bay, shucking them as soon as they were prised from the rocks. A constant stream of children ran the shucked oysters back to the large table in the middle of the grassy area beside the beach.

Lily wandered around the rock pools in the lagoon with Katarina, Tatiana and the twins. Mama was busy over at the food tent and Dad was stoking the fires in the huge drums that would cook the chickens and vegetables for the baked dinner later. The pools were fascinating, and she bent over and pointed out the fish to the children as the small creatures darted among the coral flowers. They reflected the sunlight, some silver and golden, some of the tiny ones, myriad colours.

'Oh, Lil, look at the little blue one*th*.' Katarina's lisp was pronounced when she was excited, and Lily grabbed for her as the small girl leaned too far and flailed her arms. A whoosh of air brushed her arm as someone shot past her and grabbed the back of Katarina's shorts before she overbalanced into the water.

'Gotcha!' The voice was deep, and the man chuckled as he pulled Katarina to safety. 'That was close.'

Lily took her sister's hand.

'Thank you.' She smiled at the unfamiliar young man as he balanced on the large flat rock at the edge of the pool.

'No problem.'

'I can *thwim*,' Katarina protested.

'I know you can,' Lily replied. 'But Uncle Joe and his boys haven't got the dinghies out there yet.'

'Do they act as lifeguards?' the man asked curiously as Lily stared at him. 'I'm sorry. I'm Jack Rickard.'

His dark brown eyes were friendly and full of warmth as he smiled at her. Lily held out her hand.

'Welcome, Jack. I'm Liliana Ellis and these are my sisters and brothers, Tatiana, Katarina, and that's Billy and Robbie.'

Robbie looked up at him earnestly and Billy scowled at his big sister.

'If you want to talk to Billy, you know you have to call him "Goat" or he won't answer,' Robbie said. 'You know that, Lil.'

'Got it,' said Jack. 'It's a nickname, is it? Hello, Goat. Nice to meet you. How old are you?' He held out a hand to Billy who shook it earnestly.

'We're twins and we're seven and a half.' Billy scampered away to the next rock pool, followed by Robbie and Katarina, soon losing interest in a new grown-up.

Tatiana stayed by Lily's side. 'Look, Lil, there go the dinghies now. We can go for a swim soon.'

Four long wooden boats, each with a man rowing in the centre, pushed out from the shore. A teenage boy was perched at the front end of each boat, each boy holding a long-handled net. As they watched, there was a whoop and one of the boys dipped his net into the water and scooped something into the boat.

'What are they doing? Fishing?' Jack addressed his question to Lily, and her sister rolled her eyes and jumped over the small rock pools to follow her brothers and sister.

'Clearing the bay so we can swim. We had to wait for the bottom of the tide.'

'Clearing it?' Jack watched as the net was lifted triumphantly for a second time.

'Box jellyfish. Once they've cleared the bay at the bottom of the tide, the boys sit out there in their boats and scoop in the ones that come in with the flood tide.'

'Do they sting?' Jack asked.

'Yes, they do.' Lily waited for his reaction as she spoke slowly. 'You'll actually die if you get stung. Or you probably will. No one's ever survived a sting that I've heard of.'

'Really? They can kill you? I didn't know that.' Jack shook his head. 'And the adults let the kids get in the water?'

'You're not from around here then?'

'No, I'm in the air force, but I'm from New South Wales. Down in the Hunter Valley.' His eyes were wide and Lily smiled at him again.

'Ah, so you're not even a Queenslander? No wonder you didn't know.' She beckoned him to follow her as she spied the children heading back to the beach. 'Have a look at the jellyfish when the boats come in. The rowers change over every hour or so, but between them, the local fishermen will keep a watch out until the tide changes. But don't touch them. Even the tentacles are deadly.'

'Incredible.' Jack shook his head. 'Have you lived here long? You seem to know a lot about the place.'

'I do. I've lived here all my life. Apart from going away to school, that is. Come for a walk and chat to me. I promised Mama I'd keep an eye on the kids when they were on the rocks. Once they get back to the grass near the beach, they'll be fine. The twins— especially Billy—'

'Goat,' Jack said with a smile.

'Yes, especially Goat, will disappear on a search for buried treasure or some adventure if I don't watch them. Kat! Goat and Robbie. Come on, over here.' Liliana pointed to the grassed area behind the strip of sand as she called them. Jack followed them over and waited until they were all on the grass. Tatiana followed them back. The children scampered off to their friends where a game of Red Rover was in full swing.

'Wait here.' Jack left them for a moment and came back with a blanket. He shook it and spread it in the shade beneath the huge Poinciana tree. 'A seat for you, my lady.'

Lily laughed and sat down.

Tatiana put her hands on her hips and cleared her throat.

Jack looked away from Lily with a smile. 'My apologies, a seat for you, *my ladies.*'

He sat down across from them and leaned back against the tree. 'So tell me, where do you—both—live?' He shot a smile at Tat, and Lily smiled when her sister blushed.

He really was thoughtful, and good-looking.

'We live on a farm on Whitsunday Island,' Tatiana butted in before Lily could reply.

'What sort of farm? And which island is Whitsunday Island? Tell me all about it.'

As Tat chattered on, telling Jack all about the sawmill, the pineapple plantation, and the goats, he kept his eyes on Lily. After a while, she began to feel self-conscious and turned away from his steady gaze to watch the children playing.

Tatiana kept the best for last. 'And now we have our own resort.'

'Resort?' he asked with a smile.

Lily turned back to him. 'Our parents built some palm huts along the bay a couple of years back after Hayman and South Molle islands started up their resorts. Mama cooks the meals, and Dad takes the tourists out fishing in between looking after everything else.'

'It must be busy over there,' he said.

'It is. But we all have our own jobs.' Lily picked at the fringe of the picnic rug. They were probably boring him with the mundane details of their lives.

'Are you a tourist too?' Tat asked.

'Tat, don't be rude,' Lily reprimanded. 'Jack is in the air force.'

'How was I supposed to know that? He hasn't got a uniform on.' Tat pulled a face as she turned to face Jack. 'I just was going to ask where you were staying. You could come to our island.'

At fourteen, Tat was obviously smitten. Liliana very much felt the grown-up, wise older sister. 'Perhaps.'

'That would be great. I haven't got anywhere to stay yet. We were going to ask around here today,' Jack said. 'And also, do you know if we can get back to Bowen by boat?'

'Yes. You can.' Tatiana was almost jumping with excitement and Lily frowned at her. 'The morning steamer comes by our jetty to drop off the mail and picks up guests before it goes back to Bowen.'

'Great, we'll look into that.' Jack was well-spoken and Lily wondered how old he was.

'Who's we?' she asked.

'I'm with two other men from the airfield.'

'The one at Bowen? Why are you there?' Lily sat up straight. She hadn't seen a newspaper since her trip home, and the ever-present worry rose to her throat. 'Have the Japs landed in the north already?' Her voice shook as she pointed to the children heading towards the water. 'Tat, go and look after them. Don't let them go in past their knees.'

'Yes, ma'am.' Tat scowled at her and walked off slowly towards the water. Once her sister had reached the children, Lily clasped her hands together and turned to Jack. 'Tell me honestly. Is there fighting on land already? Is that why the air force is up in Bowen? I *have* seen more planes go over in the last week or two.'

'No, I'm based in New Guinea. I'm just here for some engineering work. The action is way north of the Coral Sea.' His smile was gentle. 'Don't worry. There's nothing for you to be worried about. The Japs are nowhere near the Australian coast.'

Lily's shoulders sagged with relief. 'We're so isolated here, and it's hard to get decent radio reception out on the island. The news comes to us very late.'

He looked around and gestured to the Passage. 'This looks pretty idyllic to me. Living up here would be worth the isolation, I reckon.'

The memory of Peg calling her island home an idyllic life made Liliana's response a little waspish. 'It's far from idyllic, trust me.'

'I'd love to see your island. It's so different up here to where I come from. On our farm, we don't get very good radio reception either. Too many hills.' Jack leaned back on his hands as he looked out over the water. 'This is amazing. I've never seen anything so beautiful.'

'I think we do have a couple of empty palm huts at the moment.' Lily began to thaw and tried to make amends for snapping at him. 'We're not as busy in the wet season.'

He lifted his gaze from the water to the clear blue sky and his white teeth flashed in a smile. 'This is the wet season?'

'It is.' Lily frowned. His calm voice gave her a warm feeling in the pit of her tummy, a feeling she'd never experienced before. 'How about I take you to meet Dad and see what he says. Maybe he could take you and your friends out on a fishing trip too if you stayed with us. Then you can tell me all about where you come from.' She jumped up and headed for the cooking area with Jack close behind her.

'Dad.' Lily tapped on her father's shoulder as he leaned over the fire drum. He was a tall man, but lean, his muscles honed by years of manual work.

'Dad, this is Jack—' She paused and looked at Jack. 'Sorry, I forgot your last name.'

'Rickard, sir,' Jack finished for her and held out his hand to her father.

Admiration filled Lily. Jack's quietly spoken confidence and unassuming demeanour was very different to the drunken soldiers she had seen last week in Brisbane. As well as being interested in what she had to say, he was polite and obviously came from a good family. And he was a *real* air force man, about to go on a mission. She watched as the two men sized each other up.

'Jack and his friends have come down for a break from the airfield at Bowen. They're looking for somewhere to stay,' she said.

'Pleased to meet you, Mr ...'

'Ellis, but please call me Boyd.' Her father shook Jack's hand. 'So, you're at Bowen. I heard there was something going on up there.'

Jack shook his head. 'I'm an LAC with number 20 squadron in Port Moresby. On the Catalinas. I've been seconded down to Bowen for a couple of weeks. Roger and Charlie are construction crew. We're down here on a few days' leave.'

'We'd be happy to have you stay on the island. We have plenty of room at the moment,' Boyd said. Lily smiled as her father added, 'And how about a fishing trip out to the Passage?'

'That would be great, sir—I mean Boyd—although you'll have to show me the ropes, I'm just a farm boy. I've never been fishing in the sea.'

'Well, we'll have to remedy that, won't we?' Dad's grin widened as he threw an arm around Jack's shoulder. 'Stay and have a yarn with me, Jack. Lil, you go and help your mother with the other women.'

'Thanks for bringing me over to meet your father. The boys'll be pleased we have somewhere to bunk tonight.' Jack's eyes crinkled as he smiled at her and that funny light feeling went down her legs again.

'See you later then.' Lily made her way over to the long narrow tents that had been set up to keep the hot sun off the cold food, a bit piqued that Dad had taken away her new friend. As she walked away, Jack was asking Dad about the steam launch that would take them back to Bowen.

She'd wanted to hear more about the war. Not the specifics, just what he was allowed to talk about. Whether she should be as scared as reading the paper made her feel. Jack seemed like a nice young man, and she'd enjoyed listening to his voice. She guessed he wasn't much older than she was. He was a little more genteel than the local fishermen who visited the island. But now *she'd* been dismissed to the food tent to be with the women. Honestly, Dad was so old-fashioned.

Mama was what Dad always laughingly called 'chief cook and bottle washer', and she was in full chief mode when Lily wandered into the tent. No matter how much she fought it, Mama was chief everything in their lives. To those looking in on the lives of the Ellis family on Whitsunday Island, the family appeared happy. Boyd had come home from the First World War with a Russian wife, the daughter of a white émigré who had lost his own wife— Alexandra rarely spoke of that—and fled to Paris with his daughter and son in 1917 just before the revolution. Nor did Alexandra speak of those days to her children. Instead, she told them stories about where she lived when she was a small child, a huge house, a beautiful garden and the forest.

'Oh, how I loved the forest,' Mama would say as Lily and Tatiana sat at her feet by the lamplight in the cool of the winter. 'It was just like our island but bigger. We would pick mushrooms and berries, so many berries—strawberries, blueberries, cranberries and raspberries.'

'Who's we, Mama?' Lily would ask. 'Was it your mama?'

Mama would wave her hand. 'Oh, it was just me. I would wander by myself.' The story would finish at that point and Mama would go into the kitchen and cook until well into the night. Liliana soon learned not to ask questions.

One night, Tatiana shook her awake. 'I can hear Mama crying.'

Together, they crept to the door of their parents' bedroom. The deep soothing tones of her father's voice covered her mother's sobs. 'I do not want to remember anymore,' the girls heard her say.

Fragments of her mother's unexplained sadness lodged in Lily's soul, but the nights Mama cried became less frequent as twin brothers were born, followed by another sister a couple of years later. But when talk of war began, Lily saw the shadows deepen beneath her mother's eyes again and she became more protective of the children. Lily had to beg to be allowed to go back to school in 1939 when war was actually declared. Tatiana took advantage of Mama's fear and insisted on staying home and doing her lessons by correspondence. But despite the shadows she carried, Alexandra had taken to island life as though she had been born to it and, after almost twenty years as Boyd's wife and living on the island, she was respected and admired by the local community. The children soon learned there were times when they had to be on their best behaviour and treat Mama gently.

Laughter and chatter filled the air as the women prepared salads and then laid damp tea towels over the platters as they were filled up, but Mama's lilting accent rose above the other voices and her eyes narrowed as Lily walked across to her. 'Who's watching the little ones?'

'Tatiana is,' Lily replied.

'As long as someone's keeping a close eye on that Billy.' Her mother reached under the long bench at the back of the tent and pulled out two kerosene tins. 'Seeing you're here, you can help us out. Take these around to the spring and fill them up, please, Lil.'

Lily frowned. She had packed a book in her bag and had been looking forward to finding a secluded corner and reading now that the kids were occupied. 'Both of them?'

'Yes, both of them. And no sneaking off to read your book until after the meal is served and cleaned up. There's plenty for you to do.' Her voice was impatient. 'I don't know why you even had to bring a book anyway.'

'Do you really need the water now? I can get it later.'

'Yes, we do.' Mama's eyes narrowed further as she looked past her.

'I can only carry one tin at a time.' Lily knew there was a grumble in her tone but knowing Mama, this was a job for a job's sake. They didn't need all that water here just to wet a few tea towels.

Idle hands and all that. Her mother was the mistress of proverbs. She had one for every occasion.

'Can I help?'

Lily swivelled around. Jack was standing behind her.

'Your dad had to go in the truck to collect some more timber for the fire, so I said I'd come over and see if I could help.'

'Mama, this is Jack. He and his friends from the air force base are staying in our huts tonight,' Lily said as Mama's frown deepened.

'And your dad has kindly offered to organise for the steamer to collect us at the end of the week.' Jack turned to Mama. 'Now, please let me help, Mrs Ellis. What would you like me to do?'

'You certainly can help, Jack. Lil will show you where the spring is.' Her mother handed the empty tins to him. 'Thank you. Now, get a wriggle on, Lil. I've got plenty more work for you to do. No dawdling, please.'

Lily tried to keep the smile off her face as she and Jack left the tent. Her mother had eagle eyes and she knew that they would be on them as they walked along the beach to the spring. It wasn't often that a young man paid attention to her.

'Lil, wait!'

Uh oh. Lily turned slowly at her mother's command. 'Yes, Mama?'

'After you fill the tins, collect the kids, and then Dad can do the photo as soon as he gets back.'

'The photo!' A smile spread across Lily's face. 'Oh, yes. I nearly forgot.'

After they'd collected the water and the requisite number of tea towels were soaking—Jack had laughed when Lily started quoting Mama's favourite proverbs—the whole family gathered together for the annual family photo. Jack stayed with them while Lily and Tat walked along the beach until they found a suitable patch of sand, and Lily caught her mother watching them closely. Her mother treated her as though she was a child. If she ever found out that she'd been out in the streets of Brisbane on a Saturday night and fending off the attention of grown men in uniform, Lily knew she'd never be allowed off the island again.

Dad retrieved his six-twenty Box Brownie camera and loaded a fresh roll of film as Mama kicked off her shoes and left them on the grass. As usual, she was the only one wearing shoes. Kat was doing cartwheels on the grass as Lily and Tat smoothed the sand with the palms of their hands. Jack stood to the side and when Lily glanced up at him from beneath her eyelashes, he sent her a sweet smile.

'Be careful, Tat.' She jumped to her feet and tugged Tatiana back from the sand. Her sister was gawping at Jack and, knowing how clumsy she was, she would probably walk on the freshly smoothed surface.

'We're ready, Dad.'

Their father stood with the sun behind him as the family lined up in order of age.

Mama, Lil, Tat, Goat, Robbie and Kat. It was a memory that would stay with Lily for the rest of her life.

The annual ritual of the Ellis family footprints in the sand.

The war must be worrying her more than she realised because her throat closed and tears pricked at her eyes. Lily fought back the sob that rose in her chest and put her hand to her mouth as they waited. What if Dad had to go to fight the war too? This might be the last photo he ever took of their family.

'Rightio,' said Dad as he looked down into the camera box. 'Lil, smile. Stop looking miserable. And take your hand away from your face.'

'Wait, sir.' Jack's voice interrupted and Dad looked up. 'Would you like me to take it, so you can be in the photograph too?'

'That is very thoughtful of you, son. Just let me do this bit and then you can take a photo of all of us all together. We don't usually do that.'

Jack smiled and stepped back as Dad held the camera. Mama stepped forward and delicately placed one slender foot in the sand before stepping back slowly with a satisfied nod. 'Lil,' she said. 'Your turn.'

Lily stepped forward and placed her right foot carefully next to the imprint in the sand that her mother had made. Her voice shook as she stepped back. 'Tat.' She ignored the tear that rolled down her cheek, not wanting to draw attention to herself by wiping it away.

Tat followed suit and the stepping forward onto the sand continued until the small prints of Goat and Robbie, and finally Kat completed the line. With a fist pump and a cry of satisfaction, Dad took the annual photo.

'A bloody beauty, that one!' he said triumphantly.

'Boyd Ellis, watch your language.' But the smile on Mama's face took the sting from her rebuke as Dad handed the camera to Jack and they stood in a line for him to take the family photo.

* * *

As it turned out, there was only room for two extra on the Ellis boat that night, so Jack's friend, Charlie, went back to South Molle. Wally Bauer was home on leave for Christmas from the RAAF and would bring Charlie across the Passage to Whitsunday Island the next morning.

'Liliana. Tatiana. Come here please.' On the way back to the island, Mama beckoned them to the front of the boat. Katarina had gone to sleep with her head on their mother's lap, and Goat and Robbie yawned as they sat on the floor, their backs resting on the wheelhouse. Jack and Roger were up the back with Dad as he steered the boat past Pioneer Rocks.

'Yes, Mama?' Lily kept her gaze ahead as the launch rounded the rock and headed south towards home.

'It's past time I had a talk to both of you.'

'What about, Mama?' Tatiana sat down as their mother made room for them.

'About boys.'

'Oh, not now.' Lily stood until their mother pointed to the empty seat.

'*Time and tide wait for no one.*' Mama patted the empty bench beside her.

'What does that mean?' Tat asked.

'It means if you don't prepare for the future, you will fall behind.' Liliana rolled her eyes and added under her breath, 'Mama's going to make sure we don't.'

'I'm pleased to hear you learned something at that boarding school.' Mama's hearing was as acute as her sight was shrewd.

Her stern lecture to Lily and Tat took up most of the trip. Once when she looked away from the girls as they approached the island, Lily rolled her eyes at Tat; their mother was so prudish she didn't even use the word 'sex'. The one time she'd said intercourse to Lily when she'd had her first talk about 'becoming a woman', poor Mama had blushed for days after. Sometimes, Lily wondered how she and her siblings had ever been conceived. But the talk of the moment was more about trust and having respect for themselves. As *women* of course.

'You have been taught how to act like ladies, and I expect your behaviour to reflect that.' She looked to the back of the boat where Dad was pointing out the fishing marks to Jack and Roger. 'At no time over the next two days will either of you be alone with any of those boys—young men. Is that clear?'

'Yes, Mama,' they responded in unison. Lily wondered what Mama would say if she knew about the activities of some of her friends at All Hallows' School. If Amelia did need a sanctuary, it certainly wouldn't be here on their island.

'Tatiana. Go and sit with your brothers please.'

Lily knew there was more to come, and she tried not to roll her eyes. The gaps in her sex education—what she hadn't picked up from reading the novels that Peg had given her—had been filled in when she'd listened to the girls in the dormitory each night, but it looked like she was about to get the next instalment from her mother.

Mama smoothed her hand over Lily's hair. 'You can take that look off your face right now.' Even though her words sounded cross, they were accompanied by a smile. 'You're old enough now, Lil. And you have grown into a young woman over the past couple of years. A very beautiful young woman.'

'There's no need to talk about *that*, Mama. We learned it all at school.'

Her mother took her chin gently in her hand and Liliana met her soft gaze reluctantly. 'You might have learned about the physical aspects of *that*'—Mama's eyes crinkled in a rare smile—'but there's more to it than that, my sweet. There's one thing I want you to always remember.'

'Yes?' Lily tried to keep the scowl from her face.

'When you meet somebody, I want you to always remember this. Love is unselfish. True love, I mean. And the respect for a woman should be considered over the pleasures of the moment. A *good* man will always hold to that.'

This time the heat ran up Lily's neck and into her cheeks. No matter what detailed conversations the girls had in the dorm, this was her mother, for goodness sake.

'Yes, Mama,' she muttered. 'I need a drink of water.' She jumped up and headed into the cabin and spent the rest of the journey helping Dad steer the boat towards home.

CHAPTER
10

27 December, 1941

When Charlie arrived on the Bauers' boat the next morning, Lily and Tatiana met him at the jetty. There was no sign of life at the palm huts where Jack and Roger had bunked down last night. Charlie waved to the crew of the boat as it pulled away into the channel and turned to the girls with wide eyes.

'This is where you *live*? You actually live on a tropical island?'

Tatiana nodded. 'Yep. All our lives. All of us kids were born up there at the house. Mrs Pentecost, the midwife in Prossie, came over to help every time.' She laughed at Charlie's expression. 'Dad can handle the goats but not the *kids*. Get it?'

'Really, Tat.' Lily rolled her eyes and her tone was bored. 'Grow up.'

'No, it's fine.' Charlie's smile was infectious. 'I want to know all about the island and how you live. It's so much bigger than South

Molle. This island is huge.' He looked past them up to the volcanic peak that rose up behind Sawmill Bay. 'I come from Brisbane, but I've never even been to Moreton Bay. This is just … just amazing. Where are the other lads?'

Lily pointed to the palm huts that lined the shore. 'They're in the first one over there. I haven't seen them this morning. Maybe they've gone for a walk around the island. It's late.'

Charlie laughed. 'Not bloody likely.' A flush ran up into his cheeks. 'Oh, sorry. Not blooming likely. They'll both be snoring in there. Come on, we'll go in and wake them up.'

Tat went to follow him, but Lily put her hand on her sister's arm. 'No. We'll wait here. Mama put some bread and fruit in there for them last night. When they've eaten, we'll take you for a walk and show you the island.'

Charlie left them on the path and carried his kit bag down to the small hut. Boyd and Alexandra had thatched the huts from palm leaves, and the openings that substituted for windows had been covered with hessian sacks.

'Hey, you layabouts! I'm here and I'm ready for action.' Charlie pounded on the wooden door at the front as he called out. 'Come on, you blokes, get up and going.'

Lily waited until the door opened. Jack stood there yawning, his chest bare, and his hair tousled. That strange, shaky feeling ran down her legs and she looked away.

'Come on, Tat. We'll go and let the goats out while they get themselves organised.' She couldn't believe that they were still asleep at this time of day. The sun had been up for about three hours.

Early to bed and early to rise, Mama said. And that was the way the Ellis family lived. By another of Mama's proverbs.

'Charlie.' She pointed up the hill when he turned to her. 'Come up to the farm when you're all ready. We're going up to the goats.'

And make sure Jack wears a shirt.

As per their father's insistence that they entertain Jack, Roger and Charlie, and Mama's decree about appropriate behaviour, Liliana and Tatiana spent the rest of the morning showing off their island home.

They swam by the jetty after the boys appeared, and then walked along the shore from Sawmill Bay to Joe's Beach, heading for the bush when the water was too high to walk along the sand and mud flats. The bush was crisscrossed with myriad paths from years of the children playing, and the wider tracks had been cleared by the sawmill workers making a track to bring the logs down to the water for floating to Bowen in years gone by.

'What's all this?' Jack asked, pointing to some old rails on the side. Tatiana was leading the way, chattering nineteen to the dozen, with Charlie and Roger laughing every few minutes. Probably being polite, thought Lily. Tat's jokes were woeful, although the boys seemed happy to listen to her. She and Jack were about fifty yards behind them as they headed for the beach a couple of miles north of the house. Lily loved the history of the island and enjoyed talking about it. After living at school in Brisbane, her appreciation for the beautiful place she lived in had grown, although she knew she would leave one day—after the war was over—to see the world.

'Left over from the timber days. Our island is a timber reserve. When Bowen was established in 1861, the need for timber for housing brought timber-getters to the Whitsundays. The hoop pine'—she pointed to the towering pines on the side of the mountain—'is used for building houses and furniture. The first timber was logged here on our island. We own one hundred acres where the house and the palm huts are, and where Dad grows the crops, but from that low fence we crossed at the first gully where the creek came out, all that is a timber reserve owned by the government. It's leased to a timber company in Townsville, but they haven't worked here for a couple of years now.'

Jack shook his head. 'I can't believe that they came way out here onto the islands for timber. How did they get it to the mainland?'

'They floated it behind a launch all the way to Bowen, and then it was offloaded.'

'We used to have a mill at our farm before Dad decided it was too much work for little return,' Jack said.

'There's a few mills scattered around the islands, if you want to see a working one on one of your visits.' Lily was surprised by the depth of his interest and she was enjoying telling him about her island. 'Over at Woodcutter Bay on Hook Island, and on Long Island at Happy Bay. I'm sorry, I'm probably boring you.'

Jack shook his head. 'No, it's interesting. Our timber was all on flat land. How the heck did they get it off these hills and down to the shore?' He stopped and looked up at the steep hill that led up to the peak. 'It would have been an engineering nightmare.'

'Tat, we'll meet you at the beach. I'm going to show Jack the old sawmill workings,' Lily called out. It didn't seem to bother her sister. Tat waved and the three quickly disappeared out of their sight. Lily held her hand out to Jack.

'Come with me.' She knew she was disobeying Mama's decree, but they had behaved like genteel young ladies so far and she would continue to do so. No matter how free the girls' upbringing had been, and how much they could run wild on the island, they respected their mother and they usually accepted her word as law. Lily had got to know Jack already and it was obvious to her he was from a good family. She knew instinctively she could trust him. She'd held out her hand without thinking about it first. The warmth that travelled up her arm was only because it was getting hot as they walked up the hill.

'The pine trees grow best on the leeward side of the island and you can see the terrain is rough and steep.' Lily waited till they reached a gap in the bush and pointed to the peak that towered over the middle of the island. 'That's Whitsunday Peak. Apparently, it was a lot more heavily timbered in the old days and they say the timber-getters cleaned it out. Do you reckon you'd all be up for a climb to the top later? It's an amazing view and it will show what it looks like from the air.' She realised what she'd said, and heat ran into her cheeks. 'Oh, how stupid of me. You've probably flown over here already.'

'I have but it was cloudy.' Jack squeezed her hand. Holding his hand seemed natural now, and Lily wasn't self-conscious anymore.

Lily kept walking, trying to ignore the shaky feelings in her legs. She'd climbed up here to the old sawmill hundreds of times but this was the first time her legs had been unsteady.

Maybe it was the heat.

'Tell me about the plane you fly in. What do you do?'

Lily turned onto the old sawmill path. The bush had thickened since she'd last been up here, and the light was blocked by the thick canopy above them.

'I'm in a Catalina squadron. It's a flying boat.'

'That means it can land on water?' she asked as she let go of Jack's hand.

'That's right. Its unique aeronautical design and twelve hundred horsepower engines means it can travel for up to three and a half thousand miles without landing.' He caught up to her and frowned. 'Sorry, I'm probably boring you with technical details. It's the engineer in me. It's a small aircraft with a short body and a single fixed wing.'

'You're an engineer? You've been to university?' Lily's interest flared.

Jack nodded. 'Yes, I finished at Sydney Uni last year and a few months later, I joined the air force.'

'Oh, you're so lucky. How old are you?' Lily didn't care if she was being forthright. The more Jack spoke, the more she was getting to like him and wanted to know about his life.

'I turned twenty-one just before Christmas. What about you?'

'I'm almost seventeen. If it wasn't for this blasted war, I would have been going to Brisbane to university next year, but Mama won't let me now. I want to be a journalist.'

Jack held her gaze with his, and that funny feeling quivered in her tummy again.

'You know, she's probably right. You're much better off up here until the war is over.'

'And how long do you think that will be?' Lily put her hands on her hips and leaned towards him. It was hard to see Jack's expression as the sunlight dappling through the foliage put his face in shadow.

He shrugged. 'I don't think anyone knows. Now that the Japs have come into the war, things have changed.'

'Better or worse?' Lily tipped her head to the side.

'I don't know.' Jack's voice was quiet as he held out his hand to her. 'Come on, we've gotten off track. Come and show me this sawmill.'

Lily shook her head emphatically, ignoring his outstretched hand. 'No, I *want* to know all about it. Tell me, what do the Catalinas do? Are they bombers?'

Jack shook his head slowly and Lily sensed he was reluctant to say too much.

'No. It's pretty mundane what we do, nothing exciting. And there's nothing for you to worry about here.' His eyes crinkled as he smiled at her. 'Can I call you Liliana? It's such a pretty name, it's a shame to shorten it to Lil.'

Heat rushed up into her cheeks, and she nodded. 'Yes, that would be nice. Lil is the person who gets bossed around and told what to do. The girls at school called me Lily, but yes, Liliana is fine.' She turned and walked ahead of him along the path. 'What do you do on the plane? I only know what I've read in the *Courier Mail*.' Her voice was soft as she glanced back at him. 'No matter what you do, it's going to be dangerous, isn't it? Even just being up in the air over the water is dangerous.'

Jack looked away and Lily thought she saw him nod slightly.

'Do you get scared?' She looked at him curiously as they walked deeper into the bush.

Jack didn't answer until they reached the end of the path, where a rocky outcrop looked over a flat area on a saddle where the mill had stood. He held out his hand and Lily grasped it tightly as she jumped off the last rock.

'I am, but I'd never tell the others that. I didn't intend joining the air force.' A gust of wind caught Jack's hair and Lily focused on his hand as he pushed it back. She didn't want him to know that she'd noticed the flush on his cheeks as he put his head down and kicked at a small cairn of stones at the edge of the mill site.

'It's not that I'm a coward. Something happened and before I knew it, I'd enlisted, was in the air force and became an LAC—a light aircraftman that stands for—after I did my courses. I've been trained as an observer. And sometimes, I get sent places where there is construction work at the air fields.' He lifted his head, holding Lily's gaze and his eyes were sad. 'I've never talked to anyone like this before.'

Lily reached for his hand and squeezed it. 'You can trust me, Jack. I appreciate you being so honest with me. And any time you want to talk about how you feel, tell me.' Lily dropped his hand and crossed the clearing. 'This is where they cut the timber and milled it. In the old days, the method used for getting the timber down was hard work. Where the pine trees grow tallest, it's rough and steep, and Dad told me that they called the way they got them down the "shoot and jack" procedure. A tree would be felled, lopped of its branches and then "shot" end-on down the hillside to this gully. Sometimes, the log would be halted by rocks or standing trees. Dad said if that happened, the cutters would manoeuvre it free with jacks and levers until its downward slide was resumed. He used to work with them when he and Mama first came to the island, but they don't mill anymore. In the gully below us here, you can just see the head of Upper Gulnare Inlet and there is a tramline. The logs were loaded onto trolleys and sent on their way by gravity.'

'Cripes, that would have been fast, looking at the angle of that slope,' Jack exclaimed. The flush had gone from his cheeks now, and the intense awareness between them had faded but Lily knew that a friendship had been forged up here on the hill above Sawmill Bay.

'Yes, it was. Sometimes the logs shot down to the gullies and got stuck so firmly they had to be abandoned. I'll show you some of them if we climb the peak. How long are you here for?'

'A week. We have to go back on New Year's Day.'

'A whole week! Well then, we can show you *all* the island.'

Lily hid the excited anticipation that filled her. A week in Jack's company would be most enjoyable.

Mama had lunch ready for them when they got back to the house. Dad and the boys were out fishing, and Katarina was swinging on the old wooden swing hanging from the tree beside the outhouse. Mama's gaze was shrewd, and Lily was aware of her high colour every time Jack looked her way. She fanned herself.

'It's really hot out there today, Mama.' She turned to the three men who were sitting on the verandah steps. 'I think it might be too hot to climb the peak.'

'No. We're tough. Maybe you girls aren't up to it.' Charlie glanced at Tatiana, who burred straight up.

'Of course we are. We'll get there twice as quick as you lot,' she said with her hands on her hips.

'I think you girls can have the afternoon off and take these young men up to the peak. The view from up there is *incroyable*.' Mama's voice was soft and her smile indulgent as she stared across the verandah to the water. The early afternoon breeze had picked up and the water was sparkling where the waves were dancing in the sunlight. 'I'll never forget the day Boyd took me up there for the first time. We'd only been on the island a week, and we were living in one of the old huts over at the old sawmill.' Lily caught Jack's eye but it was obvious that he knew they shouldn't have gone there alone. He said nothing. 'I was wondering how I was ever going to survive on this island, away from everything I knew. We climbed to the top and I looked out to the most beautiful view in the world, and I knew it was all going to be all right.'

Lily walked over to her mother and hugged her. It was good to see that she was in a happy mood today. Sometimes, her unhappiness pressed on the family like a dead weight and the children knew when to stay out of her way.

'Come on, Tat, help me get some sandwiches. We'll pack lunch and have a picnic at the peak.'

Katarina jumped off the swing and ran over. 'Me too. A picnic.'

Mama reached down and picked her up. 'You and I will have our own picnic here, sweetheart. The hill is too high for your little legs yet.'

Lily smiled and pushed away the ever-present worry that seemed to have been with her since the war had been declared. At least one good thing had come from it.

Jack had come into their lives.

CHAPTER

11

December 28, 1941

Tat and Liliana led the three men, each with a pack on their backs carrying sandwiches, drink and fruit, into the bush at the back of Sawmill Beach. The men forged ahead and Tat and Lily smiled at each other in a rare moment of understanding. They would soon see how difficult the climb was. Soon, the huffs and panting reached them as the men climbed slowly through the diverse vegetation. Rainforest gullies were replaced by windblown saddles, and then, when they entered the rainforest again, the canopy provided cool shade and dappled sunlight. Halfway up, before the track turned into the strenuous haul to the summit, Lily called a halt so they could all have a drink.

Charlie and Roger were red-faced and sweating, but Jack's breathing was even and he hadn't raised a flush. There was little conversation before they took off again, scrambling over the rocky outcrops. Gradually, the trees thinned out and the peak loomed above them. Charlie and Roger had been full of chatter as they tried to show off their prowess scurrying up the peak but by the time they reached the top, they barely had enough breath to speak.

No one spoke as they stood looking down over the magnificent vista of the islands. Lily had been to the peak many times, and the beauty of the view never palled for her. In the distance, smoke curled lazily from a couple of steamers heading north, and the whitewash from their engines cut a perfect swathe in the deep sapphire water.

'You'll need to get fitter than that if you're going to fight in the war, boys.' Tatiana stood near the pile of rocks at the top of the peak. Jack was quiet as he walked across to Lily and they stood and looked out over the water. Down below, in the centre of the Passage, a grey vessel made its way north.

'It makes it real to me, seeing those navy ships in the Passage.' Lily shook her head slowly as she watched the progress of the ship. 'The world's changing, isn't it?'

Jack put his hand on her shoulder and squeezed it gently. 'I know what you mean.' His voice was determined but his words were sad. 'It makes past hurts seem very insignificant, in the big picture.' He smiled at her and lifted his hand. 'Come on, girls, you're supposed to be feeding us.'

'Look.' Roger pointed to the north after they'd sat for a while and demolished the sandwiches the girls had made. 'I'm sure that's the mountain just south of Bowen. You can almost see the town from here. There's that high island we can see from the hill in town.'

'Yes, that's Cape Gloucester. It's not far by sea. Just over forty nautical miles,' Lily said. 'When the westerly wind blows, it's almost clear enough to see the houses up there on the hill.'

'That's the way we're going back.' Jack pointed to the launch making its way north. 'By steamer.'

Tat stood and beckoned the boys over to the eastern side of the drop, but Jack stayed by Lily's side.

'Thank you for suggesting this. It's beautiful,' he said.

Lily dropped her eyes and reached for the paper that the sandwiches had been wrapped in. 'Dad asked us to show you the island. We don't get to meet many people our own age up here. Most of the guests are families with young children. All it means for us is more cooking and washing up. We don't very often get to have fun like this, so it's pretty special for us too.'

'You're pretty special too.' Jack's quiet murmur was overlaid by Tatiana's call, and Lily wasn't sure if she'd heard him correctly.

'Okay, boys. Who's up for a challenge?' Her sister's grin was cheeky as she looked at Lily. 'I bet Lily and I can beat you back to Sawmill Bay.'

'We'll see about that.' Jack's laugh was loud as he grabbed a bag and swung it on to his back. 'Come on, men. We have a reputation to uphold.'

Charlie and Roger took off with a loud whoop, and Jack wasn't far behind them as they slid down the track from the peak. Stones rattled and rolled down the hill, and Lily smiled as she heard the odd curse float up. Lily and Tat climbed slowly and steadily at a sedate pace until they reached the track. They knew the shortcut that diverted from the path at the back of Joe's Beach, where some steps had been cut into the cliff below the sawmill. They could hear the boys tearing along the path that zigzagged above them as they cut across to the bay.

By the time they reached the beach, the sounds from the bush behind them had faded into the distance.

'I thought soldiers were supposed to be fit?' Tatiana jumped onto the bow of their father's hoop pine sailing boat moored in Sawmill Bay as they waited for the airmen to catch up.

'They'll be ready for a swim.' As the men got closer and pushed their way through the overgrown track, Lily was anxious to get back to the house. She'd spotted the mail launch in the bay as they headed down and she was hoping for a letter from Amelia. As soon as they had a swim, she'd make Tat come back with her. It was time to start helping Mama prepare dinner anyway. She had been very lenient to let them have the afternoon off, *and* in the company of three young men.

Roger and Charlie burst out onto the sand, red-faced and panting.

'How did you get here first?' Roger cried. 'Not fair!'

They pulled their shirts off and flung them onto the sand before running to the water and diving in. Jack stepped onto the sand and walked leisurely across to Lily and watched as the other two dunked each other in the deep channel at the edge of the coral. He hadn't raised a sweat.

'Watch out for those killer jellyfish,' he called out.

Tatiana was on her toes poised to dive into the water from the edge of the boat. 'No, we're fine out here on our island. They're only in the estuaries on the mainland.' She shot a cheeky grin at the men before diving into the deep water behind them.

'You only have to worry about the tiger sharks out here,' Lily added dryly. 'Aren't you going to swim?'

Jack's gaze was intense. 'Are you?'

'No. I've got things I need to do.' Lily glanced over at Tatiana. She was showing off by swimming out to the middle of the deep channel at the edge of the bay.

'Do you want company on the way back to the house?'

'No. I'll wait for Tat. She has chores too.'

Jack pulled off his shirt and for a moment, Lily thought he'd changed his mind about swimming, but he laid it on the sand.

'Sit and talk to me some more,' he said.

Lily was used to the local fishermen getting about in shorts and no shirts, but for some reason, Jack's bare chest sent a flash of something unfamiliar through her again, and she moved a little further away from him.

Lily stood as Tat swam close to the jetty. 'Come on, Tat. We have to go and help Mama at the house.'

As she and her sister took their leave and walked back to the house, Lily was conscious of Jack watching her.

* * *

As the week passed, they went for more walks and swims between their chores at the house, and Lily found herself talking to Jack more often than the other two. He had good manners, and was kind, and patient with her brothers and sisters. She found Roger and Charlie a bit—well, coarse, was the word Mama would use—but Jack was well-educated and he'd read and loved many of her favourite novels.

'You've really and truly read *Gone with the Wind*?' Lily asked one afternoon as they walked back to the house after a swim before dinner. She nudged him as colour ran into Jack's cheeks.

'Yes. It was interesting.'

'Interesting?' Lily put her hand to her chest and pretended to swoon. 'It is so romantic.'

'It was interesting to read about slavery in the south.'

'Okay.' She grinned back at Jack as he smiled at her.

On the last afternoon before they left, Lily swung in the hammock on the verandah overlooking the bay. Jack sat on the steps, lost in his thoughts. The silence was comfortable and Lily didn't feel the need to keep up endless conversation. Mama had been quiet today, and had gone for a nap before dinner, taking Katarina with her. Tat had disappeared with a muttered comment about checking on the goats. Dad and the boys had been up on the hill since the twins had finished their lessons. There was always plenty to do on the farm, and they all had their own chores.

Lily's book lay unopened in her lap as she watched the boats travel south past the island. There had been a lot of water traffic today, more than usual. She wondered if it had anything to do with what old Mr Bauer had told Dad the other day. He said there was a rumour that the Japs had reached the islands, and her nerves were more skittish than usual. His uncle had seen some soldiers on the seaward side of Hook Island but Dad laughed and said that Johnny Bauer was always on the turps and made up stories.

But Hook Island was just north of their island, and Lily wondered if Dad was trying to stop them worrying.

All afternoon, every rustle from the bush had her peering into the trees behind the house. Roger and Charlie had gone down for a last swim, but Jack had offered to stay and help peel the vegetables for the early dinner Mama had planned before the three young men caught the second launch back to Bowen. Jack seemed to be slowly winning Mama around, and Lily didn't mind that he tried hard. She grinned; Jack's presence had got her out of the dinner preparation tonight. She looked up as he pushed open the door and handed her a tall glass of Mama's lemon syrup. She hadn't noticed him go inside.

'I should be looking after you. You're the guest,' she said with a laugh.

'My pleasure.' Jack took the chair beside the hammock and leaned back. He looked at her curiously. 'Will you stay on the island?'

'What, forever?' Lily shook her head.

'Maybe. Marry a local and settle here?' Jack looked across the bay, his eyes distant for a moment.

'Oh gosh, no. As soon as the war is over and Mama is happy that the world is safe again, I'll go to Brisbane. Maybe university. Unless I can get a cadetship on the *Courier Mail*.' Lily spread her arms wide. 'And then I'm going to see the world! I'll come back here when I'm old.'

Jack shook his head slowly and laughed.

'Why are you laughing? Don't you think a woman should do that?' Liliana's voice was full of indignation. 'Are you one of these blokes who think a woman's place is tied to the stove and having a child every year?'

'No. I'm shaking my head because I'm jealous that you know what you want,' he said. 'Until I joined up, I would have been quite content staying at home on our vineyard. I love the land like you love your islands. But I'm envious. For someone who grew up in such an isolated place, you know what you want out of life already.'

'I've been away to school. I'm not a country bumpkin.'

'I didn't mean that.' He looked away and clenched his jaw.

'What's wrong, Jack?' Lily reached out and touched his hand. He looked down at it and a warm shivery feeling ran through her as his thumb stroked her skin. After a moment, he lifted his head and his voice was quiet.

'I miss my home. I miss the land. I'll go back and make my peace with Dad, but I will travel the world too. That's if I survive this wretched war. I have to. I'm only twenty-one, and I haven't told my father how sorry I am.'

'Sorry?' she asked softly.

'When I left home, we'd just had an argument. I was so angry because of his attitude. I shouldn't have spoken to him the way I did that last night. He's got a short temper and my arguing always riled him. Even when I was a little tacker, I used to know how to get him angry. Then when he'd calm down, sometimes we used to talk things out. He's not a bad person, he's just set in his old-fashioned ways, and I was cocky. I stormed out with angry words and I didn't go back.'

Her neck cooled as Jack lifted his head and wiped his face with the back of his hand. 'And you know what the worst thing was that I can't forget?'

'No. What was it?' Lily kept her voice low.

'I was a proper arse. I ran over Mum's rose bushes on purpose on the way out. I was so angry with Dad, and she always took his side.' He stared at her. 'And here I am worrying about roses when my mates are dying in the war. Sometimes I feel like I'm going crazy.'

'No. It just shows me what I already know. You're a good person, Jack. Families always hurt each other. We know each other so well, and we know how to hurt those we love. You didn't do anything bad.'

When he turned back to her, their eyes met and held, and the despair in Jack's expression touched her. She made sure she didn't mention the war again. Or the future. Everything was so uncertain. No one knew what was going to happen, and it frightened her more than she ever let on. But her problems were minor when she thought of Jack heading into enemy territory.

* * *

Late in the afternoon, Lily lingered by the shore while they waited for the launch to arrive to take Jack, Roger and Charlie back to Bowen. The three men were playing cricket on the beach with Billy and Robbie and she smiled as their yells and whoops carried over every time someone was caught out.

Whitsunday Island lay under the magic of a rising December moon, a big golden orb that shone a golden haze through the clouds.

As the sun set, a glorious purple hue washed over the mountains to the west of Cannon Valley on the mainland. She sat on the jetty at the edge of the bay fascinated by the play of light on the water. Contentment filled Lily as the night sounds lulled her almost to sleep, the swish of the tiny waves on the coral beach, the mournful calls of the curlews and the chirping of cicadas. The horn blared as the launch rounded the point and she jumped up.

'Boat's here,' she called across to the beach.

She waited as the three men ran across to the jetty and picked up their kit bags. The twins scarpered back to the house. Roger and Charlie waved and were first on, but Jack hung back. He stood beside her as Wally unloaded two boxes onto the jetty.

'That's the nets Boyd ordered, Lil,' Wally called.

'Thanks, Wally. I'll tell him.' She stood awkwardly beside Jack. He'd been great company and she'd loved talking to him. It was going to be different with him gone.

He turned to her and spoke softly. 'I would rather have sat here with you, but I'd already promised the twins a game of cricket.'

'That's fine.' She looked down as he moved closer and the fine hairs on her neck tingled. 'It sounded like you all had fun.'

'We did.' Jack glanced across at the launch and Lily's gaze followed his. Roger and Charlie were leaning over the bow, watching a turtle as it bobbed up and down in the bay. 'And I didn't want to give Rog and Charlie any reason to tease you. They can be a bit rough sometimes.'

'They've been good company too.'

'I've enjoyed spending time with you, Liliana. I hope you've enjoyed it as much as I have.'

She nodded, and a warm little frisson shimmied down her back as Jack's breath touched her face. Her heart beat a little faster when he leaned in and brushed her cheek with his lips.

'I'll be back, Liliana.'

'That would be nice,' she whispered. 'I'll look forward to it.'

He picked up his kit bag, strode along the jetty and jumped aboard just as Wally lifted the rope from the post.

Lily stood and waved until the launch disappeared into the darkness of the Passage.

A sleepy smile lifted her lips as she walked up the path to the house.

CHAPTER
12

29 April, 2018

'How's my favourite girl?'

Liv looked over as Fynn appeared behind Aunty Tat's chair. Aunty Tat was still sitting at the coffee table, presiding over the teapot. Liv had moved over to a cane sofa in the warm sunshine, a glass of wine in hand, and the elderly woman was content as long as she could see her. The delicious aroma of frying onions and meat wafted over from the barbeque area at the back of the house. Contentment filled her, and her limbs felt loose and fluid. A gentle breeze blew off the water and she watched the white sails of the yachts as they sailed past the beach.

Fynn leaned over and kissed Aunty Tat's cheek, and Liv smiled when she saw the look on the older woman's face. She had been easy to talk to as they'd sat over a cup of tea earlier. She'd been quite lucid and for a while, she'd seemed to accept that she was Olivia, and not her sister, Liliana.

There was adoration on Aunty Tat's face as she looked up at Fynn. He really was a charmer, and most people seemed to fall for that charm.

Liv was wary. She didn't find him quite as open and charming with her. Ever since the comment he'd made yesterday on the *Lady May* about the serpent in paradise, and despite the spark between them, she suspected he was more interested in her involvement with Sheridan Corp.

But there was no doubt about it, he was very comfortable with this family. As she watched him greet some of the couples she'd been introduced to, and swoop a couple of the small children into the air, she knew he was more than a casual guest.

Obviously a very welcome friend.

She sat back and watched him as the conversations washed around her. As Inga had commented yesterday, he had movie-star looks, but when he was talking to others, the wariness that was in his expression when he talked to her disappeared. His face was tanned, with laughter lines creasing around his eyes. Cat-green eyes, she guessed you'd call them. What made him so attractive was the perpetual smile on his face—when he wasn't looking at her, anyway.

Fynn's laugh rang out and when Aunty Tat reached up and touched his face, Fynn placed his hand over hers. The tender moment between Fynn and Aunty Tat brought a strange feeling to Liv's chest. The close and obviously loving interactions of these people were unfamiliar to her. Even though she knew her mother loved her—who knew what her father's feelings were—there were few displays of affection shown in her family. As she looked around and saw Byron loop his arm around Louise's shoulder, and one of the younger couples exchange a quick kiss beneath the Poinciana tree, a feeling of loss took the shine off the day.

When was the last time someone had held her? When was the last time someone had kissed her? She couldn't remember. Her life was sterile, and the happiness and openness of this family brought that home to her on this beautiful sunny afternoon. The last thing Liv felt like was going back to a lonely hotel room—even though it was on a beautiful tropical island—and work on a project she was beginning to doubt.

'How did you go with Aunty Tat?' Liv hadn't notice Fynn walk across to where she was sitting. He sat down beside her on the sofa and his leg brushed against hers. She moved away a fraction.

'Good. She seems a lot happier and has been calling me Liv, but I'm a little worried about how she'll be when I leave.'

'Yeah. It's been a tough few weeks. The slight stroke she suffered hasn't caused any physical issues but no matter what we say, she seems to be locked in the past most of the time now.' His voice was sad. 'I guess losing her sister and not knowing what happened has to have done some emotional damage.'

'Yes, it would.' Liv's voice was soft as she stared over at the group sitting at the table.

Fynn touched her fingers lightly and she glanced down at his hand. On his middle finger, he wore an ornate silver ring and as she looked more closely, she realised it was two dolphins arching together around in a circular leap.

'That's an unusual ring.'

'Yeah, it was my mum's. She was the one who taught me what a special place the islands are. She gave it to me on my twenty-first.' It was the first time Liv felt that they'd had a conversation—however short—where they were both being natural with each other.

'Lunch is on,' Byron called from the barbeque. Fynn stood and held out his hand. Liv looked at it for a moment before putting her hand in his and letting him pull her up. The long table was already full of bowls of assorted salads and fruit. Byron carried over a tray loaded with steaks, fried onions and mushrooms.

Louise came over to the table, her arm laced through Aunty Tat's. 'Aunty Tat asked if she could sit next to *Olivia*.' Liv and Fynn's eyes met in a moment of shared understanding. The smile he returned left her feeling happy. It looked as though her visit had perhaps helped the older woman to settle.

Fynn sat at the other end of the long wooden table once he had settled Aunty Tat beside Liv. Lunch was eaten with lots of noisy conversation and good-natured ribbing across the table. A couple of times, Aunty Tat even explained to Liv what was happening, and she was lucid, and as sharp as a tack.

'That's Declan, he's my youngest grandson. He and Jenny are getting married at Christmas. I'm doing my best to last till then.' Her laugh was a little tinkle. 'I don't want to shuffle off before the wedding.'

Liv swallowed. 'I'm sure you'll be here for the wedding and many more. You have lots of grandchildren.'

'And a few great-grandchildren.' Aunty Tat's eyes clouded over and her gaze wavered. 'But now that you've come home, Lil, I'm not ready to die. I've changed my mind.'

Uh oh. How did you respond to that, especially when the poor woman believed you were her dead sister? Before Liv could open her mouth, two warm hands settled on the tops of her bare arms. 'Almost ready to head back across to Hamo, Olivia?' Fynn drew out her name as Aunty Tat watched them with an indulgent smile.

'Hamo?' She raised her eyebrows but returned his smile. Tentatively. 'Byron said that on the phone too.'

'That's what we locals call it.' He leaned closer and the warmth of his skin against hers was pleasant.

No sense of personal space. But as Liv had watched the affection between family members since she'd arrived, the touching and the hugging, she'd realised no one gave it a thought. It was just the way they were. It was way out of the realm of her experience.

'And I am ready. I need to go back and do some work.' She waited for his reaction but the smile stayed on his face.

Surprise filled her when he lowered his head and his breath brushed her cheek. 'Follow my lead,' he said quietly.

The nerves in her arm zinged as he stood behind her chair and helped her to her feet.

'Aunty Tat, I'm going to take this lovely lady for a ride in my boat, but I'm sure she'll come back and visit you soon. Won't you, darling?' Fynn let go of her hand and casually put his arm around her shoulder, tucking her in close to him. The fresh smell of soap and shampoo surrounded her. Liv tried to relax and not stand stiffly against him.

Darling?

Aunty Tat looked from Fynn to Liv and her lips lifted in a wide smile. 'You're going home with Fynn? To Fynn's boat.' She clapped her hands. 'Well, that's just perfect.'

'It is.' Fynn rested his head against Liv's and she tensed.

What is he doing?

Aunty Tat rescued her when she held her arms out. 'It's been lovely to see you, Olivia.'

It seemed she was back in the present with them now. Liv stepped away from Fynn and put her arms around the plump woman. 'It's been lovely to meet you too, and I'd love to come and visit again.'

Byron joined them and put his arm round his grandmother. 'Any time you're up this way again, Olivia, make sure you come and see us.'

'Will you be up again soon?' The tone in Fynn's voice was strange. She couldn't figure him out.

Liv stepped back. 'I'll make sure I am.'

* * *

'Why did you do that in front of Aunty Tat?' Liv asked when the boat was underway. After slipping the lines, she'd settled up on the fly bridge.

'It worked.' Fynn's grin was wide. 'She thought I'd found myself a lady. It made her happy and took her focus off you—her lost sister—leaving.'

'Quite the psychologist, aren't you? As well as being a fisherman, a sailing boat captain, a water taxi driver … and a waiter. You're a surprise a minute.' Liv folded her arms and stared at the water. 'Jack of all trades is right.'

Fynn was still grinning when she looked back, as though she hadn't made her smart comment. 'Dear old Aunty Tat's been trying to marry me off to each of her granddaughters since I was a teenager.'

Liv couldn't help the picture of the young Fynn that flashed into her mind. Still in his fishing clothes, his hair a mass of long sun-bleached curls, she imagined he would have been a wild young man.

'And you resisted?'

'Sure. I'm a loner.'

'What did she mean about going home to your boat? Not this one? I thought you said it was Byron's.'

'It is. My lady is much more sedate than this stink boat.'

Liv widened her eyes. 'Stink boat?'

'Simple, darlin'. Diesel smells, sails don't.'

'You live on a sailing boat?'

'I do.'

Liv looked back at the water. Fynn was like no one else she had met before and she was finding him altogether too fascinating. She settled back into the seat, lost in her thoughts.

As the boat turned east and Hamilton Island came into view, the chilly wind raised goosebumps on her arms. Liv reached down into her bag for her cardigan and when she looked up, she drew her breath in on a surprised gasp.

She leaned over and touched Fynn's arm. 'Can you slow down for a moment?'

'With pleasure.' He eased back on the throttle and looked at her curiously. 'I thought you were in a hurry to get back to the hotel and do your work.'

'I am.' Liv stared at the island on the portside of the cruiser. 'That's Whitsunday Island, isn't it?'

'It is.' Fynn throttled back and the boat idled along in the current. 'Whitsunday Island is the big one. Henning Island is the small one to starboard.'

Liv put one hand up to shade her eyes and pointed with the other. Her attention was on the large, heavily timbered Whitsunday Island. 'Those two flat-topped hills with the trees on them. Do you know what they are? Is it a place?'

'What do you mean "is it a place"?' Fynn stood beside her.

'Does it have a name? Is it called something?'

The current caught the boat and pushed it closer to the shore, and he increased their speed and turned the boat around in a circle. A wide-mouthed inlet opened in front of them. 'Not the hills as far as I know. That's Gulnare Inlet. Do you want to go in and have a look? It's almost top tide and it'll be easy to go in.'

'Yes please.' Liv looked around. Several yachts were moored further in the inlet, but her eyes were drawn straight back to the two hills at the far end. 'It's strange but I really feel as though I've been here before. I know those hills,' she said half to herself.

'Let's take you in for a closer look then.' Fynn started the motor and Liv watched as he took his bearings. 'There's a lot of hidden reef at the entrance here.'

'Oh, don't worry about going in. It's not that important,' she said.

'No. Let's go and have a look, it's an interesting place. There's a hidden creek on the south side that goes into the forest where they used to fell the timber back in the early days, and if you keep an eye out, you'll see the goats clambering over the rocks when we get to that point.' He pointed to a spur that came out at the end of the inlet. Liv realised that it actually split into a wide bay on the north and a smaller, sheltered body of water on the south side.

'As far as I know, the hills don't have a name, although it's not far from them down to the ruins of the Ellis homestead. Byron used to bring me out here to camp when I first started working with him.' He smiled at her. 'Byron said you're not related to Aunty Tat. Are you sure about that?'

'Positive.' Liv shook her head as they motored further into the inlet. 'It just looks so familiar.' Once they passed the reef at the portside of the entrance, Fynn turned the cruiser to mid-channel and they motored slowly down to the point. He waved to a couple on the catamaran moored nearby, and Liv smiled. Washing was pegged along the steel wire along the side of the boat.

'Nice way to spend a holiday,' she commented. The inlet was quiet and the water was glass-like as the hills protected it from the breeze that was blowing out in the Passage.

'Nice way to live,' was Fynn's laconic reply.

As they drew closer to the rocky outcrop, there was a splash as loose rocks tumbled into the water. He cut the motor and came to the side of the boat where Liv stood, looking at the rocky coastline. He put one hand on her shoulder, but she had nowhere to move to.

'See the goats up there?' He leaned forward and gestured to the rocks. 'They reckon they're the descendants of the goats that Byron's great-grandparents used to have here back in the 1940s. Aunty Tat's parents.'

'And Liliana's.' Liv closed her eyes for a moment. The only sound was the gentle lapping of the water on the side of the boat. 'This place is pure magic,' she whispered softly.

When she opened her eyes, Fynn was looking at her and his brow was creased in a frown. 'Gulnare?'

'No, this whole place.' Liv made a wide arc with her arm. 'The islands, the mainland, the Passage. I honestly don't think I've seen anything so beautiful in my life.'

'It's a shame you have to go back and work,' he said slowly. 'We could spend the night here.'

Liv straightened and moved away from the casual arm that was draped over her shoulder. 'The night?' Her voice was icy.

'Yeah. There's going to be an almost full moon rising'—he looked down at his watch—'in about five hours. It'll be pretty spectacular.'

'Thank you, but no. I do have work to do. And I have to go back to the mainland tomorrow. I should have taken my gear with me today. I could have stayed over there. It would have saved you a trip back.'

'I had to come back anyway, darlin'.'

She nodded and looked away to stare over the water. Casual sex was one thing Liv had no experience in. Working a fifteen-hour day, it was all she could do to go home and feed herself, let alone find time for anyone else or a social life.

'Okay, let's take you home.'

'And I owe you for the taxi,' she said as she turned away.

CHAPTER
13

30 April, 2018

By the time Liv had dressed in her navy-blue pencil slim skirt, her white shirt, her jacket with the Sheridan Corp pin and slipped on her high heels, she was a bundle of nerves. No matter how many times she'd called her father, Rod and the guy from Zenith, none of them had answered their phones. She felt disconnected; it was as though she wasn't a part of the company. She'd gone through the replacement PowerPoint, flagged any areas where she wasn't sure of the figures, and then read back through her notes. As instructed, she had left it exactly as it was. She was surprised to see there was very little information about the new location. The only difference was that the model had been moved to a different bay on the map. She'd wing her presentation, and any difficult questions, she'd simply refer to the others.

Liv had pre-booked the 7.15 am *Cruise Whitsunday* ferry to get to Port of Airlie in time to pick up a taxi, make the call, and still leave her half an hour before the meeting began. She chewed on her bottom lip as she sat in the electric buggy on the way down to catch the ferry at the marina. Her stomach churned; she hadn't been able to face a coffee yet. To add to her grey mood, the weather had turned and even though the sky was clear, the wind was blowing from the south-east at a vigorous twenty-five knots, according to the weather board in the hotel.

The receptionist had sympathised when she had dropped her room key off on the way out. 'Do you get seasick?'

'I'm not sure.' Liv shook her head. 'I've been okay out on the water over the weekend. Do you think it will be rough this morning?'

'Oh yes, very rough. The swell will be big, from the wind change we had overnight and with the wind against the tide, it's not going to be pleasant out in the Passage. And the ferry trip to Port of Airlie takes almost an hour. I'd take a seasick tablet if it was me.'

'I didn't think of that.' Liv frowned. 'Is it too late now?'

'Give me a minute. I think we've got some in the office.' The young woman walked into the back office and came back and passed Liv a small packet. 'No charge. The reps leave us sample packets.'

'Thanks.'

When Liv got into the buggy, she read the instructions packet, swallowed two of the tablets and washed them down with the bottle of water she always carried in her bag. Nothing would be worse than being sick before the meeting.

The journey across the Passage was nothing like the two days she'd spent on the water over the weekend. The ferry was a large vessel, over twenty metres long, and Liv was grateful that the passenger area was enclosed once they headed out into the open water. The vessel lurched not only up and down, slamming into the troughs between the huge waves, but a couple of times it slewed to the side when a rogue wave came from another direction. She sat on the edge of the cushioned seat, clutching her bag and her briefcase to her chest, unable to see out of the window because of the spray surrounding the ferry from the wind and the high waves. A couple of small children were crying, and the volume of their screams increased as the journey progressed. Every time one of the crew opened the door to the outer deck, a strong smell of diesel pervaded the enclosed cabin.

By the time the ferry entered the calm waters of the Port of Airlie marina, almost an hour later, Liv's head was throbbing, and her mouth was dry. Once the vessel docked and the doors were opened, her legs were shaking so much she had to support herself on the back of the seat in front for a moment before she was steady enough to walk.

With a deep breath, she joined the queue of passengers waiting to disembark. As she finally stepped off the boat onto the concrete wharf, she glanced at her watch. It was close to eight-thirty. The coffee shop in the ferry terminal building was not too busy, maybe a coffee and something to eat would settle her stomach before she headed over to Abell Point Marina, where the meeting was scheduled for ten o'clock.

Five minutes later, Liv sat at the table staring at the coffee and pastry, willing her stomach to settle and her headache to ease. Pulling out her phone, she tried her father's number. Again, it went straight to voicemail. She pressed speed dial for the office and sipped at her coffee while she waited for front reception to pick up.

'Sheridan Corp. Would you please hold the line.'

Liv tapped her fingers impatiently on the tabletop as she was put on hold. Finally, the music stopped and the receptionist came back on. 'Sorry to keep you waiting, how may I help you?'

'Hi, Gloria, it's Olivia Sheridan. Would you please put me through to my father.'

'I'm sorry, Ms Sheridan. Your father is not available.'

Liv clenched her jaw and kept her words even. 'It's extremely important that I speak with him immediately, Gloria. Please connect me to his direct line.' Liv had been asking for access to that number for months with no success.

'I'm sorry, Ms Sheridan. He's not in the office. Actually, he's not in the country. He left for China on Saturday night, I believe. Perhaps you could try his mobile?'

'Thank you.' Liv disconnected and threw her phone into her bag with disgust. She sat back and put one hand over her eyes. It looked like she was going to have to wing it.

Well, Dad. I'll do my best.

But she knew it wasn't going to be good enough.

'Olivia?'

Liv sat up straight and lifted her hand from her eyes. The fluorescent light in the café made her eyes ache and for a brief second, her vision blurred. As it cleared, she stared at the two men standing beside the table. 'Yes?'

'You arrived later than we expected.' The implied criticism stung and her reply was waspish.

'I apologise but I don't have control over the vagaries of the wind and tides.' Liv swallowed as her stomach roiled. She tried to keep her head still as she stared at Anthony Collins. He'd been her father's right-hand man for the past two years, and she'd never liked him. Not because he'd been promoted over her a couple of times, but because he was an underhanded, lying sneak. She still didn't know what his exact role was supposed to be.

'Where's Rod?' she asked.

'I'm doing Andrew's PR now,' Anthony said.

Andrew's PR?

'I wasn't aware that Rod had left. Where's he gone?' Her question remained unanswered as she gestured to the chair. 'You might as well sit down. We have an hour before the meeting and I have questions that need answering.'

The other man—Phillip Garvan, she assumed—didn't speak as he sat opposite her. His jet-black hair was slicked back from his face and despite being inside, he didn't remove his wrap around dark sunglasses.

Liv picked up her coffee, sipped and almost gagged at the bitter taste. She put her cup down and reached for the carafe of water to top up her glass. She shivered as another wave of nausea washed over her, but sipping the water seemed to settle her stomach a bit.

'Right.' She put the glass down and stared at Anthony. The other man hadn't taken his eyes off her since he'd sat down, and she felt unnerved. 'I tried to call my father, but he's unavailable, so I need some questions answered before the meeting.'

Phillip leaned forward and when he finally spoke, his voice was firm. 'You have no need for questions. All you have to do is stand up and click through the presentation. You can reiterate any data on the PowerPoint, but you give nothing more than what is up on the screen.' He finally lifted his sunglasses from his face and his eyes were cold. 'If there are any difficult questions, you'll pass them to us.'

Liv frowned as she returned his intense stare. 'Excuse me, I am the project manager for public relations. The purpose of this meeting is to make the local community more comfortable about the proposal, so of course, I'll be answering all questions. And that's where I need some clarification.'

'You'll do exactly as I direct you to.'

Disbelief flooded through Liv as Phillip reached over and took her hand. 'You will present the new file that you were emailed, and then you'll hand over to the next speaker.' His hand gripped hers tightly and the stone from his ring cut into her skin.

She tugged her hand, but the pressure increased.

'Is that quite clear?'

Liv glanced over at Anthony but there was no help from that quarter. He was looking past her. 'Is that Zenith's directive or my father's?' she asked.

'It's a directive that you'll follow if you want to keep your job.'

'How dare you speak to me like that.' When he let go of her hand, Liv picked up the serviette and wiped her fingers without breaking eye contact.

'Don't push it, sweetheart.' Phillip's voice was full of steel. 'The meeting will go well, and the community will be happy. Don't you worry your pretty little head about it. The big players know what has to be done. And you *will* do as you're told.'

'Or I'll lose my job? My father wouldn't let that happen.' She clutched at the serviette on her lap as Phillip stared her down. A ripple of fear ran down her back when he smiled at her.

'Don't be naïve. If you don't do as you're told, holding your job will be the least of your worries.'

'Are you threatening me?' Liv stared at him, unable to believe what she was hearing. She stiffened her back, but a wave of nausea rolled over her and she broke out into a cold sweat. She was so ill it was hard to concentrate.

Liv stood and the shredded serviette fell to the floor but she was too dizzy to reach down and pick it up. 'Right. Let's go and get this over with. The sooner it's done, the sooner I can go back to Sydney and sort this out with my *father*.'

She picked up her briefcase and strode to the door.

★ ★ ★

Lure, the conference centre where the community meeting was being held, was an elegant venue on the top floor of the building in the south marina precinct of Abell Point Marina. Fynn waited until most of the waiting crowd had entered before he went in and took a seat in the corner at the back of the room. The mood was tense, and a couple of small groups remained outside talking. The room filled quickly, and he nodded at a few locals as they made their way to their seats. John Blumer, the representative from the regional council, was already on the raised platform at the front of the room with a couple of other local identities but there was no sign of Liv Sheridan. For a fleeting moment, he wondered if her experiences over the weekend had brought her to the realisation that this project should not go ahead, and she'd pulled the pin.

He shook his head. No chance of that—the only reason she was up in the Whitsundays was to deliver the company's public relations spiel about the benefits of the Zenith coal loader to the local economy. Of that fact, he had no doubt. Any industry created in the region would have an economic benefit and increase employment. Since Cyclone Debbie had decimated the islands last year, the tourist dollar had taken a hit, and Sheridan Corp knew how to put the positive spin on their projects. He had no doubt that the presentation ahead would convince some of the community that this project was essential for the future of the region.

But that was not the point.

Tourism was recovering as the landscape regenerated, and the man-made structures that had been damaged were being repaired or rebuilt. Major rebuilds were still underway on Hayman and Daydream islands.

If the coal loader went ahead, the project would cause irreversible damage to the reef—a reef that was already under threat from climate change and other human activities.

Fynn settled back and waited for Liv to arrive.

By the time she walked in—flanked by two suits—the mood of the audience was tense. Byron had arrived and taken a seat in front of Fynn. Low conversations were shared between groups, and frowns were the predominant expression. The audience was mixed: tourist operators, long-term locals, and yachties, young and old. He watched as Liv took a seat at the end of the row on the podium, but Fynn couldn't help the interest that flared as he watched her.

Liv Sheridan had none of the confidence and brashness he'd expect from the public face of a company like Sheridan Corp. Over the weekend, he'd found her to be a soft and caring woman, one who'd retreated into a dignified shell the couple of times he'd gone out of his way to push her buttons. Her face was set, her bright red lipstick accentuating the pallor of her cheeks. She sat straight and stared ahead. If he hadn't have known better, he would have said she was terrified.

The Liv Sheridan up on the podium was very different from the happy and relaxed woman who had joined in at the Ellis family lunch yesterday.

Interesting.

The usual introductions and formalities were completed, and Fynn took a breath as Olivia Sheridan was introduced as the spokes-person for Sheridan Corp. A dark mutter from much of the crowd swelled as she stood. Reluctant sympathy shot through Fynn as she stumbled on her way across to the lectern.

As she stood at the microphone, the screen illuminated and the title slide saying, *Sheridan Corp. Moving the Whitsundays Forward* brought a renewed negative response from the audience.

Liv began to speak, and the crowd quieted.

'Good morning. And thank you for joining us here today. We're excited about the future of the Whitsunday region.' Her voice was steady, but as she brought up the first slide, she dabbed at her lips with a tissue.

'Sheridan Corp has an outstanding reputation globally. Australia is an important part of our business and we hold significant interests in a range of commodity industries across all mainland states and the Northern Territory. We are a major Australian employer, with over twenty thousand people working across the mining sector including coal, copper, gold, nickel, and zinc. We are very proud of the role we play in assisting the economy and creating lasting benefits in Australia, and we look forward to including the Whitsunday region in our future.'

Already, the crowd was sitting up and taking notice. Fynn wondered if they were aware of the percentage of Sheridan Corp owned by the Chinese company, Zenith. Greg's investigation had revealed some increased investment in the region by the mother company recently, but he was sitting on that information until he needed it.

Fynn leaned forward as the next slide clicked over, and again, Liv raised the tissue to her face. Frustration settled deep within him as he listened. Over the past six months, Sheridan Corp had come back with a slick answer to every concern raised. Some days, Fynn wondered if they would be successful, but then his determination kicked in. The coal loader at Double Bay would *not* go ahead. No matter what it took, they would beat it.

Liv Sheridan's spiel was practised and polished, and he could see her confidence build as she moved through the data. The figures were positive and the outlook exciting for the region, if you could believe the word of Sheridan Corp. The slide for the rail line flicked over and as Liv spoke of the benefit to the region, a man called from the centre of the audience.

'Can you please explain how a railway line to the proposed coal loader is going to bring more tourists to the islands?'

There was a rumble of support from the crowd, but the chairman moved across to the microphone and leaned forward. 'Please hold all questions until Ms Sheridan has finished the presentation. There will be ample time for questions before the next speaker.'

Liv continued and flicked through slide after slide. She seemed detached, her voice was almost disinterested. Fynn waited for the slide that he knew would cause the reaction from the audience: the proposed site of the coal loader at Double Bay. Even as he thought about the audacity of the proposal, his stomach burned. And he wasn't alone. Everyone he'd spoken to was ready to fight the development of a coal loader so close to the islands and the reef. The high attendance at a meeting on a Monday morning bore testimony to that. How the company intended to justify the location to the community was going to be very interesting.

The further Liv got into her presentation, the more Fynn was convinced that she had no passion for the content, and that she was simply going through the motions. He'd seen her spark over the weekend, but today, she was flat and there was little enthusiasm in her voice.

He fought the sympathy that rose in him. He had to remind himself that Olivia Sheridan was the opposition—no matter how interesting he found her.

His eyes widened as she flicked over to the next screen: a detailed drawing of the proposed development.

What the hell?

It wasn't at Double Bay. The 3D representation was situated at Earlando Bay.

* * *

As Liv clicked over to the slide with the 3D representation of the development, her mouth filled with saliva and silver lights pricked at the edge of her vision. For one awful moment, she thought she was going to vomit right where she was standing. She took a deep breath and clenched her fingers on the lectern, fought the dizziness and swallowed down the nausea. The noise of the crowd increased, and several people jumped to their feet before she could read off the notes that related to the slide on the screen. The council representative who was sitting to the right of where she was standing half got out of his seat and then sat back down in his chair.

As she took another deep breath and swallowed the saliva that was pooling in her mouth, Phillip jumped up and took the remote from the lectern. After he pointed it to the data projector, he walked over and took her arm, and led her back to the seat. For a moment, she thought it was because he'd noticed how unwell she was, but the low words hissed into her ear soon sent any thoughts of sympathy flying.

'What the fuck do you think you're playing at?'

As the screen behind her went black, the noise in the room increased in volume. The man who'd asked the question about the rail line walked to the front of the room, one fist clenched, and the other finger pointing at the representative from the regional council.

'John, why is the model at Earlando Bay? Has the bloody council shafted us again? Double Bay was bad enough but are you aware of the environmental impact of moving it to Earlando? It's a protected ecological environment, just like Muddy Bay was.' He turned his attention to Liv. 'Ms Sheridan, perhaps you'd like to answer that question on behalf of the company. Why Earlando Bay? Has it already been approved by our council?'

Liv went to stand, but Anthony reached over and held her arm tightly as Phillip stood behind the lectern. His voice was calm and he held up both hands in a conciliatory manner.

'May I have your attention again.' He stood there quietly until the angry voices subsided and the man sat down in a spare seat in the front row. 'Thank you. I'd like to apologise on behalf of the company.' The look he shot at Liv was full of pure venom, but he quickly schooled his face into a regretful expression before he turned back to the audience. 'Unfortunately, due to an inexperienced public relations member, your time has been wasted here today.' His voice was slick, but Liv was feeling so ill she didn't care that she was copping the blame for something that she didn't understand. She was too sick to even think about what was going on around her. All she wanted to do was for the meeting to be over, so she could—

Honestly, I don't care. Not one iota. Sack me or whatever, I don't care. Just let me get out of here.

She had no idea what she was going to do. One thing was for sure, she doubted if she would have a position with Sheridan Corp anymore. When she thought about it, her father's business ethics left a lot to be desired. It had taken her too long to accept that and realise that her sole reason for staying with the company was to gain his approval. His rude and overbearing attitude on the phone had woken her up to where she stood in the scheme of things. She was being used because she was so eager to please and always had been. Thoughts whirled around in her head as the dizziness increased and she gripped the side of the chair with both hands, forcing down the nausea.

Phillip's voice was smooth and placating as he addressed the questions thrown at him. Each question about the location of the development, and whether it had council approval, was cleverly side-stepped, and he promised that once the very sensitive negotiations that were underway were ready to be brought to the community, they would have their chance to speak for or against the project.

Disgusted calls filled the room.

'Waste of time coming here today.'

'Why did you bother coming all the way from the big smoke if you can't tell us where the bloody thing's even going to be?'

'Give the microphone to Blumer so he can answer our questions.'

Liv glanced across at the council representative. Perspiration was running down his face, and there were large circular damp spots on each side of his grey business shirt. She leaned back in her seat and looked around the room. Her breath caught as she looked to the back row.

Fynn James was sitting there. He wasn't looking at her but was totally focused on Phillip. After Phillip's swipe at her, the man in the front fired question after question to the floor. But Phillip had the answers down pat until the final question was put forward.

'Would you also please explain how the project has reached this stage of development—and I understand that the state government funding for the rail line has been approved this week—without a land use agreement from the traditional owners pertaining to the route of the rail line?'

'I'm able to tell you today that in the past couple of days, the land use agreement has been signed.' Phillip's response was cold and terse.

The man huffed in disgust and seemed at a loss for words suddenly. He sat down after Phillip's answer. Liv was thankful that this hostile barrage of questions was no longer directed at her. Her head was aching, and her mouth was dry, and the longer the discussion went on, the harder she was finding it to focus on the crowd, or even the discussion. Phillip sat down and the chairman stood and raised his hand.

'We're running short of time and we still have another speaker to take the floor.' He waited as someone approached the front but the chairman was blocking Liv's view. 'I'd like to welcome Doctor Fynn James from James Cook University, who will present his discussion of the potential damage to the reef.'

Liv's breath caught, and she stared at Fynn as he took the one step up onto the podium.

What? Doctor?

The voice that she had become very familiar with over the past two days rang out true and clear as Fynn took the microphone.

'Good morning. I'd like to say it is a pleasure to be here today, but in all honesty, I can't because that would go against everything that I believe in.'

Liv glanced at Phillip as he let out what could only be described as a scornful snort, followed by the low mutter of, 'Just another bloody environmentalist.'

But, environmentalist or greenie or whatever, Fynn held the audience in the palm of his hand as he launched into the reasons that the coal loader could not—and would not—go ahead in the Whitsunday Islands, wherever it was situated; his words made that abundantly clear.

'The Great Barrier Reef is a World Heritage Area and for the past forty years, the government and various authorities have managed it so that the communities and industries that depend on a healthy reef for recreation and their livelihoods, can be sure that it is sustained and preserved.' His voice soothed Liv and if she sat quietly without turning her head, the nausea receded. He continued for ten minutes—no notes and no PowerPoint—and his passion and love for the islands, and more than that, his depth of knowledge, showed in every word that he spoke. The crowd sat quietly as he spoke, but there were many nods as he made his points.

'So to sum up, legal challenges over the past six years have ensured that the approval of this project has met with opposition on every level. What I would like to question today, is what has changed so that we have come to this point, where the Chinese parent company, Zenith, today represented by the Sydney firm, Sheridan Corp'—he inclined his head to Olivia and the two men either side of her—'have approval for a rail line and the signing off by traditional owners before this project gains final approval? What has happened to the protection of the Great Barrier Reef? When will we be told where Zenith plan to locate this monstrosity? What hidden incentives have been provided to those in the positions that have signed off on the many objections, and dismissed those legal challenges? Smoke and mirrors might have worked in the past, but rest assured this community will continue to fight. We will not have this built at Earlando Bay. We will not have this built in the Whitsunday region.'

Fynn stepped down from the podium to a rousing cheer, and headed back to his seat as loud applause continued. The chairman leaned over to Liv.

'Would you like to respond, Ms Sheridan?'

She shook her head. Her two minders also declined when asked, and as the meeting closed, Phillip rose and stood in front of Liv, blocking her view of the rest of the room.

'Where the fuck did you get that PowerPoint from? Who gave it to you?' His voice was like steel and his cold eyes frightened her.

'Rod sent it to me.' She could barely speak with the nausea rising in her throat.

Phillip gestured to Anthony with a sharp nod, and they both headed towards the exit. He was on the phone before they reached it. The audience began to move around the room and Liv put her head down as the floor tilted. Small groups gathered, and she looked desperately over towards the rest rooms as nausea rose in her throat. Somehow, she managed to thank the chairman as he unhooked her computer from the data projector and passed it across to her.

'Excuse me.' She grabbed her computer, swung her handbag over her shoulder and dashed across the room.

Fifteen long, horrid minutes later, Liv leaned one elbow on the marble sink in the elegant ladies room and used a paper towel to wipe away the eye makeup that had run down her cheeks. Her face was pale and her lips were colourless. All she wanted to do was crawl into her bed, but the thought of getting on a boat and heading back across the Passage to her hotel room brought the nausea back. Scooping her hand beneath the tap, she drank deeply, finally assuaging the intense thirst that had hit her in the meeting room. Thank goodness the awful sickness that had come on her so suddenly was easing. With shaking hands, she smoothed down her skirt, straightened her blouse and checked for any stains, and after a final look at her face, she picked up her handbag, slid her laptop into her briefcase, and pushed open the door.

All was quiet and the meeting room was empty. Putting her head down and focusing on putting one foot after the other, she made for the door.

'I was giving you another minute, then I was coming in to find you.'

Liv stopped and turned around slowly. Fynn was leaning against the bar.

'God, Liv, you look like shit. Are you okay?'

All she could do was shake her head. Closing her eyes, she drew in a shaking breath, willing the sickness to stay away. Finally, she managed a shaky, 'No.'

Stress, fear, seasickness?

She didn't know what had made her feel so ill, but she certainly didn't want it to come back. The weight of her briefcase and her handbag lifted from her shoulders, and a firm arm supported her. 'Come on. Let's get you out of here.'

'Has everyone else gone?' The thought of having to speak to anyone brought the nausea back. Especially the two men in her father's pocket who had treated her so badly.

'They have.'

As they stepped out onto the verandah that ran the length of the top floor of the conference centre, the bright midday sun made Liv's eyes ache. With a soft moan, she put her hand up. 'Sunglasses.'

'Where are they?'

'In my bag. In the purple case.'

Before she could blink, Fynn had slipped her glasses over her eyes.

'Why are you being so nice to me?' she asked softly.

'And why wouldn't I be?'

Fynn led her along the verandah and down the stairs to the walkway along the marina. His hand was firm beneath her elbow as they walked past a coffee shop, a tour booking agency and down to a covered walkway that connected to the finger wharves. When they were almost to the end of the first wharf, he let go of her arm.

'Where are we going?'

'Are you okay to stand and wait here for a moment?'

Liv nodded and he stepped onto a boat.

The concrete wharf rocked slightly beneath her feet and as Liv grabbed for the post, her stomach knotted. A minute later, Fynn appeared on the deck of the boat minus her handbag and her brief-case. He stood on the side of the boat and held out his hand. 'Just a small step up, and you'll be right.'

Once on board, he kept hold of her hand and led her down a couple of steps to a saloon area. 'How are you feeling? Do you want to sit here, or would you be better lying down?'

'Lie down, please.'

'Do you need to see a doctor?'

Liv shook her head. 'No. I just need to sleep this off. Whatever it was.' For the first time since she'd come out of the restroom, she held Fynn's gaze and was surprised—and touched—by the concern she saw there. 'I'm sorry. I don't want to be a bother. A short sleep will fix me and then I can be on my way.'

He showed her into a cabin two steps down from the saloon and along a short walkway. Leaning down, he pulled a light blanket from a small cupboard at the side of the bed and handed it to her.

'Thank you,' Liv said.

The door closed behind Fynn and she sank onto the soft bed. Within seconds, her eyes closed and she was asleep.

*   *   *

Fynn checked on Liv a couple of times to make sure she was sleeping normally and hadn't passed out. She was breathing evenly and a touch of colour had come back into her cheeks. He touched her shoulder gently and she stirred each time, satisfying him that she was merely sleeping off whatever had made her ill. He went up to the deck and sat there thinking as the sun moved across the sky.

He felt bad about not having told her what his job was, and he was sure he would pay for that once she woke up and was feeling better, but for the time being, he was happy to let her sleep.

As the meeting had progressed, he'd seen the tension that held her as tight as a bow string, as well as the obvious lack of communication with the two other guys who were supposedly there to support her. When they'd pulled the pin on her presentation and blamed her, disgust had filled him.

He had no doubt that she was merely a mouthpiece for the organisation. As much as he sensed that Liv would like him to believe she was tough, he knew instinctively she wasn't the sort of person to be involved in the underhand deal that was going down here. He was good at judging people, and even on their short acquaintance, he knew Olivia Sheridan was a decent person. He pulled out his phone and scrolled through the contacts.

As the phone rang, he stared across the water. The marina was sheltered from the stiff south-easterly still blowing, but the wind had dropped off as the afternoon faded.

'Greg? It's Fynn.'

'Gidday, mate. I've been waiting for your call. How did it go?'

'It's been a very interesting day. Something came out at the meeting that wasn't supposed to and it's sparked a big reaction.'

'What can you give me?'

Fynn moved to the stern of the boat and lowered his voice. Last time he'd checked Liv had been sound asleep, and he'd stood there and looked at her for a few moments. Who would ever have thought that Liv Sheridan would be asleep on his boat tonight? 'A new location for the coal loader. At Earlando Bay.'

'What the fuck?'

'Yeah. That's sort of what the community said too.'

'First I've heard of that location. I don't even know where it is. Tell me everything.'

'It's the next bay north and a protected ecological area.' Fynn related the events of the day, and when he finally mentioned that Olivia Sheridan was currently asleep below decks, Greg was silent for a few seconds.

'I don't know how, and for the life of me I can't figure out a reason for it, but she was set up at the meeting to take a very public fall.' Fynn broke the loaded silence.

'You be careful, mate. The whole thing could be a set-up. They're bloody clever. She could be there to see how much we have on them.'

'She could, but I don't think so. I've spent a bit of time with her over the weekend, and she was the one set up. I'd put money on it.'

'But why? What good would that do the project? Jesus, Fynn. Who fucking knows! Andrew Sheridan is such a slimy bastard, you'd never know what he's up to.'

'Sounds like it. And the two Sheridan guys at the meeting were about the same quality.'

'Leave it with me. I'll do some digging around tonight. Anything else comes up, give me a call.'

Fynn stared out over the marina for a while, thoughts tumbling, before he headed inside and pulled out the notes he'd made at the meeting.

CHAPTER
14

Liv stretched her legs out on the cool sheets and buried her face into the soft pillow. In that delicious moment between sleep and waking, she took a deep breath and inhaled the fresh fragrance of the smooth cotton pillowcase. Soft guitar music lulled her back into a doze and a moment later, she woke fully and reached for the alarm clock beside the bed to stop the music.

What day is it? What have I got on today? She stretched further for the alarm clock before she stopped, hand in midair. She opened her eyes as the music stopped, lying still as the cold fingers of memory brushed across her thoughts. With a quiet groan, she rolled over onto her stomach and buried her face in the pillow again.

Fynn's pillow.

It was Monday—or Monday night, as the cabin was in semi-darkness—and she had made an absolute fool of herself at the public meeting today. All she could remember was Fynn bringing her back to a boat and putting her to bed. Liv rolled onto her back and sat up gingerly, testing to see if her head was still spinning. Something had made her sick today—she suspected the seasick tablets had disagreed with her—but she hoped whatever it was had gone. Swinging her legs over to the floor, her bare feet touched smooth timber. Her head was steady so far and her stomach seemed fine. She sat there for a moment and listened. Apart from the faint music, the only other noise was the occasional soft splat of a small wave on the side of the hull, sounding in time with the gentle movement of the yacht.

As Liv sat there, light footsteps crossed the deck above and then it was quiet. She stood carefully and made her way to the corridor outside the open door. Two steps led up to a wide saloon with a galley on the other side that she hadn't noticed on the way down.

'Hey there.' Fynn was sitting at the table in the middle of the saloon. 'Feeling a bit better?' He put the pen in his hand down on the pile of paper in the centre of the table, slid along the bench seat and stood. Liv bit her lip as he placed his hand against her forehead.

'Cool as a cucumber. But then I suppose you didn't have a temp before either.'

She stepped back and took a breath. 'May I have a drink please? I'm really thirsty.'

He scooted over to the small fridge at the end of a bank of timber cupboards and pulled out a small bottle. 'Water, okay?'

'Yes, thank you. That's fine.' Liv knew her voice was stilted and overly polite but she was feeling awkward and didn't know how to handle this. She hadn't known how to talk to Fynn since their first meeting.

He opened the bottle and passed the water over to her but didn't step away as she tipped the bottle up. She drank for longer than she needed to ease her thirst, taking the time to think about what to say to him. Finally, she lowered the bottle and he passed the lid over to her and she screwed it on, before placing it carefully on the table.

'So, Doctor Fynn James,' she said, folding her arms and lifting her head to hold his gaze. 'Tell me what's going on.'

He gestured to the bench seat that followed the table in a semi-circle.

'Are you happy to sit here or would you rather go up on deck?'

'This is fine.' Liv slipped along the seat and sat at the other end of the table from where Fynn had perched himself. 'Now. The truth, please. It was more than coincidence seeing you everywhere on the weekend, wasn't it? You were following me.'

He shook his head emphatically. 'No, trust me. It *was* pure coincidence. Except for the night in the restaurant. Byron called and asked me to look after you when you came down.'

'You're not a waiter there usually?'

He held her gaze steadily. 'I do spend a bit of my time at Fruits de Mer.'

She pushed. 'Why?'

'I'm part-owner.'

'And the *Lady May*?'

He had the grace to look sheepish. 'Byron's and mine.'

'And this boat?' She gestured around them.

'Nah, this baby, she's all mine. This is where I live.'

'So what's all that got to do with the "doctor" bit? And the talk at the … at the meeting this morning?' She glanced at the window; it was too dark to see anything outside. 'It *is* still Monday, isn't it?'

'Yes, but you've been asleep for hours. It's almost eight.' He pushed himself back to his feet and crossed to where a wooden ledge filled the corner. As he leaned against it casually, Liv stared at him. It was hard to reconcile this man in the board shorts and faded David Bowie T-shirt with the authoritative man who had spoken at the meeting.

He was so different from the men she met in the corporate world of suits and business that had been her life over the past few years.

'I work with the university in a research and a consultative capacity. No teaching. My area of expertise is the reef itself. Looking at what damages it, how it survives and regenerates, and identifying what threatens it. Natural and man-made threats.' He picked up a pen and flicked it against the benchtop. 'Both short and long term.'

Liv realised Fynn wasn't just the casual person she'd spent time with over the past couple of days. 'And you didn't think it was necessary to tell me who you are?'

'No, I didn't.' He held her gaze without blinking. 'Did you tell me who you were?'

'It was pretty obvious with the Sheridan Corp pin on my jacket.'

Another casual shrug and one raised eyebrow.

'And did the whole family enjoy the joke at my expense yesterday?' Liv's voice trembled, but Fynn held up his hand.

'Whoa, right there. No one was having a joke at your expense. Why would they? Byron and I were the only ones who knew you're with Sheridan Corp. And that had nothing to do with why he invited you to Aunty Tat's yesterday. He waited with me for a while to make sure you came out, but he got a call and had to go into Prossie to the council office. The shit's hit the fan there.' Fynn walked back to the table and slid in beside her. 'Our meeting at the marina, when she called out to you? How could you possibly think that was a set-up? I knew that someone from Sheridan Corp'—he said the company name as though it left a bad taste in his mouth—'was speaking today. I had no idea you'd be on Hamo. And you were nothing like I expected.'

'You were expecting a suit, I suppose? Not eye candy.' Liv knew her voice was bitter, but she was becoming disgusted with herself the more she thought about how naïve she'd been.

Sherro's daughter's got the looks. Why else would he send her out there to do his dirty work? At the time she'd dismissed that comment as professional jealousy but the truth was that her father had been using her, and the events of the past couple of days had made that very clear. She'd been kidding herself that she had ever been a part of the company. But today's fiasco made no sense. What were they up to? Giving her a presentation and then pulling the plug—literally—before she'd finished.

And what had Phillip meant? His words had been menacing. Heat ran up her neck and she put her hand up to her face. What a fool she must have looked in the meeting.

'Huh?' Fynn was looking at her, his brow wrinkled in a frown. 'Eye candy? What do you mean? Are you feeling all right?'

'Oh yes. I've never felt better. What I mean is I've been absolutely used.' Liv looked around the room. 'Where's my bag please? I need to make a call. And my computer please?'

Fynn crossed the cabin and unlocked a small cupboard beneath the corner bench. He reached in and pulled out her handbag, her briefcase and her shoes. 'Your phone rang and buzzed and dinged most of the afternoon, but I didn't like to wake you up. I checked on you a few times, but you were dead to the world.'

He watched me sleep? Altogether too intimate for her comfort.

'Thank you,' she said as he passed her handbag over. He put the briefcase on the table in front of her. She looked in and pulled out her phone. A frustrated sound escaped her lips before she could hold it back.

'A problem?'

Liv lifted her eyes from the phone and looked at him. Was he genuinely such a nice guy? Or was it all an act? After all, she was the enemy, representing everything he was against. But despite that, Fynn had looked after her when she'd been ill. He'd been kind to her and now, concern filled his voice as she stared at her phone. Why was it so hard for her to trust anyone?

'Just about a hundred missed calls and messages.' She scrolled through the list on the screen. Most were from her father, but there was one from Mum halfway down.

She glanced at Fynn. 'Will you please excuse me while I make some calls?'

'Sure.' He turned towards the door. 'You must be hungry? How about I go and grab some dinner while you do whatever you have to do?'

She nodded. 'Thank you. That would be good. And then I have to figure out how to get to a hotel.'

'Don't worry about that yet. We'll sort that out later.' He picked up his wallet and phone from the bench. 'Pizza okay, or something lighter?'

'Pizza is fine. Thank you.'

'There's a bathroom at the end of the walkway.' With a quick nod, Fynn disappeared up the stairs to the deck, and she listened as his footsteps faded away until he left the boat.

Liv went to the bathroom before she made her calls. After she'd washed her hands, she stared into the mirror. Her face was pale and deep shadows rimmed her eyes. Her braid had come loose and her hair was in a messy tangle. She rinsed her face and patted it dry on the only towel hanging there, feeling as though she was intruding on Fynn's space. As she quickly smoothed and re-braided her hair, she thought of what she wanted to say to her father.

It was going to be an unpleasant conversation, but one that was long overdue.

Making her way back to the saloon, Liv opened the bottle and took another drink of water as she sat at the table. Her tiredness had faded, and she looked curiously at the maps and charts that were spread in front of her. Double Bay and Earlando Bay jumped out at her. She looked away.

Of all people, Fynn had more cause to be against her than anyone else, and that made his kind concern even harder to understand. With a deep breath, she picked up her phone, ignoring the messages from her father and opening the message from Mum.

Livi, call me. What have you done? As long as you're OK I'm happy.

Nothing, she thought as she pressed the text to return the call.

Her mother picked up immediately and sounded worried. 'Hi, sweetheart. Are you okay? I've been trying to call you.'

'I am now. How did you know I was sick?'

'I didn't.' The worry in her mother's voice intensified. 'Sick? What's wrong? Where are you?'

'I'm fine now. I'm still up at Airlie Beach. I had a bit of a tummy thing. Why did you ask if I was okay?'

'I knew something was wrong when your father called me demanding to know where *my* daughter was. Good on you, love. You've certainly pushed his buttons. What's happened?'

'I don't really know. He's used me somehow.' Liv sighed and pushed her hair back from her face. 'I've finally woken up to myself. I know you've been trying to tell me for a long time, but I guess I had to discover it for myself.'

'A long while? Eight years, more like it! It was inevitable, Liv. You're a good person, and you have ethics and standards. It was only a matter of time before you woke up to him, but I'd hoped it wouldn't take so long. Are you going to stay with the company?'

'No, I don't want anything to do with it. Or him.' She couldn't bring herself to say 'Dad'. 'I don't know what he's doing but he set me up to look like a fool in a public meeting, and then one of his minders actually threatened me.'

'Be careful, love. I know it sounds harsh, or maybe like a disgruntled ex-wife, but your father doesn't like being crossed.'

'Don't be silly, Mum. But I didn't cross him. That's the point. I've been set up and I'm about to call him and find out why.' She shook her head. 'It's bizarre.' Liv dropped her chin into her hand. 'But you and Gran have told me often enough not to trust him.'

Her mother's voice was brisk. 'We did, but it's understandable. He's your father and he can be very persuasive when he wants to be. The conniving bastard pulled the wool over my eyes for a long time. There's a lot of things I haven't ever told you, Liv. I didn't think it was fair to make you take sides. But I will share them with you one day. You had to choose your own path, but you're probably old enough and wise enough now to hear the truth.'

Liv let out a short laugh. 'Thirty is probably old enough.'

'Okay, next time we're together. It will take wine. And we'll get Gran to come. She can fill you in too!' Her mother laughed over the phone and Liv couldn't help but smile. She was feeling better already.

'That sounds like a plan.'

'When are you coming home?'

'I'm not sure yet. I have to get back to Hamilton Island and get my things.'

'Where are you now?'

Liv looked around at the beautiful interior of Fynn's boat. She hadn't taken much notice of it before. It was an older vessel like the *Lady May* but obviously well loved and cared for. The timber work was glossy, and the galley was immaculate.

'I'm staying with a ... er ... a friend. My flight back to Sydney is booked for tomorrow but it depends how rough the Passage is. Mum, are you going out to Gran's soon? I could meet you at the farm.'

'I'm going to the farm at the end of the month. I want to plan something for her birthday. It would be lovely if you'd come out with me. We can have that chat.'

'Consider it booked.' With a farewell, Liv disconnected. She was calmer than she'd been for a few days. She should listen to Mum more often; she and Gran always managed to ground her.

Where has the time gone? It only seemed a few years since they'd held a big party at the farm for Gran's eighty-fifth. Guilt ripped through Liv. She'd been close to Gran when she'd been growing up but once she'd left home for university, her focus had moved to her studies. And trying to gain her father's respect.

If only I'd taken notice of Mum and Gran.

With a deep breath, Liv composed herself and read the text messages from her father. She scrolled through the messages, each one was angrier than the one before. By the time she scrolled to the last one where she read 'if she didn't fucking contact him within ten minutes she would regret it' she had composed herself. A set smile stretched her lips. That final message had come in about five hours ago.

Threats in the workplace? Daughter or not, those texts were enough for a harassment case. She'd keep that up her sleeve in case she needed it. Liv clicked on the speed dial and the call was picked up before it even rang.

'Olivia!' Her father's voice boomed over the phone. 'Where the fuck have you been?'

'Don't speak to me like that, please.' Her voice was icily calm and she sat straight.

'I asked you where the fuck have you been. Do you think I pay you to swan around some tropical resort?' Liv could picture the red face and the spittle flying from his mouth. 'I've been trying to bloody call you since this morning's fiasco.'

She said nothing, focusing instead on detaching herself from the angry voice at the other end of her phone. Deep, controlled breathing. Her yoga classes stood her in good stead.

'I'll give you one chance to explain yourself, Olivia. One fucking chance.'

Her calm flew out the window. 'So, Dad, did you think that the community up here in the boondocks would be swayed by some dumb blonde bimbo? Or what did I hear in the office? "Eye candy" can sway a community. What an arrogant bastard you are.'

'One chance, I said. Explain yourself.' His yell was so loud she moved the phone away from her ear.

'Explain myself? You're the one who needs to explain why your minder pulled the pin on the presentation. I looked like a fool. You give me no credit for intelligence.'

Silence. And then a deathly quiet and controlled voice. 'You *are* a fool.'

'What?' Her voice was as cold as his. 'What did you say?'

'You heard me. Now tell me where you got hold of that actual data. Who have you got in your pocket? I know all you've ever wanted is to be promoted but that was never going to happen.'

'Rod—*your* PR guy—sent me the link. The email *you* told me was coming. The PowerPoint was the most recent one in the folder I downloaded.'

'What folder?'

She ignored his question. 'That's what you think of me, isn't it? You give me no credit for any intelligence. How dare you *use* me? No matter what the economic analysis shows, this is the wrong location for the development.'

'*Rod* sent you more than the file?' His voice sent a chill down her spine. 'How long have you been in cahoots with him? Are you fucking him?'

'How dare you!' Liv gasped. Her head began to throb again, and she put her hand to her eyes.

'Oh, that's right. Little Miss Innocent, I forgot for a moment. And don't you try and justify your stuff up on some airy fairy environmental bullshit, you stupid bitch. It's your incompetence that's put this deal in jeopardy. I told you what to do and now you've interfered in something you know nothing about, and I've got to send someone else to clean up your mess. Do you know how much this contract is worth to Sheridan Corp? Do you realise this could cost us the project? Zenith is talking about dropping us because word is out about the new site before we were ready.'

'Good.' Despite the headache slamming back in, Liv kept her voice brisk. 'Perhaps you'll ultimately realise honesty and treating people with respect is more important than making money. Maybe you could take a look at the environment too.' Her breath was starting to hitch and she paused for a moment to compose herself. 'You've used my loyalty to the company, and to you as my father, and thrown it in my face. Well, you can have my resignation now. Make up my termination pay. I won't be back.'

As she drew in a breath, the smell of pizza wafted in and she looked up to see Fynn in the doorway, his eyes intense.

'You can't resign. Your employment is already terminated. Now, tell me what else you downloaded.'

'I'm not interested in anything I downloaded. I'm not interested in Sheridan Corp. I'm not interested in anything you have to say.' Liv's voice rose higher. '*I've* resigned. Please ensure what's owing is paid to me, or you'll find yourself on the front page of the papers for bullying in the workplace. And you know what? I won't be letting this go. The islands up here are not the place for your coal loader. Maybe I'll talk to the media.'

'You signed a confidentiality agreement, Olivia. You can't share anything from the company. If you do, I'll see you in court.' Liv narrowed her eyes. For the first time, a note of worry laced her father's voice.

'Go your hardest.' Her voice was firm, and Fynn nodded as she looked back at him. If she wasn't mistaken there was a glimmer of a smile hovering around his lips.

'Your computer belongs to the company you no longer work for. So does your phone. I'll organise a courier. Where are you?' Her father's voice suddenly lost its belligerent tone. 'Look, I'm sorry, Liv. I was harsh before. Just tell me where you are, and I'll send someone to get the computer. We'll forget we had this conversation. When you come back to the office, we'll discuss a pay rise for you.'

'No, we won't. I'll bring it back to the office when I come back to Sydney.' Liv glanced at the computer in front of her. 'You disgust me. For years, I've tried to live up to your standards but now I'm ashamed to call you my father. If I need to see you in court, I'm sure your texts will prove what a bully you are. Don't bother contacting me again. *Ever.* Organise my termination pay.'

Liv threw the phone down and closed her eyes. She laid her head back on the soft cushioned padding behind her.

'Bravo.' Fynn stood in the galley, unmoving, his eyes fixed on her. 'I couldn't help but overhear. In fact, I could hear you up on deck.' He put the pizza box and a bottle of red wine on the sink before he came across to the table.

Liv bit her lip and looked down; her hands were shaking. He sat beside her and his voice was soft and kind. 'Well, darlin', after a conversation like that, how can I help?'

'First up, you can pour me a wine.' Liv blinked away the moisture that was stinging her eyes. It wasn't grief, but anger, a cold anger that she knew had settled in her for a long time to come. She lifted her chin and firmed her voice. 'Then, you can accept my apology.'

Warm hands held her shoulders, and then Fynn lifted her chin with one finger so she was looking at him. 'No need for any apology.'

'Yes, there is. I accused you unfairly.'

'No, you didn't. I heard most of what you said. Not many people would be brave enough to take Andrew Sheridan on.'

The lack of food, the bilious attack and the conversation with her father overwhelmed Liv in a crashing wave of reaction. Her lips trembled and she shivered as he held her gaze.

'Can you just hold me, please?' Liv closed her eyes as Fynn pulled her close and she rested her cheek against the comforting firmness of his chest.

* * *

Liv was slim but her soft curves pressed against Fynn as he held her close. He'd been right about her moral core. The things she'd said to her father—that bastard Andrew Sheridan—had been on the mark. The two guys who had been with her at the meeting this morning had walked out on her, even though she was obviously unwell. He'd known as soon as they'd stopped her presentation that she was in trouble.

He wondered what the problem was. Something stank about the whole thing, but Greg was on it and would find something, he had no doubt of that.

When Earlando Bay had appeared on the screen, those attending the meeting had been silent for a moment before all hell had broken loose. And then that pointy-faced guy with the slick hair had pulled the power cord out and turned on Liv.

Her strength in standing up to her father on the phone surprised him. Honesty was good but after some of the things Greg had unearthed about Andrew Sheridan, Fynn wondered how wise it would be having him as an enemy.

Daughter or not.

She was still and quiet in his arms, and he stared across the top of her head to the lights blinking out on the harbour wall. Her breathing was slow and deep and she didn't say anything. Liv was Sheridan's daughter, and she'd quit his company as Fynn had stood in the galley with a box of pizza. Her words had been blunt and brave, and she'd not held back. He wondered what was in this folder that seemed to have caused the problem.

Eventually, she stirred in his arms and pulled back, dropping her arms to her sides. Her cheeks were flushed, but it was better than the earlier pallor.

Liv dropped her chin and her arms crept around to hug herself. 'I'm sorry. I guess I'm a bit fragile from being sick.' She kept looking down and didn't meet his eyes.

'There's no need to be embarrassed. You've had a pretty big day. And then not being well topped it all off.' He put his hand out and gently took her chin and she looked up. 'And then to have a conversation like that at the end of a day like you had, I'm impressed that you're still standing.'

She lifted her head higher and her eyes flashed. 'If you could have heard what he was saying ...'

'Tell me as much as you want but first, I've got a lovely supreme pizza from the best pizzeria on the Queensland coast.'

'You know, I think it might have been the seasick tablets that I took before I left Hamilton Island this morning. I think I'd rather have chanced seasickness than ending up like I did.'

Fynn was pleased when her eyes brightened and her lips tilted upwards. Her smile was shaky, but it was a smile.

His gut tightened, and he stood and reached over to pick up the pizza box from the bench, shaking his head. 'Trust me, darlin'. Sea-sickness is not pretty. Now, are you up for pizza, or will I eat it all?'

CHAPTER
15

Liv was starving, and there wasn't much conversation as she and Fynn made quick work of the pizza. Apart from a lingering tiredness and thirst, the awful sickness that had hit her this morning had disappeared. Yet despite the tiredness, in another way she was full of energy. In between eating, she stood and roamed around the cabin as she talked to Fynn.

'Maybe I should have ordered two pizzas.' His eyes crinkled in a smile as he held up the bottle of wine, offering to top up her glass. Since he'd held her, Liv had relaxed and strangely felt more comfortable with him even though it was only three days since she had met him.

She shook her head and put her hand over the glass. 'No thanks. I'll fall asleep again.'

He grinned. 'The way you've been up and down for the last half hour, it looks like you've already had your night's sleep.'

'Thanks for looking after me today.' She pulled a face. 'Anthony and that guy from Zenith must have taken off quickly.'

'Like rats up a rafter.' Fynn laughed. 'They didn't even wait for a taxi. Last I saw, they were walking around the boardwalk into town.'

'Hopefully followed by an angry mob?' she asked.

'No. But looking decidedly pissed off. And while I was waiting for you to come out, they were arguing outside and it looked pretty nasty.'

Liv sat down again. 'I'd say it was because I was given access to a folder instead of to the file I needed. I downloaded the wrong presentation. Apparently, the new site at Earlando Bay is still confidential.'

'Not anymore, it's not. No wonder your father is so pissed off.' Fynn leaned back and put his hands behind his head. 'So, what are your plans now you don't have a job?'

'First off, I have to get back to my hotel room on Hamilton Island, and see about my flight back to Sydney. Do the water taxis leave from here or will I have to go back around to Port of Airlie?'

He waved a dismissive hand. 'Don't worry about that. We'll take you back over in the morning.'

'Who's we?'

'Me and this lovely lady.'

'Who?' When Liv frowned, he grinned.

'*Footprint*, my yacht.'

'Thank you. I owe you big time.'

'I actually meant what are your plans past the next few days.' Fynn's tone was more serious now.

Liv shrugged. 'I haven't really had time to absorb all of the changes that have hit me today.'

He stared at her for a moment and his eyes were intense. 'Were you serious when you said you were going to fight the development? Using what you have to expose whatever they're doing to get all these approvals through? We could use some help, and some inside knowledge would be very helpful if we're going to beat this.'

'We?' she asked.

'Greg, my journo mate, and I have been digging away at this together for almost a year now. And Byron is with us too. You knew he was on the regional council, didn't you?'

She nodded.

'What do you mean digging?'

'I hate to be the one to tell you, but Sheridan Corp has a pretty shaky track record.' He reached for the wine bottle and topped up both their glasses.

'I need to know what exactly is happening up here. Down in the office, I'm involved with the data analysis, predominantly the economic benefits, and I guess, I really missed the human element.'

'You mean, like those who are pulling the strings?'

She shook her head emphatically. 'Yes, that's a part of it. But what I meant is the real impact that the project would have on this area. You'd have to be blind Freddie not to see that. The waterways, the tourists, the whales … I guess just the absolute pristine nature of the place. I didn't get that through facts and figures. The thought of a coal loader extending out into the sea from that bay, and coal ships travelling through the Passage—' She cut herself off and shook her head again. 'It's just not right. So, tell me what you know.'

'We know a lot of what's happening, but getting reliable evidence is almost impossible. There's corruption everywhere you turn. Money buys favours and silence, and a blind eye can be turned to legislation if the right palms are greased. Greg did an initial report in the *Courier Mail* over the weekend. He could only use the facts that he can prove but we know so much more that we can't use yet.'

'Greg Coutts? I read that article. He's your journo friend?'

'He is. He's a good man. Honest and tenacious. Like me, he knows there's a lot going on behind the scenes here. The level of corruption in the government sign off—well, just let me say, I'd find it hard to believe it if I hadn't seen the evidence that Greg has gotten hold of.'

'Could you really use me?' Her voice was soft as regret slammed through her. Regret that she'd been a part of this corruption that he talked about. It might have been unknowing, but she'd been too focused on trying to please Dad and get promoted. 'I'm ashamed of myself, Fynn. I've been naïve, and I've been duped and used. I'm going to nail the bastard.'

His eyes widened. 'That's your father you're talking about.'

'No. From now on, I'll listen to my mother and my grand-mother, they tried to tell me, but I was so ambitious and so sure I could measure up, I put up with the way he treated me. No more. He's done it and I'm angry.'

Fynn's wide smile sent a fluttering feeling to Liv's stomach. 'So why leave? Why not stay now and help us?'

She looked down at her work shirt with a grimace. 'I've got two business outfits, a sarong, swimmers, and a couple of casual outfits with me.'

'We have shops here.'

His smile really should be declared illegal.

Fynn was way too good-looking for her peace of mind. When he smiled his whole face lit up, and more importantly, he'd shown her he was a really nice guy along with the good looks. Kind and dependable.

'Unless you have a reason to go home, and then you could turn around and come up a few days later?'

Liv tucked her feet beneath her and picked up the wine glass. She looked over the rim at Fynn as she thought about what he'd suggested. There was no reason to go back to Sydney yet. She was well qualified; it wouldn't take much to find another job and get immersed in another company. Her career was her security, and it was all she had in her life.

Up until now.

'You're right, you know. I've got no reason to go south just yet. I've got nothing planned until I visit my grandmother at the end of the month, so all I really have to do is check out of the hotel and find an apartment.' Anticipation filled her as her thoughts scurried around. The holiday she'd needed for a long time, in a beautiful location, and while she was here, she could try to make amends for what her father's company was trying to do to the environment. 'So what do you think? Airlie Beach or Hamilton Island? What would make the most sense?' she asked.

Fynn's smile disappeared and he cleared his throat. 'What about on the water? I've got a perfectly good spare cabin here, and if we're going to be working together …'

'Thank you, that's a lovely gesture for someone you barely know, but who knows how long I'll stay up here. The way I'm feeling now, I don't ever want to go back to the city.'

'Well then, I think the mainland is probably the best place to base yourself. Give me a minute.' Fynn reached for his phone and punched in a number.

'Hey, Byron. You busy, mate?' He listened for a while. 'Is anyone in Shingley Beach at the moment?' He smiled at Liv and she fought back the warmth that settled in her belly. 'No? That's great. Close it off for a fortnight to start with.' He nodded and disconnected.

Liv frowned. 'Shingley Beach? What's that?'

'Byron and I have an apartment there that we holiday let. You're in luck. It's empty at the moment. You have somewhere to stay, Ms Sheridan.'

'I'll pay, of course.'

'Okay, but mate's rates. I'll be putting you to work, don't you worry.' He took her hand and his voice was serious. 'And the first thing I want to see is this folder that your father is so damned upset about.'

Liv nodded and determination filled her voice. 'Why not start now?'

Fynn was cautious. He was all too aware of the reach of those in Sheridan Corp.

'Liv, I don't want to worry you. But I do want you to be aware that you have to be careful. You've put yourself in the sights of the big boys now, and they've got a lot to lose. Do you mind if I talk to Greg first?'

She yawned as he waited for her to answer. There were dark circles beneath her eyes, and her face was still pale. 'I'm happy for you to do that.'

'Are you okay to spend tonight on board? Byron said he'd get the apartment serviced tomorrow. By the time we sail back to Hamo and collect your luggage, and then come back to the mainland, it should be ready for you.'

'I appreciate the offer. Thank you. And yes, call Greg.'

'I've already told him about the meeting, and he's looking at Earlando Bay, but I'd like to tell him you're prepared to work with us. And about these files you've got. From what you said about your father's reaction, whatever they are, it sounds like they could be crucial.'

Liv took their plates across to the galley and ran the hot water as he dialled Greg's number. As he waited for Greg to pick up, Fynn looked at her as she stood at the sink. She'd rolled up the sleeves of her corporate shirt and pulled it loose from the fitted skirt. He let his gaze linger; it was obvious that she looked after herself. Her calf muscles were toned and—

Jesus. Fynn looked away. This was not the time to be thinking about Liv like that. Even if he'd been attracted to her from the first time her cool gaze had locked with his as he'd walked her along the street at Hamo.

'Fynn.' He turned his attention to Greg when his mate picked up the phone.

'Hey, mate.' As he answered, Liv came back over to the table and slid in beside him. Her eyes stayed on his face. 'I've got something else for you. And I need some advice.' Fynn smiled at Liv as she listened. 'After the fiasco today, Liv Sheridan is leaving Sheridan Corp and wants to come on board with us.'

'Christ, mate. Are you sure that's a wise move? It's not a set-up, is it?' Greg's voice was wary. 'Or you're thinking with your—'

'No. I'm not.' Fynn cut him off. 'I'm going to put you on speakerphone now, so Liv can join the conversation. And yes, it's the right thing to do.' He held her gaze as he put his mobile onto speaker. 'I trust Liv and she's on board, one hundred percent.'

Fynn listened as Greg outlined what he'd discovered since their earlier call. 'There's something going on that's upset them. There's been a flurry of calls to and from China all day.'

Liv's eyebrows rose, but Fynn shook his head. 'Okay. Let me know if anything comes out of that.' Greg had a contact in Sheridan Corp who kept him informed. Fynn suspected that Liv was naïve when it came to company espionage. There was no loyalty that couldn't be brought down with the right incentive, or enough money. 'There's one thing you need to know, and it could be what's got them buzzing. I'll let Liv tell you.'

He nodded at Liv and she spoke slowly. 'Hi, Greg.'

'Hello, Olivia.'

'Liv, please.' Her hand was shaking as she reached up and pushed her hair back. 'I might know what's caused that upset you talked about. My father's PR guy, Rod Smythe, gave me the rights to some files two nights ago. By mistake, I know now. I wasn't sure which one I was supposed to download so I downloaded the whole folder onto my computer.'

Greg's whistle was shrill. 'Could be interesting.'

Liv glanced at Fynn and he shot her a smile. 'And to put it not so politely, it appears the shit has hit the fan,' she said.

'Where's the computer now? You've still got those files?'

'Yes. It's with us here on the boat,' Fynn answered.

'Great. Do they know you're quitting?'

'Yes. My father demanded I send the computer back now.'

Greg spoke quickly. 'Have you been online since the meeting, Liv?'

Fynn looked at Liv and she shook her head. 'No.'

'Good. Now, listen carefully. Don't log on to the internet. Your login to the company network is sure to be gone, but I'm sure they'll still be able to log into the computer if it's on a network. What you have to do is get that computer backed up before I get there. If those files are incriminating, they'll be watching and waiting for you to go online.' Liv's eyes were wide as Greg lowered his voice. 'Or more likely, they'll come looking for it. I know what those bastards are like.'

'They don't know where I am.' Her voice shook. Fynn reached over and squeezed her hand.

'Take care.' Greg's voice was brisk. 'I'll fly up tomorrow.'

Liv was quiet once the call ended. Fynn got up and filled the kettle. He held up a cup and she nodded.

'Coffee, please. White, no sugar.'

'It won't keep you awake?'

'If I have trouble sleeping tonight, I can guarantee it won't be the coffee.'

Fynn waited for the kettle to boil and once he'd poured two coffees, he gestured to the door with his head. 'Let's go up on deck. A bit of fresh air is what you need.' He waited till Liv stood and then he followed her up to the deck, and once she was settled on the cushioned seat near the helm, he passed her the coffee mug.

'Thank you.' Her eyes were bright, but her hand was steady as she sipped the hot drink. Fynn sat at the other end of the seat.

They sat up on the deck and talked for an hour. The more she shared with him about her father's end of the conversation, the more Fynn's respect grew. Liv had responded to her father's tirade in a calm and controlled manner. He didn't mention that he'd met Andrew Sheridan at a meeting at the Reef Authority in Brisbane six months earlier. He'd watched the complex corporate moves he'd pulled off over the ensuing months, bringing the final approval for the coal loader, the huge mine in the central western basin, and the rail line, closer to completion every day.

There was no doubt about the truths that Liv had told her father on the phone. He was an unscrupulous businessman who would stop at nothing to make money. And Fynn knew Sheridan would do anything it took, even if his own daughter was in the firing line. It was disappointing that Liv hadn't accepted his offer to stay on his boat after they collected her luggage, but he could understand why she'd said no. He could still keep a close eye on her in the apartment until Greg published the exposé that he was working on.

The one thing he was worried about was Sheridan's next move. Fynn didn't trust him at all. Greg had uncovered some pretty murky things about his past, and he was sure that Liv had no idea what her father was capable of.

But surely his own daughter would be out of his sights? Fynn was pleased that the two minders hadn't seen him wait for her and bring her to his boat.

CHAPTER
16

2 May, 1942

For Jack, the week of leave on Whitsunday Island after Christmas had been like living in fairyland, and while the island was now a distant recollection, the memory of Liliana's company had seen him through some difficult times. It hadn't taken him long to lose the calm that he had regained in those seven idyllic days. Now it was like the fragment of a pleasant dream that stays briefly with you on awakening, not that he had many of them these days. Once back on base at Port Moresby, the tension was palpable twenty-four hours a day. Even when the airmen weren't up in the Black Cats, danger surrounded them.

'Run for it, guys. Here comes another Charlie.' Two days ago, the urgent call from one of the Yanks on base had sent the men running for the jungle. The drone of the tired engines of the approaching Japanese Betty bombers—christened 'washing machine Charlies' by the American airmen—and the subsequent explosions of the bombs as they hit Port Moresby and the harbour, ensured that Jack had little sleep. He shared a hut with ginger-haired Megsy, the airframe fitter on the Cat.

In the first raid, three Catalinas were destroyed at their mooring and a fourth was damaged. The squadron headquarters took a direct hit in the second raid the next day, and they lost an airman. Johnny Mac was from Tamworth, not far from Jack's home in the Hunter Valley, and his death had hit hard.

For the next few weeks, the smallest sound would wake him and he'd jump from his stretcher, ready to flee the hut into the jungle. Megsy snored in the stretcher next to him as Jack lay back down each time he woke, feeling like a coward. Those two bombing raids had ended any complacency he'd held about being safe on base.

At the end of April their wing commander, John Hughes—known to the airmen as Smiley—called them into the briefing room. His face and voice were grim. 'We're pulling out, so pack your kit bags, men. The 11 and 20 Squadrons are shifting to Bowen. We just don't have the manpower here to build an airbase and the Japanese are getting too close and too fast. Tomorrow afternoon, lads. It'll give you time for a kip after your last mission out of Moresby.'

Relief rippled through the room. Over two hundred hours of flying had been done in the last three weeks, and it was unsustainable. Jack couldn't help the grin that tugged at his lips, even as guilt flooded him when he thought of how Johnny Mac wouldn't be going home. His relief soon disappeared when Smiley pulled down the map on the wall at the front of the briefing hut. Perspiration trickled down Jack's neck as the unbearable heat mingled with his apprehension.

'Captain Munford. Your crew is up for the milk run tonight.'

Jack glanced at Megsy. The airframe fitter was a stocky man and his short-cropped ginger hair was distinctive in the crowd of airmen. Last time they'd flown a milk run, they'd encountered a severe electrical storm on the way back. Their aircraft had dropped over a thousand feet without warning. Jack still had raw, weeping scabs on his elbows where he'd slammed into the side of the turret. The tropical heat meant infection set in quickly.

'Debriefing for the flight crew now.' Smiley glanced at Jack and Megsy, his expression dour and his mouth set in a straight line as usual. 'NCOs, you are dismissed. Officers, please join me for breakfast in the Officer's Mess after the briefing.'

Jack and Megsy walked out together and closed the door of the tin hut behind them. As Megsy cupped his hand around a rollie, he caught Jack's eye.

'Strewth, he's a sour blighter. Sun don't shine anywhere there.' Megsy's voice was quiet as he blew out the first puff of smoke.

'I wouldn't like to have his responsibility at the moment,' Jack replied. He looked up at the sky. Clouds tipped the top of the range, but the rest of the sky was clear, and it looked like the relentless tropical rain would stay away for at least a few hours.

'So what do you reckon? Liquid breakfast?' Megsy gestured to the tin hunt where the beer was always available and cold, despite the steaming heat and humidity. 'The toffs can sod off and have their cooked breakfast.'

The voice from behind them was quiet. 'It's necessary, Megsy.'

'Oh, sorry, Sarge, I thought you'd gone with 'em.' Megsy jerked his head back to the hut.

The tall man standing at the door shook his head. 'The rank of sergeant is non-commissioned, and we don't mix with the officers either.'

'So why do you say it's necessary?' Megsy's temper matched his hair and it looked like he wasn't going to let the matter go. 'Bloody stupid if you ask me.'

'I'm with Megsy here.' Jack held Sarge's eye. 'We're all fighting the Japs together.'

The sergeant shook his head. 'You'll soon learn, boys.'

'Boys!' Megsy squawked in protest.

'Yes. Boys.' The older man's eyes were distant, and Jack listened with interest. 'Old soldiers know that fraternising with the officers jeopardises the discipline and respect required within an armed force. You'll learn that very quickly.'

Megsy put his head down, suitably chastened. 'Want to come and have a beer with us, Sarge?'

'No thanks. I've got work to do.'

'Count me out too, Megsy,' Jack said. 'I think I'll go for a walk down to the village for a while.'

Megsy scratched his chin as he yawned. His ginger whiskers blended into his sunburned skin. 'You okay, Jack?'

Jack shrugged. 'Yeah. You?'

'Sick of this bloody heat.' Megsy's fair skin was burned raw from the tropical sun, and blisters covered his shoulders. 'Okay, I won't drink by myself. I'll go and write to the missus. Tell her that life is bloody wonderful here in the air force. Getting myself a tan too.'

Jack walked beside Megsy as far as the hut they shared. 'It's too bloody hot in that tin shed. I'll see you later.'

'Not much better outside,' Megsy said. 'Watch out for those native girls. I think they fancy a fine-looking bloke like you.'

'I've been teaching the little kids how to play cricket.'

'I miss my young blokes.'

'You've got kids?' Jack stopped in surprise and looked at Megsy. 'You never said.'

'Yeah, five and two. I miss them like crazy.'

'I'll bet.' Jack was surprised. He'd thought Megsy a bit of a lad rather than a family man.

'I hated leaving them and the missus, but you know what it's like. Why we're all here. Make the country a safe place for them to grow up.'

'Yeah. I know.' Jack's voice was quiet as he looked past Megsy.

Megsy gave him a nod. 'You're a good bloke, Jack.'

'Fills in the days,' Jack replied.

'See ya, mate.'

Playing cricket with the small boys from the village gave Jack's life a semblance of normality, between sleeping in a tin hut and spending monotonous hours in a metal tube in the air. The down-time between missions was hard to take, and the apprehension that gripped him before each take off had made him physically ill a couple of times. Most of the crew spent the long hours between missions sleeping or writing to their families, but Jack hadn't been able to write home. The longer he'd left it, the harder it became. His father was in the wrong, and he'd be blowed if he was going to make the first move. Guilt nagged at him because he knew his mother would be sick with worry, but if he wrote to her, she'd show the letter to Dad.

Rather than staying in the galvanised iron huts under Ack Ack Hill, Jack had also volunteered to help the ground crews and spent some of his days scraping the hulls of the last couple of Cats waiting to be painted black. When the metal was too hot to work on, that's when he'd wander down the road to the village to play with the kids. But now those Cats had been destroyed, cricket was his only option.

A couple of times, Jack had thought of writing to Liliana but there was nothing he could talk about. Any mention of missions or locations was taboo. Still, he couldn't stop thinking about her.

When the creeping fear took hold and claustrophobia threatened as the Cat flew the long hours over the sea, he would close his eyes briefly and imagine the blue waters around the Ellis home, and the lush green forests on the mountain behind their house. The silence was broken only by the soughing of the wind in the top of the hoop pines. The island was as close to perfection as he'd ever seen. But if he was honest, Jack knew it was Liliana he wanted to see again more than a timbered island with a few goats running on it, no matter how scenic and peaceful it was. Since the launch had steamed towards Bowen on that balmy evening when he'd left her, it had been hard to forget those pretty eyes and gentle expression. In those days on Whitsunday Island, he'd been able to kid himself that there was no war.

It hadn't lasted long. The fear had returned and worsened by the day until he thought he was going mad. The other airmen were quiet, but they didn't seem to have the fear that filled him, so Jack never talked about how he felt.

One more mission, that's all he had to survive, and they'd be going south. The fear sat in his gut like the small coconut he was using for the cricket game with the laughing children.

One more mission out of Moresby.

CHAPTER

17

Jack was in the bunk compartment of the Cat, looking down through the starboard wheel observation window with his forehead resting against the cold metal. They'd dropped enough bombs on the Japanese ships near Salamaua to slow down the advance of the navy.

Every time the Cat shuddered in the ever-present turbulence of the tropics, he grabbed for the log book as it slid along the cold metal floor beside his head. Jack swore as he bumped his infected elbow against the metal shelf at his side as he secured the log book. His attention was on the ocean below them as occasional wisps of cloud were touched by the rising sun. Coming home in daylight had the crew on tenterhooks; the Cats were painted black to avoid detection at night and the morning return was fraught with tension. As Jack leaned forward, a glint of silver flashed below. His blood ran cold, and he picked up the radio handset as he pressed his eye against the small observation window.

'Captain Munford!' Jack's voice was low and urgent as the two red circles confirmed his worst fear.

'Rickard?' It was hard to hear the captain's response over the roar of the engines as they headed for base, even though the captain was only a couple of metres away in the cockpit.

'We've got a Zero at five o'clock, sir.'

'Shit.'

The engines roared as their air speed increased almost instantly. Captain Munford was pushing the cumbersome aircraft as hard as he could. Jack knew that their slow speed and lack of manoeuvrability would turn them into a sitting duck. Bile rose to his throat and he clenched his fingers as he leaned forward, watching as the fighter plane levelled out beneath them and then disappeared. He held his breath and waited for the fuselage to rip as bullets tore through the metal.

The minutes passed slowly, and the compartment shook as the captain increased their air speed to the maximum. Jack's ears buzzed with the roar of the engines. Megsy clambered over the low divider between the radio room and the bunk compartment and dropped to his haunches, peering through the port observation window. He tapped Jack's leg and when Jack looked up, Megsy shook his head. 'Can't see the blighter this side,' he yelled. 'You?'

'No. I think he's gone behind us.'

They peered below and waited.

But the Zero with the distinctive red circle on each wing didn't reappear. Once they reached the Owen Stanley Range just north of Port Moresby, Jack stared down into jungle-clad mountains. The low morning clouds hovered over the razorback ridges of the mountain chain, and he stared, waiting for the silver fighter to burst clear of the mist. His eyes burned with the strain and he blinked as two red circles appeared beneath him. He blinked and looked again but there was nothing there. They began to descend as the water of the harbour glinted to the south. He counted down in his head as the air speed dropped and the Black Cat lost height.

The eight crew members were subdued as they landed in the harbour with a wash of spray, knowing how close they'd come to being shot down. The Cat taxied through the choppy waves to the personnel barge that was waiting to ferry them to the shore. Captain Munford waited for Jack to clamber from the fuselage and jump onto the boat.

'Well spotted, Rickard. Sighting that bastard when you did probably saved us.'

Jack held it together as they headed for the small wooden jetty adjacent to the base. They disembarked and he hurried up the hill, managing to get around to the back of the first hut before he leaned over and vomited. His knees were shaking as he straightened and pulled a rag from his back pocket and wiped the sweat from his face.

As the Cat was refuelled, Jack and Megsy grabbed their bags. He didn't look back at Ack Ack Hill as they headed to the harbour for the flight to Bowen.

★ ★ ★

14 May, 1942

Jack sat on the step at the back of the boarding house, smoking his second cigarette of the morning. Their aircraft was up on the hard stand and they hadn't flown a mission since coming back from Moresby a week earlier. The view from the top of Bowen Hill was depressing. The coal mines in the distance were as ugly as those at home in the Hunter Valley and to the south were the flat salt pans. Although some of the airmen had raved about the pastel swirling colours, it wasn't to be compared with the beauty he'd seen on Whitsunday Island.

Adjacent to the salt pans was the salt works, and to the north, an overgrown lagoon. The smell of the stagnant water drifted up as soon as the sun set each evening, along with the mosquitoes. Jack lit a third cigarette and ignored the now cold mug of tea that he'd collected from the kitchen on his way outside. He didn't care how boring it was here in Bowen, at least back on Australian soil the constant fear that had dogged him in Port Moresby had gone. Even though they had lost two Cats and both crews in the battle dubbed 'Coral Sea' the week the squadrons had moved to Bowen, being here, and close to the islands was much safer than being on the base at Port Moresby.

He tipped the tea onto the parched ground next to the back steps, then washed and shaved in preparation for the squadron morning muster. He quickly tidied the small space that served as his bedroom in the house where he was kipping with Roger and Charlie. Most of the squadron officers and ground crews were accommodated in various hotels, private houses and shops in the main streets of Bowen, and when Roger and Charlie had heard Jack's squadron was coming back, they'd found a place for him at their boarding house.

He smoothed down his uniform as he let himself out the front door. 'Bye, Mrs Atkins.'

The landlady was kneeling in the middle of the large vegetable patch that had replaced the front lawn. She'd taken great pride in telling him about her Victory Garden when he'd arrived yesterday. The tomatoes were looking sad, no wonder in this dry heat, but Jack kept his voice cheery as he walked past. 'No need for breakfast today. I'll have it down town.'

Many of the local men had volunteered and gone away to war. Those who remained struggled to maintain the crops and orchards. It was not uncommon to see a vegetable field with all women picking the crops. He wondered whether it was like that at home now. The grape harvest would be done for the year … he pushed away the thought of home. When the war was over, maybe he'd find somewhere else to establish his own vineyard, unless Dad was prepared to change his mind. Maybe he'd buy some land up here and grow tropical fruits.

Jack whistled as he crossed Powell Street, where the Denison Hotel served as squadron headquarters and officers' accommodation. The operational base unit had been established in the town to undertake administration and maintenance of the base. It was so different to the tin huts and the jungle encroaching on the base up at Moresby.

The local picture theatre had been converted to a maintenance workshop. An airmen's mess, station headquarters, and station store and guard room had taken over the adjacent shops, the locals being more than happy to help with supporting the war effort. Houses along Dalrymple and George Streets became airmen's barracks and elsewhere in the town, more private houses were converted into a hospital and dental clinic for the servicemen, as well as general equipment stores. It was an air force community already, and the town had a welcoming feel to it, but the first chance he had, Jack intended going back to Whitsunday Island.

As he walked towards the hotel, the sky was heavy with rain clouds and a low mist hung over Gloucester Island to the south. The beautiful weather of the past few days had broken and some of the men from New South Wales had asked if a cyclone was coming. The few old locals in the pub last night had shaken their heads and laughed.

'When a cyclone is on the way, don't worry, you'll know about it,' an old fellow with missing teeth had cackled. 'This is nothing but a bit of a rain shower.'

There was a division between the men who had stayed back in Bowen and not gone to war, and the newcomers. Jack could understand it. He knew how he would have felt if a lot of cocky young men had come to Cessnock and settled in as though it was their right.

Jack pushed open the door of the hotel and headed to the large room at the back that had been set up as the mission room. He took a seat in the middle, wishing his father and Richard could see him now.

Wing Commander Jim Butler entered and crossed to the table at the front. The four flight officers took the seats in the front row. Jack leaned forward as the commander turned and unrolled a map hanging at the front of the room. His demeanour, his crisp uniform—despite the heat—and his words showed him to be more formal than Smiley had ever been.

'Good morning, gentlemen. Thank you for being so prompt.' He looked to the group of men sitting behind the flight officers. 'To those of you who are new to the base, and to the new NCOs, I must remind you of the sensitivity of any information that is discussed in this room. You may think that everyone in this small country town is part of the war effort—and at this point, I am sure there is no need to remind you that we have taken over an entire town—but it is critical that you keep tightlipped on everything disclosed here. Do not trust anyone enough to discuss anything with them. Anything at all. Is that clear?'

As the men sitting in the room nodded, the wing commander took an ironed white handkerchief from his top pocket and wiped his brow. 'We know that the Japanese are moving into the south-west Pacific a lot faster than we expected. Indeed, there have been reports of Japanese coast watchers in the Whitsunday Passage over the past month.'

A couple of men in front of Jack put their hands up. 'May we ask where, sir?'

'Some of you are new and may not know the islands yet, but the Whitsunday Passage is a way for our naval ships to come north and is inside the reef.' He picked up a wooden pointer and ran it down to the middle of the map from Townsville to Mackay. 'The Great Barrier Reef itself provides a natural barrier, which will no doubt deter the Japanese from invasion on this point of the coast. But we cannot be complacent. The Royal Australian Navy is using the Passage and considering an anchorage at Cid Harbour on the leeward side of Whitsunday Island. It is a safe and deep anchorage, and will be used when they need protection from the weather on their way north.'

Jack craned forward as the commander's voice deepened. 'A couple of weeks ago, a suspicious person was spotted by some local fishermen climbing down Whitsunday Peak on the island which overlooks Cid Harbour. In fact, it looks over the whole Passage and I have no doubt that they could probably see our PBYs taking off from here if they were on the peak.'

Jack had to bite his tongue. He *knew* you could see Bowen if you were up there.

Bloody hell. That was where they'd climbed after Christmas with Liliana and Tat Ellis. No, you couldn't actually see the Cats on the ground from up there, but as soon as they took to the air, they'd be easily visible from the peak on a clear day.

He had to warn Liliana. God, she and her sisters and the young twins scampered all over that island.

'Will it be addressed, sir?' an airman from the other squadron asked.

'That is correct,' was the commander's short reply before he continued with the briefing. 'The threat of danger to the Australian mainland is creeping ever closer with the southward expansion of the Japanese. We know they're attempting to cut the supply line with America by establishing bases in the south-west Pacific islands. So, from next week, the responsibility of 11 and 20 Squadrons is tracking the Japanese fleet.'

A shiver of trepidation ran through Jack. The bloody Japanese were getting closer every day. The move to Bowen was to base and service the eight remaining Catalinas in 11 and 20 Squadrons here until the situation in the north became more secure. Roger and Charlie had been seconded to the work crew building the timber slipway for the aircraft maintenance hard stand on the harbour shore.

'Bloody hard work,' Charlie had said last night over dinner.

'We have to have somewhere to slip the boats close to the harbour.' Jack's knowledge had grown in the time he'd been in New Guinea. He waited for the wing commander to continue.

'The crew lists have been posted on the noticeboard at the back of the room. From tomorrow, you will each have three days' leave. You may go off base, but on your return, you'll be on call for missions out at any time of the day or night. Make good use of it, it may be a while before you have leave again. Rest up and prepare, men. We have a long road—and a long fight—ahead.' He nodded and put down the wooden pointer. 'Flight Lieutenant Jarvis will now take you through some protocols.'

Jack's excited anticipation soon dissipated as the officer handed a small booklet first to him and then to the three other non-commissioned officers from the two squadrons.

'We are at war, men, and the enemy is getting closer. As you are going into enemy territory, there are some protocols you must be aware of. Our country's future is in your hands.'

Jack turned over the small book. It had a dark grey cover and on the front was a heading in block letters: *THIS PUBLICATION MUST NOT BE TAKEN INTO THE AIR OR INTO THE COMBAT ZONE.*

'Over the next three days while you are on leave, I expect you to memorise every word.' His smile was tight and held no warmth. 'You will be examined on Saturday morning. Anyone who does not get a perfect score will no longer be a part of the crew. There is a need for as much labour to build the hard stand as we can get so there will be a ground-based job for any of you who do not memorise that booklet. Every word. Is that clear?'

Jack opened the book and quickly flicked through it as he nodded along with the other three NCOs. His stomach roiled as he read some of the phrases.

Be Silent!

Don't Weaken!

Keep Calm!

Rights of Prisoners of War: your most important rights are: you are not to be compelled by force or threat of force to give any information other than your NAME, RANK and SERIAL NUMBER.

'Has anyone told this to the Nips?' Megsy's voice came from behind Jack and he was surprised when he wasn't reprimanded.

'We can only hope so,' said the lieutenant. 'Officers, please join me for breakfast in the Officer's Mess. NCOs, you are dismissed.'

Megsy nudged him as they followed the officers from the room. 'I think I need a drink. What about you?'

Jack nodded. 'I'm with you, mate.'

* * *

Jack stopped drinking late afternoon because he wanted to read the booklet that was burning a hole in his pocket. In the end, the other two new blokes had joined them at the pub, and Jack had drunk way more than he was used to. Megsy's stories had kept them all entertained. It was only when the publican's wife asked if they wanted dinner that Jack realised he'd been there all day. On the way back home, he climbed to the top of Flagstaff Hill Lookout to try and sober up a bit. He looked south to the islands and thought about Liliana again; if he could get down there again, he'd spend his three days' leave on the island. It would be a quiet place to focus on learning the contents of the book before the test. He had no worry about his ability to memorise it; that was the easy part. He belched and the sour taste of too much beer touched his throat. He had to tell her to be careful.

By the time he got back to the boarding house and copped a disapproving eye from Mrs Atkins, Charlie and Roger were sitting on the enclosed back porch, shirtless and each holding a large bottle of beer. A rattan fan whirled lazily above but the air it moved was hot and humid.

'All right for some.' Charlie gave him the stink-eye too.

'I have some news,' Jack replied. He pulled out another chair and straddled it. 'I'm sure you blokes are allowed to know, because you'll be doing the servicing.' He looked curiously at Roger. 'You must be nearly finished building the hard stand?'

Roger tipped his beer and took a swig. 'It is. We've started work on the slipway, thank God. It's much cooler working in the water than on that fucking hot sand.'

'Well, I can tell you it'll be finished by Saturday of next week.'

'Yep, we're working for the next seven days straight we've been told.'

'Shame.' Jack grinned. A rare surge of happiness—maybe from the beer, or more likely from the prospect of seeing Liliana again— rose in him.

'Why's that?' Charlie stretched his arms up and pulled a face. 'Shit.'

Jack grimaced at the top of Charlie's shoulders, blistered from sunburn just like Megsy's.

'I'm going back to the islands for a couple of days. But don't worry. I'll be working as hard as you blokes when I get back. We're on notice that we'll be called out day and night.'

'I think I'd rather be working here than up in the air with you blokes. We worried about you up north. Wondered what was happening up in Moresby. Not a lot of information gets through down here. But good for you that you get to go back to the island,' Roger said quietly as he stood and pulled his shirt from the back of the chair. 'Come on, let's go and see what the old bat's cooked up for dinner.'

'Smells different,' Jack said as he waited for the other two men to put their shirts on. Roger's words had dispelled his brief contentment. 'And yes, it was pretty nasty up there.'

'It's good to have you back, mate.' Charlie followed Jack down the hall to the small dining room.

Mrs Atkins waited by the kitchen door until they all sat at the table, her mouth pursed in a disapproving line. The three of them smiled politely as she put a bowl of meat floating in grey liquid in the centre of the table.

'So back to the islands, hey, Jack? Lucky you. Think of us working up here.' Charlie pulled a face when Mrs Atkins went back into the kitchen and he dug his fork into the stew and sniffed at it. 'Jesus, that stuff smells worse than it looks.'

'When are you going?' Roger asked.

'On the dawn steamer in the morning.'

CHAPTER
18

15 May, 1942

South Molle Island was a more established resort than the Ellis bungalows at Sawmill Bay and, being closer to the mainland, it had more guests. Lily had started work in the kitchen early in the new year—Dad had secured the position for her to help the Bauers now that some of the local workers had joined the war effort, and to earn herself some money. Much to her surprise, she had settled in and was enjoying the work. Here she was treated like an adult, and the pay packet meant she could save for new books, although being at the sink for a couple of hours at a time did test her patience when it was her turn for scullery duty.

To Lily's disappointment, four months had passed since Jack's visit and she wondered if he'd ever come back. Maybe he'd moved away to another base. More likely, he'd found her a bit childish. All she hoped was that he was safe. The occasional newspaper that made its way to the island frightened her more each time she read the headlines. They'd made no plans to write to each other, and the weight of regret seemed to get heavier as each day passed.

'Lil, where are you?' Her sister's voice came from inside the house. Lily rolled over and shoved her book under the bed. For some reason, her reading tastes had taken a different turn lately, and she'd taken to raiding the bookcase in Mama's sewing room. Her dorm mates had seen *Gone with the Wind* at the Rialto theatre in West End one winter when Lily had been late going back to school. It was all she'd heard for weeks once she'd gone back to All Hallows'.

Amelia had stood on her bed with her hands clasped to her chest. 'And he said, "No, I don't think I will kiss you, although you need kissing, badly. That's what's wrong with you. You should be kissed and often, by someone who knows what he's doing."'

Peggy's shoulders had dropped along with her dramatic sigh. 'If Rhett Butler or Clark Gable said that to me, I'd be much more sensible than Scarlett O'Hara. She made me so angry, the silly woman!'

Now Lily understood what all the fuss had been about. She adored the book, and had read by torchlight until the early hours this morning. As soon as she'd woken up, she'd picked it up again.

'Lil, are you still in bed!' Tat's voice was full of indignation.

'Yes, I am. What's wrong?'

'Mama and Daddy are catching the early launch to the mainland so they can take the fish to the train. You've got to come with me, we have to bring some boxes of veggies back to the house. Hurry up, Lil. I'm not doing it by myself.'

'Okay, okay, I'm on my way.' Lily climbed out of bed and pulled on a pair of shorts and a cotton top that she tied in a knot above her waist. Her hair was loose and tangled, and she gritted her teeth as the hairbrush caught in the knots. Finally, she gave up and pulled it up into a messy ponytail and slipped on a pair of canvas shoes.

'They're already out in the shed getting the fish from the ice box. They said to let you sleep in because you're working hard. But I know you were reading, I saw the light last night when I got up for a drink of water.'

Lily wandered out, yawning and put her hands up to protect her eyes from the bright sunlight. Tatiana was sitting on the front porch waiting and she pointed to the bay. 'Look, the steamer is rounding the point already. Mama and Daddy are down on the jetty. Hurry up!'

'All right, all right, Miss Bossy Pants.'

Tatiana flashed her a grin, jumped down the steps in one leap, and then ran ahead down the grassy hill to Sawmill Bay below the house. Lily followed slowly. The clouds and misty rain of yesterday had cleared and the mountains on the mainland were clear and vivid green, promising a fine hot day. Once she'd done her chores and checked on the boys and kept Tatiana happy, she'd get her book and wander down the hill to her special place, the place they'd named Butterfly Glade when they were small children. She had four whole free days stretching ahead. She didn't have to go back to South Molle to work till Saturday and with Mama gone to the mainland, a whole wonderful day with Rhett and Scarlett beckoned.

Lily sighed. Of course she'd be expected to do chores today. She pulled a face as she walked along the path to the shore. Mama's favourite proverb was the one about idle hands. Her fears were confirmed when she caught up to Tatiana on the jetty where Mama and Dad were stacking the fish boxes.

Lily looked past them to the launch approaching across the narrow channel. Her heart jumped into her throat and she put her hand up to the messy hair that she'd scraped back into a ponytail of sorts.

Jack was leaning over the side and waving to her.

Jack.

This time, he was wearing his uniform and he looked so … so grown-up. Her heart set up a funny beat and the shaky feeling ran down from her chest to her knees, but she jumped onto the jetty and waved madly to him as the smile spread across her face.

He'd come back to see her again, just like he'd promised.

'Look, Dad. Jack's come to visit again,' Tat called out. She had spotted him at the same time. Lily caught the sharp look that Mama directed at her and then across to Jack, but Dad's smile was wide and welcoming as he hoisted the last box to the pile and waved.

'Jack, welcome back,' he called across the channel.

The launch made its way carefully between the coral heads at the head of their bay and Mama walked over to Lily.

'Liliana, today I want you to do some baking and fill the cake tins. Then you and Tatiana can clean out the pantry. Keep your brothers and Kat inside all day. They've got some school lessons to do. You can supervise them while you bake.'

Lily straightened her shoulders. 'Yes, Mama.' Nothing was going to take the gloss off her day. She didn't care what chores were thrown at her. Jack was here.

Jack. Lily relished the excitement that was running through her.

'And Lil?' Mama's voice was soft. 'Remember what I said to you and Tat about being ladies?' Lily nodded and Mama pulled her in for a close hug. 'You're a good girl.' Mama turned to Tat. 'Tatiana, you do as your sister tells you today. She's in charge and there are enough chores to keep you both busy.'

'Yes, Mama.' There was no enthusiasm in her sister's voice as she shot a cranky look at Lily.

Jack jumped off the launch onto the jetty and put his bag down. Lily watched as he shook Dad's hand and then helped him load the

crates of fish onto the raised platform at the front of the boat, anticipation curling in her tummy.

Mama took the mail from the skipper and leafed through the
envelopes.

'Lil. Mail for you,' she called, holding up a pink envelope.

Amelia!

Lily dragged her eyes from Jack and walked over to Mama.

'Take the rest up with you and put them on your father's desk,
please.' Mama held out a pile of envelopes and a *Courier Mail*. 'Who's
yours from?'

Lily turned the pink envelope over with interest. 'My friend,
Amelia, from school. She stayed in Brisbane when school finished
up for the holidays. She and Peggy volunteered to work at the
Red Cross Café instead of going back out west to their parents'
properties.'

Mama's eyebrows headed for her hairline. 'Their parents let them
stay in the city? Unsupervised?'

Lily nodded. 'They did.' She pushed the letter into the back
pocket of her shorts, tempted to tell her mother that she was sixteen years old and some girls that age were living in the city
without having their every move monitored, but she bit her
tongue.

Mama greeted Jack with a polite smile and Lily bit her lip as her
cheeks heated.

'Hello, Mrs Ellis. It's good to see you again. I hope it was all right
for me to come back and stay in the hut again?' Jack held out his
hand and helped Mama step up onto the launch.

'I'm very pleased that you wanted to come back to our island.
But where are your two friends?'

'Roger and Charlie are working at the harbour.' Jack turned his
head, and a lock of hair fell over his forehead. He lifted his hand

and pushed it back. Lily stared at him, her legs all shaky as shyness flooded through her.

Conscious of Tat's glare as she stood beside the boxes of vegetables that had been unloaded from the launch, Lily straightened her shoulders. 'Hello, Jack. Welcome back. It's good to see you again.'

'It's really good to be back.' His dark hair was glossy black and as he moved closer she could smell the mildly floral fragrance of Brylcreem. Clark Gable sprang to Lily's mind, and she savoured the pleasant shiver that ran down her back when he smiled at her.

The launch pulled out into the channel and Jack left his kit bag on the jetty and helped them carry some of the boxes up. Lily turned to Tat when they reached the house.

'There's still three more boxes down on the jetty. You start the kids on their lessons and Jack and I will get the rest. Where *are* the kids?'

Tat shrugged and walked across to the kitchen window. 'Out on the tree swing.'

'It's a wonder Billy hasn't scampered already.' Lily leaned across to the window and called out, 'Come on, you lot. School's on.'

Jack and Lily took their time as they strolled back down to the jetty. It was so good to be with Jack again; it was as though he hadn't been gone all those months.

'I love being here.' He held her gaze, but she looked down as her tummy fluttered. 'Want to go for a walk later?'

'That would be nice.'

'I missed you, Liliana.' As soon as they were out of sight of the house and the kids, Jack reached for her hand. Lily took it, and then slowed and looked at their joined hands.

'It's really good to see you again.' Jack squeezed her fingers gently. Her shyness disappeared, and she grinned back.

'I'm so pleased you've come back too. How about ... how about I show you the butterfly glade later?' It was going against all of Mama's instructions about being alone with Jack, but all at once, she didn't care. She was sixteen years old—almost seventeen—and it wasn't as though he was a stranger.

'The butterfly glade?' His voice was soft and he moved a little bit closer to her. 'I'd like that.'

★ ★ ★

The boxes were stowed in the pantry, and while Tat unpacked the vegetables, Lily cooked a batch of biscuits before she made the sandwiches for lunch. As they ate their sandwiches, the twins bombarded Jack with questions and Lily took the opportunity to quickly read Amelia's letter.

It was a long letter, Amelia's small perfectly formed words filling six pages. Lily smiled and lifted the pages to her nose and sniffed them. Lavender perfumed. The first page of the letter was bright and chatty, and full of news about the work in the café and how much Amelia was enjoying it.

That wasn't what she was looking for. Lily flicked over the pages and scanned the neat writing. Amelia wrote she'd heard from some of the other girls but there was no mention of working with Peggy. Lily held her breath as she scanned the small writing and flicked through the pages until she came to the words she was looking for.

All is well with me. It was a false alarm. I think I had myself so worried, my monthlies stayed away. I really thought I'd done my dash and was going to be an unmarried mother. I have never been so terrified in my life. Can you imagine my joy when I went to the WC at the café and I had them, Lily! I was checking my undies every hour on the hour for days and days. Even the ladies in the café were worried about me, I had to tell them I'd eaten something and I had the runs. They wouldn't let me near the food so I was on wash-up duty for ages.

Oh, Lil, you just can't imagine the relief I felt when I finally got them, but trust me I have been smiling for three weeks now. Never ever again will I ever, ever put myself through that! No more soldiers in my life. Ever!

I do have some other news though and it's not so good.

Peggy was not so lucky. I didn't even know that she'd missed her monthlies for three months. My God, Lil. She is having a baby and she doesn't even know who the father is. Her parents came to Brisbane and collected her, and the day poor Peg left the café, she told me they went up to the convent and blasted poor Mother Vincent Reilly to Kingdom come.

I am so glad we have all left that awful place even though gadding about the city at night with you was fun, and it did get me this job. I miss you and I hope you are happy back on your island and reading lots of those books you love. Please come and see me when the war is over, and I so hope you come back to Brisbane to study like I know you always wanted to. You are smart enough to be whatever you want, Lil.

Be good ... although I suppose you get no chance to be anything else in your tropical paradise. Love from a very, very, very well-behaved Amelia.

Lily shook her head and let out the breath she'd been holding. At least that was one less thing to worry about. All she needed now was for Mama and Dad to come home with a newspaper saying that the war was over, and she could stop worrying.

But, oh, poor Peggy. Even if Peggy had been unkind to her and her teasing had often been nasty, Lily didn't wish her any ill feeling. Especially not the predicament Peg had gotten herself into.

'Lil? Do we have to do more school work?' Billy's voice was hopeful.

She folded the letter and propped it against a pot of herbs on the windowsill. Later on, she'd find a good hidey hole for it in her room. Or safer still, once she'd written down Amelia's address, it could go in the stove fire.

'Just finish your maps and then you can go and play on the verandah for a while before Mama and Daddy come home.' Lily walked over to the table and took the pencil that Billy was chewing from his mouth. Pulling out the chair on the other side of Billy, she glanced across the table. Jack and Robbie had their heads together as Robbie traced around the Gulf of Carpentaria.

'You'll get lead poisoning.' Lily shivered as he put the pencil down. Ragged bits of wood exposed the single line of lead where Billy had chewed around it. 'Ugh, that's awful. Where's your map, Billy?'

He lifted his book and pulled out a tattered, folded map and Lily shook her head as she pointed to the border between Queensland and the southern states.

'Okay, you're at sixes and sevens. Sydney is the capital of—?'

'New South Wales,' Robbie piped up and Billy picked up the pencil and threw it at him.

'You don't have to show off in front of Jack,' he cried.

'Manners, Billy.'

Lily looked down at the tattered map and smiled. Robbie's work was always neat, and Billy rushed his. Next to the map of Queensland, he'd drawn a map of their island and she nodded.

'That's a pretty good map of our island,' she said with a smile. 'Although I don't ever recall seeing a pirate ship up near Turtle Rock when we've been fishing.'

'Of course you haven't.' His voice was smug, and his little chest puffed with importance. 'The pirates only come at night and bury their treasure in Turtle Cave. Maybe I could take Jack there and show him.' He shot a tentative smile at Jack, who was fast becoming a hero to the twins. Before Lily could look away, he lifted his head and caught her staring at him. He held her gaze and a gentle smile lifted his lips.

Doing school work with the children had all of a sudden turned into a pleasant task.

'You know you're not allowed to go there.' Liliana wagged her finger at her small brother and he scrunched his nose up.

'One day soon, I will. And you'll be sorry when I don't give you the jewels that the pirates will bury there.'

'I don't want jewels.' She couldn't help the retort but smiled when she saw Jack's grin.

After a few minutes of working quietly while Tat banged about in the pantry, Jack stood up and brought his chair around next to Lily's.

'Look, this is what I was showing Robbie on this map.' He sat on the chair and his leg brushed against Lily's bare knees beneath the table. Warmth shot through her and she lowered her eyes, hoping her face wasn't as rosy as it felt.

'All right, kids. You've been really good.' Reluctantly, she moved her leg away from Jack's knee and took a breath. 'Jack and I are going for a walk.'

'I'm coming too.' Tat came out from the pantry wiping her hands on her shorts.

Lily shook her head. 'You have to stay here with the kids. Mama put me in charge, remember?'

Tatiana's glare followed them down the steps.

'Okay, show me this butterfly place.' Jack's voice was carefree and his laughter followed Lily as she ran into the bush a few hundred yards up past the house. It was mid-afternoon and a breeze had whipped up. A gust ricocheted off the mountain with a crack and Jack's head flew up. A branch fell in the bush in front of them with a loud crack.

Suddenly, the tenor of his voice changed. 'Stop! Wait. Don't go any further.'

The seriousness of his cry stopped her, and Lily waited for him to catch up to her.

'What was that?' He led her off the log, looking around into the dark bush surrounding them.

'It's okay. It was only a bullet.'

'A bullet?' Jack pulled her close to him and pressed her back against a wide tree. His heart was pounding hard and Lily could feel it against the bare skin above the neckline of her shirt.

'Not a real bullet. Just what we call a bullet. It's when the wind comes roaring from nowhere. When you sail in our islands, you have to be wary of them.'

'Are you sure?' Jack looked up at the still branches above them. 'There's no wind now.'

'Bullets are pretty unique to our islands. The high hills and the winds combine, and they just come out of nowhere. It happens when—' Lily cut off the words that were on the tip of her tongue, an explanation about air temperature she'd learned in science. She didn't want to sound like a scientific know-it-all. 'This bay is one of the worst. If you want to know why it happens, ask Dad.'

'I will. Especially if our aircraft are going to fly down this way when they take off and land.'

Lily's happiness fled. Her excitement about being alone with Jack had chased away the reason for them coming down here in the first place.

'How far away is this glade?'

'About half a mile along the shore.'

'Maybe we should stay closer to the house.' Jack put his head down and rubbed the back of his neck.

'Why? What's the matter?' she said.

'I just don't know how safe it is for you—for us—to be wandering around the island.'

'For heaven's sake!' She shook her head. 'Why not? We've done it all our lives.'

Jack took a deep breath. 'But it's wartime now.'

Fear curled in Lily's stomach as he stared at her and she knew he was serious. 'What are you saying?'

'Nothing. I just don't think it's very safe to be wandering around. A young woman by herself.'

'But you're with me.'

CHAPTER
19

Liliana's eyes were wide as she stared up at Jack. He took both of her hands in his and held them close to his chest.

'But I won't always be with you. Promise me you won't climb the peak again. Promise me, Liliana, please.'

'You're scaring me, Jack.'

'I don't want you to be scared, maybe just be a little bit more careful than usual.' He dropped her hands and slipped his arms around her waist. She stood still in his hold.

'Is this okay? If I hold you for a minute?'

Lily dropped her head and rested it on his shoulder. 'It's nice.'

They stood listening to the sounds of the bush as the wind rustled through the high branches. Serenity flooded through Jack; if only he could feel like this all the time. After a moment, he pulled back and smiled down at her. 'I don't want to rush you, Liliana. I know I've only known you for a really short time, but I want you to know how I feel about you. I couldn't wait to get back down here and see you again.'

She lifted her arms and looped them around his shoulders.

'I know,' she whispered. 'I've thought about you a lot too since you left.'

'When I was up in the Cat and feeling scared, I thought about you and it made it a lot easier,' he said softly. 'You're my lucky charm.'

'Oh, Jack. Why does there have to be a war? Why couldn't things stay the same as they were? I hate it!'

'I can't answer any of those questions. But if there wasn't a war, I wouldn't be up here, and I wouldn't have met you.' He stepped back from her, gently lifting her hands away from his shoulders but he kept one of her hands in his. 'Come on, show me your glade and then we'd better go back to the house.'

She nodded and pointed to the track in front of them. 'It's just over there. We follow that track and it comes back around to a small rocky bay along the shore.'

'Nowhere near the path to the peak?'

'Why are you so worried about the mountain?'

Jack swallowed, remembering the instructions of the wing commander not to share anything off base. He'd already scared her, but he wanted to be sure she and the family stayed safe.

'If I tell you something, will you promise not to tell anyone? I'm not supposed to share anything we get told on base.'

She nodded silently.

He hesitated and then said, 'There's been some talk that the Japanese have infiltrated some of the islands and they are using the high points to keep an eye on our naval shipping.'

'The high points? So, you mean that they ... that the Japanese could even be up on our peak? On *our* island?'

'Maybe. I don't know for sure. Just be careful. Stay away from there.'

'Daddy heard that ages ago, but he said it wasn't true.' Her eyes were wide and Jack regretted saying anything, but he was pleased that Boyd had already mentioned it. 'Just don't say anything, okay.'

'I promise.'

* * *

All thoughts of the Japanese infiltrating their island fled from Lily's mind when they reached the glade. Jack sat close to her on an old hessian sack on the sand behind the beach. The vertical rock wall against their backs was still warm from the morning sun, and Sawmill Bay shimmered like a silver mirror. As they sat there, they spoke in quiet whispers as the soft dappled light filtered through the lacy foliage above. Jack drew in a breath as the first delicate black butterflies fluttered out of the forest at the end of the clearing.

'Amazing,' he said.

She put her finger to her lips and whispered, 'Wait. It gets better.'

Jack's leg rested against hers as they waited and watched. Within moments, they were surrounded by hundreds of butterflies. She closed her eyes as Jack's warm breath puffed across her cheek, shivering as his lips pressed against her ear.

'You have two butterflies sitting on top of your head,' he murmured.

'That's supposed to be good luck.' She stayed perfectly still as Jack's lips moved from her ear to her cheek, and moved softly down and across to her lips. He tilted his head a little to one side and his lips brushed the edge of her mouth. Liliana smiled as the gentle pressure on her lips increased and her stomach fluttered like the butterflies that were around them.

She turned her head to give Jack full access to her mouth, and he lifted his arm and put it around her shoulders, turning her slightly so that she was facing him. Her pulse raced as his lips took hers, and she let out a little sigh. Jack's lips were soft as they clung to hers. When his lips finally slid from her mouth and stopped on the soft spot beneath her ear, little flashes of heat tingled all over her skin.

A grown-up kiss, like Rhett Butler and Scarlett would have shared.

The sun dropped lower in the sky and the darkness of the bush that had been part of her life for almost seventeen years took on a sinister quality. Lily jumped when a branch dropped from a tree and the leaves crackled underfoot. As a bird was disturbed, it cried and the noise echoed through the now still night air. As Jack's words about the Japanese came back to her, the launch's horn blared across the Passage and she jumped up. 'Quick, that's the launch heading for the bay.'

Jack's hand held hers firmly as they walked along the narrow path to the jetty to meet the launch.

He stopped as they approached the jetty and pointed to the water. Little shimmers of light flickered as the water pushed in. 'What's that?'

'I always thought it was something magical until we learned about it in science at school last year. I'd never tell the boys and Katarina what it really is. They think it's the fairies in my stories.' A gust of wind blew her hair across her face. 'It's phosphorescent algae, but whatever the cause, it's still beautiful.'

'It is.' Jack's voice was a low murmur and a delicious shiver ran down Liliana's spine as he reached up and tucked the loose strand of hair behind her ear. He moved closer and his breath was warm. 'And so are you, Liliana.' He placed a gentle kiss on her cheek.

She put a hand to her face and moved away from him. She knew if she got closer she would want his lips on hers again.

'Find a stick. Quickly!' she managed to say as she moved away from him.

She turned and held her hand out to him. 'When I get to the end of the log, hold onto me so I don't fall into the water.'

She stepped up onto the log and tiptoed to the end of it with Jack following close behind. 'Okay.' When she stopped his hands went to her waist and held her firmly. It was easy to balance with him holding her although her breath quickened as his fingers pressed into the skin just below her breasts. Goosebumps rose on her arms and the strange quiver that seemed to be in her tummy all of the time now moved lower. She leaned forward and tipped the end of the long stick into the water.

Jack's quiet exclamation puffed past her as the algae wrapped around the stick and she moved it up and down, and from side to side, writing her name in the water. Electric blues and pink formed the letters and they hung there suspended in the still water.

'That is so super. I've never seen anything like that before.' Amazement filled Jack's voice as he kept hold of her with one firm hand and took the stick from her with the other. 'My turn.'

Their fingers brushed as he moved closer to her.

Lily's cheeks burned as she watched Jack draw a heart. In the centre of the heart he wrote 'Jack' and then 'Lily'. The shape of the letters hovered in the water until the next small wave pushed them into a swirl of colours. 'It mightn't be as permanent as names carved in wood, but I want you to remember that and think about me every time you look at the water. Until I come back next time. Will you promise me that, Lily?'

'I promise,' she said. 'And you promise me you'll come back and visit again as soon as you can.'

'I will.'

'Oh, Jack.' She turned her face into his hand so that his palm cupped her cheek.

'It will make things so much easier if I know you're thinking of me every day, Liliana.'

'You will be in my thoughts and in my prayers every day.' Her voice was a whisper, but she lifted her face to his and met his eyes as the launch headed for the jetty. 'I promise.'

★ ★ ★

After dinner that night, the children were allowed to stay up for a while. Boyd went to the shed and came back with a knife and a piece of wood and began to whittle. Jack focused on Liliana's voice as she told a story to the small children. Tatiana was sitting out on the steps staring at the sky as Alexandra sewed beneath the light of a kerosene lamp on a table by her chair.

Like the last time he'd been here, the war seemed to be a bad dream, something that was not real. If Jack closed his eyes, he could forget it. That damn book that he was supposed to memorise was sitting in the bottom of his kit bag. The longer he left it, the more reluctant he was to open it. It was too real, and it brought the danger of the war home to him every time he thought of it. Maybe if he didn't learn it, they'd send him home. But he knew there was no chance of that. He swallowed and pushed the thoughts away, focusing instead on Liliana's soft voice.

'Behind the white sand at Betty's Beach, there are all those funny little trees. Do you remember them?' She dropped her voice low and the boys looked up at her. 'The little ones with the scary, twisted branches?'

The twins nodded wide-eyed.

'One night on the full moon, a patch of silver light climbed one of those trees. That very tree was a playground for the fairies.'

'Do they swim in the water?' Robbie asked.

'Yes. The fairies hide their tiny clothes in the debris on the beach and flit out to the waves at midnight. You thought it was little fish jumping in the shallows, didn't you? It's the fairy bath and they choose their place very well. They dive to the coral garden and they pick the beautiful flowers for their homes in their secret place in the middle of the island.'

'But the coral is hard,' Billy, always the pragmatic one, protested. Liliana caught Jack's eye as she compromised, and he swallowed.

'Yes, that's right. It's to protect the garden from our fishing lines.'

He could have listened to her voice all night, but he'd already stayed way too long after dinner. It was good, sitting here in this easy atmosphere where there was no need to put on anything other than he was.

The three young children were yawning and Alexandra put aside her sewing. 'Come on, my darlings, it is time to go to bed and dream of wonderful things.' She held out her arms and swung Katarina onto her hip. 'Come on, boys. You too.'

Jack stood as she did, and she waved him back to his seat. 'Don't go, Jack. Stay and keep Boyd company for a while. Tatiana and Liliana, you can stay up later tonight too.'

Jack caught Liliana's eye as her mother walked inside, and her shy smile made his heart warm. She was so beautiful. Her voice had been mesmerising as she'd told her fairy story.

Boyd cleared his throat and Jack realised he had intercepted the look between them, but his smile was indulgent.

CHAPTER
20

19 May, 1942

The cup of tea that Jack had managed to drink as they were briefed for the mission roiled in his stomach as he leaned against the cold metal and strapped himself in. The space next to the pylon between the two engines he shared with the flight engineer was claustrophobic. He slipped on the ear muffs and focused on the small square of blue sky he could see through the small square window opposite him.

His hands shook as he put them back onto his lap and he tried to marshal his thoughts. If he could stop this bloody fear that was gripping his insides every time he boarded the Cat, he could get through this.

Bloody Dad. Bloody Richard. Bloody war.

Ever since that flight back from Salamaua, the nightmares had got worse. But being up in the Cat again was ten times worse than

any nightmare. He couldn't wake up from this. His heart was beating out of his chest, his knees were shaking and he was sure he was
going to vomit. Putting his hand to his mouth, he looked up as
Jonesy, the flight engineer, tapped his shoulder and he lifted the ear
muffs with one hand.

'Heard any good jokes lately, Jacko?'

'What?' Jack stared at him as the bile burned his throat.

'Best way to get through this, mate. We're okay. It's that bloody
Zero that spooked you, isn't it?'

Jack nodded.

'Well, it's a shit thing we have to do each mission, and I'm as
scared as you are.'

'Really?'

Jonesy was an officer and, up until two minutes ago, had never
spoken to Jack even though they'd spent hours in the same briefing
room over the past months, as well as the hours they'd spent in the
air. Megsy, who was down the back of the plane with the navigator,
and Jack were the only NCOs on board, and they'd quickly learned
their place in the hierarchy.

'That doesn't mean we have to like it,' Megsy had said as they'd
eaten in the mess before going to the airfield. 'But I've learned to
shut my mouth a bit.'

All Jack was wishing now was that he'd learned to control his
mouth at home and hadn't stormed out and enlisted. He closed his
eyes and tried to picture the vineyard at home. The vine leaves
would be turning red and most would have fallen from—

'Yep, bloody shit-scared.' Jonesy's voice interrupted his thoughts.
'It's such a blasted long time to be out over the water. I hate it
every time.'

Jack's eyes widened, and his fear began to recede as he held Jonesy's eye.

'Did you hear the one about the German soldier, the old lady, a buxom girl, and a young Frenchman?' the engineer said with a cheeky smile.

Jack shook his head and listened to the joke. Even though it wasn't funny, it had the desired effect. The nausea passed and the shaking eased a bit.

'Bloody hot in here,' he said as he wiped the sweat off his forehead.

'What did you think of Dumbo?' Jonesy asked with a grin.

Jack grinned back and his nausea eased a little. He'd noticed the grey and pink elephant with big floppy ears some wag had painted beneath the angled metal of the forward cockpit as the barge driver had taken them under the Cat where it floated on the water.

'Something to cheer you up, lads.' He'd knocked the motor out of gear and idled the engine and they drifted under the front of the aircraft. 'Meet your new mascot.'

It was a calm afternoon, and the usual easterly breeze hadn't come up yet, which boded well for a good take off. No bombs to increase the weight of the aircraft, and no chop to plough through as the captain got enough revs up to lift the cumbersome Cat from the harbour.

'We hope it'll confuse the Nips and give you blokes a bit of a laugh.'

'What's it supposed to be?' Captain Munford's grin was wide, and Jack relaxed. He wasn't sure how the officer would take it.

'Dumbo, captain.' The barge operator fired up the engine and guided the barge around to the ladder behind the cockpit.

'I beg your pardon?' This time the captain's voice hadn't held any amusement, and the bargeman cleared his throat.

'Not you, captain. *Dumbo*. It's a new movie. Just come out at the pictures. We all thought Dumbo the elephant would bring you some luck.'

The propellers started and after a few minutes, the noise inside the aircraft was deafening. Jonesy leaned over and yelled at him, and he could barely hear what he was saying even when he lifted the ear muff. 'Big breaths in, to the count of four, and then out for the same. That'll settle you, mate. And don't feel like a ninny. I still do it.'

Jack watched as the engineer went across to the other side of the narrow space and pulled the harness belt over his shoulders. He grinned at Jack and gave him the thumbs up as the Catalina began to move.

Ten minutes later, Jack was calm. The noise of the engines had settled to a just less than deafening roar, and he ignored the occasional juddering of the plane. His shaking had stopped and his breathing was back to normal. The sweat was gone as cold air came in through every gap in the metal skin. As the huge aircraft banked to the right, the pressure on Jack's harness increased and he leaned forward with the movement to ease the pressure. As the plane dipped lower, he caught a glimpse of the sky. Purple clouds were lined with golden shards of sunlight as the sun sank behind the mountains to the west. He took another deep breath. There was no point being scared; it wasn't going to make any difference to the outcome of the night. If they came across a Japanese fighter, worrying about it wouldn't change the outcome. He had to stay vigilant. As the plane banked in the other direction, Jack caught a glimpse of blue water and shadowed islands below, and wondered if Liliana would hear them fly over.

What would be would be. He was doing his bit for the war effort. And he'd do it for as long as he had to.

If he didn't die today, maybe he would write to Mum and tell her he was okay.

★ ★ ★

Lily had woken up early and slipped out of bed quietly. Last night just before sunset, she'd heard a plane fly over. She knew Jack was on it and she'd put her fingers to her lips and prayed that he would stay safe through the night. She'd pushed her feet into her canvas shoes, and walked down to the shoreline in her pyjamas. If it hadn't been for Jack's visits and her worry about him on the missions, she could almost have forgotten there was a war on.

It was one of those perfect autumn days in the islands when the water was that special colour—not blue or green but a glorious mix of sea colours that enticed you to touch it, dip your fingers into the warmth and let the water caress your fingers as it ran over your skin.

The palm huts were empty until next Saturday. Family life was back to normal, Dad and the boys had gone fishing at sunrise. She'd heard them in the kitchen before daybreak, and she hadn't been able to go back to sleep after they'd left. When they came back, she'd make sure she went with the boys to the goats later this morning. She might have promised Jack she wouldn't say anything, but she had been extra vigilant when the twins were outside.

Her book was sitting unread beneath her bed. Every time she'd gone to pick it up, her thoughts had turned to Jack and she'd lain in bed dreaming about him instead of reading. She put her hand up to her face and trailed her fingers down her cheek. Jack's kisses filled her dreams. Her *good* dreams.

The night he'd left to go back to the base, she'd woken with a start, heart pounding as she'd dreamed of the war. Japanese soldiers had been up on the peak building a hut, and in her dream, they had come down to raid Mama's vegetable garden. Jack had been in every dream, looking out for her and chasing the soldiers away with one of Dad's whittling knives.

Lily sat there staring over the water. The noise around her increased as the day brightened. Small fish plopped in the shallows with tiny splashes, and the parrots began to squawk as they sought the nectar from the blossoms on the trees in the veggie garden at the top of the hill. In the distance, she could see Dad and the twins in the fishing boat in the channel and from the frequent whoops coming across the water, they must be catching fish. Maybe she could go to Proserpine with Dad if the catch was big enough and pick up a newspaper from the railway station. She hadn't seen a current paper for almost three weeks now. If there was a mention of the Japanese infiltration, she could show Dad, and that wouldn't be breaking the promise that sat heavily in her mind. Being isolated on their island, not knowing what was happening in the war, made her feel helpless.

The low hum of a motor vibrated in the still air and she looked across the Passage, expecting to see the steam launch coming, although it was way earlier than it usually arrived. Lily jumped to her feet as the noise increased, until it became so loud she could feel it in her chest. She held her hand to her throat and as she looked up, a shadow crossed the peak. A plane painted black dipped slowly towards the bay. It was so close as it approached, she could see the propellers spinning, and the huge wing span. As it swooped lower, she wondered if it was going to land. It was one of the amphibious craft that Jack had told the boys about. Their eyes had been wide when he had told them how the Catalinas could land on the water. As she watched the aircraft, it seemed to hang in the air above the island. Slowly, ponderously, with a huge roar of engines, it flew over the jetty where she was standing and as she stared up, she could see the white faces of the men on board through the windscreen. There were two windows where faces were peering out: one tucked beneath the wings and the other lower and further back. Lily ran to the end of the jetty and waved both arms madly as she realised that Jack could be on board the plane. It dipped one wing down and then headed out across the channel before turning in a wide, slow arc and heading back towards her. As it came closer to Whitsunday Island, it flew right over Dad and the twins in the boat, dipping the other wing as they passed over the channel where they were fishing.

It was Jack!

Lily was sure of it. She waved again as the huge plane flew over her and then headed across the island and north into the Coral Sea. Happiness swirled through her, and then trickled away to be replaced by worry when the Catalina got further and further away until all that remained was a black speck on the northern horizon. As it disappeared from her sight, Lily turned and walked slowly up the path to the house, fear running through her veins. The log that Jack had helped her across was in shadow as a cloud crossed the sun. As she climbed over it she ran her fingers over the mossy bark. Next time Jack was here, she would bring a knife and make sure they carved their initials in the tree. Despite the warmth of the morning, she shivered and rubbed her arms, thinking of how the letters Jack had drawn with the phosphorescence had swirled away until there was nothing.

Please, God, let there be a next time.

* * *

Lily and Dad had been over to the mainland to drop off the fish catch. He jumped off the launch and held out one hand for Liliana to grab hold of. Dad had bought a new radio at the general store in Prossie, and now it was tucked carefully under his other arm. The best purchase of the day for Lily was a week's worth of newspapers.

'Tell your mother to put the jug on. I'll be up in a minute. I just want to check the crab traps over on Sawmill Bay.' He let go as she landed lightly on the jetty. 'Crab will be just the go with that fresh bread for tea. My mouth's watering already.'

Lily didn't care about fresh crab sandwiches. She hurried up the path, looking forward to reading the newspapers. All she wanted to hear was that the war was being won. What she'd managed to read on the launch on the way across the Passage had frightened her.

'We're back, Mama.' The minute she walked into the kitchen with a couple of loaves of bread from the Prossie bakery under her arm, Lily glanced over at the pot of mint on the windowsill and knew, without a doubt, that Mama had found Amelia's letter.

Damnation and blast it all. How stupid was I to leave it sitting there.

She'd been too busy mooning over Jack to remember to put it away from prying eyes. The late afternoon sun shone through the glass and reflected myriad rainbow colours on the tea cups and ornaments that Mama had lined up on the sill, but there was no letter leaning against the herbs. She edged around the kitchen, keeping one eye on Mama as she stood at the sink. Lily stood on her toes in case the letter had dropped behind the leaves. But there was no sign of any paper. But more ominously, there was no sign of Tat or the smaller children. Mama's back was straight, and her head was still as she stared through the window. Tension radiated from her. Lily placed the loaves on the table quietly, clutched the three newspapers to her chest, and tiptoed to the door, wanting to escape to the sanctuary of her verandah room.

'Stay there, Liliana.' Mama's voice was cold and hard as she turned slowly from the window. Her mouth was set in a straight line and her lips were pale, but it was her red-rimmed eyes that hurt Lily the most. For a brief instant, Lily forgot about the letter and worried that there had been bad news, but she quickly dismissed that. The only news would have come via the afternoon steam launch, and she and Dad had been on it. She let her temper build. Mama had no right to read her private letter, so she had no right to get stuck into her for the content.

'Daddy said would you put the jug on please. He's gone down to the bay.'

'I want you to come into my bedroom. *Now.*'

Lily gulped and swallowed as Mama led the way to the sacrosanct room. Each of the children knew that Mama and Daddy's room was private. It was their personal space and the only time they entered it was when they were sick and allowed to lie on the big bed with the feather pillow and soft eiderdown—such a treat after their own scratchy wool blankets in the winter. Mama closed the door and leaned against it as Lily stood there, not knowing where to look. The sweet smell of lavender was overlaid by the smell of moth balls and Lily's nose began to itch. She lifted her chin as the silence lengthened and shifted her gaze to meet her mother's.

'Do you know how disappointed I am with you?' Her mother's voice was quiet but cut through the silent room like steel. She lifted a white lace-edged handkerchief and dabbed at her eyes, but Lily refused to soften. Mama was brilliant at getting her own way with Daddy by turning on the tears, but it wasn't going to work with her.

'Why? *I* have done nothing wrong.' Her chin lifted a bit higher. 'You're the one who is showing a lack of respect.'

'Don't you speak to me in that tone, young lady.' Mama reached into the pocket of her calico apron. One of the aprons that Lily hated to iron when it was her turn to stand in the laundry with the smell of starch, the steam billowing around her in the tropical heat. She closed her eyes and wished she was back at school in Brisbane.

'What is this?' Mama's hand was shaking as she held the letter out to Liliana.

'You know very well what it is.' Lily welcomed the rage that flowed through her.

'What does it mean about the nights that you were "gadding about the city"?' Mama ignored her protest. 'Did you indulge in the same wicked behaviour that your two *friends* obviously did? I have never been more disgusted or more disappointed in you.' Her voice rose as she continued and now the tears were rolling down her face. Her words hardened something in Lily's heart. She had done nothing wrong and she was angry that Mama would think badly of her so readily.

'I have done nothing wrong,' she repeated. Lily folded her arms and sat on the bed. 'And how dare you, Mama. You had no right to read my personal letter.'

'How dare you question my right! I am your mother and you are sixteen years old. I thought I had brought you up with moral values, and yet you behave like this.' As Mama's distress increased, her accent thickened and the words ran together. She threw the letter onto the dressing table and a bottle of scent tipped over. As the cloying smell of lavender surrounded them, Lily watched the words run into black splotches on the pink paper and the lavender oil soaked the pages. She stood and crossed to the table and picked up the sodden letter, trying to save it. 'I believe this is my property.'

She turned and blinked as her mother's hand rose in front of her face. Disbelief filled Lily as Mama's palm connected with her cheek in a stinging slap. She caught her breath as her mother raised her hand again. Grief and hurt lodged in her throat like a stone and she backed away as Mama put her hand to her mouth.

'*No.* Oh, Lily, Lily, don't look at me like that.' Lily had no idea what the expression on her face was. She was still in shock; it was the first time her mother had ever lifted a hand to her in her whole life.

'Oh, *mon Dieu*, I'm so sorry.' Mama's eyes were wide and her lips were bloodless. She turned from Lily and sat on the edge of the bed and dropped her face into her hands. There was no sound as her shoulders heaved in silent sobs. Lily took a step towards her mother, with her hand held out. The hoarse sobs were frightening her.

'You don't know. You can't know. I never wanted you to have to know.'

'Know what?' Lily tentatively placed her hand on Mama's shoulder. 'It's all right, Mama. Everything is going to be all right.'

'No. It's not. You do not understand why you have to be careful. You cannot know that horror that I felt when I read that you put yourself in danger. You need to know these things, but I didn't want you to know.' She repeated the last words in a harsh whisper. 'I didn't want you to.'

Danger? Lily had never been in any danger. Although those two soldiers who had been insistent that night in Brisbane did come to her mind.

Finally, Mama lifted her head and her eyes were empty, dark windows of despair. 'I manage not to think of it, but when I read of soldiers and young women, it all comes back to me. There are bad men in the world. When I was in Paris, I was like you, I believed in good and I was trusting. After my father was killed, two men accosted me one night—'

Lily widened her eyes as horror filled her. Mama bit her bottom lip so hard a trickle of blood ran down her chin. She quickly crossed the room and crouched in front of Mama, the pages of the letter falling unheeded onto the wooden floor. She uncurled Mama's fingers and took the handkerchief from her hand and dabbed at her mother's lip, watching as the red blood stained the white handkerchief.

'Mama, I'm sorry. Oh, please don't cry. It's all right.' She fought back the tears that were clogging her voice.

'They raped me, Liliana. Two soldiers. In an alleyway in Montmartre. I'd been to Friday mass at the Sacré-Coeur. I still feel the cobblestones beneath my back when I think of that day. I wanted to keep my girls safe.'

'I really didn't do anything, honestly. Please believe me. I was a sympathetic ear for Amelia when she thought ...' Her voice shook and Mama reached out and caught the first tear as it rolled down Lily's cheek. 'When she thought she was having a baby. I didn't even know what the girls had ... what they had done. All I did was leave the school—only once, Mama—I promise you. And it was only because I wanted to read the newspaper. I wanted to see what was happening in the war. I wanted to know you were all safe up here.' Her voice hitched. 'I didn't do anything that would make you ashamed of me. Really. I promise you, Mama.'

Trepidation tightened her chest as Mama pulled her close. 'And what about Jack?'

'Jack is my friend.' She held Mama's eye steadily. 'And that is all, you have my word.'

'Good. I knew he was a fine young man. He is thoughtful and considerate, and I trust him to be a gentleman,' she said.

The hardness in Lily's chest eased even as her cheeks filled with heat. 'I like him very much,' she said softly.

'I know you do, sweetheart, and that's why I want to talk to you.' Mama let go of her but held her eyes. 'First love is sweet and fresh, and a wonderful thing. I just don't want to see you hurt. Jack will leave the base, and I pray to God each night that wherever he goes he will stay safe.'

Lily swallowed. The thought of Jack being in danger was one that was with her every minute that he was gone. Until she heard the Catalina fly over every morning when he was away, she couldn't relax.

'But, Lil darling, you need to know this. It's wartime, and awful things happen, and people change. And life changes very much after a war is done.'

Lily shook her head. She didn't want anything to take that lovely feeling away—the sweetness that had been there since Jack's lips had settled on hers.

'Be prepared. Jack will change, and he will go back home when the war is done. You will change, you will go off to university, and you will see the world you dream about.'

Lily stared as surprise filled her. Mama was treating her as an adult.

'And you are only sixteen years old. Too young to know your own mind yet.'

'I'll be seventeen next month.'

Mama's voice had a faraway quality as she looked past Lily. 'I was seventeen too. I pray that you never have to go through what I went through. Your father was my salvation. My circumstances were very different to yours. I want you to be happy.'

'I know it's wartime, Mama.' Lily's voice was soft and sad.

'You have a family who loves you, Lil.' Mama brushed her eyes. 'When we left Russia and moved to Paris after my beautiful mother died, it was very hard. That alone was enough to fill me with despair. But when my papa and my darling brother were killed not long after we arrived, I was alone.'

Lily drew in a breath. How was it that she was sixteen years old, and had known nothing of her mother's tragic past? Those nights when they had heard Mama crying in her bedroom, and her fear for the safety of the children began to make sense for the first time. And Dad's gentle care for his beloved Alexandra. 'I'm sorry, Mama.'

'Your father was in the street where they were killed by a runaway horse. He saw it coming and he grabbed me and pulled me from its way. He took care of me for the first few days when I was grief-stricken. Then only a few weeks later when I was attacked, he did not leave my side for days. I will never forget what your father did for me, and I will love him till the day I draw my last breath.' Mama's eyes lost their bleakness as she smiled at Lily. 'He saved my life, he saved my mind from the darkness that threatened to suck me down, and he has given me a wonderful life here. What I want you to think about is to give yourself a chance to find the person who will give you a wonderful life too. Someone who loves you like your father loves me.' She reached for Lily's hand again as she stared at her, her eyes full of love. 'Jack is a lovely young man, but I don't want to see you get hurt.'

Lily nodded and as tears filled her eyes, she put her head in her mother's lap and closed her eyes, relieved as a shaking hand smoothed her hair from her forehead. A door slammed outside, and Mama paused.

'I am so sorry I hit you. Will you forgive me, Lil?'

Lily looked up and nodded. 'I was rude and disrespectful to you. I'm sorry too.'

They both looked up as the door to the bedroom opened and Boyd stood in the doorway.

'I wondered where everybody was.' Boyd took a step into the room and stopped dead. 'What's the matter? What's happened? Where are the children?'

Her mother put her hand up. 'It's all right, Boyd. Just some female business we had to discuss. I became upset, and Lil bore the brunt of it.' She stood and straightened her shoulders and her voice was calm. 'The children are all up with the goats, and I promised we would go and help once you came home.'

Boyd crossed the room and Lily's heart clenched as he put his arms around Mama. 'Alex, are you sure you're all right?' His voice was low.

She looked at her mother. Her eyes were overly bright and there was a deep flush on each cheek.

'I am.' Mama lifted her chin and her smile was tremulous. 'Liliana has reassured me, and I know my girl. I have nothing to worry about.'

Lily bit her lip again as Dad looked from her to Mama.

'Daddy? Mama?' she said. 'I promised Jack I wouldn't, but I have to tell you.' She shook her head as Mama's eyes widened. 'No, Mama. It's not like that. I know more than you have ever told me. I am not some young silly girl like Peggy. Trust me. Please.'

Mama smiled. 'I am sorry, my sweetheart. I have to remember you are a young woman now.' She reached for Lily's hand and squeezed it, and looked up. 'Boyd, Lil is almost as old as I was when I met you in Paris. I will remember that from now on.'

Lily's eyes filled with tears as she made the decision to tell her parents. Her first loyalty was to her family. 'I promised Jack I wouldn't tell you. I don't want him to get into trouble, but I must tell you what he said.' She shook her head slowly and looked at her father. His eyes were kind but full of concern. 'What I read in the paper on the boat this afternoon just made me certain I have to tell you. The Japanese are coming. They might already be here. We have to be very careful. Maybe the children shouldn't be up alone with the goats.'

She turned to her father. 'Daddy ...'

Boyd stepped forward; it was the second time she'd called him Daddy today. 'Daddy. I think you had better keep your gun handy.'

'What?' Her father's brow wrinkled with concern.

'Jack told me that the Japanese might be using Whitsunday Peak as a lookout.'

'No.' Mama's cry was heart wrenching as she jumped up from the bed. 'The children are up at the goats now. I have to get them. And then they are not to leave the house.'

'It's all right, Alexandra. I'll go. Liliana can come with me.' Her father reached out and held Mama close to him as she tried to push past him towards the door. 'Stay here and put the water on. We have a treat. Fresh bread and fresh-caught crabs.' Despite his calm words, worry crossed his face as he held Liliana's eyes. 'We'll talk about this tonight after the children go to bed. I don't want to frighten the little ones. It's enough that *we* have to worry. But we will have to watch where they go.'

'And make some rules,' Lily said.

Mama's eyes were bleak. 'I can't do it again. Oh, Boyd. Not again. I can't bear it. And our children. I can't bear it. If the war and turmoil is going to come to us on this isolated island, where in the world is safe? Nowhere!'

'Hush, my darling. It's going to be all right. We are safe here. There is nothing to worry about. If there *are* any Japanese here, they aren't interested in us. They'll be watching the shipping in the channel. It's nothing like Russia at all.'

Mama began to cry softly, and Boyd held her tightly.

'Not again.' Mama's whole body was shaking now. 'I can't do it again.'

He turned to Lily as he held Mama close to him. 'Lil, go and get the children. Make sure all the doors are locked after you come in.'

She fled, slamming the door behind her. Her feet had wings as she flew across the house paddock and up the hill to her brothers and sisters. The evening darkened and in the pine forest, she saw shadows she had never noticed before.

★ ★ ★

Life resumed a semblance of normality, and Lily was happy when Jack's visits became more frequent. On the mornings she was home, as soon as the morning chores were done, she would run down to the jetty and wait for the mail launch. A couple of times she caught Mama's eye on her as she pulled the screen door closed, but her smile was indulgent for once. The days that she glimpsed the khaki-shirted airman sitting at the bow as the launch approached the bay, her happiness was complete.

The next time he turned up was on the mail launch just after breakfast.

'You're early, Jack. You must have taken the night launch down to Cannon Valley from Bowen and picked up the mail launch?' Dad looked up as he sorted through the fishing nets that were strewn along the verandah.

'No, I drove down.' Jack beamed as he held Lily's gaze and a ripple of anticipation warmed her.

'Drove?' Dad frowned.

'Roger and Charlie and I threw in two quid each one day last week,' Jack told Dad as he threw his kit bag onto the verandah. 'We were out on Mrs Atkins' porch and an old codger with no teeth and a box full of rotten, pulpy tomatoes pulled up in the street. Smoke was pouring out of the engine and he got out and kicked the tyres with a tirade of language like none of us had ever heard before. Strewth, the air was almost blue! He saw us sitting there and he asked if we wanted to buy the old truck or the tomatoes so he could go to the pub.' Jack put his head back and laughed along with Dad.

Lily stared at him and moistened her lips. She loved seeing Jack laugh. It didn't happen often.

'The old bloke sold us the car, and then gave Mrs Atkins the stinking box of rotten tomatoes for the seeds before he hurried off to the pub. Between the three of us, we got the old beast going. The deal is Roger and Charlie drive it around the town, and when I've got leave, I can drive down here.'

'Where is it now?' Dad asked.

'Parked over at Cannon Valley, near the spring.' Jack smiled at Lily. 'Close to where I met Liliana and the kids at the picnic on Boxing Day. I've got to go back first thing tomorrow and drive back to Bowen by mid-afternoon.'

Dad shook his head as he picked up the nets and threw them over the verandah to the grass. His eyes narrowed as he looked at Jack. 'You're keen to drive all the way down here to visit us for just one night. I know how bad that road is, especially after the rain we had last week.'

As the heat ran into her face, Jack's reddened in a self-conscious flush. Lily didn't know who had the pinkest cheeks.

* * *

Each time Jack had at least two days leave, he headed to the island, but it was harder to settle each time he returned to the base. Sometimes he thought he was going crazy; it was like living two lives. One day he'd be on the island with Liliana, watching butterflies in the glade, herding goats or having a leisurely cup of tea on the verandah overlooking Sawmill Bay, safe, happy and cocooned within the warmth and the routine of the Ellis family. Then within twenty-four hours, he'd be out over the Coral Sea, imprisoned in a cold metal tube, jolted about by turbulence as the Cat engines roared. He would peer through the observation window, looking for Japanese fighter planes whose single goal was to shoot down the aircraft he was in. If he wasn't peering down to the sea, he'd be recording the number of bombs they dropped over a harbour on that mission.

Each time Jack left the island, he worried that it would be the last time and that he'd never see Liliana again.

On the return from his fourth visit, he parked outside Mrs Atkins' house after the long drive up from Cannon Valley. Roger and Charlie were sitting in the dark on the front verandah with half a dozen empty bottles on the floor beside them. Jack sat on the step and looked out over the town. He could see the Cats on the hard stand from here.

'You're quiet tonight, mate.' Roger belched as he reached for the bottle that he and Charlie were sharing.

'I'm thinking about the next mission, and the next one, and the one after that ...' He gestured with his head towards the harbour. 'Do you have any idea what it's like to be up in one of those metal contraptions? Not knowing if it's going to get off the water with the weight of the bombs on board. Always on the lookout for a bloody Japanese fighter, and then the run home, wondering if you're going to be shot out of the sky.'

He reached into his pocket for a cigarette and shoved it between his lips, but his hands were shaking too much to strike the match. Roger took the matches from Jack, pulled out another cigarette, cupped his hand around it until the tip glowed and passed it over to Jack. 'Sorry, mate. It's pretty easy for us here on base.'

CHAPTER
21

1 May, 2018

Fynn tapped on the cabin door as the first rosy fingers of dawn tinted the eastern horizon.

'I'm starting up the motors. We'll be out into the channel in the next ten minutes,' he called.

By the time Liv stretched and climbed out of bed, Fynn had gone back up on the deck and the motors were vibrating beneath the cabin floor. She had a quick wash and grimaced as she pulled on her skirt and Sheridan shirt. Padding barefooted up the stairs, she paused and looked out over the water. Fynn was at the helm, and the boat was under power on a flat sea. It was hard to believe it was the same Whitsunday Passage that she'd crossed in the ferry yesterday morning.

'We'll motor across and then the wind should be up by the time we come back. It should be a good sail back later this afternoon. The sou' easterlies have finally arrived.'

'Is that why it was so rough yesterday?' Liv knew her voice held a little bit of trepidation. She didn't want to have a repeat of the sickness from yesterday. 'It won't get rough like that again today, will it?' The wind was puffing gently this morning and the sky was clear. The turbulent water of yesterday had settled into small waves, only the occasional one breaking in a burst of white foam behind the yacht as Fynn steered them into the Passage.

'It'll be fine, don't worry.' He turned with a smile. 'Make yourself comfortable, it'll take us a couple of hours to get to Hamo.'

She settled into the small lounge area behind the helm and stared out over the water as they passed a huge mansion on the point at the edge of the bay. Her thoughts were stuck on the events of yesterday. The words she'd had with her father replayed in her mind, but she didn't have any regrets. The more she thought about it, the more determined she was to help Fynn and the journalist as best she could. Eventually, she put her head back on the cushion and drifted off, the movement of the boat lulling her into a light doze.

Fynn woke her as they were entering the marina at Hamilton Island, and Liv went below deck for her shoes and jacket. She smoothed her jacket, tucked her hair back into a tidy roll, and went back up on deck carrying her high-heeled shoes, her bag and her computer. Fynn had secured the boat at the last mooring near the channel.

'We can only stay here for a couple of hours. It's where boats come in to top up their water,' he said as he locked the saloon door behind her. 'I'll come with you. We'll grab a buggy,' Fynn said. 'Did your father know where you were staying?'

Liv nodded. 'Not directly, but the company booked my flights and accommodation, so he'd be able to find out easily enough.' She bit her lip and frowned. 'Do you really think there could be a problem?'

'I think we need to be careful. Until we see what's on your computer and get it backed up, anyway.'

'Will I bring it? Or leave it here? Or do you think that's a bit risky?' She looked around nervously but the marina was quiet. Apart from a deckhand pushing a trolley along the finger wharf two wharves along, there was no sign of life.

He ran his fingers through his curls. 'I don't know. It should be safe if I lock it downstairs but I'm reluctant to let it out of our sight.' He looked across at the building. 'I'll take it to the marina office and get them to lock it away. I know the girls in there really well.'

Despite the tension tugging at her, Liv lifted an eyebrow and couldn't help smiling. 'Really well?'

He grinned and waved his hand. 'You know what I mean.'

It took less than half an hour for them to go to the hotel. Fynn waited in the living room while Liv had a quick shower and changed into the one pair of shorts and T-shirt she'd packed.

She walked into the living room rubbing her wet hair with a towel. 'I really appreciate this, you know.'

'What's that?' he said with his trademark grin as he looked around the room. 'A luxurious hotel room?'

'No. You looking after me. Bringing me over to get my stuff. I'm sure you had other things to do today.'

Fynn walked over and took the towel from her. He put it on the side of the cane lounge before he held both of her elbows and looked down at her. 'Until we know you're safe, and we get that data safely off your computer, I'll be looking out for you, Liv.' He reached up and tucked a wet strand of hair behind her ear. 'I'd already told Byron I was taking some time this week to work with Greg, after we heard what Sheridan had to say at the community meeting.'

'And you didn't expect what you heard either.' Liv's arm tingled where his fingers touched her skin, and she held his eyes for a moment before she stepped back. 'I'm going to do the best I can to help.'

In less than half an hour, they were back at the marina. Fynn collected her computer from the office and handed it to Liv before he took her suitcase from the buggy. The wharves were busier now and she looked around nervously as they walked to the boat, but there was no sign of Phillip or Anthony. She shook herself mentally. Of course there wouldn't be. They'd be back in Sydney now, reporting to her father.

'Where do you want me to put my bag?' Liv looked around as she stepped onto the yacht. The deck was small and the saloon where they'd sat last night didn't have much room to spare.

'I'll put it in one of the cabins.'

'Wait. Before you take it down.' Liv held her hand out for the bag, and he passed it to her.

'To new beginnings.'

He smiled as she pulled her Sheridan work shirt and jacket out of the suitcase and put them in the bin on the portside of the deck.

'You don't want to think about that?' he asked with his usual smile.

'Unless you have a need for some cleaning rags on *Footprint*?' She zipped the bag up again.

'No. Only the best quality for us, so no old Sheridan shirts for my lady.'

Liv put her computer on the table on the salon and followed him back up to the deck.

'I'll put the mainsail up when we get out into the Passage. I'll get you to help with the ropes,' he said as he lifted the fenders. 'We can take our time to get back to Airlie.'

'I'd love to. I used to sail when I was a teenager, but not in anything as big as this.'

'Same principle. Wind and sail.' He grinned at her and Liv shook her head as she headed towards the stern.

The mood between them this morning was light and full of banter after the drama of yesterday. As the boat sped over the smooth water, Liv sensed that Fynn was working hard to keep her spirits up. She chuckled as she walked up to the helm and stood beside him once they were underway. 'You know all about me, family warts and all, so now it's your turn, Captain Jay. How long have you lived in the islands?'

'All my life, apart from my uni days and a few trips overseas. My parents are yachties and my mum went into labour with me out in the Passage. We didn't make it to shore. They're in Vanuatu these days, they've turned into landlubbers.' Fynn rested his forearm on the wheel and leaned back to look at her. 'I was born on their old yacht in Muddy Bay. The bay's gone now, or most of it. Another win for progress. It's where you came in on the ferry the other day. Muddy Bay is now Port of Airlie, a multimillion dollar marina development. The locals fought that development too, but we lost out. Thirty-eight hectares of mud flats were reclaimed and the impact on the wildlife was immeasurable.' A frown creased his brow. 'But a coal loader will have a much greater impact.'

'No wonder you're so passionate about the place, living here all your life. I've only been here a few days and already the thought of a coal loader plonked out there in that pristine water is unthinkable.'

'It is,' he said quietly. 'And we're going to fight until we beat it. If this mine and coal loader get approved, it'll be the death knell for the reef. They've kept very quiet about the dredging required, and the creation of a port to manage the increased volume of shipping. We already know the ecological damage that overdevelopment and natural predators have caused. Half of the coral making up the reef is dead or dying. Pesticide runoff, muddy sediment from land clearing, predatory starfish, and coral bleaching have had a detrimental impact. This coal mine development will pose a dire threat to a reef that can take no more.' He glanced down at her as she leaned against the side of the deck. 'I'm pleased you're going to work with us, Liv. And not just because of what you might be able to bring us.'

Her face heated and she turned away into the breeze. 'I hope I can help.'

His smile was wide as he held her gaze. 'Oh, don't worry, darlin'. I'm sure you will.'

As they sailed past Gulnare Inlet, Liv stared at the eerily familiar flat hills at the end of the bay. Maybe she'd seen them on *Getaway* or some other travel show.

She turned away and yawned as the boat sailed past the inlet and pushed north past Whitsunday Island. Despite sleeping most of the way across the Passage, she was still tired from yesterday. It had taken her ages to get to sleep in Fynn's cabin last night. He'd insisted on taking the smaller cabin on the other side of the boat. Her thoughts had been full of the conversation with Greg and his insistence about keeping the computer—and themselves—safe. Phillip's veiled threat yesterday had worried her. Dad might be a ruthless businessman, but surely he wouldn't hurt anybody?

Once she'd managed to get to sleep, her dreams had been about snorkelling through the shoals of beautifully coloured fish that darted in and out of the coral. When she was a small child, her favourite story book had been one about a tiny fish living in the coral. She'd forgotten all about it until now. Or had it been a colouring book? Funny, how old memories surfaced when you were stressed.

As unfamiliar as these islands might be, Liv was quickly falling in love with the Whitsundays. Exhilaration filled her as she moved to the front of the yacht, Fynn's *lady* as he affectionately called her, while he steered them back across the Passage. The brisk wind whipped Liv's loose hair around her face as the yacht almost flew across the deep blue water.

An hour later, *Footprint* was moored back in the pen at Abell Point Marina.

'You grab your handbag and computer, and I'll bring your suitcase. It's only a short walk around to the apartment block.' Fynn secured the last rope. 'I'll text Byron. He's going to meet us there with the key.'

* * *

The aroma of barbequing meat and onions drifted into the apartment from the balcony. Aunty Tat sat on the sofa in Liv's new apartment, her handbag clutched on her lap, as Liv tipped a packet of salad into a bowl that she'd found in the well-stocked kitchen. A loaf of bread was warming in the oven. Her laptop was sitting on the benchtop charging, but she had made sure it wasn't turned on.

'It was very thoughtful of you and Byron to stock the fridge and pantry for me.'

Aunty Tat pulled out a lace-edged handkerchief and fanned herself.

Liv walked back to the entrance foyer. 'If I can figure out how, I'll switch the air conditioner on.'

'Have you been back home yet?' the older woman said.

'I came to visit you last Sunday. Remember?'

'No, Lil. Not my place. Home to the island, to see Mama and Daddy.' Her voice was querulous. 'I need to take some groceries out there too.'

'No,' Liv said slowly. 'I haven't had a chance yet.'

'Did they take you back to Japan?' Aunty Tat's eyes were intense. 'What did you do there? Couldn't you write to us?'

Liv's eyes pricked with tears as she heard the sorrow in Tat's voice. She walked over and sat beside her on the sofa. Aunty Tat put the handkerchief in her lap and picked at the lace with her long fingernails.

'I'm here now. You tell me all about your family, about your grandchildren.'

'No. I don't want to,' she said stubbornly. 'I want to know why you didn't come back. Daddy talked to all the boys on the launches, but none of them had taken you off the island, so we knew you were there somewhere. I looked and looked, every day.' A sob broke from her throat. 'Then I heard Daddy telling Mama about the Japanese coming to our island and I knew they had you. And that they had taken you away.' She dropped her voice to a whisper. 'Don't tell Daddy, but I even climbed up to the top of the peak where Jack told us the Japanese were hiding.'

Liv didn't know what to say, so she lifted the old woman's hand from her lap and squeezed it gently. Lily of the Valley perfume surrounded her as Aunty Tat moved over and put her head on Liv's shoulder.

'But you weren't there. So, you know what I did then?'

'No. What did you do?'

'Every night, I would sit in your hammock and I'd tell the little ones your story about the fairy garden. I told them that I would tell it to them every night until you came home.'

'That was very kind,' Liv murmured.

'Yes, they loved that story.' Gradually, Tat calmed and when Fynn called out that the meat was cooked, she sat up with a smile. 'Good. I'm hungry.'

'Would you like me to set the table inside or out?' Liv stood and crossed to the door and took in the view from the balcony. *Balcony* was an understatement. The outdoor area was as large as the rest of the apartment, and to her delight, a small lap pool was set along the edge that faced the bay. An elegant and huge outdoor dining setting sat in the middle of a tiled area, and a profusion of brightly coloured flowers spilled from glossy black pots set along the glass wall that edged the balcony. From the doorway, she could see Fynn's boat in its pen in the marina below, and that was reassuring.

Not that I should feel lonely.

Liv had lived alone in her apartment in Sydney since the first year she'd started work at Sheridan Corp. It had only been a short walk along Pitt Street to the office and often she'd gone for weeks without getting her car out of the underground parking area. If she was going to stay up here for a while, she'd have to see about getting a small car to get around. The way she was feeling, she was even considering looking for a job up here. As strong as she'd been with her father, the whole experience had left her feeling pretty shattered and, if she was honest, a little bit lost. Not that she'd admit that to anyone, except maybe Mum. Sheridan Corp, and her work there, had been her life for a long time, to the exclusion of every-thing else. It was going to be strange to find a different focus. In the meantime, she'd do all she could to help Fynn and Greg.

'Outside would be good.' Fynn's reply pulled her from her thoughts. Liv inhaled the fresh, salty air before she went back to the kitchen to load the plates and cutlery onto a colourful wooden tray she'd found on the benchtop. A ripple of excitement ran through her. She had a lovely apartment to stay in, with a view to die for. She'd made some connections up here already and had been made to feel very welcome by Byron and his family. And there was Aunty Tat. She looked over at the elderly woman with affection as she stood beside Fynn, telling him how to place the meat on the tray.

And then, there was Fynn James himself.

A frisson of anticipation fired long-neglected nerve endings and Liv tipped her head to the side as she walked out to the balcony. She would be wary, and she would be careful, but she was looking forward to spending more time with him. There were some things to organise. Her computer was charging, and she needed to go shopping. Fynn and Byron had gone out of their way to look after her, and the apartment was beautiful, but she needed to get to town—apparently the shopping precinct was a short walk around a boardwalk—and buy herself some clothes, and an external drive to back up her computer, and then she could settle in and relax. Another thrill of anticipation shot through Liv and she smiled as she placed the tray on the table. It was the first time for many months that she could honestly say she felt happy. Not worrying about the next meeting, or what was ahead of her at work for the day. Not trying to impress her father or gauge the mood he'd be in.

Fynn must have noticed her smile. 'Our Whitsunday air is working its magic already, I think,' he said as he pulled out the chair beside her.

'It is. I think I could settle in for a long time.'

'That's what we like to hear, hey, By?'

Byron nodded. 'As the tourism rep for the council, what more can I add?'

Sitting around the table was relaxing, the conversation was light-hearted, and the company was entertaining. Byron made them laugh with stories about the Tuesday night sail he'd won last week at the yacht club, even though he'd had inexperienced backpackers as his sailors. Aunty Tat sat quietly, but with a constant smile on her face. After the elderly woman insisted on helping Liv clear the table while Fynn cleaned the barbeque, Byron signalled it was time for them to leave.

'See you next Sunday at our place, Liv? We'd love to have you visit again. Please come.'

'I'd like that very much.' Liv smiled and stepped forward as Aunty Tat opened her arms for a hug. A sweet floral fragrance engulfed them.

'Oh, Lily. It's so good to have you home.' Aunty Tat held her close, her soft papery skin brushing Liv's cheek.

'I'll see you soon,' Liv said quietly as she walked to the lift with them.

Byron caught her eye above Aunty Tat's head. 'Thank you,' he said.

'I'll take the stairs.' Fynn stood beside Liv as Byron and his grandmother waited for him to step in. 'So, you've got everything you need?' He turned to her as the lift doors closed. Liv watched as he reached his hand out to her and then suddenly pulled it back.

'Yes. I thought I might walk into town this afternoon.'

There was an awkward silence between them and then they both went to speak at once.

'You first,' Liv said with a laugh.

Fynn cleared his throat. 'When you go out, you be careful.'

'Don't worry, I will. I think you and Greg might be overreacting, but I'll keep an eye out.'

'It's not an overreaction, Liv.' Fynn's voice was quiet. 'You've made it clear which side you're on, and you have quite an intimate knowledge of the project from the inside, not to mention the data that you now have in your possession. That's not going to sit well with … with some people.'

Liv shook her head. 'It's my *father*, Fynn.'

'Still, make sure you lock up the apartment, and put your computer in the safe. Or I could keep it on the boat for you.'

Liv shook her head. 'I don't think there's any need to be so extreme.'

'Just be careful, okay? Make sure you lock it in the safe when it's charged. And set your own combination.'

'All right. I will.'

She stood at the top as Fynn ran lightly down the stairs. He stopped when he reached the landing halfway down and called up to her. 'I'll come over and see you when I hear back from Greg. Enjoy!' With a final wave, he disappeared down the stairs. Liv turned thoughtfully and went back into the apartment.

And locked the door behind her.

CHAPTER

22

21 May, 1942

The cloud was heavy and ominous and, for a brief time, the sun slanted through a hole in the heavy mass, lightening the green forest on the mountain in the centre of Whitsunday Island to a soft tint. The full moon of the night before was now a memory, one that Lily cherished. Last night, she and Jack had wandered down to the jetty after dinner to watch it rise over Whitsunday Peak. Charlie and Roger had been with him this trip; they'd been granted leave and had jumped at the chance to come back to the island with Jack, although for the two days they had been there, the weather had been uncooperative.

Since Jack had kissed her, they became closer every time he visited. 'I can't stop worrying until *Dumbo* flies over the Passage on your way back.'

'There's nothing for you to worry about. And apart from the noise, there's nothing unpleasant about being up there. It's quite boring.' Jack pulled her to him, and she tried to push aside her worry, she knew he was making light of going on the missions. She'd read more in the *Courier Mail* about the war in the Coral Sea than Jack had ever told her. They stood together quietly as the moon crept above Whitsunday Peak. A mass of dark cloud was approaching from the east and the moon slipped in and out of the clouds running before the wind.

'Look at that. The sky is strange tonight and the shoreline is spooky,' Lily whispered as she pointed across the bay. Grotesquely shaped mangrove trees rose up, broken boulders overhung the banks poised to fall. Dark-shelled crabs scurried on the mud flats as the tide ebbed and the moon seemed to sail through the clouds. As they watched the play of nature, a beam of light crossed the water and the noise of an engine reached them. Lily moved away from Jack and walked to the edge of the jetty as the launch from South Molle Island came into the bay.

Lily looked up at him as fear skittered through her. 'Do you think they are going to tell us something about the Japanese? Do you think they've landed on the coast? I'd better run and get Dad.' She stepped away from Jack, torn between waiting to hear what the boat was doing here at night, and knowing that Dad would want to hear any war news.

'Let's just wait.' Jack reached for her hand and held onto it tightly. He didn't let go as the sound of footsteps coming down from the house reached them. A light bobbed up and down on the path approaching the jetty and they waited as Dad appeared with Roger and Charlie by his side, and they hurried along the timber planks.

'I saw the lights of the boat coming around the point,' Dad said. They all walked to the end of the jetty and waited together as the launch drew closer. The engines cut when it was about twenty yards away and Owen, the youngest Bauer boy, climbed to the front of the launch.

'Are you going to come into the jetty?' Boyd called out, holding the light aloft.

'No, I just needed to let you know there's a big blow on the way. You'll need to secure your house and sheds. They reckon it's going to be a bad one.'

'What do you mean?' Boyd called back. 'Who said that?'

'They're predicting gale force winds,' Owen called as he kept the boat steady, a couple of feet away from the jetty.

Lily looked at Jack with a frown. 'How can they possibly know that?'

'The met service in Brisbane telegraphed the base up at Bowen to tell them to secure the aircraft.' Owen's reply answered her question. 'The base has telegraphed all towns north and south of us for a couple of hundred miles. Prossie stationmaster telegraphed South Molle, and we're calling in to all the islands tonight before the wind brings the Passage up.'

'Thanks, Owen. They must think it's going to be a big blow.'

'So they say.' He looked over at Jack. 'There'll be no launches on the Passage for a couple of days. Do you need a message telegraphed to the base?'

'We'll have to get a lift to Proserpine and take the train back north,' Jack said. On this trip, the three men had come down on the launch as they had four days before they had to return to base.

Owen's teeth flashed white in the lamplight. 'There'll be no boats going to the mainland, either, mate, if this wind gets as bad as they are saying. I'd offer to take you but it's bad enough having to get back to South Molle. We'll just have to bunker down until it blows itself out.'

Jack waved an acknowledgement. 'Then yes, please. My last name is Rickard. Just let them know the three of us will get back as soon as we can.' He turned to Roger and Charlie. 'I wonder what they'll do with the aircraft.'

'I'd say that they'd have them up on the hard stand on the harbour and secured by now. Just as well we got it done before this.' Charlie's eyes were wide. 'I've heard what damage these tropical storms can do.'

Lily looked up at the moon as the diesel motor revved. The ghostly cloud that surrounded the orb was eerie and as she focused on the cloud backlit by the moonlight, she pointed upwards. 'Look, Dad. Even though it's not windy here, the clouds are fair scudding up there.'

They stood and watched the launch as it headed back over the bay. It was so still, there wasn't a ripple on the water. Boyd scratched his head as they turned to walk back to the house.

'I guess that's the first good thing that's come out of this blasted war, anyway.'

'What's that, Dad?' Lily had been pleased that Dad hadn't commented on Jack holding her hand.

'A weather warning. First time that's ever happened to my knowledge. I hope this storm's not going to turn into a bloody cyclone. It's May, should be way too late for one anyway.'

They were quiet as they walked back to the house.

★ ★ ★

Next day, when the Ellis household stirred just after dawn, it was hot and the air was thick, like the tin of syrup Jack had seen Liliana's mother put in a pan of water in the pantry to stop the ants climbing into the sweetness.

A patchy curtain of autumn mist hung over the mountains on the mainland. Ants were scurrying about, and a long black line crawled up the post on the side of the front door. Others had built cones of sand and earth around the entrances to their nests on the track down to the jetty. Mrs Ellis had told Roger, Jack and Charlie to come up to the house for breakfast, as they'd offered to help with any storm preparation. Jack had called Roger and Charlie down to the jetty at dawn, and already there were white caps out in the Passage, although strangely, the water around Whitsunday Island was still smooth.

'Maybe we could take one of the boats across?' Charlie said when they went up for breakfast. 'I'm a bit worried about not getting back to the base when we're supposed to.'

Boyd shook his head. 'Trust me, you don't want to be out in the Passage in my small launch if that wind comes roaring in.'

The scrubbed table that took up most of the kitchen was full, and they listened as Boyd gave out a list of jobs. 'If we do get this blow'—his voice was sceptical because there still wasn't a breath of wind outside and Sawmill Bay was like glass—'there's a few chores that we need to get done now.'

He nodded at the twins. 'You pair, get up there and get those nanny goats in with the herd before they look for shelter. If there is a blow coming through, they've probably gone already and it's probably too late to lock them up.' Boyd kept the baby goats, about thirty of them, in a large wire enclosure up the hill from the house on a flat rise. The milking mothers had the freedom of the hill to graze. It was the boys' job to herd the mothers to their offspring every morning.

Jack was intrigued, being used to the independence of horses and cattle. 'I'll give the boys a hand. If you tell me what to do, I'm another pair of hands.'

'Another pair of legs is what you'll need up there, Jack.' Boyd nodded with a grin. 'Okay, Lil, you go too. You can both help the twins. You might have a chance of success if there's four of you.' The twins jumped up from the table with a whoop and Boyd turned to the others. 'Roger and Charlie, I'll get you to give me a hand up on the roof of the stone shed. The iron has been flapping. We'll get up there and secure that. Alex, you and the girls pick up anything loose lying around the house yard and secure it in the shed.' He scratched his head as he looked up at the sky. It was clear and blue, and the only sign of wind was the thready white clouds up high. 'Crazy. That's what it is.'

Liliana strode ahead of Jack up the hill. 'We have to round the kids up first.' She jumped over rocks and stubby tree stumps with an agility that surprised him. Bleating carried on a stiff wind met them at the top of the rise, but their attention was drawn to the sea to the east. The sky was sheet-metal grey, and a long dark roll cloud stretched along the horizon as far as they could see. The swell pushing to the beach was much bigger than he'd seen it before. Jack followed Liliana as she turned and hurried over to the twins.

'Come on, you pair, hurry up. We need to get this done and then get back down to the house and help Dad.'

Billy and Robert were already between the baby goats and the edge of the cliff. The herd was at the last fence before the hill ran in a steep overhang to the beach south of the jetty. The early mist had cleared and from the top of the flat hill, Jack could see the houses scattered along the mainland to the west. The sky westwards was blue, in complete contrast to the angry sky on the seaward side of the island. The air was so clear, it was as though you could almost reach out and touch the houses on the coast.

'Is the fence to stop them going over the cliff?' Jack asked as they approached the goats.

'No, it's to keep them contained. The goats were here when Mama and Daddy first moved here and built our house. Apparently, the goats were put on the island to provide food for shipwrecked sailors, or that's the way the story goes. They cause dreadful damage to the bush and the ground, so Daddy has confined them to a small part of our land. The fence is to protect the island, not the goats.' Liliana smiled as she held his eyes.

'What are you thinking about now?' he asked.

'I'm surprised that Dad worries about the goats so much. A couple of years back, on Christmas morning, the twins got up early and crept out to the tree. We were all woken up by the most awful yells and screams. One of the baby goats had got through the fence, climbed the steps and pushed open the screen door. It had unwrapped all the Christmas presents. Dad shook his head and said that's what you get for keeping goats.'

'It's never dull here, is it?' Jack pulled the gate shut as the two small boys chased the last of the kids in. It was very different to his home in the Hunter Valley. There was always laughter in the Ellis house, and always something happening here on the island, although they were the only family that lived here apart from the occasional guests in the bungalows.

Growing up on the vineyard had been about work, not family. Life at home was always serious and it was about making as much money as could be made from the grapes, the cattle and the small horse stud.

'That's all a matter of perspective. You try living here all the time. You just get to see the fun parts. When the war is over, I'll head back to the city.' Liliana pushed the gate open and they entered the enclosure. The twins had the goats contained in one corner. She picked up a couple of long sticks and passed one to Jack. 'There's never much money to spare. That's why Dad built the bungalows, to try and make some more money to pay for boarding school for all of us.'

'What about the fishing? I thought that the fish would get a good price at the markets?'

Liliana laughed again. 'Dad says the fishermen here in the islands are either stony broke or blooming millionaires by Christmas every year. It all depends on the run of kingies in the winter.'

'Kingies?'

'Striped tuna fish. When they're on, his catch is railed to Brisbane from Proserpine. But Dad says you can't put all your eggs in one basket, so we have the fruit trees and pineapples and the goats. We do okay most of the time.'

Liliana was close to her father, a relationship Jack was unfamiliar with. Maybe if he'd tried harder instead of having to suggest improvements as though he knew best, he could have had an easier relationship with his father. He had learned a lot about dealing with people in the air force. Maybe after the war, he could go back home and try again. Collaboration ...

It didn't take long to secure the enclosure, but by the time they'd finished, a strange, hot wind had begun to blow straight off the ocean. Jack stood on top of the hill and pointed to the ominous cloud on the horizon. 'Look. I think that Owen bloke might have been right.' The cloud was rolling in and getting closer to the shore.

Liliana reached up and pushed a wayward strand of hair from her eyes. She frowned and stood staring at the sky. 'I've never seen such a peculiar cloud, or felt a hot wind off the sea. And look at the way the wind is whipping the waves up already. You can see the wind line not far out where the water changes colour.' She turned to the twins who'd shinnied up a tree at the edge of the bush. 'Come on, you pair. Dad's going to need our help down at the house now. And securing the boats in the bay as quick as we can by the look of that wind line.'

As they hurried down the hill, the branches whipped in the wind that was getting stronger each minute. The deathly still of the morning had gone, and Jack looked up as the wind keened through the tops of the trees. As they reached the gate that led to the house yard, Tat came running up past the side of the house.

'Jack, Lil. Come quick. We need you. Daddy's hurt.'

Liliana wrenched the gate open and took off after Tat, Jack close behind her. 'Where is he?' she yelled.

'Down at the jetty. Mama's with him. He got his leg caught in between the boat and the jetty while he was trying to tie the ropes off. This huge wave came in and pushed the boat onto him and he slipped between the boat and the planks.'

'Is he still caught?' Jack called as he ran past them both.

'No, Roger and Charlie got him onto the jetty, but he can't walk. Mama's with him down on the jetty.'

By the time they ran down the path and reached the bay, Boyd was standing on one foot, bracing his weight with one arm on Roger's shoulder, and the other on his wife's. His brows were drawn in pain, and his lips were set in a straight line.

'Do you think it's broken?' Jack asked as he stood beside the taller man and offered his shoulder for Boyd to lean on.

Mrs Ellis stepped away. 'No. I think he's just wrenched it when he pulled it out between the boat and the jetty.' As they stood there, another large wave pushed up on the side of the boat and Boyd groaned.

'If it gets much worse, my boat's not going to hold. I didn't get it tied off at the stern.'

'Where's Charlie?' Jack looked around.

'He went down to the bungalows to get our bags when we came down here,' Roger said.

'I told them to come and bunk up in the house with us. Those bungalows weren't built to withstand a strong wind.' Boyd looked up at the trees that were bending in the wind. 'Owen's right. This is going to be a nasty storm.'

Jack nodded to Lily. 'Roger and I will get your dad up to the house and then we'll come back down and finish the job if you can tell us what to do.' He had to raise his voice to be heard over the now howling wind.

It was a slow convoy that got Boyd back to the house. Mrs Ellis ran ahead with the twins and by the time Jack and Roger had helped him up the hill, Boyd was drenched with perspiration. They lowered him onto a chair on the verandah, and he issued directions from there, frustration lacing his voice.

The heat was intense, and the thick air almost suffocating. The clouds were rolling in from the north and every few minutes Liliana would throw an agitated look at the sky. Rumbles of thunder presaged the fast-approaching clouds. An hour later, the boat was secured as best they could manage, and Roger and Charlie had helped Jack drag the two dinghies up into the bush and weighted them down with rocks as Liliana had suggested. The bungalows were as secure as they could be, and the sheds around the house were locked up, with all the loose implements from the yard and vegetable patch locked away inside. They pushed their way along the path back to the house, ducking below the whipping branches. The clouds were dark and boiling, but it wasn't raining yet.

'Jeez,' Charlie yelled. 'I wonder how long this bastard'll blow for.'

'Might be stuck here for a week or more.' Roger's grin was wide. Jack wondered if there would be any consequences for them not coming back. They should have tried for the mainland before the wind hit. There might have been time, but they wouldn't have been able to help the Ellis family prepare for the big blow.

Liliana was waiting on the verandah and she held the door open for them as they went inside.

Even though it was only early afternoon, the room was dark. Someone had lit the lamps on the tables near the windows. A rosy glow came from the huge wood stove in the kitchen, and Mrs Ellis stood there stirring something with a tantalising smell. Boyd was sitting at the table with his leg stretched out on another chair, a couple of cushions elevating his foot.

'Boats are all secured.' Jack crouched down beside him. 'How's the ankle?'

'Not too bad, just bruised. I just can't put my weight on the damn thing. Pull up a chair and have some lunch. We waited for you.'

'We'll just go out and have a wash,' Jack said. 'Come on, lads.' Liliana smiled at him as they headed to the laundry room.

When they came back, the three sisters were sitting at the table with their father. Boyd nodded at Jack as he pulled out a chair. 'I'd like to thank you lads for everything you've done to help out today. We would have been in real trouble if you hadn't been here.' Boyd shook his head. 'I still can't believe they were able to predict this storm down in Brisbane.'

His wife walked over from the stove with a pot of stew and placed it on the table on a cork mat. 'Lil, can you slice the bread please. Tat, go and get your brothers. I told them to come straight back here after they had a wash.' She jumped as something landed on the roof with a bang. 'I think this is going to be worse than the storm of '28, the one we had the year Tatiana was born.'

As their mother turned back to the kitchen, Tat came in from the side verandah with Robbie. Her brow was wrinkled in a frown and Jack watched as she gestured to Lily to come out on the verandah with her. Robbie's lip was trembling and his face was streaked with tears. Jack followed them out to the verandah. Tat had hold of Liliana's arm and her whispers were distressed.

'I don't know how far. Robbie didn't know, but he's been gone more than an hour.'

Jack walked over, and a shiver went down his spine as Liliana looked up at him, biting her lip and her eyes full of worry.

'What's wrong? How far what?'

Liliana's voice was low. 'Bloody little larrikin. Goat's gone.'

'Gone where?' Jack frowned as he looked out at the turmoil that the wind was creating in the bush at the edge of the fenced house yard. The trees in the forest were whipping from side to side and as he watched a large branch tore off and landed on the cleared area inside the fence not far from the house.

'Robbie said he doesn't know for sure. He said something about checking his cave.' Tat looked into the house. Their mother was making her way across to the doorway.

'What cave?' Jack asked. If Goat was out in this storm, he was in danger.

'He sets up cubby houses and then moves on to another one. Always reading about pirates and hidden treasure,' Liliana whispered as she ran her hand through her hair.

'Where are these caves?' Jack asked.

'He's got them all over the island. They're in the cliffs on the seaward side, and there's one up near the old timber workings behind Gulnare Inlet.'

Liliana's mother pushed open the door. 'Come inside, you three. Your lunch is on the table.' Liliana tried to compose her face, but her mother obviously knew her well. She looked past them to the end of the verandah.

'What's wrong?' Her eyes darkened as a frown crossed her fore-head. 'Where's Billy?' she said slowly.

Jack crossed to the door and took her hands in his. 'Don't worry, but it looks like he's gone off for a bit of an adventure. The lads and I will go out and look for him before we eat.'

'He must be here somewhere. I'll go and look in the sheds. You know how he likes to hide.' Mrs Ellis stood at the door. 'He knows the rules.' She reached for the oilskin that was hanging by the door. 'I'm going to find him.'

Jack stepped over and put his hand on her shoulder. 'You stay here, Mrs Ellis. We'll go.'

Boyd jumped to his feet and winced as his bad leg took his weight. 'What's wrong? Go where?'

'Goat's taken off, Dad.' Liliana lifted an oilskin from the hook by the door. 'He's out on the island somewhere.'

'You're bloody joking. In this weather!' Boyd sat down again and put his leg up. 'I wondered where he was.' He tapped his hand against his thigh, frustration in his voice and movement. 'I know what he's like. He could be anywhere, the little bugger.'

'Robbie, did he say where he was going?' Liliana asked.

'He said he had to get something from his cave before the storm blew it away.'

'Which cave?' Liliana threw a worried glance at Jack.

Boyd spoke slowly. 'There are caves over at Turtle Rock.'

'No,' Lily said. 'That part of the island is riddled with crevices.'

'He probably saw the storm coming and he's gone for shelter.' Boyd's face was set. 'I'll deal with him when he comes home. He has to learn to do as he's told, especially since we heard there could be Japanese on the island.'

Jack stared at Liliana and heat prickled his neck as she looked away.

The wind screeched outside, and something banged against the side of the house. Jack had to raise his voice to be heard as he beckoned to Roger and Charlie. 'We're going out to find him.'

'Jack, he'll be fine. Even if he has to wait the storm out. He's a sensible little tyke and he'd know this whole island better than the rest of us. But I'll tan his hide when he gets back, that I can promise.'

Mrs Ellis shook her head. 'The wind is so strong, it will blow him off the cliff if he goes near the edge.'

Jack took charge. 'He knows better than that. Tat, you get your mother a cup of tea. Liliana, come and look at those maps the boys were working on and show us where these caves are. We'll head out.'

He stared at her as she shook her head. 'You'll never find them by yourselves. I'll come with you.'

Boyd nodded. 'She's right, you know.'

'How far are the caves?' Jack asked. He moved across to the table and Roger and Charlie followed him. The twins' maps were sitting at the end of the table, and Jack knew that he had seen a map of the islands on the visit when he had helped with their lessons. He'd smiled that day when Goat had added a pirate ship and a couple of treasure chests to his map of Whitsunday Island.

'Here it is.' He slid out the map as Liliana came to stand beside him. The four of them stared down at Goat's map, and as Jack watched, Liliana traced a path with her finger. She pointed to the two treasure chests he had coloured in.

'This one is where there is a cave about half a mile to the south. It's pretty easy to find at the head of Gulnare Inlet. I know he's had a cubby house there for ages. He's even let us visit that one.' She lifted her finger and made a wide arc to the other treasure chest. 'This one is up at Turtle Rock. He's always pointed it out to us when we've been fishing out to sea, but he's not allowed to go that far from the house.' She lowered her voice. 'It's on the other side of the peak and the cliff that faces the east is full of caves. It's really high above the sea. If he's gone that way ...' Liliana cleared her throat and Jack frowned.

'If he's gone that way?' he asked quietly, and Roger and Charlie looked at each other.

'It's really dangerous.' Liliana lifted her chin. 'You'll never find it from the map. It's a good couple of miles away and there's no track.'

Jack thought for a moment. 'How about Roger and Charlie go to the one south and you can take me to Turtle Rock?'

'Yes. That's the best plan.' Liliana glanced over at her parents and lowered her voice. 'But just tell Mama we're all going to stay together and go to Gulnare. She's worried enough as it is.'

Jack nodded briskly. 'Rog and Charlie, get Tat to find whatever oil slicks and lanterns that she can. Maybe some hats to protect our heads, if we can keep them on in this wind. Liliana, can you grab us something quick to eat and drink and we'll head off before this storm gets any worse.'

He walked over to the sofa and squatted down beside Boyd and Alexandra. 'Lily's going to take us out and we'll find him.'

Boyd put his hand on Jack's shoulder. 'Thank you.'

'No.' Alexandra's eyes were wide and her voice was shrill. 'Lily is not going with them. I don't want two of my children out in that storm.'

Boyd's voice was low and calm. 'She has to, sweetheart. She'll be able to take the men straight to Billy's hidey hole.' He lifted his head to meet Jack's eyes. 'Take care of her, Jack. But follow Lil's guide. She knows the island as well as her brother. There are some more oilskins and kerosene lanterns out in the shed—'

Jack lifted his hand. 'The lads are getting them now. And don't worry, we'll find Goat and bring him home safe.' As he reached over and took Alexandra's hand, she lifted her face to him. It was pinched and white, and her lips were bloodless. 'I promise you that, Mrs Ellis.'

Jack stood but before he turned for the door he caught Boyd's eye and lowered his voice. 'Don't worry. If it gets too bad, we'll take shelter and wait till it blows out to bring him home. Once it gets really dark, we won't risk being out in the storm.'

Boyd reached up with his left hand and gripped Jack's hand. 'Thank you, Jack. Be careful. As careful as you can in that monstrosity.' They both looked to the window as another strong gust of wind roared in like a freight train. The house shook for a moment, and then the wind dropped back again.

Jack nodded and crossed to the kitchen, where Liliana handed him a bowl of stew and a mug of tea. He took it and looked at the two plates on the bench. 'Have you eaten?'

'I can't,' she said. 'I'm sick with worry.'

'You have to eat if we've got a few miles to walk.' Jack dipped the bread in his stew as Roger came through the door. Roger used both hands to hold the door against the wind, and Tat hurried in, soaking wet, her hair plastered to her face. Charlie was behind her, arms full of oil slicks. The smell of linseed oil pervaded the kitchen as he dropped them next to the wood fire.

They quickly finished the stew and drained the teapot empty. Liliana reached for a couple of brown paper parcels, handed one to Roger and held onto the other. 'I made some sandwiches in case we have to stay out overnight. There's some biscuits in there too.' She picked up the oilskin and gestured to a small door behind the wide stove at the back of the kitchen that Jack hadn't noticed before. 'Come on. We'll go out the back way.'

Jack looked over. The two younger sisters were sitting at their parents' feet and Robbie had climbed into Boyd's lap, his thumb in his mouth. If it hadn't been for the worry on their faces, it would have made a happy family picture. The three men followed Liliana over to the door and the bolt made a loud snap as she drew it undone.

'The lanterns are against the back of the shed. One each, but only put one on at a time for each pair to conserve the kero,' Charlie said as he passed an oil slick to Jack. Roger was already pulling his over his head. One by one, they slipped through the narrow, low doorway and Jack gestured for Liliana to follow the other two to the shed as he secured the door. There was a rusty bolt on the outside and as he forced it shut, his hand pushed against the timber and dislodged a piece of wood and he swore as the splinter buried deep in his palm. Putting his hand to his mouth, he dashed to the shed to join the others.

CHAPTER
23

The four of them stayed together as they pushed their way down to the jetty. Beneath the hill, the wind wasn't as strong as it was up at the exposed house. Lily had never seen anything like it. As they'd fought their way from the shed to the path, the wind had stung her face, and her hat had been blown off before they'd crossed the house yard. Trees were being whipped into a crazy dance of branches, bending and swaying, and twice they had to run as a crack above warned them of a falling branch. The tide was out but the sea was churning, and she pointed to the jetty.

'Quick, down here. I'll tell you where we have to go.' She ran ahead of them and stood out of the wind behind one of the wooden pylons beneath the jetty. The water was still a few yards away from the last pylon, and the space beneath the jetty was wide enough for them to get some respite from the wind but Lily had to shout to make herself heard. Even though it was mid-afternoon, it was hard to see in the darkness brought early by the low clouds and the driving rain. Jack held the lantern up and the shadowed light created grotesque shadows on their faces.

Once she was sure Roger and Charlie could hear her, she pointed to the south. 'If you follow the beach along to the end, you'll see a track as soon as you reach the end of the sand. Follow that for about five hundred yards and then it splits into two. Take the right fork, but watch out for the water. With this wind and the tide turning, there might be deeper water than usual in the mangroves. Once you go around the head of Gulnare Inlet, go around to the other side and you'll see the tracks where the old railway brought the logs down. Follow that until the end of the track and you'll see a big cave tucked into the cliff facing the water.'

'If he's there, do you want us to try and get him back to the house?' Roger's voice was muffled by the wind.

'Wait and see what the wind does. With any luck, this will blow itself out in a couple of hours.' Lily reached up and pulled the wet strands of hair from her lips. 'Stay there until it does.'

Jack shook his head and yelled over the noise. 'If it is a cyclone, there'll be a lull in the middle when the wind will stop, so wait a while, because the wind will come roaring back from the other direction.'

'Okay. We'll see you soon, I hope.' Charlie and Roger ducked from beneath the jetty and ran to the end of the beach, but it was only seconds before they disappeared into the driving rain.

'Ready, Liliana?' Lily looked up as Jack's warm breath puffed on her cheek. She nodded as he took her hand. 'Before we go, tell me exactly where we're going, just like you told the others, in case we get separated. I don't want to lose you.'

Lily quickly described the course through the forest that would bring them to the middle of the island on the seaward side, where Turtle Rock protruded from the cliff face. 'It's going to take us a good hour or two to get there. Depends on how windy it is once we get away from the lee of the island. The best thing is we can skirt around the peak and it's mostly flat, with a lot of cleared areas where they took the hoop pines from the low areas when they first started felling the timber.'

'Don't let go of me, okay?' Jack yelled.

By the time they'd fought their way through the driving rain and into the swampy mangroves at the base of the last hill, Lily was exhausted. Jack's grip was firm and when she stopped to catch her breath, he stood in front of her in an attempt to shelter her from the incessant rain.

He lowered his head. 'Do you want to stop for a while?'

'No. I'm fine. I just need to catch my breath.' She looked down at her feet. One shoe had been sucked from her feet by the black sticky mud in the mangrove swamp, and she didn't tell Jack that a root had cut the sole of her foot and it was throbbing with pain.

It was more important to get to the cave and see if Goat was tucked up there, although Lily had begun to doubt that he would have come this far, knowing the storm was about to break.

'Come on, we haven't got far to go.'

As they climbed the hill, the rain stopped and the wind began to ease. By the time they reached the base of the volcanic plug that formed the protrusion that the Ellis children had named Turtle Rock, glimmers of watery sunlight were breaking through the clouds.

'Do you think it's over?' Lily squinted as she looked west into the setting sun.

'No.' Jack's voice was concerned. 'Look to the east.'

She did. To the east, a mass of black cloud was moving quickly towards them. From there, they could see the sea beneath them, and it was a mass of angry white caps as the waves crashed against the cliffs far below. Lily swallowed, praying and hoping that Roger and Charlie had found Goat, or that he'd made his way home himself.

Jack held out his other hand and pulled her up to the flat rock at the top of the cliff. 'Come away from the edge. We're in the eye of the cyclone, and it will be worse once the back end of the storm hits us.' Jack held Lily tightly and despite her wet clothes, the storm and her throbbing foot, pleasure filled her.

She wasn't going to give up. 'Come on, the cave is only about a hundred yards along the cliff top.' She pulled away from Jack's hold and bit her lip as she put her weight on her foot.

'Billy,' she yelled. 'Goat, are you in there?'

The cave mouth was hidden ahead behind low scrubby bushes. 'I haven't been here for ages. I didn't even know Billy had discovered it until I saw that map he'd drawn with the pirate ship on it.'

She watched as Jack cocked his head and his eyes narrowed.

'What is it?' she said, leaning forward. 'Can you hear him?'

'No, quickly, run!' As soon as he finished speaking, the roar of the wind hit Lily with a physical force. Jack grabbed for her hand as she was almost knocked off her feet by the wind gust. There was a huge crack above them and a massive tree hit the ground at the base of the rock with a reverberating thud. Small rocks bounced and skittered around the mouth of the cave. Jack waited until the rock fall was done and then dragged her along to the entrance. Tears stung Lily's eyes as the cut on her foot ached. Jack pulled back the low branches covering the opening.

'Billy!' Lily yelled.

There was no answer.

Jack strode past Lily and paused just inside the dark space until Lily hobbled beside him. The air was musty and still, and the cave was in total darkness.

'He's not here.' Lily put her hand to her mouth and held back the tears, unsure if the emotion clogging her throat was relief or disappointment.

'He'll be fine. I think you're right. He probably went to the cave closest to the house. Robbie did say he was going to a cave, and unless he has any more secret places, he's probably with Roger and Charlie right now.'

'Will we go back?'

Jack moved back to the cave entrance and fiddled with the lantern. 'I don't think it would be wise. That wind is twice as strong as before.'

As the flame caught, the space inside the cave was filled with light. Liliana gasped.

CHAPTER

24

1 May, 2018

The holiday atmosphere in the main street of Airlie Beach relaxed Liv. How could she not chill, surrounded by smiling tourists enjoying a holiday in the tropics? Her heart lifted as she strolled through the shops. She lingered on the foreshore beside the huge lagoon pool, indulged herself with an ice cream as she stood in the shade beneath the massive fig trees, watching the children squealing in the pool, and simply enjoyed the freedom of being out in the open air. While she was surrounded by people, she felt safe but she still kept an eye out for anyone watching her.

Laden with shopping bags, Liv caught a taxi back to the apartment late in the afternoon. By the time the taxi turned onto the road that ran past the marina, the sun was setting in a spectacular palette of pinks and golds. Liv paid the taxi driver and lifted the shopping bags filled with clothes and shoes. She looked at the staircase and changed her mind, opting for the lift. When she stepped out at the top floor, the corridor was in semi-darkness but a night light illuminated the door to the apartment. Placing the bags on the floor against the door, she dug into her pocket for the keycard. As her fingers closed around the hard plastic, a soft creak came from the door. As it swung open slowly the plastic bags fell sideways into the apartment with a rustle.

Liv paused, frowning as her heart kicked up a few beats. As she slid the keycard into her pocket, the back of her neck prickled. Despite the warm breeze blowing through the open sliding door to the balcony—the door that she'd closed and locked before she'd left earlier—goosebumps rose on her arms. She left the bags on the floor and stepped quietly into the apartment, her new canvas slip-ons making no sound on the tiles.

As she reached the bedroom, her breath caught. Her suitcase was open and the contents were scattered over the bed and floor. As she stared at the disarray, something hit the floor in the ensuite bathroom with a tinkle.

'Shit.' The muttered oath came through the half-open door to the bathroom and Liv froze.

Turning on her heel, she tiptoed to the foyer, then hurried through the door and stepped over the bags. She cursed as the breeze caught the door and slammed it shut behind her. Whoever was in there would see the shopping bags and know she'd been there. Dragging in a ragged breath, Liv looked from the lift to the staircase that was now in darkness. The stairs would be quicker than the lift, and the thought of closing herself in there and someone waiting for her at the bottom sent a fresh spike of fear running through her. Her hands were sweating, and they slipped on the rail as she negotiated her way down in the darkness, hoping that one of the other tenants would come home and turn the light on.

By the time she got to the bottom of the second flight, footsteps were pounding down the steps above her. She flung the door open and ran into the car park, desperately looking for somewhere to hide, but all that was ahead was an open expanse of lush green lawn leading down to the sand of Shingley Beach.

Grateful that she'd changed into her new shoes, Liv ran across the lawn and onto the beach, praying that it joined the boardwalk that led to the marina. She expelled a relieved breath as she reached the end of the curved beach. The sun had set, and the beach was not as well-lit as the lawn or the boardwalk and she hurried into the shadows of the rocks. Catching her breath, she looked back at the apartment block, but there was no sign of anyone following her. At the edge of the sand, a short ramp joined the boardwalk that led onto the finger wharf where Fynn's *Footprint* was docked.

Please be there, please be there. Her whisper was in time with her footsteps as she ran the two hundred metres along the timbered walk to the south marina, not daring to stop and look behind her. Nothing in her life had ever been as welcome as the sight of Fynn sitting up on the *Footprint*'s deck. As she turned down the timber ramp, and along the finger wharf, he looked up.

'Liv! What's wrong?'

By the time she reached the boat, he'd jumped onto the wharf and she ran into his arms. Her throat ached as she drew in great gasps of air, struggling to speak as he held her close.

'Is there anyone following me? Did they see where I came? They mustn't know that I'm here.' Her words were short and jerky as the fear settled deep within her. Someone had broken into the apartment. How did they even know where to find her?

As far as the company knew, she should have been on a flight back to Sydney. A shiver ran down her back; she'd come very close to whoever was after her.

'I can't see anyone on the boardwalk.' Fynn's arms held her close. 'Calm down, Liv. Take another deep breath. It's okay, I've got you. You're safe.'

By the time her panic had subsided and her breathing was easier, Fynn had led her onto the boat and down into the saloon. He let go of her briefly to open the fridge and pass her a bottle of water.

Liv placed the cold bottle against her forehead before she opened it. Fynn took her free hand again and held it. She appreciated the warmth of contact as she drank. The ache in her throat eased.

'I haven't run that fast since I left high school,' she croaked and cleared her throat.

'What happened?'

'I got back from shopping and the door was open. I went inside, and my suitcase was open and everything was on the bed or the floor. Then I heard someone in the bathroom.' Her voice shook and she took another deep breath. 'I took off down the steps and I heard someone running above me, but I ran as fast as I could.'

'You did the right thing.'

'I just hope they didn't see me come to the boat.' Liv looked up as she put the water bottle onto the table.

Fynn's jaw was tight and his usually smiling lips were set in a straight line. 'If they did see you come here, we'll deal with it.'

'Thank goodness I locked my computer in the safe. I just hope they didn't find it.'

'I shouldn't have let you go to the apartment. Greg said it wasn't safe, but damn'—he slammed his fist onto the tabletop and Liv jumped—'I didn't think they'd be so fast.' He pulled her into his arms and dropped his chin to the top of her head. 'Look, Liv, you've pissed off a very powerful company. They know you've got some-thing on your computer that may incriminate them, and they'll do their damnedest to get whatever it is. It's time we had a look at what's on it. We can't wait for Greg.'

'If it's still there.' Liv shook her head. 'God, I hope it's still there.'

★ ★ ★

Fynn focused on keeping calm in front of Liv. When he thought about how close she'd come to being hurt—and he had no doubt that they would have hurt her to get hold of her computer—he clenched his hands. If they'd taken the computer, it would be a damn shame, but at least Liv was safe.

'I'm going to call Byron, and I'll leave you over with Lou while Byron and I go to the apartment and get your stuff. You're coming back here.'

'No.' Liv stepped back out of his hold and folded her arms.

'It's not safe there. I'm hoping that they mightn't have had time to look for the safe with you interrupting them. They may have thought you took your computer with you. Did you see anyone following you in town?'

She shook her head.

He tapped his bare foot against the floor as Liv lifted her chin and her mouth set in an obstinate line.

'I'm coming with you,' she insisted. 'Whoever it was will be long gone by now. They're probably expecting me to call the police. And I will call them too.'

'All right. But we'll wait for Byron to come first. Safety in numbers.'

Byron was at home when he called, and Fynn was pleased to see the headlights of his Prado when he pulled into the five-minute parking space above the marina only a short time later. Liv followed him to the car and he held open the back door for her. Byron shot him a look as he pulled himself into the front seat. 'What's happening, Fynn?'

'I just need some backup. Someone's broken into the apartment. I'll fill you in later.'

Byron parked on the road across from the apartment block, and Fynn took Liv's hand as he helped her from the four-wheel drive. He was pleased when she didn't pull away when he kept hold of it. As they crossed the usually quiet street, a dark sedan cruised past them and the light streaming down from the street light illuminated the front of the car. A man looked at them from the passenger seat, and Fynn paused as Liv drew in a quick gasp.

'What's wrong?'

'I'm sure that was one of the security staff from the office in Sydney. I can't believe it.'

'I'd say he's after you or your computer. And I'd hazard a guess that he hasn't found it, and they're waiting for you to come back.'

Liv's fingers squeezed his. 'In that case, I'm glad you're both with me. I feel like I'm in some sort of spy movie. It's surreal.'

'I was going to suggest you waited out in Byron's car, but after seeing those guys, I think you'd better come inside with us.'

'I'm not arguing.' A slight smile lifted her lips and Fynn grinned back at her.

'That'd be a change, darlin'.'

He pulled out his phone and opened speed dial before he handed it to her. 'If we have any problems at all, hit six. It's a shortcut to the local police station and it's only over the hill from here.'

Liv's shopping was still scattered outside the entry and Fynn bent to pick up the plastic bags. Byron went in first, checked the rooms and called them in. 'All clear.'

Fynn locked the door behind them as Liv crossed to the safe and keyed in the security code she'd set.

'Thank God,' she said as she lifted her briefcase out. 'It's in there.'

'Gather up the rest of your things. We're not staying here.'

'Okay.' The look they shared when Liv readily agreed needed no words.

'Did you check in the shower and toilet?' she asked Byron, flicking a nervous glance towards the ensuite.

He nodded, but Fynn headed through the bedroom. 'I'll check again.'

After he'd checked the bathroom again and opened the sliding door of the wardrobe, he called out to Liv, 'All good.'

As she walked past him into the bedroom, she paused and held his arm before reaching up and brushing her lips across his. 'Thank you.'

Byron was in the kitchen, unpacking the fridge.

'By the look of things, they've been through this too.' Byron turned to him. 'Chuck me the sponge.'

Fynn picked up the sponge and a couple of plastic bags. He held them open while Byron emptied and wiped out the fridge.

'How serious is this, Fynn?' Byron kept his voice low.

'Very. Liv doesn't think her father is capable of seeing her hurt, but Greg's getting ready to expose them, and I think Sheridan is getting desperate. There's something on that computer that they want back.'

'Greg's article in the paper last weekend got the politicians backpedalling.'

'Yeah, he said that was just a strategic move before the community meeting. He changed the focus of the article to the environment so they didn't twig to what he was actually investigating.'

Byron nodded. 'The regional council has called a meeting tomorrow. If you find anything that I can use to argue against any approvals, let me know.'

'I will. Greg called me a couple of hours ago and said he's flying up on the early flight tomorrow, but Liv and I will have a look at the laptop tonight.'

'You need to back up the computer, in case there's another incident.'

'Yes, Greg said that too. I should have done it before we brought Liv to the apartment, but I didn't think they'd move so fast. I've got my external drive on the boat.'

'I bought one today too,' Liv said as she came out of the bedroom carrying her suitcase. Byron stepped forward to take it from her.

'Thank you.'

Fynn held the door open for Liv as she followed Byron into the foyer of the apartment block. He didn't miss the nervous glance she flicked at the shadows in the stairwell as they crossed to the lift.

'You want my take, mate?' Byron pressed the button to take them down to ground level. 'I think you need to get on *Footprint* and head out to the islands. I can pick Greg up at the airport and bring him out on my boat.'

'Not a bad idea. How would you feel about that, Liv? We can sail to somewhere isolated, bunker down in a bay, wait there until Byron brings Greg out.'

Liv nodded. 'I think I'd feel safer out there than I would here in town or in the marina. I'm seeing shadows in every corner here.' Her face was pale. 'I'm having trouble dealing with the fact that my father might be behind this.'

Fynn put his arm around her shoulders as the lift headed down and she leaned into him.

CHAPTER
25

Liv stood up on the deck as Fynn steered the boat into the channel. She'd been nervous about going out into the Passage in the dark, and when Fynn had glanced at her, he'd changed his mind.

'We'll moor at the front of Cannonvale Beach tonight instead of going out to the islands. We can cross the Passage at first light like we did today. The tide's still good early.'

Liv bit her lip and nodded. 'Thank you. I know I'm a scaredy-cat, but that trip over from Hamilton on Monday wasn't a good experience. I don't know how I'd be doing it in the dark.'

'No point pushing your boundaries.' He grinned at her. '*Yet*. But I will make a Whitsunday sailor out of you before you leave.'

'We'll see. It's a bit different to the inland lake I'm used to.' Not being able to see out in the dark Passage added to her fear of what—or who—was in the shadows.

'Anyway, the best thing is we'll have phone service this close to shore and I can give Greg a call after we eat. I want to let him know what we're doing.'

'Okay.' She smiled up at him as his stomach rumbled.

'I don't know about you, but I'm starving.'

'Not really.' Liv shook her head. 'My stomach hasn't stopped churning since I realised someone was in the apartment.'

'Luckily, I stocked up the freezer when you were at Byron's on Sunday morning. Once we moor, I'll cook something to tempt your appetite.'

They motored to only a few hundred metres off the front of Cannonvale and once they'd picked up a mooring, Fynn pointed out the lights of Aunty Tat's house.

'She's such a sweet thing. It's sad to see how her mind comes and goes from the past to the present,' Liv said.

'Dementia is cruel.' Fynn nodded as he cut the motor. 'We're not far from the shore here, but far enough out that it'll give us time to move if a boat heads towards us. I'll turn the gas on, and get dinner started.'

She summoned up a smile. 'Sounds good. But let me help. You've done so much for me today.'

Working in the small galley was cosy, and a couple of times, they bumped into each other. Liv was aware of Fynn's proximity but it wasn't awkward. He kept her busy chopping and dicing while he thawed some beef in the microwave, and mixed together a marinade. It wasn't long before a fragrant aroma permeated the galley and Liv's stomach gurgled loudly.

She laughed when Fynn looked sideways at her from the stove. 'Not hungry, hey? Looks like my famous marinade has done the trick.'

'Maybe I am a *little* bit hungry after all.'

Fynn poured her a wine while he attended to the stir fry, and Liv raised her eyebrows when he took a bottle of water from the fridge.

'None for you?'

'I don't drink when I'm at sea,' he said. 'Even this close to shore, you have to keep your wits about you. We don't want to wake up and find we've slipped the mooring and drifted to New Zealand overnight.'

'Wouldn't be too bad,' Liv joked. 'I've always wanted to go there.' She sat at the table and watched as he stir-fried the vegetables she'd chopped. His eyes lit up and he grinned back at her.

'Maybe I can sail you there one day.'

'Maybe.' Liv nodded and took a sip of the white wine, tucking her feet beneath her. It was strange, since she'd kissed him briefly back at the apartment, something had changed between them. Even when there was silence now, it was a comfortable silence.

'As soon as we eat, we'll boot up your laptop.' Fynn drained the rice into the sink and put the empty pot onto the chopping board.

'It's time to have a look.' Liv swallowed as she wondered what they were going to find. She put her hand over her mouth as a yawn threatened.

'You tired?' Fynn opened a cupboard and lifted down two bowls.

'Sort of, but I'm wired. All I've done lately is drift off to sleep.'

'You can't beat being rocked off to sleep on the water.'

'I won't be able to sleep until I know what we've got.' Liv watched as Fynn spooned the stir fry into the bowls and a delicious aroma filled the saloon.

'Hopefully something that will put the project back some more,' he said.

'Yes.' She nodded and looked around. 'How long have you had *Footprint*?' Liv looked around. 'It's beautiful.'

'She.'

'Sorry. *She*'s beautiful.'

'I bought her when I was nineteen. My parents loaned me the money, but she didn't cost much. She was an old wreck and I've spent the last fifteen years doing her up.'

So he's thirty-four.

'Well, you've done a great job. Do you spend much time on her?'

Fynn raised his eyebrows. 'I live on her.'

'All the time?'

'Yep. Unless I'm travelling away for the university, I'm on board.'

Liv sipped her wine and tipped her head to the side. 'I can't imagine living on a boat.'

'It gives you a sense of freedom that you just can't imagine when you live on land. Some nights, I sit out on the deck and watch the birds diving for fish. The only sound is the wash of the waves on the side, or the splash of a fish in the bay. The nights in the marina are special too. When the wind comes up, the clanging of the halyards can sound like church bells. Every day is different and if I get sick of the view, I simply move on to another bay. I can work anywhere.'

Fynn painted a picture of a serene lifestyle Liv could barely imagine.

'So the downsides? Are there any?'

'Let me think.' He tapped a finger on his lip and smiled. 'You learn to cook a lot of one pot meals.'

'Anything else?'

'Nope. I wouldn't live anywhere else.' Fynn slid both the bowls along the table and sat next to her before he lifted up his water bottle. 'Cheers and welcome aboard, officially.'

'Thank you and cheers.' She touched her glass to the bottle.

They were almost finished eating when Fynn's phone rang. He reached for it and nodded when he looked at the caller ID. 'Greg. Good timing.'

Liv frowned when the tone of his voice changed almost as soon as the phone went to his ear.

'What? Are you serious?' He stopped talking and listened for a couple of minutes. As he listened, he rubbed the back of his neck with his free hand. 'Are they sure? Jesus. I can't believe it.' Fynn turned and looked at Liv and his eyes were bleak. She put her fork in the bowl and pushed it to the middle of the table, keeping eye contact with him. Her stomach clenched as he put his hand over his eyes.

'Greg's in hospital.'

CHAPTER
26

22 May, 1942

Jack lowered the lantern as Liliana stood there with her hand over her mouth.

'What is it? What's wrong?' he asked, hurrying over to where she was standing in the middle of the cave.

'He's not here, but look at this.' She held out one hand and pointed to the hollow at the back of the cave half in shadow from the lantern but light enough to see the little camp set up there. 'He's been here recently. Goat's set up a home away from home.'

Jack walked across the surprisingly large space to the smaller section at the back where the roof dipped down. In the centre, the cave was high enough that he didn't have to lower his head when he was standing. The rock floor was flat and covered with a fine layer of sand and leaves.

In one corner, a couple of old blankets were spread on the floor. Next to them was a small box containing a variety of trinkets and shells and shark's teeth, and a couple of lumps of grey coral. He put his hand on the small pile of grey ash.

Stone cold.

'Looks like he's made his own treasure chest.'

Liliana shook her head. 'If I wasn't so worried about him I'd smile. Little bugger. I wonder how long he's been coming here. Dad will wallop him if he sees this.'

Jack walked back to the entrance and lifted the lantern. He stepped back quickly as the wind caught the flame and it almost died. 'It's almost dark and the wind is getting stronger. How long do you think the storm will last?'

'It's hard to say, but it will probably blow itself out overnight and pass over,' she said as she stood beside him.

'At least we're out of the wind here and it's dry.' Jack turned and as he followed Liliana, she hobbled over to a large rock in the other corner and sat down.

'What's wrong with your foot?' He put the light down and squatted beside her.

'Nothing. I just stood on a root in the mangroves when I lost my shoe.'

'Show me.'

She lifted her foot and he took it gently in his hand trying not to wince as he stretched the skin of his palm where the splinter had buried itself deep.

'Cripes, Liliana. You've got a good gash there.' Jack dug in his pocket for the clean handkerchief he knew was in there. 'I'll go and get some water and clean it. There's mud in the wound.'

'Don't go too far.' Her voice quavered and for the first time Jack realised she was scared. He reached down and cupped his uninjured hand around her cheek.

'It's okay, I'll just lean out and the runoff from the cliff face will soak it in no time.' He held the handkerchief up with a rueful smile. 'It's almost wet enough already, even with the oilskin on.'

'I'm soaked, too,' she said with a grimace. 'At least it's not cold. Just icky and uncomfortable.'

'Stay there. When I clean your foot, we'll check out Billy's blankets. We can get dried off a bit and maybe I can get a fire going. He's left a small pile of wood by the ashes.'

'Don't you think we should head back to Gulnare?'

Jack shook his head. 'I think we should wait until the back of the storm passes. There's too many trees coming down out there. It's blowing even harder now.'

* * *

Lily reached up and undid the oilskin before slipping it off her shoulders. She laid the coat on the ground, reached up and squeezed the water from her hair before she ran her hands over her face. Trying to wipe wet skin with wet fingers wasn't at all successful. Her cotton blouse was sodden, and she tried to pull it away where it was stuck to her chest. In the end, she gave up and sat there, waiting for Jack to return.

And now here they were, seeking shelter in a rock cave until the storm blew out. It was only a minute or so before Jack returned with the handkerchief soaked with rainwater. He shrugged out of his oilskin before he sat on the ground next to the rock she was sitting on. Liliana looked at the top of his head as he lifted her foot onto his lap. His hair was wet and small dark curls stuck to his neck. She was tempted to reach out and lift the wet strands from his skin, but shyness stopped her.

She sat and watched as he gently cleaned the debris and sand from her foot. 'Tell me if I'm hurting you.' He looked up and heat rushed into her cheeks as he hurriedly averted his gaze from her wet blouse. She hadn't put a brassiere on this morning, and knew that everything she owned—not that there was much of that—was clearly visible through the saturated white cotton.

Jack cleared his throat and he put her foot down, and she was pleased he'd looked away; he was a gentleman and she trusted him.

'All good now. Although it's going to be hard to walk home on that foot,' he said.

'Maybe I'll have to use one of Billy's blankets to wrap it up.'

'Or I might have to piggyback you.' His laugh dispelled the awkwardness between them.

Lily reached over and picked up her oilskin. 'Pass me yours. I'll drape them over a rock and they might dry out a bit.' She dug into the pocket and held up the brown paper wrapped parcel. 'Are you hungry? I don't know what state these sandwiches will be in.'

'As long as they don't taste like linseed oil,' Jack said with a grin. 'Before we eat, let's get a bit organised.'

He stood and Liliana in turn averted her gaze from the wet trousers that were plastered to his thighs. Unfamiliar feelings were running through her.

When he'd held her cheek before, all she could think about was the first time he'd kissed her at Butterfly Glade. It had pushed her worry about Billy aside and made her more self-conscious about being here with him.

Jack put the lantern on the rock as Lily stood. 'I'll try and get the fire going while you have a look at Billy's stash of blankets over there. Maybe we can get ourselves a bit drier.'

Half an hour later, cosy firelight flickered on the shadowed walls of the cave. Jack had lit a small fire near the opening so they didn't get smoked out, and Lily had spread one blanket for them to sit on, and they'd shared the other to dry themselves as best they could.

He raised his eyebrows with a smile when she passed him a sodden and squashed sandwich.

'Dinner is served, sir.'

'Looks delicious, madam.'

After they'd eaten, Jack balled up the paper and threw it onto the fire.

'Ouch.' He flexed his fingers as the paper sizzled into a pile of white ash.

'Did you burn yourself?' Lily reached for his hand and turned it over. 'Oh, Jack. Look at that splinter. When did you get that?'

'It's nothing. It'll come out by itself. I've had worse working in the vineyards.'

Lily kept hold of his hand and he moved closer to her. 'Lean back on me. You look uncomfortable.'

She moved across and leaned back against him as Jack stretched his legs either side of hers. Lily listened quietly as Jack took a deep breath and pulled her closer to him. 'Liliana?' His breath puffed against her cheek and she knew his lips weren't far from her skin.

'Yes, Jack.' She moved a little bit closer.

'When the war is over, I'd like to see you.'

'See me?'

'Oh, I know you have plans, but I don't think I could bear it if we didn't see each other again.'

She turned her head slightly and looked up at him. 'Me too.'

'And one day, maybe one day, when you've done all the things you want to do—' a chuckle rumbled up from his chest—'and I've gone back home and made my peace with Dad, and bought Mum a new rose bush, maybe we can start a life together.'

Joy burst through Lily's chest and she turned around so that she was facing him, but the angle was awkward. Jack put his arms beneath her elbows and lifted her so that she was sitting across his lap and facing him. The fire warmed her back, but it was the expression in Jack's eyes that sent heat coursing through her.

'Yes. I would like that very much,' she whispered. She slid her arms around his waist and put her head on his chest. Closing her eyes, she listened to the slow steady beat of his heart beneath her cheek as he breathed deeply. They sat together like that for a long time, as she thought of what a future with Jack would hold.

'Are you sleepy?' His voice broke into her happy dreaming.

She lifted her head and met Jack's gaze. A smile tilted his lips and he cupped her cheek with his hand.

'A little bit.'

Their eyes held, and Lily's heartbeat picked up as Jack lifted his other hand and both of his hands held her face. His thumb brushed her skin slowly, up and down, up and down, and an exquisite sensation pooled low in her belly. She closed her eyes as he lowered his head and his lips gently brushed hers. He went to pull away but this time, she lifted her hand and pulled his head back down to hers.

'Don't stop. Please.'

This time the pressure of his lips was firm, and Lily opened her mouth with a sigh. The crackling of the low flames and the keening of the wind outside faded into the background as the intensity of Jack's kiss deepened. Her tummy fluttered as tenderness turned to passion. Lily lowered her hands and slipped them beneath his shirt, and he drew a quick breath against her lips as her fingers caressed the silky bare smoothness of his back.

Now Lily understood the words she had read when Rhett Butler had kissed Scarlett, but this was so much better than reading the words on a page. The same wild tremors and new but wonderful sensations consumed her whole body.

Jack pulled away and his breath was ragged. 'This isn't a good idea. You don't … you can't understand what this is doing to me. We have to stop.' He took another breath as she caressed his back. 'Before it's too late to stop.'

'But I … I don't want you to stop, Jack.'

His lips were back on her cheek sliding slowly and softly towards her mouth. His lips vibrated against hers. 'Just one more kiss then, and we'll stop.'

This time his lips were hungry, and Lily moved her hands forward and knotted them in his shirt, pulling him hard against her. She smiled as his erection pressed against her stomach before he tried to move the lower half of his body away.

In that moment, she made up her mind. Mama had been right when she had said about war changing things. Nothing was more important than being with Jack.

Who knew what the future would hold for them?

* * *

The sky was a brilliant blue and raindrops glimmered on the leaves in the forest as they walked back to the house the next morning. The wind had blown itself out and only the fallen branches on the track bore evidence of the massive storm that had crossed the island last night. But Lily didn't notice, nor did she feel the soreness of her injured foot, or the tenderness between her thighs, because every time he helped her over a fallen log, Jack took her in his arms and kissed her. As he lifted his lips from hers for the last time at the top of the hill before they reached the house, Lily took in the entire scene around them, and knew that the memory of this morning would stay with her forever. The fresh smell of the forest, the pure sapphire blue of the Passage, the curve of the bay and the sighing of the wind in the hoop pines settled into her soul.

This morning, when she had woken up in Jack's arms, the fire had gone out and the cave was dim, as soft shards of sunlight crept in through the fissure in the rock.

'I just want you to know that last night was very special for me.' His voice was soft.

'And for me too,' she whispered. Shyness flooded Lily despite what she and Jack had shared through the night. Very few words had been exchanged but the whispering of their bodies had been enough, as Jack had shown her he loved her.

'I want to marry you, Liliana. Soon.'

As they hurried down the path—as quickly as Lily could limp with her injured foot and no shoes—trepidation dampened her happiness as she worried about Billy, and what her parents would say about her spending the night in the cave with Jack. But her worry was for nothing. Tat ran down the steps with a happy cry as they made their way down the path towards the house.

'There you are!' When Lily reached her, Tat grabbed her hands. 'Charlie and Roger found Billy. He was safely in the cave at Gulnare.'

Tears welled in Lily's eyes and she turned to Jack with a wide smile. 'Oh, thank goodness for that.' She clung onto the post as she climbed up the steps, Jack keeping a respectful distance behind her. They had agreed not to say anything to the family yet. It was all too new, and they both wanted to hold their happiness to themselves. Lily was worried about Mama's reaction and her all-seeing eyes, but still she hugged the knowledge to herself. She was a woman now, and no one could take that from her.

'Where is everybody?' Jack looked at the house where all was quiet.

'They didn't get back here till a couple of hours ago,' Tat said.

'Waited the storm out like we had to.' Jack glanced at Lily and she dropped her eyes.

'Then Mama cuddled and kissed Billy.' Tatiana's lip rose with disdain. 'He thought he was a hero until Daddy walloped him and then he cried himself to sleep. Then Mama had one of her "things" and now Daddy's in there with her.'

'What about the others?' Lily asked, relieved that her parents weren't about.

'Roger and Charlie are packing, and the littlies are doing their lessons. I've been in charge.' Tat smiled and stood straight.

'I'd better go and get packed too. I guess we'll take the launch back as soon as it gets here.'

'What about your car?' Lily asked.

'It can stay at Prossie for a while. I think we need to get back as quick as we can today.' Her heart skittered up a beat as his lips tilted in a smile, just for her, and the laughter lines creased at the corner of his eyes. Jack looked happy, happier than he had in all the visits he'd made to their island home. He put his hand over hers on the post at the top of the stairs. 'I don't want to leave, but I'll be back as soon as I can get leave again. I'd better go and see the lads.'

* * *

The launch pulled in at the jetty early in the afternoon. Dad said goodbye to the men at the house—Mama hadn't reappeared, much to Lily's relief.

'Thank you. All of you, and you too, Lil.' Dad reached out and put his arm around her shoulders as Jack and Roger and Charlie hefted their kit bags to their shoulders. They'd spotted the launch as it made its way across the Passage. 'I'll never forget what you did last night, looking for that little tyke in that storm. Whenever you want to stay, lads, make sure you come back as often as you want. Consider this your second home.'

He shook Roger and Charlie's hands, and they headed off to the wharf with Tatiana chattering beside them.

Dad held his hand out to Jack, and held it for a long time in a firm grip. 'I know we'll see a lot more of you too, Jack.' Dad glanced at Lily and she felt the blush creep up her cheeks. 'Take care, son. You'll be in our prayers.'

Lily stood on the jetty with her two sisters and the twins. Looking down at the grey weathered timber as though something of deep interest had suddenly appeared on the jetty, she fought to hold back the tears that threatened. The children scampered around, calling out to the crew on the launch as they brought it to the end of the short pier. Happiness filled the air. The storm was gone, Billy was over his sulks and the children's laughter drowned out the squawking of the gulls that flew over the water. The Passage was calm and peaceful this afternoon and mirrored the mountains overhanging the mainland near Shute Harbour. Jack walked over to Liliana and stood beside her as she stared at the water beneath the wooden pier. The depths were a mix of blues and greens, and she looked into the still water as he stood beside her and took her hand.

'Liliana, I'll be back. I promise.'

She lifted her head slowly. Jack's eyes held hers as he lifted her hand to his lips.

'May I kiss you goodbye? Would that be all right?'

'It would.' She nodded and lifted her face to his. His lips clung to hers in a gentle kiss. He held her hand until they walked to the launch and he stepped onto the boat.

'Bye, Liliana.'

'Take care, Jack.' She lifted her finger to her lips and blew him a kiss, and Charlie and Roger whooped, breaking the mood.

Lily was proud that she smiled until the launch was out of sight. Closing her eyes, she let the tears roll down her cheeks.

CHAPTER
27

May 1, 2018

Liv waited as Fynn lowered his hand from his eyes and stared at her. His lips were in a straight line and he rubbed his fingers over the back of his neck again. Liv followed the movement; the tendons were standing out on his neck and the pulse was visible.

'What's happened? Is Greg okay?' Fear crawled from her stomach up into her chest and she swallowed. Images of a boat making its way silently across the dark water filled her mind and she darted a nervous glance to the small window above the sink. 'What did he say?'

Fynn reached out and took her hand. 'I know you're a bit nervous about crossing the Passage in the dark, but we're going to head out tonight. It's not safe to stay here.'

'What did he say? What does he know?'

'It wasn't Greg.' Fynn stood and looked through the hatch before he sat down again and took her hand. 'It was Jill, Greg's partner.

She was calling from the hospital.' He took a deep breath. 'Greg was involved in an incident on the way home this afternoon. His car went over an embankment and he's in hospital.'

Liv put her other hand on top of Fynn's. 'Oh, God, no. I'm so sorry.'

'Apparently, a man walking his dog across the road saw it all. He got to Greg and called triple zero.' Fynn put his arm around her and pulled her close. 'I've got to keep you safe, Liv. It wasn't an accident. The witness said his car was deliberately rammed by a vehicle that sped away.'

Liv buried her face into Fynn's shoulder and they sat close together. It was surreal, an experience totally out of what she was used to.

When Fynn moved back, he brushed his hand lightly over her hair. 'So, we're out of here tonight. Until I can talk to the police in Brisbane, we're going to hide in a safe spot I know. It's going to be tricky getting in there with the tide now, but I think we'll be right.'

To Liv's relief, the trip across the Passage was fast and smooth. Fynn hoisted the sails as soon as he'd slipped the mooring, and the boat flew silently across the water. If there had been no concern about Greg, or a fear that someone was watching them, it would have been magical. As they approached the dark shape of Whitsunday Island ahead, the sky brightened and Fynn made his way along the deck to where Liv was sitting on the roof of the cabin below.

'Come over to the helm with me, this is going to be pretty spectacular.' His voice was low. Jill had texted to say there had been an improvement, and Greg's condition had been downgraded to stable. Still a concern, but the test results had shown the prognosis for his recovery was good.

Liv followed Fynn to the stern and stood beside him as she steered them along the western coast of Whitsunday Island. The sky brightened until a silver sheen danced on the water and she looked from the water to the sky. The light was so bright she could see the trees on the island, even though the moon had not yet crested the hill.

'Almost.' Fynn reached for her hand and held it. Liv drew a breath as the edge of the moon peeked over the hill ahead of them. As she watched, the huge orb rose, a deep yellow ball moving quickly into the sky above the tree line. As it rose higher, the moon turned silver and the sea beside them took on an eerie blue hue. The rays were so bright making a path to the water Liv could imagine them touching her skin.

Fynn turned his head to hers. His lips brushed her forehead and serenity filled her. She put her arms around his waist and looked up at him. His eyes were shadowed in the moonlight, his brow was furrowed with worry.

'It's going to be okay,' she whispered. 'Greg's improving. We're safe and we have the computer.'

We can deal with it.

'We'll deal with it, whatever happens.' Fynn's whisper echoed her thoughts.

'Whatever happens,' she repeated.

Liv lifted her face and time stood still as he lowered his head, until his warm breath fanned her lips. He slipped his hand beneath her loose top and splayed his fingers on the bare skin of her back, pulling her closer. A delicious shiver raised the hairs on Liv's neck as his lips held hers. A surge of desire spiralled through Liv and settled low in her belly as he deepened the kiss, but eventually Fynn pulled back.

'We'll explore this later.' His voice was low and held a promise.

Liv nodded as his eyes held hers. 'We will.'

He looped an arm around her shoulder and held her close, his chin resting on top of her head as he steered them towards their sanctuary.

*　*　*

It was after midnight by the time they were ready to look at the folders Liv had downloaded. She removed the SIM card from the laptop and Fynn turned his router off.

'I'll see if I can get any network service on my phone, just to make doubly sure there's no internet service that would let them see your computer come online.' He held his phone up and clicked away before he grunted with satisfaction. 'No service at all.'

'So, all right to boot up?' she asked with her eyebrows raised.

'Right to go.' Fynn nodded and slid into the seat beside her.

Before motoring into the bay, he'd lowered the sails and waited until the tide was rising before he steered *Footprint* carefully into Gulnare Inlet, keeping an eye on the chart spread out beside him, and the wind speed and depth indicator. Even at full tide, there were still a few shallow spots on the way in. Going through the narrow channel in the dark had been dangerous and he'd breathed a sigh of relief once they were past the reef at the entrance. He'd motored slowly into the Upper Gulnare Inlet and then turned the boat into the small creek that came out at the head of the inlet. It was shallow at half tide and once the tide was dead low, they wouldn't be able to get out, but he had no fear of them being followed to this isolated bay in the middle of the night. Despite that certainty, he'd still kept his eye out on the water as they'd crossed the Passage—and the sky—but there'd been no other vessels or helicopters in sight. Two catamarans were moored in the main inlet of Gulnare, but he knew that it was used as an overnight anchorage as bareboats from the charter companies made their way to the more popular diving spots. He'd sussed them out as he'd quietly motored past.

The laptop screen came on and Liv took a deep breath. 'Ready?'

'Ready and waiting. First thing we'll do is back them up.' He handed her the external hard drive he'd removed from his computer.

He leaned over as the folder copied across so he could see the screen too. On the desktop were a neat row of folders and he smiled to himself; he knew that Liv would be organised. On the far right was a folder labelled 'presentation file', and Liv pointed to that one.

'That's the one Rod sent me the link to. I downloaded it and that's where I chose the wrong presentation from. Look.'

'Who's Rod?' he asked.

'Dad's PR guy.' Then she shook her head. 'The previous one, I mean one of the guys at the meeting was his new one. They don't last very long. Dad is a difficult boss.'

'Interesting,' Fynn mused. 'Maybe you were set up?'

'It *was* a bit fast. Rod had only emailed me the day before Anthony turned up before the meeting and said he was Dad's new PR man. I asked about Rod but he didn't answer me. I didn't give it a thought at the time.'

'So you weren't ever told why the other guy moved on?'

She shook her head. 'I was never told much about what happened in the company.'

'A few things to think about there,' Fynn said thoughtfully. The data transferred quickly, and he unplugged the external drive and put it on the shelf behind the table. Now there was a back-up copy, he felt more secure.

Liv clicked on the folder with the wireless mouse. Within the folder there were a series of other folders with varying names. 'I didn't have a look in any of the others. I was too peed off at Dad's attitude telling me what to do. I downloaded it and then headed off to the *Lady May*.'

'So why did you pick that presentation? It obviously wasn't the one you were supposed to use.'

'The file name was Community Meeting and Monday's date. I had a quick look at the others, but they were all older dates, so I opened that, had a quick look and it was almost identical to the one I already had. I noticed that the new location—Earlando Bay—was on a slide, but Dad had told me on the phone that the new location had been approved on Friday, so nothing seemed wrong to me. He also told me that the rail line had been approved but that *wasn't* in the slides.'

'Are you sure about that approval?'

'Dad said it had. He was really pleased.'

Fynn sat up as alarm bells began to ring for him. 'I can't believe the rail line's been signed off by the traditional landowners. There was massive opposition there, and we were sure that would be the sticking point for the approval.' He let out a low whistle. 'Wait till Greg hears that. Let's have a look at these other folders.'

Liv read the folder names out. 'Earlando Bay, CQRC, John, Pol_ Don, and the last one is called Reimbursements.'

'CQRC will be Central Queensland Regional Council.' Fynn pointed to the folder labelled Reimbursements. 'We'll come back and look at the others one by one.'

Liv clicked on the folder and groaned when it asked for a password. 'Damn, it didn't do that for the Presentations folder.' She typed a password in, but it came up 'incorrect password'.

'Maybe we can't get in after all,' Fynn said. 'Looks like they were panicking about nothing after all.'

Liv turned to him and her smile was devious. 'Don't give up on me yet.'

As he watched, she typed a long string of letters and numbers. She turned to him with a huge smile as the folder opened to reveal a list of spreadsheets and word documents.

'Good guess,' she said. 'I watched Dad type his password last Friday when I was standing behind him, and I memorised it.' She shook her head. 'Would you believe he uses Mum's full name and birth date? They've been divorced for almost twenty years!'

'Clever lady.' He leaned over and dropped a kiss on her cheek, and left his arm around her shoulder as they stared at the screen.

'I had no idea I'd need it so soon.' Liv clicked on the first spreadsheet, and again it was password protected.

'Sure looks like these are highly confidential, doesn't it?' Fynn lifted his head and then sat still as the noise of a motor drifted across the water. He put his finger to his lips and spoke quietly. 'I want you to go down to the cabin and take the hard drive with you.' He closed the laptop and stood. 'Quickly. Lock the door from the inside.'

The sound of the motor outside was getting louder and he switched off the saloon light as Liv hurried downstairs to the cabin, clutching the external drive to her chest. He grabbed a flashlight and went up to the deck and slipped into the shadow of the mast. The moon was bright enough for him to see a small tender crossing the bay. As he watched, it headed to the southern shore, and after a few minutes, a flashlight lit up the mud flats. He let out a sigh of relief and headed below deck and tapped on the cabin door. 'It's okay, Liv. Just some yachties after crabs.'

She took a deep breath and shook her head. 'I cannot believe I'm scared of my own father. It makes me so angry.'

Her eyes were wide, and Fynn couldn't stop himself from reaching out to her. She nestled in his arms and he could feel her heart beating against his chest.

Liv and Fynn had worked into the early hours, opening and reading each document. Her eyes widened as they dug deeper into the files. Fynn shook his head in disbelief as he typed up a series of brief dot points to send to Greg as soon as he was well enough to deal with what they discovered. His satisfaction—and certainty that they could stop the coal loader project approval—grew as the hours passed.

'This is pure gold.' Fynn almost whooped as they read each incriminating document. 'Payoffs, bribes, political donations and expensive holidays for various councillors from more than one regional council in the north.'

Liv shook her head. 'I can't believe my father's audacity. And he thinks he is untouchable. He kept them on the company network!'

'And the dates of the donations to the council are dated after the state government changed the legislation late last year. It was one of the factors that Greg suspected once the corruption commission alleged that councillors were influencing the outcome of council decisions on development applications, but each investigation led to a dead end.' Fynn leaned back and stretched. 'Greg is going to love this. Zenith are dead in the water with the stuff we have here. No wonder they want it back.'

'No wonder my *father* wants it back.' Liv yawned and put her hand over her mouth.

'You look worn out. Why don't you go down and grab some sleep?'

'I don't think I can stay awake any longer.' She nodded and slid out of the seat. 'And I'll sleep in the cabin where you put my bag. It's not fair that I take yours.'

He looked at her for a long moment. 'Fair enough. We could be out here for a while. We'll stay here till Greg is well enough to come up. I've got enough provisions to do us up to a week, but we'll have to go easy on the water. The old girl doesn't hold that much.'

After Liv went below decks Fynn packed up the laptop and put the hard drive in a cupboard in his cabin. He was wired and he knew it was going to be hard to go to his bed, knowing that Liv had slept there. Not to mention the overwhelming temptation of the attraction that he was feeling; it was way out of his experience, but he had decided to take it slow. Liv was beginning to trust him, and she was in his care, and he wouldn't be doing anything to compromise that.

No matter how tempting it is.

He stayed up on deck, leaning against the cushioned seat, and he dozed on and off as the moon crossed the sky. The occasional splash of a fish jumping, and the wail of the stone curlews as they patrolled the mangroves in search of crabs were the only sounds to break the silence. Gradually the clouds turned pink as dawn approached and he stood and stretched.

'Good morning.' Liv's voice was soft and he turned around in surprise.

'I thought you were still asleep.'

'I've been awake for a while. Thinking. Trying not to worry. Planning.' She smiled as she came across to him and put her arms around his neck. 'I just put the kettle on the gas, and I figured out how to light it. I'm getting used to this boat living.'

'That's good.' He dropped his head and brushed his lips over her cheek.

'Would you like me to bring you up a coffee?'

'Yes, please, and grab some shoes. We're going to take a walk.'

Fynn went below decks and brought up the external drive, wondering where to put it so it would be safe. As he stared across the mangroves, an idea came to him. It might seem over the top, but from the events of the past few days, he wouldn't put anything past Sheridan Corp. It was only a matter of time until they crossed paths.

As they sipped their coffee up on deck, Fynn pointed to the shore. 'See the bird in the shallows? He's a white-faced heron and he's getting his breakfast. And over there on the beach you can see a couple of ruddy turnstones.'

Liv shook her head and smiled at him over the rim of her coffee cup. 'How do you remember all the names?'

Fynn shrugged. 'I guess because I've always been out here. Being part of this landscape is as necessary to me as breathing.' He regretted his words as her expression tightened.

'It's something that's sadly lacking in my life. Now, anyway. I used to love going out to my grandparents' farm but all that stopped once I started university, and then for the last eight years, I've been trapped on the bloody corporate treadmill. I've really lost sight of what's in life. Spreadsheets, projections, data analysis. It's all artificial and it can be made to justify whatever we want.'

'We certainly saw that in those files.' Fynn nodded, his eyes intent on Liv's face as she kept talking. Her cheeks were flushed and her eyes were bright.

'It's been even more of an eye opener for me and I'm determined to take the company on. You know, I was hoping it was Zenith that was behind the corruption, but those letters to the guy on the council were signed by Dad.'

'And the donations to the council were from his personal account. Byron's going to be very interested in all of this.'

'You know, at uni I had a close friend, and like everything else, I've lost touch with Bec since I've been working for Sheridan Corp. Bec used to say that everything happens for a reason, that we're all on a journey and grow through our experiences. We used to joke with her and say it was all the spirituality stuff she was into.' Liv put her cup on the deck and stood before she came over and sat beside him. 'So, I'm going to be honest. I've been kidding myself for too long. I came up here to do a job, but if I go with Bec's idea that there was another purpose for me coming here, I'll just accept it.

'My father might have sent me up here to carry out his dirty work, whatever it is, while he had his bribes and corrupt behaviour going on in the background, but there have been so many more positives that have come out of this experience for me. Maybe I've been able to help Aunty Tat be a little bit happier, thinking she's found her sister.' She dropped her gaze and her cheeks became a little pinker. 'And I've enjoyed meeting you, Fynn. And I've learned that you can trust someone by following your heart.'

She lifted her head and the look that they shared was intense.

When she looked away, he stood and held out his hand. 'Come on, put your shoes on. We're going for a ride.'

He pulled her up and Liv put her arms around him. 'Thank you, Fynn. For keeping me safe. I really appreciate what you're doing for me.'

His voice was sombre. 'It's not over yet. Once Greg's better, we still have a lot of work to do. Don't think that the exposure of what's going on will automatically stop them. They'll fight every inch of the way. You can see what they've done already. How many unlikely people do they have in their pocket? I know John Blumer, and I always thought he was a decent bloke.' Fynn undid the ropes on the tender and lowered it into the creek.

'Greed can be a strong motivator,' Liv said as she stepped down and settled on the front seat. He swung himself down to the boat and started the motor.

'We could go ashore here, but I want to go out through the bay and see if the two boats that were there have gone.'

The motor puttered as he steered them across the first semi-enclosed bay. Fynn nodded with satisfaction as they entered the wider bay of Gulnare Inlet. There were no boats there.

The tide was ebbing now, but the wind was with them as they left the inlet and motored along, close to the shore. As they reached the rocky headland, he turned the boat into the beach on the other side. Liv watched as he tucked a parcel inside his shirt and stepped into the knee-deep water.

'No Irukandji here?' Her grin was cheeky.

'Not this time of the year. Would you like me to lift you out?'

She waved a dismissive hand. 'I'll be fine, thank you, captain.'

'This is Sawmill Beach.' He pointed to the southern end. 'Just on the edge of the beach there, you can see the pylons of an old jetty. It was where the Ellises used to moor their boats. Aunty Tat grew up in a house up on the hill.'

The pathway was overgrown. It was years since he'd been here with Byron but Fynn was hoping the old shed was still there. They reached the clearing at the top of the path and he pointed to the top. 'There's your two hills from a different vantage point.'

Liv frowned and shook her head. 'I must have seen them on TV.'

Fynn strode over to the old stone shed near the ruins of the house. 'This was where they used to keep their food cold. I thought it would still be standing.' Only a few stumps of the house remained, and a few fence posts showed where the house yard once ended.

'It's so sad, isn't it?' Liv walked along behind him. 'To think a family once lived here. And now this is all that's left. Ruins and Aunty Tat's memories.' She turned to look at the water. 'What a beautiful view to look at each day. I'd never get sick of it.'

Fynn pushed open the door of the old shed. Liv went to follow him but stopped in the doorway. 'Ergh. Too many cobwebs! What are you doing anyway?'

'It might be overkill, but if anyone comes looking for your computer, we can safely hand it over.' He pulled the waterproof bag from inside his shirt and held it up. 'I'm going to put the external drive in here. We'll leave it here for as long as needed. I'm sure it will be quite secure.'

'Seeing you've backed it up, what do you think of me calling my father and saying I am going to send the computer back? Maybe that would stop whoever it is trying to get it.'

'I think that's a good idea. We'll stay here for a couple of days and then go around to Hamo. I've got a sat phone on board and I'll call Jill later to see how Greg is, but I don't want to give Sheridan Corp any idea of where you are.'

'Sounds good to me.'

As they walked down towards the boat, Fynn reached for her hand. *Slowly. Slowly.*

CHAPTER
29

July 16, 1942

High-tailed and wide-winged, Catalinas flew roughly at the same slow speed as they climbed and landed. Jack lay back in the passage next to the blister turret trying to sleep, but the thoughts whirling through his head kept him awake. They had finished their run and *Dumbo* was making the slow and ponderous journey back to Bowen. That night, they had covered a cruiser and two Japanese destroyers, and dropped flame floats at the bow of the cruiser.

'Take that, ya bastard.' Megsy and Jack had grinned at each other as Eric, the LAC manning the turret, had dropped the first flame float. As they peered down, the fluorescence from the float lit up the wake from the churning propellers in the sea beneath them. Their job was done. They'd located the Japanese naval vessels by a square search plotted by Jack that night and made the cruiser a ready target for the Liberator bombers not far behind *Dumbo*.

The sporadic anti-aircraft fire from the destroyers hadn't reached them, and Jack knew it was a miracle that there'd been no Japanese fighters in the vicinity. Armed only with the .30 calibre machine guns, they had no chance against the speedy Zeros. Since January, the Nips had taken Rabaul, New Britain and New Ireland and those locations had now become the main targets for Squadrons 11 and 20 out of Bowen.

Megsy had tapped his shoulder about an hour ago as they had reached the point of no return and turned back to base. 'I'll take over watch while you get some shut-eye, mate.'

'Thanks, Megs.'

Usually, once they were on the way home, Jack's anxiety faded as he focused on his responsibilities; plotting the drop zone, and recording accurate and detailed records of the flight and knowing the danger was behind them, and he had survived another mission. But he couldn't settle tonight. His thoughts were full of Liliana and the guilt he'd carried since he'd left her at the island.

He loved her, but Jack knew he should have resisted the temptation in the cave. It hadn't been the right thing to do, no matter how willing she had been. Worrying about the consequences, he'd set aside some money and a letter for Liliana, leaving it in a prominent position on the bureau in his room at Mrs Atkins' house.

He remembered how he'd once reassured her that his brief was reconnaissance and transport. If he'd told her the truth about shadowing the Japanese fleet and timing mine releases on mine-lay runs, it would have worried her so much, knowing how close the Nips were getting to the mainland of Australia.

Wing Commander Butler had called the squadron crews into the briefing room yesterday, not long after they had disembarked from the steamer bringing them back to base from Whitsunday Island. The wing commander's voice was more sombre than usual. 'The war in the south-west Pacific is intensifying. All leave has been cancelled for now. You'll be going out more frequently, men, as we try to locate the Japanese fleet in the Coral Sea.'

As soon as he got his next leave—and that looked as though it could be a long time away—he would go down to the island. Why wait until the war was over to get married? The way the Japs were taking over the Pacific, the war could go on for years, and Jack's fear that he wouldn't survive was with him constantly. As soon as he could, he would speak to Boyd. Lily would be seventeen at the end of July, and he could promise her a good life wherever they chose to settle.

Coming to a decision eased his anxiety, and Jack pulled down his jacket and rolled it beneath his head as he yawned.

'Wake up, mate.'

Jack pushed himself out of a restless sleep as Megsy shook him. He frowned as he sat up and rubbed his eyes; the note of the engines was different. 'Are we landing already?'

Megsy's voice was flat. 'Yeah, we're stopping at Horn Island to refuel. We have to go back out to the Palau Islands.'

'What for?' Jack asked.

'Don't know. Captain said he'd fill us in when we got there.'

'Damn. The Japs will be active once the Liberators finish that bombing run, and it's getting light.'

'I know. I don't like the feel of this.' Megsy pulled a small dog-eared photo from his shirt pocket and stared at it.

'What's that you've got there?' Jack leaned forward in the dim light.

'My boys.' Megsy handed the photo over and Jack stared at the photograph for a moment before passing it back. Two rosy-cheeked children, a toddler and a baby, smiled at the camera.

'It makes you think about why we're up here, doesn't it?' Jack said.

'It does. It's worth it. Every minute of it. And we just have to keep the faith we'll survive.' Megsy put the photo carefully back into his pocket and buttoned it up.

The two men exchanged a long look, no more words were necessary. They both knew how many of the Cats had been shot down over the past month.

As they got closer to their destination, *Dumbo* descended, and Jack knew something was happening, as for the last two and a half hours they had flown only fifty feet above the sea. They were so low, the moonlight flashing off the waves had an almost hypnotic effect on him as he stared down through the observation window. He prayed that whichever of the three pilots was in charge of the cockpit knew what he was doing. A short while later, Captain Munford climbed over the metal barrier to the turret and squatted beside them.

'How's it going back here, men?' His voice was jovial but there was no accompanying smile.

'Good, sir.' Megsy gestured to the sea not far below them. 'What's going on?'

'Jack, I want you to work out exactly how much fuel we need to get back to Horn Island—the absolute bare minimum. We've got a big payload to pick up on Peleliu Island and we need to be as light as we possibly can.'

'Payload, sir?' Jack asked.

'Eight men to pick up. It's going to be a crowded and uncomfortable trip home,' Captain Munford said. 'I'll be taking the controls for take off. We need to jettison as much as we can, and quickly. Fuel and ammunition to counter balance the extra weight we'll be taking on.'

'Yes, sir.'

'Let me know as soon as you do the calculation.' The captain stood and lowered his head as he ducked beneath the bulkhead. 'We're about ten minutes from landing.'

Jack opened the log book and turned to a blank page, working out distances and fuel calculations. By the time he had the required figure, the note of the engine changed as the pilot throttled back. He walked past the radio operator and up to the lower cockpit.

'Done, cap—'

The urgent voice of the other observer interrupted him. 'Captain! There's a Jap sub lying broadside in the middle of the bay. Straight in the middle of our landing run. Abort?'

'No. We'll stall her and drop.' Captain Munford's voice stayed calm despite the tension in the cockpit. Jack didn't look down as he stood waiting. Ice filled his veins as he waited. The pilot's hands were white on the controls.

'How much can I jettison, Jack?' The captain turned to him.

Jack quickly gave the figures to the captain as the other pilot brought *Dumbo* in low over the submarine, stalled the engine and dropped down in a whirl of spray. Jack reached for the metal wall and hung on as the flying boat bobbed to a stop on the choppy water. Ahead were two dinghies, each carrying four men.

'Get that anchor out,' the captain said quietly. 'Otherwise those poor buggers'll have no chance against the slipstream. And worse still, the Nips know they're there waiting for us now. We have to move fast.' His quiet and controlled instructions sent a measure of calm through the crew as each carried out his assigned tasks to secure the Cat. As they waited for the men to paddle alongside in the two dinghies, everyone was silent. The newcomers climbed into the Cat one by one. The men were told of the enemy nearby before the dinghies were slashed with a knife and allowed to sink.

'Cut the anchor line too,' Captain Munford commanded as he took over the controls in the cockpit. 'We don't have time to pull it up. Everything unnecessary, ditch it now, over the side.'

The engines roared and the Cat taxied away from the submarine. The bunk area and the blister compartments were crowded with the extra men and Jack stayed in the cockpit. He would go back to his observation post once they were airborne.

If they could get airborne with all that weight.

The sky was bright pink as the sun cleared the horizon and Jack swallowed as the top of the submarine glinted in the early morning sunlight. His stomach was roiling and bile touched the base of his throat. The engines thundered as the overloaded flying boat strained desperately, trying to clear the water.

'A few degrees to port.' Jack was close enough to hear the captain's quiet order.

The control column was hard back, and the captain gunned the engine to full throttle in an attempt to get the nose up, but the weight on board was too heavy. 'Get rid of some more fuel before I come around,' he yelled this time. All Jack could think of was the submarine sending a torpedo in their direction.

Minutes later, they were off again at full throttle. Jack could hear the flight engineer pleading with the captain to reduce power because the engines were overheating. Jack kept his eyes on the dials that the flight engineer was staring at. The needles were well into the red; there was obviously a problem.

What would be the least painful way to die? A crash or a torpedo? All of the flight crew were white-faced and white-knuckled, but the captain kept going, and finally after a couple of tail clips and a final bump, the plane was airborne and he throttled back. The submarine below quickly became a speck in the distance as a cheer went up through the plane.

'Thank you, gentlemen. It's going to be a slow trip back to Horn to refuel. I'll have to take it slow with such a low fuel load over the distance. Back to observation posts.' Captain Munford dismissed them with a nod. 'Extra vigilance as the enemy will certainly know where we are.'

Jack made his way to the blister turret. Three of the men they'd picked up were sitting silently, their backs against the metal wall. He nodded as he leaned down to the narrow observation window beside them. There was no point speaking with the roar of the engines in the confined space. The Cat banked as the captain took them lower over the island of Southern Peleliu.

Sitting on the narrow metal bench in the Black Cat, Jack froze as he peered down at the water below, always on the lookout for the small Zeros. The nightmare of the war returned in full force.

Silhouetted against the golden-red ball of sun that hovered over the eastern horizon, four Japanese Zeros dropped out of the red flame as they flew towards *Dumbo* in perfect formation.

Jack craned forward and caught a flash of dull green wings with red rising suns and the pilots in black helmets. Bullets ripped through the fuselage of the plane and horror filled Jack as a burst of blood sprayed from the man in the turret beside him. The aircraft slewed to one side as a burst of fire from the Zero tore the starboard engine apart, pieces of the engine exploding in a ball of flame. The captain struggled to keep control, but it was useless.

'Grab something and hang on, boys. We're going in.'

CHAPTER
30

July 18, 1942

Almost two months had passed since Jack's last leave, and Lily became more listless every day. There was no word from Jack, and no smiling face greeting her on the launch as she waited for him to arrive each time the mail launch came in. No visits from anyone on the base, and to top it all off, there had been no newspapers on the mail launch for a few weeks.

On the morning of her seventeenth birthday, Lily waited on the jetty for the Catalina to return. As the sky lightened with the first pink flush of the autumn dawn on the third morning, she'd pulled on her shoes and run down to the jetty in her pyjamas. Three nights ago, when she had lain in bed the flying boat had roared over the island on its trip north into a danger that her imagination now imbued with all sorts of dreadful possibilities, she'd squeezed her eyes shut but still the tears had run down her cheeks. It had taken her till the early hours to fall asleep as she held Jack's face in her thoughts, and worried about how he was feeling, what he was doing, and if he was safe.

'No news is good news, Lil,' Dad had reassured her yesterday. 'If anything had happened, we would have heard about it down here.'

Last week the plane had roared over each night and returned each morning, but for three days, she had waited on the jetty, and for three mornings, the sky had been empty.

The occasional splash of fish breaking the silvery surface of the calm water was her only company this morning until Tatiana wandered down.

'Happy birthday, Lil. Mama said to come up when you're ready. She's making fried bread, your favourite.'

'Thank you.' She held her cheek up for Tat's kiss. 'I'll come up in a while.'

'Good. I'll have a quick dip.'

Even in July in the tropics, the mornings were warm, even though the grey sky was heavy with threatening rain. Lily clenched her fingers as she strained to hear the distant roar of the engine as it approached the Passage.

Waiting. Waiting.

She counted slowly in her head, blocking out Tat's incessant chatter as she dived off the jetty, swam around to the end, climbed out and then dived back in, bombarding Lily with questions that she couldn't answer. Roger this, Charlie that. When were the boys going to come back and visit them?

Tat's voice was like an incessant buzz in Lily's head and she closed her eyes. The welcome splash as Tat dived off the jetty guaranteed at least one minute of silence as she swam around to the other side.

'Do you think they'll be here this weekend?'

Liliana jumped as Tat dropped water onto her face as she flicked her wet hair over her shoulder.

'Oh for God's sake, Tatiana, put a sock in it and bloody shut up.'

'I'll tell Mama you swore.'

'I don't care. Bloody grow up.' Lily stood and slipped on her canvas sandshoes. The thought of Jack being caught somewhere out in the ocean, entombed in that metal tube, combined with the hot sun on her bare head was making her dizzy. She gagged and ran to the end of the jetty, holding her stomach as she leaned over the bush.

'Oh, Lil. I'm sorry. I didn't mean to upset you.' Tatiana caught up to her and put a gentle hand on her shoulder. 'Here, take my towel and wipe your face.'

'Thank you.' Lily raised a shaking hand to her face. Her head was still spinning, and she was seeing stars. She'd sat out in the hot sun for too long.

Hot tears slipped from her eyes and she swiped at her cheeks with the towel. 'I'm scared, Tat. I don't know if they've come back. Where are they? Where's Jack?'

Once she let the tears fall, they turned into sobs. Tat held her hand tightly as they made their way back up to the house as the sun climbed high and the water of the Passage shimmered.

Lily crawled further into her shell as the weeks passed. She didn't know what was worse. Had Jack been killed? Or was he up in Bowen and had he just decided he didn't want to visit anymore? It was her punishment for what she'd done with him in Goat's cave on the night of the storm.

On a clear night on the first day of August, the Ellis family sat together on the verandah, watching the sun set over the mainland. The sky was painted in purples and mauves, and as the sun dipped behind the hills, an arc of gold bathed the clouds in an almost celestial light. Mama was sewing buttons back onto the twins' shirts.

'Come and sit by me, Lil.'

She crossed the verandah and sat on the mat in front of her mother's chair. Leaning against Mama's knee, Lily closed her eyes as Mama gently brushed her hand against her hair. 'I pray every night for your Jack and that the war will be over soon.'

My Jack.

It was the first time that Mama had acknowledged that she knew how Lily felt.

'I worry that he has gone.' She stared at the sky as Mama's hand caressed her hair. 'That he's dead. Or he doesn't want to come back here.'

'Lil, it's wartime. Communication is difficult. Since the air battles over the Coral Sea, I'm sure there's no leave for the boys and no time for them to write. Stop worrying yourself so sick.'

'Your mother is right.' Dad looked up from his whittling and smiled at her. 'It'll be all right. Before you know it, the three boys will be back for a visit.'

Lily looked up at him and she knew he didn't believe his own words.

'You are fading away, darling.' Mama turned to Dad. 'I think it is time that Lil stopped working over with the Bauers. It's too much for her.'

'No.' Lily shook her head. 'It gives me something else to think about it.' Going to South Molle Island to work was her escape. Lily knew she was being dishonest, but she was terrified that Mama would guess the other worry that was consuming her day and night. Last month, she had washed the linen rags that she always used when she bled, although there had been no need. Mama would have noticed if she hadn't.

On a Monday morning two weeks later, Lily was in the wash house lighting the fire beneath the copper when Tat's cries reached her. She had stopped going down to the jetty each morning; the disappointment when the launch had docked at the jetty time and time again with no one on it, no smiling face to greet her had become unbearable.

'Lily! Lily! The boys are here.' Tat's voice was shrill with excitement. 'Come quickly.'

Lily threw the taper to the dirt floor and ran to the path, her heart beating hard as joy flooded through her.

Oh, God. Thank you, God. At least one of her prayers had been answered. And if her other prayer remained unanswered—if the curse didn't arrive this week—at least she could tell Jack her fears and share her worry that she was pregnant with his child.

Dad was already down there unloading the crates of supplies from the launch. Roger and Charlie stood beside Tatiana. For the first time, they were wearing their air force uniforms and were looking very grown-up and serious.

Lily ran along the jetty, her eyes darting from the boat to the men. 'Jack? Where's Jack?'

As Roger stepped forward, Dad walked over to Lily and put his hand on her shoulder.

Lily looked at Tat, and noticed the tears streaking down her face.

'What is it? Where's Jack? Why isn't he here too?' She barely managed to get the words out as her breath caught and the heavy weight of grief crushed her chest.

Dad's arm went around her as Roger stood in front of her. His stance was respectful, almost formal. 'On the sixteenth of July, the radio operator from the Cat that Jack was on reported that the Catalina was under attack in the Mariana Islands by anti-aircraft fire. The crew had reported a submarine, but managed to avoid any action. They left Peleliu Island and headed home.'

Hope filtered through Lily for a brief moment until she saw the bleakness in Roger's eyes. Charlie stepped forward clutching a small parcel tied with string.

'After it took off, they broke radio silence with a standard signal. "We are forced to alight on the sea." *Dumbo* failed to return to base the next morning. It is believed that the Cat has been shot down over the Mariana Islands and the fate of the crew is unknown.' His voice was formal. 'We've waited for confirmation but there's been nothing. We knew we had to come and tell you ourselves. Your family was so good to Jack, and to us.'

'No. Please no.' Dad supported Lily as disbelief slammed through her. 'Maybe they just landed somewhere and stayed there?'

'I'm sorry, Lily. I know that you and Jack were really good friends. He left this for you...' Charlie's voice shook as he held out the small package and put it into her hand. 'In case he didn't come back.'

Roger took her hand. 'Lily, never ever give up hope. We know there are thousands of prisoners of war out there, and the Allies are doing their damnedest to end this war in the Pacific. Since the air raids on Townsville—'

'Townsville?' Lily's voice was shrill. 'What air raids?'

Roger and Charlie looked at each other. 'You haven't had the news this week?'

'No.' Boyd shook his head. 'We've not been over to the mainland for a couple of weeks.'

'Townsville's been bombed. Three air raids. The last one only four days ago.'

Lily drew a breath so quickly that she almost choked. 'Townsville, that's not far north.' She leaned against Dad as he held her close. Even Tat's eyes were wide and her lip quivered.

'Are the Japanese going to come to our island. Daddy, what will we do?' Tat grabbed his arm. 'Where will we hide if they come?'

Boyd put his other arm around Tat and held both his daughters close. The lump in Lily's throat was making it hard to breathe.

'Stay strong and believe that Jack is ... alive. Until we hear otherwise, we will believe.' Roger stepped back and turned away from them, but his shoulders were shaking.

Lily held her head high and straightened her back, ignoring the pain that was slicing through her. Not only from the despair that settled in her chest but a physical pain as her belly cramped as it did every month.

How ironic that this news came at the same moment that her other prayer was answered. Dad's arm was firm around her shoulders, but she pulled away and straightened her back.

'Thank you, Charlie and Roger. Would you like to come up to the house for a cup of tea? I know Mama was baking this morning. She must have had an inkling that we would have guests. We don't get many these days.' While ever she could keep the conversation normal, Lily was determined not to break down. She slid the small parcel into her pocket and turned towards the path. Tatiana slipped her hand into hers, and she gave a sad smile as her heart shattered into a thousand pieces.

★ ★ ★

A soft and mauve dawn crept over the eastern horizon as Lily made her way to an inlet on the leeward side of the island. A small creek wound across to the east before it petered out into a swamp. Its banks were a dense mass of vegetation, but where it met the sea, a large flat rock was exposed on the ebb tide.

She sat there silently on her rock, and waited.

Yesterday's cramp had been nothing, and the sad realisation that her life was about to change made her physically ill. The harsh bitterness that consumed her was like one of the box jellyfish that Jack hadn't known about. She hitched a sob and blocked him from her mind.

None too soon, dawn flooded the eastern sky. The inner islands of the Whitsundays hovered like jewels above a pearl-like sea as the low clouds turned golden. The sun rose higher as she sat and wondered what to do.

How can I tell Mama?

They would send her away, and she didn't think she could stand that. The wind picked up and the blustering breeze caught her hair in a swirl. She vowed never to forget the blue of the sea, the gold of the sky and the smell of the salt that morning. Sadness filled her as she feared that she would only remember the evil-smelling mud, banked up day by day by each incoming tide, coating the ugly roots of the mangrove trees on the banks of the creek, and covering the new green shoots of life. The haunting cry of the curlew, the lament that was a portent of death, echoed her sadness. The first time she'd heard a curlew cry, that high-pitched lament, she had been four years old and she had cried with it. Mama had lifted her onto her knee and soothed her. 'Hush, Liliana, it is only a bird.'

Regret for what might have been flooded through her, fed by her grief. As she looked up at the sky, now bathed in the pearly light of a Whitsunday dawn, the peak loomed above her, still dark and shadowy on its leeward side.

Lily stared at it and pushed herself to her feet. Up there, closer to the sky, was where Jack had last flown over the island. With determination, she made her way around the bay and headed for the path past the old sawmill. She would climb the peak, and she would say goodbye to him.

CHAPTER
31

May 7, 2018

'We're going to have to go across to Hamo tomorrow,' Fynn said late one afternoon as Liv lay in the hammock he'd strung up on the deck. 'We're almost out of water.'

'It should be safe now, surely?' Liv frowned. No one knew where she was, or that she was on Fynn's yacht. They—whoever *they* were—would have no idea where to look for her.

He shrugged as he looked across at her. 'We'll still need to be careful. They've probably been watching the airport.'

They'd spent a week moored in Upper Gulnare Inlet. A call made last night from Fynn's sat phone had garnered the information that Greg was back in a general ward. Fynn had texted the points he'd taken from the folders, and Greg had replied almost immediately.

As soon as I am discharged I'm on a flight up. Saturday probably. Not even a broken leg will stop me.

'Watch the airport? Do you really think they'd go to those lengths? It sounds like something out of a movie.'

'Ask Greg's opinion on that when he gets here.' He looked up at her from where he was leaning with his back against the side of the boat. 'There's millions—no, billions—of dollars to be made if the coal loader is approved. They've already demonstrated that they'll do anything to stop that information getting out there. Until Greg's exposé is published, we'll keep a very low profile. Once we get to Hamo, you can call your father and send the computer back to him. Hopefully, that'll take the pressure off you.'

'It'll be interesting to hear what he has to say.' Liv put her head back and looked out over the water. 'I'll give Mum a call too. She'll be worrying.'

Fynn put his hands behind his head, tipped his head back and closed his eyes. It was still hard to believe that she'd spent the past five days out on his yacht with him.

'Thank goodness Greg's okay.' Liv ran her hand through her loose hair. It was stiff with salt and her skin was tinged pink with sunburn, but she was happier than she'd been for a long time. Her confidence had increased as the days passed, and the time spent with Fynn had been stimulating. He was an intelligent man with strong principles, and she had learned to trust him.

They'd spent the week exploring the island, climbing Whitsunday Peak yesterday morning. The day before, they'd hiked across the island to Whitehaven Beach.

They'd come across the workings of an abandoned sawmill in the bush, and Fynn had examined the rusted equipment with interest. 'It's amazing how they got those huge pine logs down from the steep hills in the days before chain saws.'

'It was a whole different life back then, wasn't it?' She glanced at Fynn curiously as he held his hand out for hers but before she could take it, he'd dropped it again. Seeing the places where Aunty Tat had spent her childhood in the war years had been sad.

'It was.' Fynn held a branch back as she ducked her head. 'A hard life with no luxuries.'

Liv had stumbled as she stubbed her toe on a log and Fynn had caught her and held her close for a minute and then let her go. It was like being a teenager again, this dance of 'will he' or 'won't he'.

Liv bit back a smile as she looked at him now. He certainly was a fine-looking man, and a decent man too. She'd sensed his withdrawal over the past few days. Not in his conversation, but Fynn had seemed more careful not to brush against her, and had kept more physical space between them.

She jumped out of the hammock. 'I'm going for a swim. You coming?'

Fynn opened his eyes and his smile was lazy. 'You go first. I'll come in when I summon up the energy.'

★   ★   ★

Fynn tried not to stare as Liv stood and peeled her T-shirt off to reveal her brief white bikini. Her skin had taken on a rich coppery glow over the past few days, and his mouth dried as he caught a glimpse of the small piece of jewellery in her belly button. It was a very different Liv from the terse corporate woman he'd encountered that first day. He closed his eyes and pulled his cap over his eyes again so she wouldn't catch him staring.

'Tell me what the water's like,' he murmured.

He opened his eyes and sat up once he heard the splash of her entering the water. Pushing himself to his feet he leaned on the side of the boat and watched as she swam towards the small sandy bay at the side of the inlet. She waded into the shallows and wandered along the shoreline, bending occasionally to pick up something and examine it.

Spending a whole week in the company of an attractive woman was something he hadn't done for a long time, but as he watched Liv walk along the edge of the water, Fynn admitted to himself that his feelings for Olivia Sheridan were growing by the day. He narrowed his eyes as a low squeal reached him. She ran to the water and waded out before she began to swim quickly back to the yacht. Without hesitation, he pulled off his T-shirt and dived off the side. It only took a few strokes before he reached her.

'What's wrong? Did you see someone?' Fynn reached out and held her as they both trod water.

She shook her head and water droplets flew from her hair as a giggle erupted from her lips. 'No. I heard a noise and when I looked up there was this huge black goat behind the rock I was heading for. I wasn't going to hang around to say hello.' Liv lifted her arms and looped them around his neck. 'Did you come to rescue me?' Her eyes held his and a shaft of need hit him in the solar plexus.

'I did.' A low groan came from his chest as she moved her head closer to his while she still held his eyes. 'What are you doing, Liv?'

'Thanking my rescuer.'

Cool soft lips brushed against his, and all Fynn's good intentions dissolved like the vapour trails in the sky above them. As she kissed him, they sank beneath the water and he felt her lips tilt in a smile when the water closed over their heads. He kicked hard and they broke the surface.

'My pleasure, darlin'.'

* * *

As they prepared dinner together in the galley that evening, the air was charged with sexual tension. Liv stood closer to him than she usually did, and a couple of times, Fynn put his arm around her when she stood beside him.

'Our last night on the water,' she said wistfully. 'I guess we'll go back to the mainland after we go to Hamo?'

'Depends when Greg flies in. Once we get into phone range at Hamo, I'll give Byron a call too. Just to make sure it looks safe.'

Later that night as they lay on the deck, it seemed natural for Fynn to put his arm out. Liv nestled her head against his shoulder as they watched the stars. A meteorite flashed through the sky and split into a shower of sparks over the Passage.

'It's going to be so hard to go back to the land. Back to real life,' she murmured. 'I feel like I've been in a magic place for the past week.'

'You don't have to be a landlubber. It'd make a lot of sense for you to stay with me on the boat if we're going to be working together.'

She rolled to her side and he looked down. Her eyes were bright in the dim light. 'Would that be all right, do you think?'

As he lowered his lips to hers, he said quietly, 'I think it would be just fine.'

*   *   *

Sharing the same cabin meant that they got a much later start the next morning, although Fynn assured Liv that he'd only slept in because he was waiting for the tide to rise. As he climbed out of bed—reluctantly—she put on a mock pout and fluttered her eyelashes at him.

'You do wonders for a girl's confidence.'

'Come on, wench. It's time to help me hoist the sails.'

He waited as Liv climbed out of bed and he pulled her close. Her skin was warm against his chest and he nuzzled his lips into her neck. 'Are you nervous about heading back to civilisation?'

'No. I'm looking forward to starting this fight. Maybe we could have stayed on the mainland and got a head start.'

'Better to be safe than sorry.' Fynn trailed his fingers down her bare back and glanced back at the bed. 'Maybe we should rest a little more to store up some energy.'

'I thought you were in a hurry to get going.' Her smile was enticing as she moved away and her breasts brushed lightly against his chest.

Reluctantly he reached for his shorts. 'Yeah, I guess the tide won't wait.'

The wind was only light, so they hoisted the headsail and the main before motoring out of Gulnare on the rising tide. As they turned towards Hamilton Island, Fynn cut the engines.

Liv went to the cabin and brought her phone up as they approached the island. As soon as she turned it on, the messages began to ding.

'Your father?' he asked with a frown.

'Most of them but I'm going to ignore his texts.' She nodded towards the screen. 'But poor Mum wants to know where I've been. I'll call her now.'

'Hang on. Is it your own phone or a work phone?'

Her eyes were wide. 'A Sheridan Corp phone.'

'Damn. Turn it off in case they have a track on it.'

'Really?' Her brow furrowed as she switched it off.

'Yeah. I didn't think.' Fynn clenched his hands on the wheel. 'You can send your mother a text from my phone. And maybe email your father and say you'll courier the laptop back.'

'It'll be fine.' She darted a nervous look his way. 'Won't it?'

Fynn radioed the harbourmaster for a berth and as soon as they were allocated one, he motored into the marina, pleased to see they had the end berth at the last finger wharf.

'Just to be on the safe side, you go down to the cabin while I head into the marina. Call your mum. My phone's on the cupboard next to the bed.'

Liv disappeared below deck and he motored into the channel, his eyes scanning the public mooring looking for anything out of the ordinary.

It didn't take long to fill the water tanks and as soon as he was done, Fynn called up the marina office on the radio to charge the berth to his account. He didn't want to leave the boat or let Liv out of his sight. He started the motor and eased the boat back into the channel. Once they were a few hundred metres off the island, he hoisted the main sail and then called down below.

'Come back up now. All clear. Can you bring my phone up too please?'

Liv came up and crossed the deck. She stood next to him looking across at Hamo.

'Mum wasn't too worried. Dad's been hassling her, so she knew I was avoiding him.'

'That's good. I'll call Byron while we've still got service. Can you take the helm? Just keep us in a straight line between the two islands.'

Liv pulled the phone from her pocket and passed it over. Fynn took it and headed to the bow where he could keep an eye ahead while he made the call.

'Gidday, mate.'

'Hey, Fynn. I thought you'd surface soon. Everything okay?'

'More than okay. We've got some information that's going to blow the regional council apart. So much dodgy stuff going on you'll be gobsmacked. And we've got proof. Names, deposits, and dates all set out nicely in a spreadsheet.'

'Is John Blumer involved?'

'Got it in one, mate.'

'Bloody hell, the bastard. What else have you got?'

'A nasty bit of corruption to do with the approval of the rail line route, and a lot of payoffs made there too. It looks like the site relocation to Earlando Bay had more to do with the rail line than any concern for the environment. These bastards seem to think money will buy them whatever support they need. And, By, they got to Greg and put him in hospital.' Fynn glanced back at Liv but she had her eye on the channel ahead. 'He's okay, but I'm worried about Liv's safety.'

'Fuck. Where are you now?'

'Just heading to Chalkies to moor for tonight, and we'll come back to the mainland tomorrow. Greg's hoping to come up on Saturday.'

'Right, mate. Take care.'

Fynn took over the helm but Liv stayed by his side. 'It's okay over there. I told Byron we'd be back tomorrow.'

She stood staring out over the water, the sun playing on her reddish-gold hair, but her expression was sad. He reached out and put his arm around her.

'You okay?'

'Yes. I'm fine.' Her voice was quiet as she leaned into him. Even though Liv was tall, she was a perfect fit against him. 'I guess it's just coming back to reality that's hit me after a week in paradise.'

'You're still in paradise. Go and get comfy on the lounge. We'll have a swim'—he winked at her—'and maybe an afternoon nap after we moor.'

She nudged him with her shoulder. 'Build up our energy, hey?' Her smile was cheeky.

'Nothing like an afternoon nap, I always say.' Fynn let go of the helm and put both arms around Liv as she leaned back against his chest. They stood quietly for a few minutes until she yawned.

'See, I told you you'd need a nap.'

'How about a coffee now?' she asked. 'Now that we've got water again.'

'Sounds good.' Fynn found it hard to take his eyes off her as she went below deck again.

It wasn't long before they were past Plum Pudding Island and as he turned east into Fitzalan Passage, Liv came back up with two cups of coffee and a packet of gingernut biscuits.

'Just as well this is our last day. This is the last of the bikkies,' she said with a smile. Fynn took the cup, pleased to hear her voice back to normal. The wind gusted in and the headsail billowed in the fresh sou' easter. The wind had changed direction since they'd left the marina and he frowned. The tide was still flooding in and Solway Passage might be tricky. He'd seen a yacht under sail spin a full ninety degrees with the whirlpools on the flooding tide bucked by a fresh south-east trade wind.

He peered ahead as they swung into the passage that would take them past Whitehaven Beach. The waves were standing up and he debated whether to use the motor. As the wind pushed them further in, it eased and the waves became smaller. Deciding to stay under sail, he kept a watch on the conditions ahead. Liv came back to stand beside him and he finished his coffee and passed her his cup.

'Is it a bit rough?' she asked nervously.

'It's just the wind against the tide. Once the tide stops flooding, the waves will drop right back, but it's only a short trip around to Chalkies, and out there it will be just a rolling swell.'

Liv turned to take the cups back down to the galley and stopped, staring behind them. 'They're going a bit fast, aren't they?'

Fynn checked ahead before he turned to see what she was talking about. A huge black powerboat was bearing down on them. As he watched, it almost flew above the waves and slammed down on the next swell in a huge spray of white water. 'Power gives way to sail, buddy,' he muttered as the boat came closer. It was directly behind them. It was going to have to bear to the portside to avoid running right over the top of them.

'Bloody hell! Hang on, Liv,' Fynn yelled as he wrenched the wheel to starboard.

The powerboat swerved at the last minute and Fynn swore.

'Shit. You bloody idiots.' He raised his fist as the boat passed so close he could have reached out and touched it.

But instead of roaring past them, the driver flung the boat into a three-sixty turn directly in front of *Footprint*.

'What the fuck are you playing at?' Fynn called out to the man behind the wheel. The sunlight reflected off the windscreen of the powerboat and Fynn put his hand up to shade his eyes as the wash from its wake caught *Footprint* and slewed her around.

The boat tipped precariously, and Liv stumbled. She dropped the cups as she fell to the deck and they rolled along the timber floor to the stern. Clambering back to the side, she pulled herself up as the powerboat roared past between them and the shore.

'Bloody WAFI,' the man beside the driver yelled out with a whoop. Once more, the boat turned and circled them. Once again, *Footprint* was caught in the wash. It was like being caught in a giant whirlpool. As the powerboat roared past and headed back the way it had come, the current caught his yacht. Fynn clenched his jaw and fought with the wheel. She was heading straight for the rocky point at the northern end of Pig Bay.

With a muttered curse and not taking his eye off the rocks ahead, he reached down and started the engine, desperately turning the wheel as his boat drifted closer to the rocks.

'Come on, baby. Come on, you can do it.' At the last minute, the yacht turned and the wind filled the sail. A minute later, they were through the passage and bearing south along Haslewood Island. Fynn glanced across at Liv to check she was okay before he motored around the point and into the sheltered bay at the western end of the beach. She was sitting against the side of the boat with her knees up against her chest, her arms wrapped around them.

He swung the bow into the wind and dropped the sails and lowered the anchor. As soon as the anchor took up, he went across to Liv. Her face was white and her eyes wide. He held out his arms and when she stood Fynn held her close.

'It's okay. We're safe. We made it.'

'What's a WAFI?' she asked as she looked up at him.

Fynn grimaced. 'It's what the powerboaters call a sailor. It stands for "wind-assisted fucking idiot". It normally makes me smile, but not today. His reckless behaviour could have had us on the rocks. I was so busy trying to stay off them I didn't even get the name of the boat.'

'That guy with the sunglasses. It was the same guy.' Liv's voice shook.

'What guy?' Fynn frowned as he looked down at her.

'The one I saw in the car last week. The security guy from the office in Sydney. Do you think they'll come back?'

CHAPTER
32

South Peleliu Island
16 July, 1942

The captain succeeded in ditching *Dumbo* in a bay on the other side of Peleliu Island. Jack, Megsy and four of the crew in the lower cockpit survived the landing despite the flames that had filled the plane when the bullets from the Zero had hit the engine.

'Open the blister.' Megsy's frantic yells had saved their lives. He and Jack had put their heads out into the air rushing past the opening. The metal skin between the blister and the cockpit was melting with the heat as they headed towards the sea below, and Jack knew they had to hit the water before the fuel tanks blew up. Jack's head hit the bulkhead as he hauled himself from the burning wreck. Jack, Megsy, Captain Munford, the two other pilots and one flight engineer scrambled from the plane and started to swim ashore.

Jack turned back to the plane. His vision was blurred and he squinted as he looked for the other men who had been in the blister turret with him and Megsy. 'What about the others?'

Megsy grabbed his arm and pushed him forward. 'No point, mate. The men in the bulkhead behind us didn't have a chance.' Black smoke billowed from the Cat as it slowly sank into the calm blue water.

Once on shore, everything that they had had drummed into them at briefings about what to do if they found themselves in enemy territory fled from Jack's mind. His ears were aching from the crash, and he stared in confusion as the other crew began to divest themselves of their jackets and flying boots. He raised a shaking hand to the perspiration running down the side of his face, but his hand came away wet with blood.

'Down to your shorts and shirt, man. Quickly!'

Bemused, Jack did as the captain instructed and watched as one of the flight engineers gathered up the clothes and boots and hid them in the low trees in the lush bush edging the sand.

Jack's knees began to shake and he grabbed for Megsy. Only half aware of the conversations around him, he closed his eyes as a searing pain sliced through the left side of his head.

* * *

South Peleliu Island
3 July, 1943

Twelve months had passed since the bayonet had sliced the skin on Jack's right arm and he had regained consciousness to see a Japanese soldier yelling and gesturing to him. Megsy sat beside a tree, his hands tied behind his back. There was no sign of the other crew members. Megsy told him later that they had left him with Jack when he had lost consciousness, and they'd headed off in search of coast watchers. Captain Munford had said there was an outpost— part of a wider coast watching network spread across the South Pacific—manned by New Zealand civilians on the island. All they could hope was that the crew had escaped the Japanese.

'Captain?' the Japanese soldier had yelled at Jack and kicked him. 'Where captain?'

He looked over at Megsy and held his eye as the other man gave a barely noticeable shake of his head.

Jack looked up at the soldier and shrugged. 'No captain.'

After two days of marching—and with no sign of the other surviving crew members—Jack and Megsy were thrown into a makeshift prison camp on the south of the island and put to work with other prisoners building the airstrip that the Japanese believed would enable them to hold the north Pacific.

Having Megsy beside him in those dreadful months on South Peleliu Island helped Jack keep his sanity. And he knew that he provided that same support to Megsy.

His arm had festered and turned putrid, but he'd constantly washed it out with salt water and it had eventually healed, leaving a long red scar from his elbow to his wrist.

For more than a year, they dug and prepared the ground for the runway.

'Bloody island is made of coral. How the hell are we supposed to dig this away?' Megsy lifted his hand to wipe the perspiration from his gaunt face.

Too much talking, and a Japanese guard would have no hesitation in knocking them down with the butt of a rifle or the heavy bamboo staff they each carried.

At the end of each day, it was all they could do to stagger into the rough hut with the other prisoners. Exhaustion would claim them both after the long days working in the hot sun constructing the new runway. Food was scarce. The enlisted men were given barely enough to give them the energy to work through the days. The officers were given meagre rations.

At last, explosives were brought in and the runway was almost complete. Some of the work crews were working up in the hills of the islands, making a network of caves and bunkers and sniper holes ready for the Allied invasion that the men prayed for and the Japs feared would come.

Jack focused on keeping Megsy in line. Megsy's sole focus was on escape.

One night as the tropical rain drenched them while they sat in the quadrangle eating the meagre bowl of maggot-ridden rice that would keep them going for the next twenty-four hours, Megsy dropped his voice to an urgent whisper.

'Tomorrow, Jack. At the end where we're digging, there's a small drop off. If we can create a diversion, we can drop into that and take off. That whole end of the island is riddled with caves. We can hide there until we're rescued.' Megsy pulled out the now tattered photos of his sons, and a lump rose in Jack's throat as tears ran down the red-headed man's burned and blistered cheeks. 'I want to go home, Jack. I want to see my boys grow into young men. We have to escape.'

'No. We wouldn't make it.' Jack shook his head. 'Patience, mate. They're getting desperate and the word is that the Nips are losing hold of the Pacific.'

'How the hell do we know that, stuck in this bastard of a place?' Megsy's voice rose and one of the guards turned to look at them. The attitude of the guards was antagonistic without riling them further, and the men had quickly learned to keep quiet and do as they were instructed.

Jack dropped his head and picked up the last grains of rice in his fingers.

When the guard walked away, Megsy's voice dropped. 'We could make a break for the jungle instead?'

'With any luck, we'll be sent up to the cliffs to work when the runway is done. I think that we'd have more chance up there. At least we could see more of the island,' Jack said.

Every night the conversation was the same, and Jack prayed for sleep to overtake him so he couldn't hear Megsy's sobs on the other side of the tin hut that they shared with eight other men.

The only similarity of their location to Whitsunday Island—the place that came to Jack in his dreams most nights—was that South Peleliu was land surrounded by sea. The water was blue, but it didn't have the sapphire colour of the water around Liliana's island. In his memory, everything on Whitsunday Island was bright and lush. The heat here was stifling and the intermittent rain brought little relief. The coral rocks absorbed the sun in the day and it was barely cooler in the nights. The jungle encroached on the camp and trapped the heat.

Jack slept very little, but when he did his dreams were of a better place and happier times.

His dreams of Liliana and their time together kept him sane.

As his arm healed, and he watched the other men succumb to *beri-beri*, dysentery and ulcers, Jack dreamed about a life on the island with her after the war was over. In his mind, he built a house for them, log by log. After the war, he would stay on Whitsunday Island, where it was safe. He would tell Liliana that there was no need to see the world. One thing he'd learned was that until you have lost what was precious to you, you don't appreciate what you had. He dreamed of his mother and hoped that Liliana had written to her as he had asked.

CHAPTER
33

May 9, 2018

'If Greg flies into Hamo, he can get the ferry across to the mainland.'

'With a broken leg?' Liv glanced up at him. Her hands were still shaking three hours later as she packed a small bag to take ashore. Fynn had a long cylindrical waterproof bag and once he'd put his computer and his valuables into it, he held his hand out for her small bag, and the briefcase holding her laptop. He slipped them in and pulled the drawstring tight and put the bag into the tender.

'Probably easier on the ferry than getting on and off *Footprint*.' Since Liv had told Fynn that she'd recognised the security guy on the black boat, he'd been quiet. He'd changed his plans and they'd motored straight back to Airlie Beach and moored off the beach at Cannonvale before sunset. On the way past Hamo, he'd called the water police and reported the incident.

'They must have tracked us when I turned the phone on,' she said as he held his hand out to help her into the small inflatable boat to go ashore. 'You were right all along, Fynn. What are we going to do now?'

The same dark blue helicopter had flown over them a couple of times as they'd crossed the Passage, and a shiver had run down her back as Fynn had stared at it.

'It's not a local helicopter,' he said as he steered for the mainland, taking the shorter route through Unsafe Passage.

Liv fought the fear that was clawing at her stomach. The serenity that she'd enjoyed over the past few days had flown.

'They want your computer. Hopefully, if you hand it over, that'll be the last we see of them.' The doubt in his voice belied his words.

'It won't, you know. I know how tenacious Dad is. He hasn't acknowledged the email I sent him.'

'Wait till we get over to Aunty Tat's house and call your father. Tell him you're sending the computer back. We'll organise a courier this afternoon.'

'What if he asks me if I've seen the files? Or if I've made a copy?'

Fynn rubbed his hand across his chin before he started the small outboard. 'Be upfront with him. We might as well put the fear of Christ into him.'

He pulled the tender up on the shingled beach and secured the small anchor before they walked through the gate to Poinciana House. There was no one on the wide verandah but the back door was wide open. Fynn gestured to a chair and stood at the door while Liv sank into the soft sofa.

'Anyone home? Aunty Tat?' He passed his phone to Liv and called up the hall.

'Looks like there's no one here.' Fynn walked over and sat beside her. 'Byron has told everyone who collects Aunty Tat to lock the door, but it never seems to happen. Are you right to call now?'

Liv swallowed and nodded. 'Yes, I just want to get it over and done with.'

Fynn took her hand after she called the company. She was so nervous she couldn't remember his mobile number.

'It's Liv Sheridan. Would you put me through to Andrew, please.'

She pressed the speaker button so Fynn could listen in when the call was picked up.

'Dad.' She kept her voice brisk. 'I got your messages. I've been out of phone range.'

The silence was deadly.

'Are you there?'

'I'm here. So you think one phone call and you can just waltz back into your job, Olivia?'

'No. I told you why I don't want to work with the company anymore. I'll come and see you when I come back to Sydney.'

'And when will that be?'

'Oh, I don't know. I'm having a good time up here. I just rang to tell you now that I'm back in town, I'll send my work computer and phone back.'

'About bloody time. Did you get into the folder?' His voice held the usual belligerent tone.

'Of course I did. And I can't put my disgust into words.'

'You're naïve, Liv. Let it go. This is how business works up with the big boys. I'll send someone to meet you. Where are you?'

'So, Anthony is still up here?' she asked, trying to sound surprised.

'No. But I have a couple of staff up there doing some more research.'

In a big black boat. Or a blue helicopter. 'I tell you what, Dad. My friend lives near the police station at Cannonvale. I'll drop the computer there and they can collect it.'

'What friend?'

'No one you know.'

'Listen to me, Liv. I know where you are and who you're with. You can tell Mr Pretty Boy that we're watching him too.'

'And others too, I hear.' Her voice was cold as ice ran through her veins. 'While I've got you there, tell me why Rod went. Did you sack him because he gave me access to the file? Was it an error or did Rod get sick of the dishonesty and corruption too?'

'He was very foolish to tell you what he did in that email, but unfortunately, we'll never know why. Poor Rod had a car accident on the motorway last weekend. He didn't survive. I've sent the company's condolences to his family.'

Fynn caught the phone as it slid from Liv's numb fingers. She gripped his other hand with hers as the ground seemed to tilt beneath her feet, even though she was sitting on the cane sofa.

'Rod's dead.' Liv could barely speak.

'Holy shit.' Fynn's whisper was harsh as he disconnected the call. 'He thinks he's untouchable.'

'Oh, how lovely.' Aunty Tat's words reached them as the gate opened. She walked up the path followed closely by Byron. 'I have visitors!'

Liv pushed herself to her feet. 'I have to go to the bathroom.' She ran up the hall and closed the door before grabbing the cold porcelain of the basin, forcing back the nausea that threatened to choke her.

★ ★ ★

Byron looked across at the door and rolled his eyes. 'I'm guessing the door was open when you arrived?'

'It was,' Fynn said distractedly as he heard the bathroom door close.

'Liv okay?' Byron frowned. 'You're a bit pale on it too, Fynn. What's happened?'

'It's not good. She's pretty upset.' He shook his head slightly as Byron went to speak. 'Later. We've just got a trip to make to the police station to drop off her computer. I've backed up the files, but I might grab another external drive and make another one just to be doubly sure.'

Byron glanced down at his watch as he crossed to the desk and picked up a flash drive 'They'll close in about twenty minutes, so you'll want to be quick.'

'I think we may be there for a while. I think it's time we got the police more involved. I'll tell you when we get back.'

'Okay, not a problem. Have you got any plans for tonight? Lou and I are cooking dinner here for Aunty Tat.'

'You don't have to now. Lily's here and she can help me cook.' Aunty Tat's voice was excited.

'Sounds good.' As Fynn replied, his phone buzzed with an incoming message and he glanced down.

'Good news. Greg's been discharged early. He's flying into Mackay on the late flight tonight and hiring a car. Jill's with him. They're going to stay in a motel tonight, but they'll be here first thing in the morning.'

'That's good.' Liv walked from the bathroom towards him. Although she was pale, her voice was composed and her eyes were bright. Fynn put his arm around her.

'Okay?' he asked in a low voice.

'Still shell-shocked but I'm okay. Talking to him was much harder than I thought it would be.' She clung to his arm and he found it hard to stay calm as anger choked him. How the bloody hell could a man do that to his daughter?

Aunty Tat's wavering voice broke the tension. 'Lily. We're going to cook dinner for the boys. Do you know if there's any goat legs left in the ice chest?'

Byron crossed to the elderly woman. 'It's all under control, love. You sit down and have a rest.' He glanced over at Fynn. 'Aunty Tat has been a bit nervous and Lou and I have spent a few nights here with her since you left.'

Aunty Tat put one hand to her eyes. 'Those rude men came to my door looking for you the other day, Lily. I told them you were missing and the Japanese had taken you away.' She put a finger to her lips and her eyes were wide. 'But I didn't tell them that you came back. That's our secret.'

Fynn and Liv exchanged a glance.

'They won't come back now. It was just someone looking for my computer. That's what we're about to drop off at the police station,' Liv said.

'We'll be back in a while. Dinner sounds good. Okay with you, Liv?' Fynn put his arm around her waist and could feel her trembling against him. 'We might sleep here tonight instead of going out to the boat.'

Liv rested her head on Fynn's shoulder. 'Sounds good to me.'

Byron raised an eyebrow. He looked at Aunty Tat and they both smiled.

★   ★   ★

As always at Aunty Tat's, there was an open door and family came and went as the word of a barbeque got around. Fynn helped Byron cook while Liv sat and talked to Aunty Tat and Louise.

'Looks like you've made a hit there.' Byron nudged Fynn as he stirred the onions over the heat.

'Just lookin' out for Liv.'

Byron smiled. 'About time you found yourself a woman and settled down.'

'Whoa there. Like I said, I'm helping her out.' Fynn looked over to where Liv was deep in conversation with the two women. 'But she is a pretty special lady.'

'You were serious about sleeping here tonight?' Byron's smile disappeared. 'Lou and I have to go to Mackay early tomorrow for an appointment.'

'Sure. I'd feel a bit safer with Liv here rather than out on the boat.' Fynn had already told Byron about the black boat that had harassed them in Solway Passage. 'That wind's come up too, and it'll be a bit rolly out in the bay.'

'Everything should be okay now that Liv's handed the laptop over, shouldn't it?' Byron scraped the barbeque plate as Fynn lifted the last of the meat and onions onto the tray. 'Or is that hoping for too much? You two haven't done anything else to come onto their radar, have you?'

'No. We've been lying low for the past week, but Greg's "accident" shows they mean business. I'm gonna be really careful, especially with Liv around.' Fynn's voice was quiet as he stared out at the water.

After dinner, Fynn and Liv sat outside chatting with Byron and Louise. As the breeze picked up, the temperature dropped and Aunty Tat came over to Liv and tucked a pashmina around her shoulders.

'Look, Lil. It's your favourite colour,' she said as she tucked the purple scarf around her shoulders.

Fynn smiled as Liv reached up and took Aunty Tat's hand.

'It is too,' she said with a smile. 'Thank you.'

It was after midnight before Byron and Louise left, and Aunty Tat led Fynn and Liv to the guest room at the back of the house.

She turned to Fynn as she opened the door. 'Jack, you and Lily can sleep in here. But don't tell anyone. I don't want to get into trouble from Mama.'

Fynn looked at Liv over the top of Aunty Tat's head as he hugged the elderly woman. 'Don't worry, Aunty Tat. No one will get into trouble.'

Fynn and Liv waited until she crossed the corridor to her bedroom.

'I'm just going to check everything's locked up.' His muscles were tense and he rubbed his neck. He hadn't been able to settle since they'd left the boat, jumping every time there was an unfamiliar noise.

'I'm going to have a quick shower,' Liv said.

Fynn crossed to the window in the guest room after he'd checked all the doors and windows. He stared out over the water as he waited for Liv to finish in the bathroom.

All was quiet. The harbour lights off Abell Point Marina flashed red and green. Way out in the Passage, the lights of a passing cruise ship lit up the night sky. As he reached up to close the window, a brief flash of light caught his attention and he stared at his boat. He leaned forward and held his breath as he waited.

There it was again. There was someone on *Footprint*, and this time the light from the flashlight reflected off a boat bobbing on the swell behind the yacht.

'Bastards,' he muttered under his breath as he moved quickly across the room. On the way to the door, he tapped lightly on the bathroom door. 'Liv, I'm just going out to the boat to check on something.'

Steam billowed from the bathroom as the door opened.

'Is everything okay?' Liv peered around the edge, clutching a white towel to her chest.

'Yes. Just a quick check. You go to bed.' There was no point worrying her. 'I'll be back soon.'

★ ★ ★

Liv frowned as she came out of the bathroom. She put aside the boxer shorts and T-shirt she'd been going to wear to bed and pulled her jeans back on. Picking up Aunty Tat's pashmina, she wrapped it around her shoulders and went to the back door. Opening it quietly, she let herself out and crossed the yard to the small wooden gate that opened to the beach. For a moment, she could just make out Fynn in the tender as he made his way to the mooring and then the dark night swallowed him.

Why did he have to go back out there so late? The wind was cold as the low putt of the tender's engine cut off and Liv shivered. The leaves of the trees beside the house rustled and she frowned as the noise of another boat reached her. She gasped and put her hand to her mouth as the whitewash behind a dark powerboat reflected in the moonlight as it roared away from Fynn's boat.

Suddenly, a boom echoed across the water and a silver flash lit up the night sky. There was a whoosh and grotesque shadows played over the dark water as flames shot high on Fynn's yacht. Liv gasped as she ran towards the water, scanning the bay, desperately searching for the tender. Searching for Fynn in the water. She dug into her pocket for her phone, but she'd left it in the bedroom.

'Lily! Lily! The Japanese have landed.' Aunty Tat's childlike voice came from behind her. Her eyes were wide with fear as she grabbed for Liv's hand. 'They killed Jack. We have to hide. I don't want Fynn to die too. Don't let them take you away again.' Aunty Tat started to cry, her sobs drifting away on the night air.

Liv took a deep breath. She'd heard him cut the motor, like he always did as the tender reached the back of the yacht. Then he'd throw the rope over and swing himself over the stern. All she could picture was Fynn pulling himself up onto the back of the boat as the flames engulfed the boat.

Oh, God.

Liv put her arm around the elderly woman and led her back to the house, trying to keep her voice calm despite sheer panic holding her in its relentless grip. Her chest tingled and it was hard to take a deep breath in.

Aunty Tat's eyes were clouded and Liv knew she needed to bring her back to the present.

'Aunty Tat, it's okay. Listen to me very carefully. You need to help me. It's not the war anymore. But sweetheart'—she held the elderly woman's cold shaking hands—'can you ring Byron for me? Tell him we need him. He'll come and help us find Fynn.' Her voice shook as Tat hurried up the hall towards the kitchen where the phone was. Liv ran to the bedroom and grabbed her mobile phone and pressed triple zero, holding it to her ear as she raced outside and back to the water's edge. Sirens sounded from the street behind her and she shoved the phone back in her pocket. The alarm had been raised.

While she was inside, a small crowd had gathered along the edge of the water, and as they watched, a couple of yachts motored close to the burning hull. Liv looked over her shoulder as a car roared into the driveway. A door slammed and Byron ran across to her.

'Liv? It's Fynn's boat, isn't it? I heard it go up from our place on the hill.' He looked around at the crowd gathered on the sand.

'Where's Fynn? Don't tell me he's gone out there. There's nothing he can do to save it.'

Liv dragged in a deep lungful of air, trying to push away the panic attack that was threatening. 'He … he … went before the explosion. In the tender.'

She stared at the burning boat until her eyes watered. Her back was rigid as the cold from the wet sand seeped into her bare feet. 'He must be in the water.' Her voice shook. If anything happened to him too, another 'accident', it would be her fault.

Byron reached out and held Liv as her knees buckled. She couldn't take it. The thought of Fynn on the boat, caught in the roaring flames, made her physically ill. Guilt seared through her; she had no doubt that the explosion was at her father's direction.

First Greg and Rod. Now Fynn.

Am I next, Dad?

Anger roared in, superseding the raw grief and the muscles in her legs quivered. Heat flushed through her body and she stood straight.

He will not break me.

'Liv, look!' Byron released her and pointed to the water.

She lifted her head and looked to the sea. From the swirling smoke, backlit by the orange flames, a small tender appeared. Fynn sat high on the back of the small boat, steering towards the shore.

She ran and by the time the tender reached the shallows, she had waded in and held her arms out to Fynn as he stumbled from the boat, trying to drag it onto the shingly sand.

Once the tender was safely on the sand, she turned to him.

'He blew up my boat, Liv. The bastard blew up my lady.' Fynn's whole body was shaking and she held him tight against her.

Strength and determination flooded through her. And in that moment, she knew that she had fallen in love with the man who she held in her arms.

CHAPTER

34

Liv stood next to the bed, watching Fynn as he slept late the next morning. His lips were slightly open as he breathed slowly and deeply. It had been almost 3 am before the police had left, and even though they'd gone to bed, he hadn't fallen asleep until almost dawn. Liv hadn't slept at all and now her throat closed as she realised how close she had come to losing him.

A tap on the front door signalled the arrival of the community worker who was picking up Aunty Tat for her weekly bingo game at the senior citizens' club. Aunty Tat seemed to have no recollection of last night, and Liv didn't mention it. After she saw Aunty Tat safely onto the bus, Liv made a coffee and carried it outside. A bench seat sat on the edge of the lawn just inside the wooden gate and she could see across the Passage out to the islands when she sat down. She took a deep breath and sat straight. The events of the past few days had been difficult, but she was determined to stay strong.

Greg Coutts was on his way up from Mackay, and she'd promised to wake Fynn when he arrived. But until then, she wanted to think over the conversation with her father yesterday. Something was niggling at Liv and she was trying to remember what he had said that she'd reacted to. Once her father had told her about Rod's death, she had shut down and the explosion and subsequent destruction of Fynn's boat had taken over her thoughts.

She blinked hard as tears threatened but refused to give way to them. There was too much work to be done to indulge in emotion. A car door slammed, and she tipped out the coffee that had gone cold as she'd stared over the water.

Fynn came out of the back door, hair wet from the shower, at the same time a man on crutches came through the side gate. A dark-haired woman followed him up the path, and Fynn reached over and kissed her cheek.

Greg and Jill.

Liv watched as Fynn held out his hand and Greg shook it. By the time she reached them, they were deep in conversation, but Fynn held his hand out and put his arm around her shoulders.

'Greg, Jill … this is Liv.'

Jill smiled at her, but Greg's expression was impassive. Liv couldn't blame him. What he knew about the Sheridans must have tainted his opinion of her. It was up to her to prove her worth.

An hour later, they sat around Aunty Tat's dining room table. Fynn had loaded the documents into Greg's laptop, and Greg had read them, alternatively shaking his head and then smiling. He'd looked curiously at Fynn as they'd sat there. Fynn was either holding Liv's hand, or had his arm around her shoulders as they spoke.

'So. What's next?' Greg closed the computer and ejected the flash drive.

'What you have here is enough to put some of them in jail.' Greg shook his head as he stared at the flash drive. 'Even the breach of the new legislation in relation to the regional council alone will take any approval process back to the beginning for them. Not to mention the bribery with the rail line relocation.'

'I still don't understand how this all went wrong for them. Why was Liv set up? Until we know that, I won't feel as though she's safe.' Fynn squeezed her hand.

'Until we know that, I won't reveal any of this publicly.' Greg turned to Liv. 'Why do you think you were given the wrong presentation, Liv?'

'I wasn't. I was given a link to the folder and it was my mistake. I downloaded the one I thought I was supposed to present.'

'Tell me about Rod.' His voice was sympathetic. Fynn had told him of the phone call with her father yesterday. 'Do you think it was deliberate? Was he trying to get the information out there? What did he say in the email he sent?'

'That's it!' Liv jumped to her feet. 'That's what I picked up yesterday and couldn't remember. My father said something strange about Rod's email and I wondered what he meant.'

'What did he say when he emailed you the folder?'

Liv had crossed to the door. 'That's just it. I didn't read what he said. I was in such a hurry, all I did was click on the link. I didn't ever go back to the email and read the message.'

'What did your father say about it?' Fynn had followed her to the door.

'He said Rod was very foolish to tell me what he did.'

Fynn slammed his fist against the doorframe. 'And we can't check it because you left the computer and phone at the police station for his henchmen.'

'I didn't.' Liv's voice was quiet and Fynn stared at her.

34748

ANNIE SEATON

'I saw you do it.'

'I left the computer, but the phone case I took in was empty. The phone is safely in my room. I kept it because if I ever need to go to court, I wanted to keep the texts he sent me after the meeting.'

'Can you access the email if they've disabled your access to the network. I'm sure they've done that by now.' Greg's brow was furrowed.

Liv smiled. 'I had my email set up so that my company emails were automatically forwarded to my Gmail account. I can read it anywhere.'

Liv paced slowly up the walkway from the jet to the terminal. She was a very different woman to the one who had boarded a plane for Hamilton Island in her corporate uniform six weeks before. Smiling, she stood near the entry and watched as her mother's eyes passed straight over her. She waited for the double-take, and sure enough seconds later, Mum turned her head back and stared. Her mouth dropped open and she hurried across to Liv, her arms wide.

'Well, look at you!'

'Hi, Mum.' Liv put her bag down and hugged her mother.

The usual fragrance of Chanel surrounded her as Mum held her close. 'It's been ages, Liv.'

'Too long, Mum. But the new Liv won't let that happen again.'

Her mother stepped back but kept hold of her hands. 'I like the look of the new Liv. You look so ... so well. And happy. And tanned.'

'There's a lot to catch up on, but let's wait till we get to Gran's. Then I'll only have to tell it all once. What time's our flight to Mudgee?'

'We'll go straight over to the regional airline now. I booked us on the early flight so we didn't have to wait too long at the airport.'

'Good thinking.' Liv picked up her bag and looped her arm through her mother's and laughed as Mum shook her head.

'I think someone is impersonating my daughter.' Her smile was wide. 'But I like her.'

The flight to Mudgee was only forty minutes, and as the small plane crossed the Blue Mountains, Liv put her head back and closed her eyes.

She was missing Fynn already. For over three weeks, they'd sailed around the islands and he'd introduced her to the beauty of the reef and the coral. She'd walked on the pure white sands of Whitehaven Beach, and explored the outer islands.

Greg and Jill had spent three days at Aunty Tat's house. Greg was an intense and quick-thinking man who knew a great deal about the intricacies of Sheridan Corp and hidden companies, and Fynn had relaxed as the evidence mounted against the company. The email from Rod had simply said that he couldn't condone the corruption anymore and that Liv might be interested in the content of the folders. He'd also included the password to access the protected folders.

As they'd discussed the situation over endless cups of coffee, Greg had concluded that the way the information had got out with Liv showing the incorrect PowerPoint had been the best way.

'What would you have done if you'd simply read the email?' he'd asked Liv.

'I suppose I would have confronted my father.'

'And that would have been the end of it.' Greg had nodded.

Fynn had his arm around her. 'Another reason you came to the islands, Liv. Remember Bec's philosophy.'

Once the investigation into the loss of his beloved yacht was underway, Fynn had accepted that his lady was gone.

'I have a new girl now,' he said one night as they moored in Tongue Bay around from Whitehaven Beach in the smaller yacht that he owned.

'This boat?' she'd asked with surprise. It was a small boat without the beauty of the yacht that had been destroyed in the explosion.

'No, a flesh and blood lady. And you know what? I love her more than I loved my *Footprint*.'

Liv had turned in his arms that night and held his face in her hands. 'Do you really mean that? So soon?'

'I do,' Fynn had said softly.

Happy tears had filled her eyes. 'It's been a long time since anyone told me they loved me.'

Their nights had been spent up on deck, watching the sunset over the mainland and early mornings watching the first rosy flush of a Whitsunday dawn tinge the eastern sky. Laughing together as they'd worked side-by-side in the galley, Liv had fallen in love with Fynn more each day.

On the last night before she left to visit her mother and Gran, they moored at Sawmill Bay next to the jetty ruins, not far from Hamilton Island for her flight the next morning.

Liv put her head back as the engine of the plane droned around her. Last night after dinner, Fynn had smiled that cute smile when his dimple appeared and held out his hand. Liv took it and followed him along the short corridor, up to the galley and saloon and down the steps to the main cabin.

She opened her mouth to speak but he'd shaken his head and opened the door to the cabin and stepped inside, smiling.

'Oh wow! Where on earth did you find them?'

ANNIE SEATON

Two jars were filled with roses; yellow, red, and white. She put her hand to her chest as she looked at the bed. Red rose petals covered the plain white bed cover, and a bottle of wine and two glasses sat beside the bed.

'There's an old, overgrown rose garden where the Ellis family lived. Aunty Tat talks about it and I went exploring. I've been waiting for them to flower. I picked them and left them in the tender and then brought them inside while you were in the shower.' He put one hand on her shoulder and gently pulled her closer. 'I wanted it to be a surprise.' His lips were a whisper away from hers.

Happiness, excitement and anticipation ran through Liv.

'I wanted you to be sure when I asked you to stay with me. I didn't want it to be when you were vulnerable. I want you to be as sure of me as I am of you. From the first time I saw you, Liv, you had me in your heart. That feisty woman who wanted her jacket back held me in her thrall from that moment.'

Liv had held her breath as his lips touched hers in the lightest kiss, and then he'd pulled back.

'I want to know that you'll come back to me after you visit your family. Am I asking too much?'

For the first time since she'd met the smelly fisherman, Fynn's confidence was missing. She raised her arms and put them around his neck.

'Will I come back?' She'd lifted her lips to his and murmured against his mouth. 'Nothing would keep me away.'

'Liv?' Her mother's voice intruded into her thoughts. 'We're about to land. I thought you were asleep.'

'No, just thinking.' She couldn't stop smiling.

Gran was waiting in the small terminal at Mudgee airport. Despite her age, she was still tall, her shoulders were always straight, and she held herself with a regal bearing.

'Livi.' Gran held her tight and Liv blinked back tears at the special name that Gran had always had for her.

Why have I left it so long?

'Oh, Livi, it's so good to see you.'

'And you too, Gran.'

Mum stood on the other side of Gran, holding her elbow as they waited for their bags to come in from the small plane.

'I've decided we're going into town for coffee before we go out to the farm. I haven't done any baking for a while, so we can treat ourselves at the bakery.'

Liv caught her mother's eye and raised her eyebrows.

'And don't go jumping to conclusions,' Gran said in a waspish voice. 'I'm quite well but there's no point baking if no one comes to visit.'

'Consider ourselves suitably chastised, Livi.'

'Your daughter has an excuse, Rhoda. She has a career to worry about. You could easily drive up and visit more than you do.' Gran pursed her lips and for a moment her expression reminded Liv of someone. She grinned; it was herself. Gran reminded her of herself when she was cross.

'That's a whole new story, Gran. I've got a lot to tell you over coffee. Both of you.'

An hour later, their bags had been collected, coffee and cake consumed, and Liv had brought them up to speed with the events in the company.

Except for the things that couldn't be proved, like Rod's death.

'Hallelujah,' Gran exclaimed when Liv told her that she had resigned from Sheridan Corp. 'About time you saw some sense, young lady. I bet the conniving bastard was furious.'

'You could say that,' Liv said quietly.

As they drove towards Cooyal, Gran glanced over her shoulder to Liv in the back seat. 'So, what are you going to do now?'

'Mum! Watch the road!' Her mother was nervous enough about Gran driving but Gran wouldn't hear of either her daughter or granddaughter taking the wheel.

'I'm perfectly capable of listening and driving at the same time, Rhoda.'

Liv leaned forward and rested her arms on the back of Gran's seat. 'I'm going to help Mum organise your birthday party, and then I'm going back to Airlie Beach.'

'What beach?' Gran slowed the car as it rattled over the cattle grid.

'Airlie Beach.' Liv smiled as she saw the colourful roses at the end of the drive. 'The Whitsundays.'

Gran pulled up at the front of the house, got out of the car and marched towards the front door.

'She never changes, does she?' Her mother shook her head as they took their bags from the back of the SUV.

Liv followed Mum up the steps. 'But we love her just the way she is. Acerbic, a tongue like vinegar sometimes, but with a heart of gold. I wouldn't change her for the world.'

They walked into the long cool hallway but there was no sign of Gran. They both turned to the rooms that they knew would be ready for them, and then walked into the kitchen together.

Gran was standing at the sink looking out the window. Her fingers were white where she was gripping the benchtop.

'Mum, are you okay?'

A nod. 'I'm just waiting for the kettle to boil.' Liv and Mum looked at each other. Gran's voice was thick and full of emotion.

Rhoda went over to her and put her arms around her mother. 'I'm sorry, Mum. I won't leave it more than a few weeks before my next visit.'

Gran shook her head. 'It's all right. You do what you have to do, both of you.' Her voice quavered. 'Livi, can you feed Boycat please. He'll be asleep in the living room. He's so old, he forgets to eat.'

'Of course. Are you sure you're okay, Gran?'

'I'm fine. I was just being a silly old woman for a moment. Heaven knows I'm almost old enough to be entitled to do that.'

'*Almost*,' Mum and Liv said at the same time.

Liv went to the fridge and took out the small bag of topside mince in the tray that had been on the bottom shelf of the fridge for as long as she could remember.

Nothing but the best for Gran's cats. Boycat was the last of a long line. She walked into the living room. Gran's walls were covered with small sketches and paintings that Gran had done over the years. Liv looked around, letting the memories of her happy childhood days come back. She'd spent a lot of time here when Mum and her father had divorced.

'Where are you, Boyc—' A gasp escaped her lips and the bag of mince slid from her fingers. She stepped closer to the wall in front of Gran's chair and looked at the paintings.

A perfect representation of the two flat-topped hills with the lacy-leaved trees sat in the middle of the wall. As Liv let her eyes roam to the other paintings around it, she stared at a jetty tucked at the side of a bay, a rose garden surrounded by a white picket fence, and last of all, a timber house with a small stone shed at the back corner.

Liv put her hand to her lips as her mind whirled.

No. It wasn't possible.

She backed away and by the time she got to the kitchen, tears filled her eyes. *No.*

'Gran?'

As soon as she met her grandmother's eyes, she knew the truth. Her grandmother's resemblance to Aunty Tat confirmed what the painting told her.

'Gran?' Liv's voice was shaking. 'Tell me your name. Your *real* name. It's not Amelia, is it?'

'What?' Mum stood still in the centre of the kitchen watching them both, her lips open. 'Liv, what's wrong?'

Gran stood straight but her hands were trembling as she reached out first to Rhoda, and then to Liv.

'No, Amelia was my friend. I took her name when I left.'

'Mum?' Rhoda's voice shook. 'Sit down. You've lost all your colour. Are you all right?'

Gran stared at Liv. 'I took her name so my parents would never find me. The shame would have killed Mama.'

Rhoda led Gran to the chair and Liv sat next to her. Her legs were shaking as she tried to process what was going on.

Gran's bottom lip was shaking 'You're Liliana, aren't you?' Liv held her hand and stared at the faded blue eyes that were so like Aunty Tat's.

Gran nodded, and a tear rolled down her face. 'I never told Jack's parents my real name. I told them I met Jack in Townsville. I didn't want Mama and Daddy to find me. I didn't want Mama to know what I'd done. Richard was the only one who ever knew the truth, and he kept my secret until he took it to his grave.'

★ ★ ★

South Peleliu Island
26 December, 1943

Gunfire and shouting woke Jack the day after Christmas Day. He lay there waiting. The men knew better than to leave the hut until they were summoned to the quadrangle by the guards.

'Maybe the Yanks have arrived?' Megsy sat up and his eyes were bright for a change. 'I'm going to see.'

'No. Wait. Don't go out there.' Jack stood and walked over to Megsy. He was pulling on the tattered boots that had been given to them.

'Today's the day, mate. It's now or never. If it's not the Yanks out there, I'm taking off today. If I can find a Cat in the water, I can be home in time to see the boys tonight.'

As Jack got closer, he realised it was fever in Megsy's eyes and delirium in his words. His jaw was slack and his eyes were two black holes.

An unearthly scream came from outside as he sat beside Megsy. Jack dropped his head to his knees and blocked out the sound. Most of the time he could cope but he was worried about what Megsy would do. The older man had lain back down and was muttering as he tossed restlessly on the grass mat.

Jack knew he had to stay strong but for the first time since they had been captured, he began to doubt the future. He opened his eyes as Megsy made a sudden movement beside him. Before Jack could get to his feet, Megsy had jumped up and run across to the door of the tin hut and pushed it open.

'Jesus Christ.' Fear settled in Jack's gut as he took off after him. He followed Megsy to the quadrangle, but the attention of the guards was on the scene in front of them. One of the sergeants from the work crew that Jack had been assigned to was kneeling in the middle of the square. A narrow rope confined his arms against his body and a white edged blindfold covered his eyes. A Japanese officer stood poised with a sword raised above his head. Jack stopped dead and watched in horror as the sword sliced down.

In that moment, he knew Megsy was right. The only way they would survive was to make an escape. He stepped back slowly towards the hut, looking around to see where Megsy had gone. A chill consumed him when a movement flashed to his left as Megsy took off running across the open yard. A soldier raised his rifle and the shot rang out. Megsy fell to the ground. Jack could see he wasn't dead, as he slowly dragged himself to his hands and knees.

Jack knew he had to help him, and he took off running. As he kneeled beside his stricken mate, the officer strode to where Megsy lay, blood staining the ground around him. Jack froze as the sword came down, the sunlight playing on the steel. The sword flashed again and Megsy was gone.

Sick with disbelief, rage flooded through Jack. If only he had a weapon he would kill the bastards. He lunged at the Jap, trying to wrestle the weapon from him, however months of starvation, infection and the brutal work had left him weak. Several soldiers ran across and grabbed him, and he was thrown to the dusty ground.

'You escape? You die too.'

Jack fought with every ounce of energy left in his weakened body as he was dragged to the middle of the quadrangle and forced to kneel. He looked away from Megsy's body and lifted his eyes for a final glimpse of the blue sky, as blue as the skies over Liliana's island. The blindfold shut out the light as it was pushed roughly over his head.

'I love you, Liliana.' Jack's whisper hung in the humid air.

CHAPTER
36

June 10, 2018

It was one of those glorious still mornings when the Passage was calm and the water myriad greens and blues like the feathers of a kingfisher. Once they were on board the yacht Fynn had borrowed and he had settled his passengers in comfort—Gran had insisted on travelling up on deck so she could see her beloved island as it came into view—they set off.

Liv bit her lip as she watched the two elderly women sit side-by-side on the lounge at the stern of the catamaran. Her grandmother sat straight, her shoulders square, her long white braid sitting over one shoulder as her sister held onto her hand as though she would never let her go. Aunty Tat—Livi couldn't think of her as Great Aunt Tat—had been Aunty Tat to her since the minute her great aunt had called out to her when she had arrived in the islands three months ago. Since the reunion of the Ellis sisters when Gran had flown into the island yesterday, Tatiana and Liliana had been inseparable.

'Fynn's a good man, Livi.' Liv jumped when her mother touched her shoulder, pulling her from her thoughts. She turned as Mum settled beside her on the roof of the cabin, and took her hand.

'He's wonderful with your grandmother and Aunty Tat.' Rhoda shook her head. 'I'm still finding it hard to reconcile my thoughts. A whole unknown family up here. It's hard to imagine what Mum went through when she found out she was having me. To leave all she knew and head off to look for Jack's family. And to change her name so her parents would never find her. I can't believe how brave she was ... but how sad it is.'

'To be seventeen years old and head off for the unknown, leaving all she knew, and in wartime too.' Liv shook her head. 'How did she get away without anyone knowing where she went?'

'She said she didn't want anyone to follow her, so she planned it carefully. Jack—my father—had left some money and his parents' address. Apparently, a young man from another island took her to the mainland and she swore him to secrecy. He took her across the Passage and to the rail line. By the time she was missed, she was way down the coast.'

'She must have been a very strong young woman,' Liv said.

'She's always been strong. I remember when she fought the mine that eventually resumed our vineyard in the Hunter Valley.'

'Do you think she had a happy life, Mum? Gran always seems so private, and often not happy.'

'I think it was that generation, although from what she's told me in this last week, her early years with the Rickards weren't easy. By the time they heard after the war that Jack had been ... had died in the prisoner-of-war camp, his parents had already insisted that she marry his brother. At least when they all passed away, she had financial security in her life. And I grew up believing Richard was my father.'

Liv squeezed her mother's hand. 'It's been a tough week for you too, Mum.'

Rhoda shrugged. 'Richard was killed on the farm when I was only a small child. I barely remember him. I'm going to do some war research and see what I can find out about Jack. *My* father and *your* grandfather. It's so much easier these days, and I think it will give Mum closure too.'

Liv looked over at Liliana. 'I just can't understand why she never told her family where she'd gone, and that she was safe.'

'You have to understand that things were very different in those days. Falling pregnant before you were married was one of the worst things that could happen to a young woman. And she told me that her mother was very religious, so the shame would have been compounded.' Rhoda sighed and lifted her hand from Liv's shoulder and brushed at her eyes. 'Poor Mum will never know if they would have accepted her situation.'

'It's so sad that her family never had closure. Their grief must have been unbearable. I can't begin to imagine it.' Liv sniffed and dug for a tissue. 'They really believed that the Japanese had taken her. I'm sure there would have been no forgiveness needed if she had stayed. From the way she speaks of them, she had loving parents.'

Rhoda put her arm around Liv's shoulder and dropped a light kiss on her cheek. 'I love you, Livi. I don't tell you enough. And it's wonderful to see you so happy.'

'I am happy.' Liv leaned against her mother and looked over at Fynn as he stood at the helm. Most of his blond curls were tied back with the usual leather tie and he stared ahead, hands firm and sure as he steered the boat from Abell Point Marina.

Fynn caught Liv's eye and she smiled when he winked at her. 'He's taught me patience, and he's shown me what's important in life.'

Her mother looked at her curiously. 'Will you go back to Sydney? Back to the corporate world?'

Liv shook her head as she stared at Fynn. With respect for the special guests he was taking to Whitsunday Island, he wore knee-length white shorts and a navy-blue polo shirt with a collar, rather than his usual tattered and faded denim shorts. His tanned, muscular arms gripped the helm as he steered the boat towards the Passage and his blond-tipped curls lifted in the slight wind that had come up as they rounded the Molle group of islands.

Out on the water. In his element.

'No. I've found my home.' Certainty and a surge of love for this man filled her chest just as the morning sun was caressing her skin with warmth. 'I won't be leaving here.'

'What about work?' Rhoda squeezed her hand.

'I'll work with Fynn.'

Rhoda laughed. 'Byron told me Fynn has quite a few business interests up here.'

Livi gave a rueful smile. 'He does. If you'd seen him like I did the first time—smelly, stained fishing clothes and attitude oozing from him—you never would have guessed it. But he owns a couple of charter yachts as well as this one, a fishing charter boat, a restaurant on Hamilton Island and another one on the mainland. But that's all secondary to the work he does with the university to save the reef. He wants to restore another yacht to replace the one he lost in the explosion.' Liv stared at her mother. 'You know, I still can't accept that Dad had anything to do with that.' She hadn't shared the worst of it with her mother, but it was obvious that she knew what he was capable of.

'Trust me, darling. I have no doubt that he would have … and more. Anything to get his way. Nothing has ever mattered more to him than making money. Not even life or love. I did love him, you know. Just remember that.' Rhoda's eyes were sad as she stared past Liv. 'Have you heard from him since you left Sydney?'

'No.' Liv had no desire to have any connection with her father. He had never treated her with love or respect, so she was not going to mourn the loss of any relationship. 'You were right, Mum. It was all about the money. He used me for his own ends, but it's come back to bite him.' She stared past Fynn to the island that was in the distance. 'He's been out of touch since things went pear-shaped for Sheridan Corp. He's overseas somewhere, but Greg—Fynn's journalist friend—said he will have to come back to Australia to face the corruption enquiry.'

'Zenith are blaming Sheridan Corp for the corruption that saw the project come so close to approval, and they're not giving up on it. Since Greg did his latest article for the *Courier Mail*, the government has taken a lot more notice of the local community, and the environmental concerns about the reef. So we'll just keep fighting and working at raising the concerns as widely as we can. It's going to be a long fight. Sheridan might be out, but we'll win in the end.'

'I read Greg's article.' Rhoda closed her eyes and Liv stared as her mother quoted the damning content from memory. '"Sheridan's tentacles stretch into government. Since Zenith severed relationships with Sheridan Corp, there are many nervous politicians watching with interest to see if Andrew Sheridan will face criminal charges." I hope he does.'

Liv nodded. And murder charges too, she thought. They had told the police what Rod had done and said.

They were both silent for a while before Rhoda put her arm around Liv's shoulder.

'And what will you be doing up here with Fynn? What sort of work do you want to do?'

Liv's voice was quiet as she shifted her gaze to her grandmother and great aunt. Gran was staring across the water to the island that was ahead of them, her face set but her eyes were shining. 'I'll use my knowledge and qualifications to do everything I can to save the reef.'

'It's wonderful to see you so happy, Livi.' Her mother reached up and smoothed Liv's hair back from her face. 'A permanent smile on your face.'

'I'm happy, Mum. For the first time in a long while.'

'Love will do that to a woman.' Her mother's smile was cheeky.

'It will.' Liv hugged her mother. 'Look, we're almost there. Go and sit with Gran, I just want to have a quick word with Fynn.'

Her mother's look was indulgent as Liv walked across to Fynn and put her arms around his waist.

They all waited in silence as they approached the bay and her grandmother called out to her.

'Give me your hand, Livi.'

With Liv's help, Liliana stood and made her way to the side of the boat. Aunty Tat wasn't far behind them. An ache settled in Liv's throat as she kept her eyes on her grandmother. Her hands gripped the side of the boat and her eyes were fixed on the island as they drew closer. As the two flat-topped hills behind Sawmill Bay came into view, Liliana drew in a quick breath.

'Oh, Tat. It's just the same. I wonder if the goats are still there.' Her voice was shaking, and Rhoda stepped across to them and took Liliana's elbow.

'Are you sure you want to do this, Mum?'

Liliana nodded. 'I must,' she said simply.

Tatiana shook her head and a tear rolled down her wrinkled cheek. 'It *is* just the same, darling. Come on. I'll take you to see Mama and Daddy, and Goat and Robbie, and Katarina.'

* * *

'I can walk up a hill. I walked this hill hundreds of times when I was a girl. It might have been seventy years ago, but remember I still play tennis twice a week and look after the horses at home.' Lily shook her head. Her ninety-third birthday might be approaching, but she took pride in her excellent health and her fitness. 'I might be a little bit slower than I was back then, but I will do it.'

'More than seventy years, Mum.' Rhoda frowned at her but Lily ignored her.

'I'm coming too.' Tat grabbed her arm. 'But I can't go fast like you, Lil.'

Lily couldn't help the teasing remark that came from her lips. 'You always did like your food, Tat.'

Tat poked her tongue out, and Lily felt like a teenager again. A carefree teenager, before the war, before the decisions she'd had to make that changed her life forever.

'But I would do it all again, Jack,' she whispered.

'What was that, Gran?' Livi walked along beside her.

'Just the thoughts of an old woman, darling. Come on, my dears. I have a family to say goodbye to,' Lily said.

'Wait, Lil!' Tatiana called to her as Lily walked briskly along the wooden jetty. 'I have to tell you something before you go to the house. You have to know. They're all gone.'

Lily turned to Tat and smiled. 'It's okay, Tat. I know.'

'But I have to explain.' Her face crumpled, and she started to cry. 'Oh, Lil, the house has gone too. They're all gone.'

Fynn crossed the jetty and put his arms around Aunty Tat. 'How about you three girls walk up first, and I'll follow with Aunty Tat.'

As they walked along the path to the top of the hill, Lily focused her thoughts on her family and the love she had been cocooned in when she had been growing up on this island. She lifted her eyes to the cloudless blue sky before dropping her gaze to the lush vegetation. In the mossy crevices of fallen hoop pines, small ferns and creepers poked their green leaves out, reminding her of the soft green of the forest when she was a child. The rainbow bee-eaters swooped catching insects on the wing. The light filtered through just as it had in the days she had shown Jack the old sawmill. She closed her eyes and pretended that it was Jack's hand that was holding hers tightly. A slight breeze stirred the treetops far above them but down here in the bush, it was still, as if the island held its breath waiting for the return of the lost daughter.

At times, fallen hoop pines blocked the path, and Rhoda and Livi held her hands tightly as they guided her off the path and around the fallen trees. A small waterfall tinkled from a creek that she didn't remember, and Lily sighed. It was the same, yet it was different. The memories that had kept her going in those early days when she had arrived in the Hunter Valley, and Jack's parents had welcomed her as Amelia, with reserve, were different. She had held this idyllic paradise in her thoughts to help her through those early years when she had married Richard, and he had agreed to bring Rhoda up as his own daughter. Times had been hard, but she had accepted losing two more children at birth as her punishment.

The bush thinned and as they stepped out into the light, Rhoda gasped. 'Oh, Mum, it's beautiful. Just like the stories you told me about the fairyland when I was a child.'

Liv nodded. 'That's what niggled at me when I first came past here in Fynn's boat. I recognised the two flat hills with the lacy trees but I couldn't place it. It wasn't until I saw that painting at your house that I realised where I knew it from. And I've remembered you used to tell me stories about an underwater fairy garden too.'

But Lily wasn't listening. She pulled her hands from their gentle grip, and took a hesitant step forward, grateful that Liv and Rhoda stayed where they were as she approached the small white picket fence surrounding the small graveyard.

The gate creaked as Lily pushed it open. It was the same place where the gate had been to the goat enclosure all those years ago. She pulled a white lace-edged handkerchief from her pocket, although she was determined to stay strong.

Three white headstones faced the sea.

She took a tentative step to the first one and walked around to the front. A white urn sat in the shade beneath the headstone and tears blurred her eyes as she smelled the violets—Mama's favourite flowers. It was a miracle to see them grow here in the tropics. With shaking fingers, Lily traced the letters in the marble.

Boyd Edward Ellis. Born 21st December, 1897. Left this life to be forever in the ever-loving arms of his beloved Alexandra, 16th February, 1987.

Liliana smiled. She was past the age that Daddy had been when he died. Still living and fishing on the island, Tat had told her proudly.

Alexandra Maria Ellis. Born 15th July 1900. Departed this life 23rd October, 1966.

Finally she couldn't hold back the emotion as the tears sprang from her eyes. Tatiana had told her of Mama's grief when Robbie and Goat had both lost their lives in the Battle of Long Tan in the Vietnam War. Her heart had broken, and she had passed later that year.

She moved to the third headstone and touched it gently.

Katarina Anne Ellis. Born 30th April 1937. Taken from this life, 4th March 1958. Forever loved by her family.

Her baby sister had been killed in a car accident in Brisbane not long after Tatiana had married her Charlie and settled at Cannon Valley Beach. Tatiana was the only one who had continued the Ellis line. And she'd insisted on keeping Ellis as part of her surname.

Oh, Mama and Daddy. You had such sad times.

Lily sat by the headstones for an hour, telling her family about her life. Telling them how much she loved them, and how much she had missed them.

'Maybe if I'd been brave and stayed, things may have been okay, but Mama, I didn't want to break your heart. It was better that I left.'

The sun was hot on the top of her hat, and she closed her eyes, listening to the wind keening in the pines. She smiled as a goat bleated in the distance and for a moment, she was sixteen years old again.

'Gran. It's time to go.' Livi touched her gently on the shoulder. 'Are you ready?'

Her granddaughter held out her hand and helped Lily to her feet.

'I am. I've said my goodbyes.'

'Fynn wants to get across the Passage before the tide changes.' Livi steered her gently towards the gate where Tatiana, Rhoda and Fynn stood waiting for them.

Lily held her arms out to Tat.

'Come on, Lil. We have to get back down the hill. Mama wants us to peel the potatoes.' Tat's voice quavered as she hugged her sister back.

Lily knew her eyes were sad as she looked at her daughter and her granddaughter. 'Yes, Tat. Come on. We'll go back down the hill and help Mama.'

As they left the small harbour that she and Tat had swum in as teenagers, they passed the rock where Lily had sat and made the decision that had changed her life all those years ago. Now that she had bid farewell to her family up on the hill, the ache in her chest had eased and the tears had dried. Serenity filled Lily for the first time for many years.

The choice she had made in 1942 had been difficult, but as her daughter and her granddaughter supported her on either side while Fynn guided the boat towards the Passage, Lily knew she had been right. If she'd stayed on the island, she would probably have been sent to Brisbane and made to give up her baby. She might have achieved the dreams of her youth of seeing the world, of being a journalist but she wouldn't have these two wonderful women in her life. A smile crossed her face as she remembered how she'd wanted to interview a member of the French Foreign Legion. Life had taken a very different path, but the loss of her family—and the love of her life—had been eased by the love of the two strong women standing each side of her.

'Jack,' she whispered softly as the boat passed the jetty where she had sat knowing that she had lost her love on that dreadful morning when the Cat hadn't returned.

Liliana closed her eyes and put her fingers to her lips and blew a soft kiss up into the sky. If she listened, she could hear the roar of a Catalina as it passed overhead.

* * *

Fynn stood by the gate and Liv wiped away a tear as she leaned back against him.

'I missed the greatest reason of all, didn't I?' she said.

He leaned down and dropped a quick kiss on the top of her head. 'What was that, darlin'?'

'The real purpose I was sent up here. I was sent up here so that a family could be reunited.'

'And so you could fall in love with the reef and join in the battle to save it.' Fynn lowered his head so his cheek was against hers. 'And you were sent up here so I could fall in love with you,' he added softly.

'And ditto.' Liv turned her head so that her lips brushed his cheek. 'That's the most important reason of all. I found you.'

'We found each other,' Fynn said as they watched Liliana look up to the sky.

AUTHOR'S NOTE

Some historical sources must be mentioned as they provided a background for the early days of the region, the war years, and the base for 11 and 20 squadrons at Bowen in 1943.

CATS at War: the story of RAAF Catalinas in the Asia-Pacific Theatre of War. This series of anecdotes compiled by Coral Gaunt and Robert Cleworth, first published in June 2000, by J.R. Cleworth, provided a close insight into the daily life of the Catalina crewmen.

The Whitsunday Islands: An Historical Dictionary by Ray Blackwood (Central Queensland University Press, 1997) provided information on the timber industry and the early settlement of Whitsunday Island.

Fangs of the Sea by Norman Caldwell (Quality Press: London, 1937)

The Last Islands by John and Mia Bates (Broadreach Press: Australia, 2016)

Welcome to the Whitsundays by Neville Smith (Koala Books: Proserpine, 1996)

I must also acknowledge the Coral Sea Display and Catalina Memorial at the Bowen Aerodrome, and the Qantas Founders' Museum at Longreach, where I was able to crawl through and explore a restored Catalina flying boat.

There was a Catalina base at Bowen in World War II, however some of the events in *Whitsunday Dawn*, relating to the establishment of the Flying Boat Maintenance Unit at Bowen, and the missions of the Catalina of which Jack was a crew member, are a creation of the author and not historically accurate.

ACKNOWLEDGEMENTS

The Whitsunday Islands, part of the World Heritage Great Barrier Reef on the east coast of Australia, are a stunning landscape. During one of our many visits to the region, the idea for *Whitsunday Dawn* was born, and gave us an excuse to spend three months in the islands researching the story in 2017. The writing of *Whitsunday Dawn* has been another chapter in my fabulous writing life, fulfilling my lifelong dream of being an author. With this book, I was able to combine my love of history with my desire to preserve our beautiful Australian landscapes for future generations. Travelling through the country, from coast to outback, and talking to people who care for our pristine landscapes provides inspiration for many more stories. I have been supported by many people in the writing of this book. I would like to acknowledge them here. Firstly, to my fabulous agent, Haylee Nash of The Nash Agency. I could not have done this without your support and hard work. A huge thank you! Many thanks to my publisher, Rachael Donovan, and the rest of the awesome team at Harlequin. A special mention for my editors: Laurie Ormond, Alex Craig and Libby Turner; my story is richer for your wonderful editing. To the many friends I have made in the writing world who constantly support me on my journey;

I often say I have found my 'tribe' and I value the daily contact with like-minded people all over the world. A special mention and thank you goes to my critique partner, Susanne Bellamy, and to my proofreader, Roby Aiken. To the many friends I have made in the Whitsunday region; if it wasn't so far from family, I know I would make my home in the islands. A special mention for Geoff Rudd, a long time local, who described for me the war years at Cannon Valley, and provided a rich tapestry of life in the region when it was only a tiny settlement of farms and fishermen. And thank you to Errol Hurst, who told me of the fishing and the growth of the resorts in the early days in the islands.

It would be impossible to write without support in your personal life: To Ian, the love of my life and my partner in research, as we travel this magnificent country seeking stories each winter. I could not do this without you. To our children and their partners, and our grandchildren: thank you for your love and support. Again my love and appreciation goes to my wonderful aunt, Maureen Smith, who not only supports me, but supports so many Australian authors by reading, loving and sharing their stories.

And to you, the reader. Thank you for choosing this book. I hope when you read *Whitsunday Dawn* that you love it and talk about it, and that maybe you will want to see this wonderful part of Australia for yourself. Drop me a line at annieseaton26@gmail.com. I would love to hear from you.

Turn over for a sneak peek.

UNDARA

by

Annie Seaton

Available August 2019

PROLOGUE

Emlyn tried to look out over the bright-white sand to the water, but her head was aching, and her eyelids were too heavy to open. Her arms burned as the tropical sun seared her skin. 'Pass my hat … please.'

She reached out to the beach mat to see if he was still there beside her.

Shimmering, blinding light.

Damn eyes, why can't I open them? She raised her hand to her face and tried to force her eyelids open. She drew in a shaking breath, but her hands were still by her side.

'Am I asleep?' she asked. 'David?'

No answer. Of course he wouldn't answer. She hadn't spoken to him since they'd left home. They'd hardly spoken at all since the fight about the wedding.

The first fight they'd ever had.

Why can't I hear the water anymore? Where is everybody?

Only low voices surrounded her. Maybe they've gone back to the bungalow for a nap.

Panic bubbled in her chest and she willed her eyes to open. Fear took her voice and her lips wouldn't shape the words.

'David. Where are you?'

No words. There was only a vibration in her chest where they formed.

'She's coming around.' The unfamiliar voice was calm.

She fisted her fingers into the sand to lift herself, but firm hands gently pushed her shoulders back.

'It's all right, Mrs Barber.'

No. There is no Mrs Barber. Not anymore.

Pain rolled over Emlyn Rees in waves, as conscious thought slammed back and she turned into the pillow.

My heart can't bear it.

As quiet surrounded her, she opened her lips to catch the hot saltiness of the tears that trickled down her cheeks.

It's not real.

It's a dream. Only a dream.

CHAPTER

1

Hidden Valley, New Year's Eve, 2018

Emlyn Rees frowned and tapped her fingers on the steering wheel of the Troop Carrier she'd picked up in Townsville. The directions on the map that had been emailed to her, outlining the route to the Hidden Valley cattle station, were detailed. Exactly thirty kilometres past Conjuboy, she'd turned left off the Kennedy Developmental Road onto an unsealed road, but there'd been no sign of any property name at the intersection. She'd been driving along the road for almost half an hour and was beginning to think she'd turned off too soon, when it narrowed, and she had to grip the manual shift and change down a gear. As the road became little more than a goat track, dense thickets of black tea-trees edged it, and the front tyres of the four-wheel drive dropped into a deep rut that was obviously cut by torrential rain.

Biting her lip, she glanced over at the printed email that now lay on the passenger seat beside her. A stand of fig trees formed a canopy over the track ahead, and with an impatient huff, she accelerated out of the rut, steered the vehicle to the side and switched off the engine.

Reaching for her water bottle, she took a deep swig before rolling the cool glass over her forehead; despite the air-conditioning, she was still perspiring. The humid air pressed in close and sticky as a bank of dark cloud edged the sky ahead. Frustration filled Emlyn and she frowned, ignoring the uncertainty that settled heavily in her chest. Flipping up her sunglasses, she reached for the printed map. She traced her shaking finger over the route from Greenvale, the last town she'd travelled through, and then along to the small square that was marked 'Hidden Valley'. This was the right road, although it was hard to believe that this narrow track could lead to one of the largest working cattle stations in the Einasleigh River area. The station was located halfway between the Undara Volcanic National Park and the tiny town of Einasleigh, almost four hundred kilometres west of Townsville in the tropical north. Emlyn had read up on the tourist facility—the Undara Experience—where some of the lava tubes were open for public viewing. The caves and tubes on Hidden Valley had not been explored and were not part of the national park.

After another kilometre along this track, she should go around a sweeping curve past the river, where the homestead would be on her left.

With a shake of her head, Emlyn put the map onto the dashboard. Despite only being mid-afternoon, it was quite dark. For the first time since she'd picked up the hire car, her unease grew, moving up her spine and making a home at the base of her neck.

The tension spread to her temples, a headache threatened, and her arm ached as it always did when she was tired … or stressed.

For a fleeting moment, she considered digging out a paracetamol capsule, but shook her head. She'd had enough painkillers—and anti-depressants—over the past months to last a lifetime; a simple headache wasn't going to kill her. As soon as she was settled in, she'd relax, and a good night's sleep would put paid to any tension.

With a determined set to her lips, she started the car and drove carefully down the track. Travis Carlyle, the property owner, had assured her that there would be someone at the homestead to meet her and take her across to the accommodation. His email assurance had been at odds with the disinterested tone of his voice in the three brief telephone conversations they'd had during the three months of planning. Making his preference to organise details by email very clear, it had seemed that Carlyle had done his best to delay the start of the research, which originally had been scheduled for late October. Carlyle had always had a reason each time he'd postponed the start date.

It was the first time Emlyn had been involved in negotiation with property owners, which was usually coordinated by the university; it hadn't been an easy experience. The delays now meant that their arrival coincided with that of the 'green' season, when the rainfall could potentially be high, and they would have to work quickly as the threat of flooding in the tubes would hamper their efforts. The initial agreement was for a three-month minimum stay and the six team members would be living in the dongas in the old resource centre.

The road ahead curved as she'd expected, and as soon as she left the river, relief eased the ache a little as a homestead appeared, perched high on the hill just past the fork in the track. The sun broke through the heavy cloud for a few seconds and she caught a glimpse of water past the house. Gripping the wheel, Emlyn took the right-hand turn that led up to the building and pulled the car up outside the gate of the small house yard. Although there was no obvious need for a gate; the dilapidated fence did little to separate the front yard from the road. The building was surrounded by acres of dry brown grass, broken only by dead tree stumps and the rusting bodies of old cars. A water tank at the side of the house leaned drunkenly on uneven posts.

She shook her head. This was supposed to be the main house of one of the largest pastoral stations in North Queensland. Maybe this was a worker's house, and the main homestead was further ahead. She glanced at the map on the seat and wondered what to do.

Grey and box-like with flat fibro walls, the place looked to be uninhabited. David would have smiled and called it a 'doer-upper'. She closed down that line of thought before it could take root in her tired brain. A couple of small windows sat either side of a front door that was located at the top of a flight of stairs. As Emlyn looked up, the late-afternoon light left dirty blood-red shadows on the rusting roof and one of the curtains twitched. She blinked and then stared; maybe she'd imagined it?

Another shiver ran down her spine and she fought off the fingers of panic that threatened to take hold. Despite the heat, goosebumps prickled her neck, and she forced herself to breathe deeply as the bands of tension tightened around her temples.

A flash of movement caught her eye, and as she turned a red kelpie shot down the stairs towards her vehicle. Emlyn sat back, waiting for someone to follow the dog through the half-open door, but there was no sign of life apart from the dog now yipping and jumping at the wheels. Someone must have opened the door to let the dog out. Eventually, the kelpie lost interest and slunk off to the shadows at the side of the house. Emlyn laid her head back on the head rest and waited until someone appeared.

And waited.

A couple of times, she'd swear she saw the same curtain move, but no one came outside. Normally, being alone didn't bother her—in fact, it had been her preferred option over the past year—but the stillness of the landscape and the eerie light through the strange brownish-hued clouds were unsettling her. Not a sound and not a breath of wind.

The dead grass stretched to the top of the hill, broken only by the decaying bodies of the old cars. She brought her gaze back to the house and the dog's eyes glinted in the half-light as he watched her.

Glancing at her watch, Emlyn considered her options. There was no way she was going to get out of the car while the dog was around; she'd been terrified of them ever since she'd been bitten as a child. The red kelpie kept lifting its head and watching her. Maybe she'd keep driving and try to find the resource centre herself, but she needed a key to get in so that wasn't an option. Sleeping in the car wasn't terribly appealing, although if it came to that, she'd do it.

Damn, she'd just have to go up to the house and knock on the door. She knew there was someone inside, and she'd pound on the door until she got a response. Emlyn turned around and picked up the large umbrella off the back seat. If she needed a weapon to keep the dog away, that would have to suffice. Digging deep for courage, she smoothed her damp hands on her jeans and reached for the doorhandle. The dog lay in the shadows at the base of the water tank, but it was still very close to the bottom of the stairs.

As she opened the car door, a puff of dust indicated an approaching vehicle. The dog took off down the hill, and Emlyn climbed out of the vehicle and waited. It was a motorbike, and when the rider saw the Troop Carrier parked by the gate he roared up the road towards her, closely followed by the yipping dog.

Emlyn swallowed. Surely it wouldn't bite now that its owner was there?

'Bits!' the man called to the dog as he stopped the bike close to her bull bar. He pointed to the dirt and the dog sank in the fine red dust beside the motorbike. He then swung his leg over the bike and walked over to Emlyn.

She leaned the umbrella against the car door and held out her hand. 'Travis Carlyle?'

He ignored her outstretched hand, shaking his head. 'Sorry, I'm filthy. You must be Emlyn Rees.'

'Yes.' She shoved her hands into her jeans pockets and waited for him to continue, but he just stood there watching her without speaking. Looking up at the dark clouds above them, she forced her voice to stay firm. 'Can you take me over to the accommodation, please?'

With a shrug, Carlyle whistled for the dog before he turned back to Emlyn. His words were curt. 'Follow the bike. It's another five kilometres west.'

What a charmer.

Shaggy fair hair in need of a cut surrounded a rugged face that held no welcome. He was younger than she'd expected—probably in his early forties—but even less personable than he'd come across in the terse emails and phone conversations. With a sigh, she put the umbrella back into the car and climbed into the front.

* * *

The last thing Travis Carlyle wanted was a bunch of damn scientists poking around his property. Times were hard enough, and if it hadn't been for the payment already made by the university, he would have given this woman short shrift. He threw an irritated look towards the house as he kickstarted the bike. Gavin was inside, and he could have at least come out and taken her down to the dongas. He'd be on that damn computer, and too shy to come out to meet a stranger.

In the months since the boys had gone back to their mother in Townsville at the end of the last school holidays, Gavin had barely left the study. Dreaming about bloody cryptocurrency and how he was going to make them a fortune when he should have been out helping Travis in the paddocks. At least the boys helped him with the cattle when they were home. That was the only way the station was going to make a living, although any chance of a fortune had long gone with the fluctuations in the cattle industry. Hard work and skill weren't enough anymore. And only having the boys home in the school holidays made it so difficult. Custody arrangements were informal, and in the end, Travis had agreed to school-holiday access. He had no other option when his wife—as they were still married—lived six hours away by road.

There were cattle to be moved from the middle paddocks before the rain hit; Travis looked up at the sky and frowned. That was the last thing he needed, having the herd washed away in a flash flood. And rain it would, he had no doubt about that. As well as the dark clouds building since late morning, his right knee had been giving him gip since he'd got out of bed before dawn. With any luck the tubes would flood, and these bloody scientists could go back to their laboratories and leave him in peace.

He glanced behind him and slowed the bike as they passed the vine thicket where the first lava tube crossed his land. The tubes functioned like giant storm-water drains as they collected and carried much of the summer rains. He had a feeling that Ms Rees—or professor or doctor or whatever she was—had disappointment ahead. He'd tried to tell her it was the wrong time of year to be poking about the caves, but like a typical woman, she'd dismissed his objections when he'd tried to put them off till autumn.

He muttered as he recalled the German blokes who'd first come looking at their place a few years ago. The Undara tubes fifty kilometres to the east had been discovered back in the sixties before Travis and Gavin had been born, and his grandfather and father had watched as the government had resumed part of that property as a national park. As kids, he and Gavin had played in the caves on their station and they'd taken for granted the strange beauty of their surroundings. Five generations of the Carlyle family had worked this land since one of their forebears had secured the pastoral lease over one hundred and fifty years ago. Now with the scientific interest in the caves, and the ongoing struggle to keep the property viable, the chances of holding onto the family land were becoming less certain every year. So when the university had offered a substantial payment for their research visit, he'd had no option but to accept. He shrugged; the three months would pass quickly and they could get back to normal.

While ever there was breath in his lungs, he would not let the property go; he'd do anything to save it for the boys. There was too much history, too much family, to walk off the place. Travis gripped the handle bars as he went down the last hill and waited for the Troop Carrier to catch up.

He hid the smile that tugged at his lips as the woman parked the large vehicle. She stared at the neglected dongas for a moment before she crossed to where he waited on the bike. The buildings had sat empty for five years; no one had been here since National Parks had built them when they'd charted the area around his caves. There'd been little feedback after they'd moved on, and the only communication had been a short email referring to the area as an undeveloped national park. He'd not followed up; if they forgot about it, that suited him well.

Large dark eyes smudged with shadows in a delicate face held his as the woman stood beside his bike. For a brief moment, he felt sorry for what she had ahead of her in the filthy dongas, but then he shrugged it away. It wasn't his problem. One of those university types, her hair—cut close to her head at the back with longer strands covering her forehead and reaching her chin at the front—screamed trendy at him. He looked down at the sturdy work boots and the brand-new, full-length khaki cargo pants. As he watched, she raised a shaking hand to her head and smoothed her hair flat against her cheek.

'Come on, I'll show you around.' Travis led her to the side of the first building and reached beneath the steps to locate the magnetised tin that held the keys. 'This is the main building. You'll find the refrigerators and the stoves in the back room, and there's office space in the front. I think you'll also find a land line in there, if you need it. As far as I know, it's still connected.'

'And the others?' She gestured to the five smaller dongas.

'The sleeping quarters.' He gave a short laugh as she took the keys from him. 'Don't know why they bothered locking them when they left. No one ever comes out this way. I suppose it keeps the kangaroos, snakes and bats out.'

'Thank you. I'm sure it will be fine.'

'Are the others far behind you?' He looked back at the road; there was no sign of dust from any other vehicles. 'You'll need a bit of a working bee to get it clean enough to stay in.'

'They'll be here soon.' Her voice was cold.

Travis narrowed his eyes and held out his hand for the keys. 'You can't stay here by yourself.'

'Oh, and why would that be?' She put the keys in her pocket and folded her arms.

As she lifted her head and stared at him with eyebrows raised, he noticed the fine tracing of silver scars on the left side of her forehead. When she became aware of him looking, she lowered her head until her hair fell forwards again.

'Because it's not safe,' he said.

'The bats and the kangaroos? Believe me, Mr Carlyle, I've worked in much more dangerous environments than this.'

'I don't mean here. I mean in the caves.'

She lifted her head and held his gaze. 'I won't be going into the caves until the rest of the team arrive. I'll be getting the set-up here ready and taking delivery of provisions from Mt Surprise. And I believe we've signed an agreement that absolves you of responsibility for any accidents that may occur on your station, so you have no need to worry about me.'

'I'm not worried. I don't want you here and I'm not responsible for you, but if anything happens I'm the one who's going to be called out to help. And I don't have the time with the wet about to hit.'

Nature supported him as the first drops splashed the tin roof above.

'Don't worry. Your help won't be required.'

Travis stared at her. 'So how many days exactly until they get here?'

'When I find out I'll make sure I let you now. They're leaving Brisbane tomorrow.' The raised eyebrows pushed him into not giving in, even though he didn't give two hoots about what was happening here.

She lifted her head and held eye contact with him. 'I believe there is mobile phone service, and you've agreed to let us log into your satellite internet connection.'

'That's right.'

'Then thank you, Mr Carlyle. I'm sure you want to get back before the rain gets heavier.'

She was dismissive, and Travis fought the need to have the last word. With a terse nod, he walked across to his motorbike and rode off without a backwards glance.

There was no doubt about it. Emlyn Rees was as cold as ice. But she and the rest of the university bods were the least of his worries, and the money that the university had deposited would stave off foreclosure for at least the next three months.

LET'S TALK
ABOUT BOOKS!

JOIN THE CONVERSATION

HARLEQUIN
AUSTRALIA

@HARLEQUINAUS

@HARLEQUINAUS